CHRISTOPHER
ROSOW

VITAL
DECEPTION

BEN PORTER SERIES **BOOK FOUR**

VITAL DECEPTION
Ben Porter Series – Book Four

For information about this title, contact the publisher:

Quadrant Publishing, LLC
354 Pequot Avenue, Southport CT 06890
QuadrantPublishing@gmail.com

Library of Congress Control Number: 2022905775

ISBN: 978-1-7347147-7-7 (print)
ISBN: 978-1-7347147-8-4 (e-book)

2 3 4 5 6 7 8 9 0

AUTHOR'S NOTE

WHILE THIS STORY is constructed in the real world, including but not limited to referencing actual companies, places, news outlets and articles, events, and things, it is a novel, and it is a work of fiction.

However, it's not entirely far-fetched.

PROLOGUE

MY NAME IS BEN PORTER. I'm thirty years old. I work under cover for the FBI.

Glamorous, right? Action movie pending, right?

Yeah, um, no. Because now, right now, I'm lying in a hospital bed. And I'm looking at the readouts on the electronic vital signs monitor above my shoulder, and it's indicating that I'm in medical distress. Dying, maybe?

No, I don't have the coronavirus.

Honestly, the few times that I've been coherent enough to have a phone conversation with a colleague or family member, that's the first question that I am asked. It's a sign of the times, I guess. Covid-19 news is reported ad nauseam by whatever flavor you favor for your source of information, so it's a logical question to ask. Maybe it will be a relief to you that my story has nothing to do with Covid.

I can tell you that I didn't get shot at again. That's also a reasonable assumption for you to make, if you've already met me. You see, on paper, I am a former Special Agent of the Federal Bureau of Investigation. And, five months ago, while working subversively, under cover for the FBI, I was, indeed, shot. That's an entirely different story, of course. Suffice it to say, I remain off the books.

But that detail is important because I think it partially explains why I'm in civilian care, at the George Washington University Hospital in Washington, D.C., instead of being treated at a military or service hospital as an active member of the law enforcement community.

Or maybe I'm here because what happened wasn't in the line of duty, either on or off the record. It was a car accident.

The accident was two weeks ago. I am pleased to be able to put that sort of day/date/time calculus together. Thinking has been difficult. And though I have a television in my room, I don't watch it that often. I can't focus on the TV. It hurts too much. Too chaotic; too many quick cuts and loud voices. I can only tolerate it for a very short time. However, from the hushed voices of the nurses, I learned that today is a Presidential inauguration day: Wednesday, January 20, 2021.

Being able to put a name on a day is a big deal to me, given that my brain aches. My thoughts run together, my memories come and go, and sometimes I feel like I'm . . . detached from myself. And now, I'm beginning to worry because the vital signs monitor device that is suspended over my hospital bed by a plastic, articulating arm has ceased its previous, almost hypnotic regular beep-beep-beep. Now, that noise has become a frantic, irregular beep. It's a *be beeep bp beeeeep bp beep bep beeeeep* . . .

You get the point. Maybe you can imagine hearing the noise. But you can't see—like I can—the visual readouts on the monitor's screen.

Respiration, charted in blue, and temperature, a number displayed in red, both seem normal. But—the green oxygen saturation plot is trending down. And—most worrying—my heart rate plot and the orange blood pressure graph are both irregular and dropping, and the electrocardiogram trace is erratic. Haywire. Hyperactive!

And what's very concerning, and really elevating my anxiety, is that no one seems to care that the electronic gizmos hooked to my body are reporting that I am in trouble. When I've seen this light show on the monitor before, it results in a flurry of activity. The nurses and doctors should be gathering at my bedside. There should be concern in their eyes, and they should be saying, with sharp tones to their voices, "The patient is medically deteriorating."

But—there's nothing. There are no shouts of "Code Blue!" in the hallways. No crash carts being wheeled through the door. Nada. Zilch.

I study the monitor intently, and those colorful lines begin to blend into a kaleidoscope of dazzling patterns, twisting and spinning and turning. And then I realize: *It's happening again. Oh, no! Not again . . . They're coming. They're coming for me.*

I close my eyes tightly.

It's of no use. It's never been useful all those times before. I might be able to shut out the kaleidoscope temporarily, but the ghosts still appear. In black and white. In greys and smoke. Their claws grab me, and their wings envelop me, and the terrifying apparitions pull at me and take me away . . .

CHAPTER

1

AFTER A ROUGH MONTH confined to a bed with scratchy sheets, I felt good, or at least as good as I could feel while wearing a backless gown.

I was ready to get the hell out of here and to have a proper meal, with, like, a real fork and knife instead of the flimsy plastic utensils they gave us here in the hospital. Putting that into perspective, I decided that if I could concern myself with cutlery, I could confirm that my brain was working, my heart was beating, and my lungs were . . . doing whatever lungs do.

My body and mind were mended. I wanted to put the past in the past, and I hoped an opportunity to move myself forward might be imminent when the door to my fifth-floor private room at the George Washington University Hospital swished open.

"Porker!"

My gut tightened, and I knew I showed offense on my face because my tan-skinned, five-foot-eleven visitor immediately started laughing. "Just kidding, Porter. Sorry. Haven't used that in a long time. Don't take it the wrong way."

"Yessir," I replied dutifully. After all, this was my boss: FBI Deputy Assistant Director Bradford Macallister, who had given me my big break back in 2017, who had shepherded my career since then, and who had supervised my most recent operation while I was under cover.

He grinned at me before examining my quarters. Beige painted walls, white ceiling tiles, grayish-white linoleum floor. A single bed, which I lay atop, fortunately with the guardrails lowered. I had not had any hallucinations for the past couple of weeks, and the nurses had relented this morning when I had asked for the rails to be dropped. I did not want to look like a child in a crib to my boss.

Macallister peered at the beeping vitals monitor above my left shoulder and nodded, humming, "Good, good. Looks good." I learned over the years that Macallister typically liked to act as if he were the smartest person in the room, and I guessed that examining the monitor would be something he thought that someone smart would do. But, despite that apparent snobbery and Macallister's often-bumbling vocabulary, I also discovered that even though he took time to process data, evidence, and theory, and while that pace made him appear to be slow-witted, he was, instead, thoughtful.

Sharp-dressed, too, and in his natty navy-blue suit, pressed white shirt, and striped tie, he stared dismissively at the small, brown-vinyl covered, oak-armed chair nestled in a windowed alcove created by a jog in the building's exterior wall. "That the only place I can sit?"

I smirked. "Obviously. Unless you want to sit on the bed with me."

"Yeah. No, thanks." Reaching the chair after weaving around the foot of the bed, Macallister sniffed haughtily before settling into the creaking vinyl. He set his brown leather briefcase on the floor. Straightening his tie and crossing his legs, exposing conservative, dark socks, and almost touching the bed with an impeccably-polished black wingtip shoe, Macallister focused on me, saying in a serious tone, "That Porker thing was meant as a joke. Apologies again. You've lost weight. You doin' okay?"

"Pretty much."

"I pulled your chart. Told the doc that the hippo took a back seat to national security."

I blinked, thinking, *What? Hippo? Oh, wait, another Macallisterism. He means HIPAA.* Blinking again, I offered, "I thought the health laws prohibited disclosure of private medical records even if national security was at stake. And besides, why am I a national security interest?"

"Well," Macallister hummed, "on the first thing, the hippo thing, the Director of the FBI himself signed the documents to give us access to your chart. That was a while ago. We had Bureau people monitoring your recovery. And that brings us to the second part."

"National security?"

"Yep. Before we get to that, let's talk about your chart. Your diagnosis. The doctor made a note in your records that the hallucinations have stopped. Tell me about them."

I nodded and closed my eyes. "Okay, I guess. I told all this to the doctor. It would start with colors. Vivid, bright, swirling colors. Things would change shape. Then my world would go dark. And creatures would appear, in black and white. Nothing I can explain. Like out of a horror movie. These things, these apparitions, would also change shape like they were ghosts or made from smoke. But they had hands or claws, and sometimes wings, and they would drag me into an abyss or into blackness. And then, nothing, like I didn't exist, until suddenly, I'd be back here, in this bed, and I'd be lucid. Until..." My voice faded off. *Until the next time,* I thought, but I didn't dare mention that to Macallister.

Thinking that I'd gone too deep with my boss, I snapped my eyes open and quickly added, "You know, some shiny lights, some dreams. No big deal."

"Fun," Macallister commented dryly. I didn't respond. It was not fun, but I didn't want to appear weak in front of Macalister. I realized those fears were unfounded as Macallister ignored my unease as he went on, "The doc says that your chart says that all your vitals are perfect, now. Back then, however, it appears that you got shook up pretty bad. Near-death, they said. You flatlined twice."

"You've been watching too many movies or TV shows without good medical advisors."

"What?"

"Saying that I 'flatlined' infers that I died. I suppose the term has become shorthand for being in medical distress." I eyed Macallister; his expression was noncommittal; I concluded he didn't care about my brief lesson in terminology. "Anyway," I continued, "they told me I required emergency stabilization twice. However, there were way more episodes of hallucinations. A dozen, at least, as far as I can remember."

"That's also a concern. Memory loss. I got some questions for you."

I stared at Macallister before asking, in an accusatory tone that I immediately regretted, "That's what this is all about? This meeting? You're not here to check on me. You're here to quiz me."

"Settle down, Porter. But, yeah, that's it. You've always been good at figuring stuff out quickly. Can we get started?"

I took a deep breath and replied, "Sure."

"Who did you work for?"

"The FBI," I replied.

Macallister chuckled. "Who was your latest assignment with?"

"Quadrant Procurement Group."

"What was your title?"

"Um." I hesitated. I started Quadrant, but I never gave myself a title. I stammered, "Ah, let's call my role the CEO. The chief executive."

"What did this Quadrant thing do?"

I hesitated. *This could be a trick question,* I thought, before realizing something else. Something more sinister, and I asked Macallister, "Ah, sir, are you sure we should be discussing this stuff? Here? In this room? It's not at all secure, and this is sensitive, classified information."

Macallister cleared his throat before saying, "Good point, Porter. Good work. Thanks for the reminder," he admitted as leaned toward his briefcase and snapped it open. He withdrew a device about the size of a paperback book and fiddled with it as he spoke. "This is an audio nullifier. It will defeat any listening devices, including exterior lasers that measure vibrations on window glass." He set the device on the small bedside table and repeated his question, "Now, what did this Quadrant do?"

Macallister knew, of course, what Quadrant had done; he had been instrumental in its creation. But pleased as I was with my security reminder—something that my boss should have been more aware of—I wasn't ready to gloat. This was a test, and I figured that if I wanted to get out of this bed, I had to ace it. I explained, "Quadrant was formed as a shell company under the aegis of the FBI. It never showed up on the books, but it was authorized by the Director of the Bureau and the Attorney General of the United States."

"Why was it called Quadrant Procurement Group? What did this company, um, procure?"

"Nothing. It didn't procure anything. The name was meant to appear bland so that if it had popped up on some government record, it would look like some bureaucratic thing."

"How was this thing funded?"

"It was financed by utilizing invisible offshore funds that were appropriated in the course of the apprehension of a criminal."

Macallister had been nodding, and I knew that I was passing the test as I waited for his next question. "Good. Be more specific. What does this Quadrant do currently?"

"What day is today?"

Scowling, Macallister replied, "What the hell for? Monday."

"I meant date. What is the date?"

"February 22, 2021. Why?"

I groaned. I couldn't believe it was almost March. Macallister watched me carefully as I spoke. "Quadrant doesn't do anything currently. The operation was shut down about two months ago. December 21, 2020."

Macallister blinked several times. *Odd*, I thought. *He's up to something.*

Pursing his lips, Macallister said, "Let's move to past tense. Gimme a history lesson. What did this Quadrant thing do prior to being shut down?"

"The mission that Quadrant was formed to take on was limited to one operation, which was concluded in August of last year. My team and I had been overseas conducting an international investigation. Do you want me to go into the details?"

"No. That's a rather involved story. Exciting, too. I liked the title of your final report. Do you remember that title?"

I smiled. "Of course, I remember. 'Subversive Addiction' was the name I gave the case."

It was Macallister's turn to grin, and he rewarded my answer with a quiet, short round of applause. "Golf clap. Well done. Let's fast forward. Pick it up in August of last year."

"We had been working from a 235-foot yacht that was also appropriated in the course of the apprehension of a criminal—"

"What's the name of the yacht?"

"*Almaz*. May I go on?" Macallister bobbed his head once, and I continued, "We returned to the States in August and docked the vessel in the Potomac River just south of the Capitol. We continued to work from the yacht as we documented our mission and subjected ourselves to endless interviews by the suits at the FBI's headquarters within the J. Edgar Hoover building. *Your* building."

Macallister grinned. "Mindless bureaucrats. The place is teeming with 'em."

"Yep. Pencil pushers. Like you." I raised one eyebrow and winked. Macallister had been drawn into the corridors of power in D.C. because of his investigatory skills, but at heart, he remained a field agent. I had no doubt that under the navy-blue suit coat, which he had not removed, was a shoulder harness cradling a fully loaded, Bureau-issued Glock Model 22 pistol.

"Go on, please."

I guessed that we departed from humor mode and returned to the test. "Paperwork and investigation re-cap from August through the beginning of December. And then, when we completed that task, you decided that Quadrant had served its purpose. You decided that Quadrant had attracted too much attention, and too many people inside the government had learned about it. You shut it down. Sent us our separate ways. Told me to put *Almaz* on the yacht market and dump it. It was over." I belatedly realized that my tone had been sharp, but I thought deservedly so. The Quadrant operation was my brainchild, and I had been—no, still was—sad to see it disbanded.

"And then what?" Macallister's voice was soft. Friendly. He wasn't going to address my bitterness, and therefore I guessed what he wanted to hear next.

"You said we needed to meet. You and me. After the Christmas holiday. After New Year's. To decide my fate. My future."

"When was that meeting scheduled?"

I closed my eyes. Everything changed that day. "The sixth of January, in 2021."

Macallister waited a moment and then said, "Tell me what you remember about the sixth of January."

CHAPTER
2

THE SIXTH OF JANUARY, IN 2021

I WOKE, AS USUAL before the dawn, the nightscape dark beyond the portholes of my stateroom aboard the 235-foot expedition-style yacht *Almaz*. Outside, I knew that the mid-winter Washington, D.C. air would be brisk. I also knew that this would be a difficult day.

As I padded toward the commercial-kitchen-style galley aboard *Almaz*, my bare feet soundless on polished wood floors in the corridor, I mentally reviewed my morning. *7:00 AM, breakfast. 8:00 AM, meeting with Macallister in the Hoover building. Without traffic, it's a twelve-minute drive to HQ. With traffic, probably twenty. Plus, I gotta park. And clear security. And—*

Reaching the galley, I remembered, thanks to the bulkhead-mounted television screen that was tuned to CNN. *Right,* I thought, *They're certifying the election today in Congress, and they are expecting protestors. That's why Macallister moved the meeting up to eight. I better leave at quarter past seven. No time for breakfast.*

I could miss a meal, I concluded. I've always struggled with the scale, ranging from "somewhat overweight" to "slightly husky." The holiday excess had not helped. I considered the coffee mug that I was topping off. *Caffeine is an appetite-suppressant, right? I'll grab another cup before I leave. That will be my breakfast.*

Those difficult decisions behind me, I prepped myself for the conversation with Macallister. *Let him lead it.* I was ready to pitch him with a concept for a reincarnation of Quadrant, but I wanted to hear from him first. Maybe he had an assignment for me. And if he did not, I could step in with my idea.

Dressed in my best suit-and-tie combo, the buttons on the jacket straining only slightly around my gut, I climbed the stairs to the main deck of the sumptuously outfitted, four-deck superyacht. This vessel—which would soon be listed for sale—had been my home for over a year, and I knew it—sorry, her, in nautical parlance—intimately. I knew I was going to miss her.

The main level of the yacht, known as deck three, included common areas and a high-tech "situation room," bristling with screens and connected to the terrestrial data and communications network by an always-on, high-speed satellite link. Below my poorly polished brown loafers, on deck two, were the bedrooms—staterooms, we called them on the yacht—and the galley. The lowest level, referred to as deck one, housed stores, machinery, and small cabins. Finally, above my head was the topmost level, deck four, where the captain's quarters and the bridge were located.

Outside, on the main deck level and toward the rear of the yacht, was a helicopter pad, currently vacant because our Eurocopter EC155B1 was in for scheduled maintenance before being sold, and under that helipad was our vehicle garage, also currently vacant, with our two four-door, four-wheel-drive, top of the line Jeep Wranglers offloaded for the team's use in D.C.

One of those two Jeeps had been taken to the Boston area for the holidays by our yacht's captain, Miles Lockwood. He was accompanied by Anastasia Volkov, a former-but-reinstated FBI Intelligence Analyst, whom Macallister tasked to report to the FBI Boston Field Office. A third teammate, also absent, was Abdul Hamid, a Special Agent who also happened to be my former roommate when we trained together at the FBI's Quantico, Virginia New Agent Training program. After graduating from Quantico, Hamid was assigned to the Albany, New York FBI Field Office, and therefore that's where he returned when the Quadrant mission was deemed complete.

In short, and having risked boring you with that long outline, my once-vibrant Quadrant team, aboard our once-well-equipped yacht, was mostly gone. The only remaining member of Quadrant aboard, other than me, was Heather Rourke.

Injured in the line of duty as a Special Agent, Rourke retired from active service to the Bureau. I recruited her to Quadrant, estimating that her youthful energy would be valuable as not only our logistics coordinator but also as our helicopter pilot. I certainly didn't expect that Rourke and I would become romantically involved, but that's exactly what happened during the previous operation.

However, now we were no longer, um, together. A relationship that began in, dare I say, the heat of the moment, exhausted itself, probably due to the monotony of paperwork that we suffered through for almost five months.

Rourke was nursing a coffee cup at the ginormous third-deck dining table as she swiped at the screen of a tablet. I cleared my throat timidly. "Do you have the keys for the Jeep?"

"I have 'em," she answered without making eye contact. "But I need 'em."

Awkward.

Technically, I was Rourke's superior. I could easily overrule her and demand the keys to the vehicle that was an asset of my soon-to-be-defunct organization. However, I'd been tiptoeing, admittedly cowardly, around Rourke since our breakup, not wanting to spark the fiery, spunky redhead into any sort of anger.

I glanced at my watch. 7:18 A.M. "Dammit, I'm gonna be late," I whined. Gathering my courage, I demanded, "Why do you need the car? I gotta go."

Rourke grinned one of her maniacal grins and told me, "I need the Jeep to run out to the hanger to do a check flight with a potential buyer for the chopper. That's my toy, remember? I'm your pilot, so that machine is my responsibility. But— grab your coffee. I'll drive you to the Hoover building."

"Fine. Fine. *Fine.* Whatever. I don't wanna to be late, so let's go."

Rourke snatched a key fob from the polished top of the lacquered coffee table in the main living area aboard *Almaz* as she barked in my general direction, "What's the temp outside?"

"Now I'm the weatherman?" I shrugged my shoulders and guessed, "Forty degrees? It's not cold, and it's not hot."

"Great," Rourke replied as she snagged a Patagonia fleece jacket from the back of a chair and tugged it on. "I don't need gloves. Don't remember where I left them." I followed, my hands warmed by cupping a tall, insulated plastic, lidded to-go mug of coffee, not daring to sip it while trotting across the rich carpet.

Hustling outside, we descended the metal gangway to the dock, the white-painted hull of *Almaz* towering above us. Leaving the yacht behind, I spotted the matte-black Jeep in the parking lot, and I angled to the shotgun side, realizing that I was happy to let her chauffeur me through the morning D.C. traffic while I sipped my coffee and steeled myself for Macallister.

I watched through the window glass as Rourke grabbed the door handle and yanked on it with her right hand, with no effect. She pulled at it again. Knowing that she was not looking at me, I dared a grin; she had not unlocked the car. I watched her squeeze the key fob with unnecessary force with her left hand, and I could hear the Jeep's locks snick open.

"Helps to unlock it before trying to open the door, Rourke," I taunted as we climbed into our seats.

"Fuck you, Porter," she retorted.

Hurling an f-bomb was unnecessarily aggressive, I thought. I realized I had started to perspire, for some reason, and I dabbed my forehead.

Rourke was doing the same, almost, as she wiped a bead of sweat off her right eyebrow. As she jabbed the car's ignition button, she muttered, "Sorry. That might have been a little harsh."

She kept her eyes averted from me as she jammed a white cord into the base of her iPhone and manipulated the device's touch screen to call up directions. This was a routine that we knew well; even though we'd driven to the Hoover building countless times over the past five months, we'd learned to place our blind trust in the overlords at Google or Apple to dictate our route, especially with morning traffic. While waiting for the algorithm to decide how we'd mix it up with our fellow commuters, Rourke rubbed her eyes.

I glanced at her. "You okay?"

"Yeah, yeah. Somethin' in my eye, I guess."

"Funny. Me too. I'm hot but my eyes are dry. Must be the climate on the boat or something."

"Huh," she grunted, examining the in-dash screen of the Jeep as it lit with a CarPlay map. "Spy Museum route. Appropriate, I guess."

I slurped at my coffee, side-eyeing Rourke. Her tone had changed; it trailed off and sounded tired instead of irritable. I wondered if she regretted snapping at me, but I chose to keep my mouth occupied with my coffee instead of responding as Rourke piloted the Wrangler north.

The Hoover building was located north of the Washington Mall, and our dock location on the banks of the Potomac River was to the south of the Mall. We had three route options to cross the Mall. The fastest drive was usually 12th Street Southwest, where we would get a perfect view of the Washington Monument towering to our left, but occasionally the mapping app would route us on 7th Street Southwest, giving us a glimpse of the US Capitol building to our right. A third route, which we had nicknamed as such because it passed the Spy Museum, started us on 7th and then turned us left on Frontage Road Southwest—and often we would bypass snarled traffic.

As we approached the I-395 overpass, I held my coffee cup in my right hand, using my left hand to poke at my eye, feeling like there was some sand on my pupil—and the Jeep nailed a pothole at speed. Jostling my coffee one-handed, narrowly averting a spill onto my suit pants, I whined in protest, "Slow down, Rourke. We got time."

She didn't respond as the Jeep surged faster, toward the traffic light at the Frontage Street intersection, at the far end of the overpass. "Rourke," I called, staring at her.

Rourke's face was red, and she was pawing at her eyes with both hands, her left knee wedged under the lower radius of the steering wheel. She was ignoring the road as the Jeep's left tires skimmed across the double yellow line painted on the concrete surface of the overpass bridge.

"Rourke!"

A horn blared as I felt the Jeep accelerate, and through the windshield, I could only watch helplessly as the blunt, gray-and-red snout of a D.C. Metrobus smashed into the left front hood of the Jeep with the renting squeal of steel-on-steel, instantly followed by the synchronized noises of shattering tempered glass and the ear-drum-bursting *BAM* as the airbags deployed...

CHAPTER 3

MONDAY, FEBRUARY 22, 2021

I OPENED MY EYES to the beige-colored walls and white ceiling tiles of the room that had become familiar to me at the GW Hospital and to Macallister's concerned stare.

"Porter?"

"Yeah. Sorry," I mumbled. "I've been trying not to think about that day."

"That's okay, Porter. My turn to say sorry. I didn't mean to reopen the wounds. For what it's worth, you passed the test. You obviously remember Quadrant, and…"

His voice faded off before he added, respectfully, his eyes downcast to the floor, "Heather Rourke."

I could only nod in response, briefly unable to speak as I swallowed to rid myself of the lump in my throat. Since learning the news that Rourke was killed in the accident, I did my best not to dwell. Like, *What if I had driven?* Or, *What if I had just demanded those keys and taken the Jeep solo?* I had come to understand that this kind of second-guessing was common after tragedy. Survivor's guilt, perhaps.

Regardless, while Rourke and I were no longer dating, for certain she remained a friend. A colleague. A teammate. I mourned the loss, but at the same time, I needed to move forward with my boss. I licked my lips and mumbled, "It's still difficult to process and to talk about." I cleared my throat and offered, "I'll be okay."

Macallister asked kindly, "Who told you?"

"One of the doctors."

"Which doctor?"

"Um, Curtis. A Doctor Curtis."

Macallister hummed, "Hmmph. Curtis. When?"

"Another memory test question?" I shook my head in dismay, annoyed that Macallister would use this opportunity to quiz me. "Sometime last week. I don't know what day since I don't have a calendar on the wall in here. But I remember the conversation perfectly. This Doctor Curtis told me that Rourke died at the scene of the accident. That there was nothing the paramedics could have done."

The memory test wasn't done, apparently. "Do you remember what happened after the accident?"

"No," I spat. "I told you what I remember, up to the time when our Jeep hit the bus."

Macallister stood and turned his right shoulder to me to gaze out the window. He addressed the glass, not me, as he said, "Okay. I figured as much. There's quite a bit to discuss with you, and I think you're ready. Hang on." He pulled an iPhone from his right jacket inside breast pocket, tapped it, stared at the screen, and began swiping and typing.

With amazement in my voice, I complimented Macallister. "You look like you know what you're doing with that thing."

"Yeah," he mumbled in response, barely slowing his motions, "I figured I had to get with the times. I've gotten pretty good at this tech stuff." From his obviously familiarity working at the screen, I had to agree; this was a new development for my previously technologically challenged boss. As he slipped the device back into his pocket, he turned his gaze back toward mine and explained, "I just texted Doctor Curtis. He'll be here in a few minutes. While we wait, I'll tell you what *really* happened on the morning of the sixth of January."

CHAPTER

4

AS I WATCHED Deputy Assistant Director Bradford Macallister turn from the window, I decided to preempt another rehash of the sixth of January. "Do we have to go over that again?" I knew I sounded exasperated, but that was fine with me. That was a message I wanted to send: to put the past in the past. Time to move forward.

Macallister lowered himself back into the creaky vinyl chair at the GW Hospital. "I'm surprised that you remember the events preceding your accident with so much clarity. Doctor Curtis thought you'd be suffering from retrograde amnesia." Macallister said those two last words pompously; he was clearly impressed with his newfound medical acumen. "Curtis said that a concussion victim wouldn't remember what happened before the trauma."

"Good for me, I guess." I wasn't sure where Macallister was going with this line of conversation.

I realized that he was stalling because he leaned forward, planted his elbows on his knees, and said, "You were conscious when the first responders pulled you from the wreckage."

I didn't reply. Sitting back in the chair, Macallister continued, "Rourke crossed the double yellow line and intersected a bus, almost exactly at the midline of the Jeep and on the driver's side of the bus. The impact was at a combined speed of about eighty miles per hour; the bus was traveling at twenty-five miles per hour, and the Jeep was doing well over fifty. There's an electronic data recorder in the Wrangler. Rourke's foot was mashing the accelerator, apparently."

"I know," I confirmed. "I felt that acceleration. She wasn't paying attention to the road. She was scratching at her face as the Jeep sped up."

Macallister nodded. "After impact, the Jeep was twisted by momentum to its right, and it rolled once. Landed on its tires. First responders were able to get you out of the passenger side of the vehicle. However, the left side of the Jeep was mashed. The jaws of life were required to get at Rourke. Not that it would have mattered," he said bitterly, adding morosely, "She was pronounced dead at the scene. And—"

Macallister stopped speaking suddenly as the door to the room swung open. He tensed, his right hand instinctively slipping under his suit coat toward his holstered Glock, but he visibly relaxed as a tall, white-lab-coated, white-haired, white-mustachioed, white-skinned physician entered, saying precisely and formally, "Good afternoon, Deputy Assistant Director Macallister."

I couldn't help myself as I smiled. *He's a dead ringer for Leslie Neilson playing Lieutenant Frank Drebin. Talks like him. And other than that perfectly trimmed mustache, looks like him.*

Macallister nodded and replied, "Good to see you, Doctor Curtis."

"And Mister Porter. You're feeling well today?"

"Ah, um, yes," I stammered, trying to shake the image of Frank Drebin from my head. At least it wasn't another hallucination. Reminding myself that Macallister was watching intently, I asked, "Ah, Doctor Curtis. Obviously, we've met before. Talked before. But I'm confused. Why is it that Macallister texted you? What's your role, exactly?"

"I should explain that, actually," Macallister interjected. "Doctor David Curtis is not a resident doc here at GW; he is a pathologist at the Walter Reed National Military Medical Center. Over at Reed, he was responsible for the autopsy on Rourke, and he assumed oversight of that investigation, reporting back to me. It became a logical step to have him moonlight from Reed to monitor your care here."

I held up a hand and wondered, "Why is that a logical step?"

With the available seating in my room maxed out, Curtis leaned against a beige wall, crossed his arms, and addressed my question. "I'll cover that. I've been waiting for your hallucinations to stop. I expected them to fade by, oh, about ten days ago. And you are right on schedule, especially because you have not presented any additional episodes over the past week. They will not happen again. You're in the clear."

Unintentionally mimicking the doctor, I crossed my arms and inquired, "Rarely do I hear a doctor speak with such certainty. Usually, in my experience, limited as it may be, doctors qualify their predictions. What makes you so sure, Doc?"

Curtis appeared surprised at my statement. "That sounds like an accusation."

"No, no," I quickly countered, immediately regretting my outburst. "Not at all. I meant, like, you're very specific and confident. Just wondering why."

The doctor huffed. "This is my specialty. Risking pomposity, this is what I studied at Harvard medical school and beyond. I am a pathologist, and I specialize in toxicology. Going one step further, I am sure of my diagnosis because I know why you've been having the hallucinations."

"Because of the accident, right?"

"No."

Curtis uncrossed his arms and sat primly at the foot of my bed before saying, cryptically, "At first examination, the accident and your hallucinations would not appear to be related. However, that is not the case. The catalyst for both the accident and for the hallucinations is one and the same."

He paused, and then he announced, "Heather Rourke—and you, Mister Porter—were both poisoned."

CHAPTER
5

"I WAS POISONED?"

I uttered those three words in a dumbfounded manner. Actually, I didn't mean to say them out loud. Curtis and Macallister did not react until I asked the obvious and quite logical follow-up question: "Poisoned by who?"

With two fingers, Curtis rubbed his mustache and said, "By whom."

"Yeah," I shot back. "By who?"

The doctor was shaking his head back and forth. "No, no, no. The correct grammar uses 'whom.' The question you're asking is, 'poisoned by whom'?"

"Really, I don't give a shit. I'm not all that good with grammar or proofreading or stuff like that. Lemme ask it this way. Who poisoned me?"

Chuckling softly and looking at the bedspread, Curtis murmured, "Well, that is a question for Deputy Assistant Director Macallister, I suppose. But I can say what poisoned you." Pulling his eyes up to meet mine, he said, "Diethyl phosphonate. It's a chemical."

He stopped. I spun my left forefinger in the spiraling circle, urging him to continue as I impatiently asked, "And?"

Curtis glanced at Macallister, who explained, "When you were a no-show at the meeting we had scheduled, I figured you were held up by the mess at the Capitol. On the Mall. The Bureau got word of the accident since we were on high alert for any sort of incident, and I finally put two-and-two together. By then, the Washington cops were ready to clear the accident scene. The bus driver had minor injuries, as did a few civilian riders, but the bus was far from full, and it was obviously far bigger than your Jeep, so the Jeep took the brunt of the damage. I wanted to get the Jeep out of sight. It wouldn't look good in the press that two former FBI agents were involved in a morning wreck. I arranged for the Jeep to be transported to our lab over in Quantico, Virginia, and the D.C. police informed me that you had been taken to the closest emergency room, which was here at the GW Hospital."

I looked at Curtis, but Macallister was shaking his head. "No. Curtis was not involved at that point. The ER docs here did all the usual workups on you, along with the trauma treatment. But, because Rourke is a former Special Agent and was carrying federal identification, protocol dictated that her body was brought to Walter Reed. Turns out that was pivotal because she would be under Curtis's roof."

The doctor took over the narrative. "At Reed, I was assigned to Rourke's case, and I began my examination in the morgue. When I identified diethyl phosphonate present in Rourke's blood, I had a hunch this was not a run-of-the-mill car accident. I asked my superiors why this particular body ended up in my morgue." Curtis inclined his head toward Macallister.

Macallister elaborated, "Doctor Curtis contacted the FBI. Rourke's file, of course, flags me, which is ultimately how I got connected with Curtis. I told the doctor that the passenger in the vehicle was alive and was being treated at GW." He pointed at me, and then he looked at Curtis.

The back-and-forth conversation was like watching a tennis match. I turned my head toward Curtis, who said, "Given the diethyl phosphonate discovery, I requested your medical records, and I suggested to Macallister that he investigate the vehicle."

Macallister held up a finger. "Remember, the mangled Jeep was at Quantico. That's a state-of-the-art laboratory, you know. After Curtis explained his suspicions, I authorized a forensics investigation, and the

technicians at Quantico found a substance on all four of the Jeep's door
handles. The substance was especially concentrated on the driver's
door handle. In addition, that substance was very clever. Imagine a
light application of moisturizer cream, in a small enough amount that
you might assume it was merely a slippery door handle."

I looked down at my own hands and recalled, "Yeah, I kinda
remember that. I remember wiping my hands."

"It wouldn't have mattered," Curtis said. "You could have washed
your hands, but it would have been too late. The poison would already
have been absorbed into your skin. Then, your own actions would have
spread it further. That same substance was found in trace amounts on
Rourke's right hand, on the vehicle's ignition button and steering wheel,
and around her eyes."

"I remember my eyes being sorta dry," I offered. "Rourke was rubbing
her eyes, too."

"Indeed. Rourke's body, which of course was static and available for
exam at the Walter Reed morgue, presented exactly as you'd suspect,
with a concentration of foreign matter on her hands, face, and around
her eyes," Curtis confirmed. "I'd postulate the same for you, but by the
time all of this became evident, you had been cleaned up. However, it all
came together after I was permitted to see your records at GW, which
gave me access to your blood sample, which was obtained shortly after
your admittance to the GW Emergency Room. That sample presented
diethyl phosphonate."

Curtis stood, stretched his legs, and resumed his leaning posture
against the beige wall. "Rourke's cause of death was the blunt force
trauma of the wreck, but it is clear that the poison caused the crash.
You see, the compound found on the door handles would have been
absorbed through the skin on your hands. But let's say you wore gloves.
Eventually, perhaps you'd touch your face with a contaminated, gloved
hand. Symptoms from an initial contact would manifest first in your
eyes, which are very sensitive. Your eyes become red and scratchy—"

"And that happened to both Rourke *and* me," I interrupted.

"Yes. We've established that was the case. Moving on in the sequence
after exposure, typically, a victim would vomit. You didn't, probably because

your digestion shut down because of the wreck, and sadly, Rourke was already dead by the time symptoms would have progressed to this stage. You, however, survived the crash, and you suffered from hallucinations as a predictable progression from exposure to the chemical. During two of those episodes, you coded and required medical intervention. You're very lucky that you are not dead. It's my estimation that if you had driven the car and had therefore received the amount of diethyl phosphonate present on the driver's side door handle, even absent a car crash, you would not have survived the hallucinations. You would be dead."

With a sideways glance at Macallister, Curtis concluded, "The good news is that the chemical loses its potency over time. Your hallucinations tapered off as expected. As I stated before, with confidence, I'm certain you're in the clear."

"Any further questions for the doctor?" Macallister had risen to his feet as Curtis was speaking. I did, indeed, have more to ask, but I immediately sensed that Macallister was dismissing Doctor Curtis, especially when the Deputy Assistant Director proffered a hand to shake. Curtis received the message; he nodded to me curtly and departed.

"That was sudden," I commented.

"We need to move on," replied Macallister. "We have more to review, and the doctor does not have the security clearance for *that* discussion."

As I considered that, I closed my eyes, and Macallister asked, "You tired, Porter? You done with this today?"

Without opening my eyes, I replied, "Not in the least. Because here's what I don't understand. Game it out, Macallister. Let's say you wanted to poison me. You're like, cool, let's wipe some poisoning goop onto the door handle of Porter's car. But here's the problem: that's a really loose technique. I mean, if you had any surveillance on me, you'd know that I used one of two identical-looking Jeeps. That at least four people regularly used those Jeeps. It was just dumb luck that Lockwood happened to take one of them, leaving Rourke and me as the only potential drivers. But let's say you had that surveillance, and you wiped your poisoned moisturizer, or whatever, on the driver's side door handle—what happens if I don't drive? You miss me, and you get collateral damage? Maybe the target was Rourke. Maybe the target was—"

"I get it. I get it," Macallister interrupted. "Like I said before, we need to move on."

My eyelids popped upwards, and I examined Macallister. "Understood. Go on."

He snorted. "The doctor has released you. You're clear of the hallucinations. You've demonstrated that you don't have memory loss. And, in sum, that means that it's time for you to go back to *Almaz* and to get back to work."

I was confused, and I let it show. "Go back and do what?"

"Quadrant has a new mission, which you have apparently considered and accepted. Without my consent, I will add." Macallister was standing imperiously over me, staring down at me, weak and backless-gowned in my hospital bed.

"I have?" I was shaking my head, now feigning confusion, but with my gut tightening to a knot. *He couldn't possibly know,* I thought. *No one knows.*

Scowling, Macallister wasn't buying my act. "Yeah. I talked to Genevieve Sullivan. She told me that she tasked Quadrant for its next mission. In August. *August!* Were you planning on looping me in, Porter?"

Oh, shit. He does know.

Sweeping the hem of his suit coat backwards, Macallister jammed his hands into his pants pockets as he scolded me, in a gravelly, pissed-off tone, "You want to bring me up to date, Porter, and tell me about Genevieve Sullivan?"

CHAPTER

6

I SLID MY BODY as far upright as I could in my hospital bed, hoping that the backless gown would sorta stay in place so that I could gain a little vertical height and try to meet my boss' withering stare. My intent probably had little effect, but I bought myself a bit of time to organize my thoughts.

It's time to come clean, I decided. *He already knows about Sullivan.*

I began with a command, trying to take control. "Sit. Please. I'll be transparent, but knowing you talked to Sullivan means nothing. I don't know what she told you. Versus, of course, what she told me. And anyway, it's all moot now, isn't it?"

Macallister settled himself slowly into the chair. He adjusted the knot of his necktie and made an unintelligible noise. A *harumph*, perhaps.

I took that as a signal that he did not want to answer my question, so I proceeded. "Genevieve Sullivan is the Under Secretary for Political Affairs. She's a direct report to the Secretary of State, and she allegedly has complete, unfettered access to not only the Sec State but also to the President—"

"Not *allegedly*," Macallister corrected. "She has that access, for certain. She's a lifer. Been a career bureaucrat for twenty, maybe twenty-five years. She's survived every political appointee because she knows what levers to pull and when. She knows where the bodies are buried."

Macallister's tone has changed from confrontational to conversational. I decided, *That's a good sign.*

"Right," I continued. "As far as I can tell, she's one of the most powerful players in D.C., and possibly, I'd guess, in the world."

"You ever meet her? In-person?"

"No," I admitted. "I've only interacted with her electronically. Phone and email, mostly. All secure and encrypted, of course. And, as you might recall, twice via video conference."

"Describe her."

I thought that was an odd question, but knowing that I was on thin ice with Macallister, I did my best to answer. "She's got a squeaky, thin voice. She's white-skinned, lined skin, a bit droopy with age. She's got white hair. And she's short of stature."

"Four-eleven," Macallister clarified. "I've met her in person. What I'd like to know, Porter, is how you became so familiar with the Under Secretary for Political Affairs."

"She called me. In August. I was watching the sunset from the situation room aboard *Almaz* as we crossed the Atlantic Ocean to return to Washington, and I was drinking a nice, ice-cold beer when the secure link satellite telephone buzzed. I took the call."

"Go on."

"We talked about the last mission, which she, of course, had been involved with, and then she told me that she had a task for me. For my team. I remember her words exactly. She said, *'I could use the resources of the blandly but cleverly named Quadrant Procurement Group—and Ben, I could especially use your unique and creative talents. This is a matter of the utmost importance. It threatens the very security of the United States of America.'*"

I paused and examined Macallister. He squinted at me and said tonelessly, "Well? What's the deal? You gonna tell me what the punchline was?"

"Well, rock, meet hard place," I offered. "The problem is this: I don't know if I'm supposed to reveal the next part to you. Obviously, you know that I've talked to Sullivan. But she demanded secrecy."

Macallister actually laughed. "Typical, Porter. You've gotten yourself stuck. What are you gonna do about it? What have you been doing about Sullivan's task for the past six or seven months? Seems pretty weak to me."

I replied, perhaps a little too defensively, "I'd been doing your paperwork, and I told Sullivan that I couldn't do anything for her until we wrapped up and closed our prior investigation. Then—as you might recall—you decided to shut down Quadrant. I passed on that news to the Under Secretary."

"What did she say?"

"She was pissed. Angry. I told her it was out of my hands. That I couldn't proceed with Quadrant without the blessing of the Attorney General or the Director, or you, Macallister."

Macallister was eyeing me suspiciously. "And that's it?"

"Yeah. Because, as you also might recall, then apparently I got poisoned, concurrently or coincidentally with a car crash, so I've been sitting here on my ass for almost two months. I haven't had any contact with Sullivan since December. Since I told her that she'd have to find another solution to her problem."

"Well, well, well," Macallister grumbled. "Sullivan contacted me. In mid-January. She had heard about the wreck. She had heard that you survived. She wanted me to know that she needed the unique abilities of something like Quadrant. Or, better yet, so we didn't have to start over, of Quadrant, reconstituted. Reimagined."

"What did you tell her?"

Macallister sat back in the chair and crossed his legs. Stretching his arms out wide, he brought them toward the back of his head, cradling his skull with intertwined fingers. "I told her you were critical to Quadrant, that I had an inside line on your medical diagnosis, and that you'd recover. That I'd be interested in discussing it further."

"It?"

"Sullivan's mission."

I remained silent for a beat, wondering if I was walking into a trap in disclosing what Sullivan had told me back in August. I cautiously probed, "Can you gimme a hint? Her mission. Something that you know, so I know that you know."

Tilting his head up to look at the white ceiling tiles, Macallister waited for a moment before lowering his eyes to meet mine and answering, "Sullivan said it was like a cancer, growing on a critical organ within the United States government. If left unchecked, it would spread. And then the damage the cancer would be unfathomable. It needed to be addressed. To be *resected*. That was the word she used."

"Humor me with one more clue," I begged, not quite willing to concede the oath of secrecy that Sullivan had insisted that I take but knowing that Macallister's answers thus far were all correct.

"The Central Intelligence Agency."

He does know, I thought, before deciding to say the name.

I spoke slowly. "Yes. Sullivan has evidence that the Director of the CIA has ties to a foreign power, that she is acting in collusion with another government, and that she must be stopped. Back in August, Sullivan told me that Quadrant has to expose and take down Hazel Ginachere."

Looking back, when I said that name out loud, I set both him and me on a perilous, deadly course—and it was the biggest mistake I ever made.

CHAPTER 7

COMFORTABLY ENSCONCED in a coffee-colored, button-tufted, top grain leather chair, a man hunched at a polished wooden desk, scribbling notes in a left-handed, flowing cursive onto a pad of legal-size, lined yellow paper. Brow furrowing, he paused, then reached a hand to a laptop computer trackpad. Tapping several times, he sat back in the chair, absent-mindedly rotating side-to-side as he slipped a large pair of headphones off his skull, running his fingers through gray, thinning, combed-over hair.

Considering the inked pad and leaning toward the desk once more, he tethered a smartphone device to the computer. He manipulated the trackpad once more, calling up a Tor browser and then a voice-over-Internet-protocol communications application. Selecting the appropriate connection code and then an encryption sequence, he settled to wait, idly considering the erratic flicker cast from a marble surrounded fireplace. Unlike the pleasant crackle of a natural, wood-burning fire, this natural-gas-fueled fake fire made no noise.

Instead, the man listened to the hiss and pops of the connection initiation progression for three minutes and nineteen seconds, until a voice sounded a single word command from the laptop computer speakers: "Report."

Out of habit, the man picked up his ballpoint pen and fidgeted with it as he spoke. "Porter and Macallister. A very lengthy discussion. In Porter's hospital room, of course."

"Topics?"

"After pleasantries, Macallister quizzed Porter. Interestingly enough, it was Porter who first expressed concerns about security. Macallister enabled an audio nullifying device, but he obviously doesn't know how to use it. It was not configured to randomly modulate the wavelength, so I was able to defeat it and pick up most of the conversation, which was essentially a memory test."

"A memory test?"

"I'd venture that description, yes. I'll transmit my notes to you. I'd offer that Porter's recall was excellent."

"Interesting," the computer speaker squawked. "Anything else?"

"The doctor—Curtis— was also there. He explained the discovery of diethyl phosphonate. Then he gave Porter the all-clear. He will be discharged from the hospital."

"That's fine. That's all to be expected. Now you must ensure that the hospital room is sanitized immediately. No one can find your listening device." With the longest response yet during the connection, the voice had remained even but dropped deeply in tone as the voice-altering software attempted to keep up with the rapidly spoken instructions.

"Understood," the man replied. "Not a problem."

"It is a problem. He's still alive."

Even though the connection was audio-only, the man was shaking his head. "No. That is not a problem. We deal with outcomes as they arrive. He may not be dead, but we have come to understand weaknesses in the alternate methodology for the protocol, though we did realize one success. This is impressive progress."

A mean-spirited laugh boomed from the computer speakers. "You're a stubborn one. You never take responsibility for a mistake, do you?"

"In my line of work, nothing is guaranteed. As you must know."

"Very well. I won't push it. But I will expect significantly more precision. Going forward, we will proceed with the original protocol."

"Understood," was the man's response, repeating a non-committal agreement that he found effective. "Do you have further instructions?"

"Not at this time," came the quick response. "Clear the scene and stand by."

With that, the active connection indicator on the man's computer screen switched from green to red.

CHAPTER

MONDAY, MARCH 1, 2021

I FELT LIKE MYSELF AGAIN, back aboard *Almaz*.

Seven days ago, Macallister towered over me in a hospital bed. Four days ago, I was discharged from the GW Hospital. And on the first Monday in March, for the first time since January, I took my usual seat at the head of the black, polished, horseshoe-shaped table in the third-deck situation room.

Exhaling, I said, "It's good to be here."

There was no response, of course, for I was the only occupant, so far, in the situation room. Absentmindedly, I ogled the gently curved interior aft wall that was dominated by three giant screens, all currently blank. Above the screens, a series of red-numbered digital clocks indicated times at locations around the globe, with the local time shown at the centermost display. The left and right edges of the outermost giant screens were each flanked with three slightly smaller screens. On the right, the top small screen displayed a view of the bridge, the middle showed an electronic chart that moved with the yacht's position, and the third, lowest screen was cluttered with numbers that indicated the yacht's speed and course, as well as air and sea temperatures, fuel status, and several other data points. On the left, screens displayed forward- and aft-facing camera views from the antenna mast, plus an interior view of the engine space. Naturally, all those image feeds could be changed to whatever was mission-critical. For example, any screen could show the feed from the camera that was installed in the nose of the currently pilotless Eurocopter EC155B1.

Each of the seven seats at the table was equipped with a small console of switches and buttons as well as a recessed computer monitor, keyboard, mouse, and headset.

Rotating my chair to face forward, I admired the view out the expanse of the forward-facing, five-foot-tall, three-foot-wide series of windows that looked out to the bow of *Almaz,* and I sipped from a cup of coffee as I waited for my team to arrive.

I heard the door click open, and I spun my chair around to greet Miles Lockwood, the captain of *Almaz* and the hero of a past sailing adventure—a man who had defied the odds stacked against him and who had proven to be not only a capable and calm mariner but also a loyal and steadfast friend. Lockwood was fair-skinned with medium-length, dark-ish but graying blond hair, and today, clean-shaven. I asked, "Miles, you met a razor? Where's the usual salt-and-pepper stubble on your chin?"

"I heard that we're going to have a special guest coming to meet us today," he said laconically as he took the seat to my left, his hazel-green eyes glinting brightly. "Figured I'd clean up. And—Ben, look at you. Baggy clothes. You're … thinner."

Even as the door opened a second time, I replied to Lockwood, "An intravenous diet for a while and then having to eat with a plastic spork does wonders for weight loss," I replied, smiling. "Now I just gotta get stronger while trying to keep the pounds off."

"Well, we got ourselves a Peloton bike," announced Anastasia Volkov, the Intelligence Analyst who sat to my right, her voice lilting with just a hint of a Russian accent, an effect left over from her upbringing in her native Ukraine. She pushed an olive-skinned hand through her caramel-blonde, long straight hair, adding, "You should check it out. It'll be good for you."

"Easy for you to say," I snorted. Volkov was always fit, not only of body but also of mind. Indeed, she was a brilliant computer expert—so much so that her vast expertise insulated her from the effects of an ill-advised foray into nefarious purposes. Ultimately, the benefit of her talents outweighed her lack of judgment.

Because of that shaky history, Volkov and I were once at odds with each other. However, I'd come to respect her, and she, truly, worked tirelessly to atone for her sins. *Put the past in the past,* I reminded myself. Without a doubt, Volkov proved herself time and again to be a crucial member of my team.

Well, my mostly-reconstituted team. I asked Volkov, "Where's Hamid?"

As if on cue, a voice boomed from the still-open door to the situation room. "I got the answer for you, Benny-boy," called Special Agent Abdul Hamid, a swarthy, bulbous-nosed, dark Middle Eastern skinned Special Agent who had been recalled to my team from his duties in Albany. "I heard you talking about that Peloton thing. No way, man. Not for you. All you gotta do is give up the longneck Budweisers. Those are empty calories, bro."

"Never," I replied with feigned indignation.

"I ain't done," Hamid complained as he took his seat to Volkov's right. "Give up the Buds, and go with the Bud Light. Easy."

I rolled my eyes. "Whatever, man. And that's quite a cliché. I think Rourke would—"

I caught myself. Heather Rourke would have piled on with some biting, sarcastic comment, and I glanced at what would have been her usual seat to Lockwood's left.

There was a moment of silence, unprompted and unspoken, and what frivolity had been present dissipated. I inhaled deeply through my nose and decided to plow ahead. "We don't have much time before our guest arrives. Can we do a quick sitrep? Volkov, can we start with you and our operational status?"

"Sure," she replied quietly. "Situation report is pretty close to normal as we restart. Our financial status is stronger thanks to investments we've made with our seed funds. As of last Friday, our accounts totaled just north of eight hundred and sixty-one million dollars."

"That's a helluva war chest," I said with some awe in my voice.

Hamid was nodding his agreement as he added, "Let's talk about an actual war chest. Our arms stores are stocked as usual. Various handguns, a couple of sniper rifles, five submachine guns, and accessories. Comms gear, body armor, grenades, explosives. You want it, we got it."

"And if you want to go anywhere, we got that, too," Lockwood added. "Fully provisioned and fully fueled with a ten-thousand nautical mile range. However, we are still short one vehicle, and while the helicopter service work is complete, our chopper remains at the airfield. We need, as you know, a new pilot."

"I know," I said somberly. "But since we're not going anywhere soon, all that can be dealt with in due course."

"There's another item," Volkov murmured. I wasn't sure what she was referring to until she elaborated, "An investigation. *That* investigation. The Bureau has, of course, been actively collaborating with the D.C. police, but neither has a clue as to who poisoned you. And—"

Not completing her sentence, Volkov closed her eyes. Hamid, however, was unfazed as he jumped in to complete Volkov's sentence. "And Rourke. Like she said, we gotta run an investigation. We can't tiptoe around it."

Bobbing my head up and down, I agreed, "I'm glad to hear that you guys are looking into it. Any progress?"

"Of course, we're 'looking into it,' Porter. More than that. Way more than that," Volkov said defensively. "It's all we've done since we got word that we were being recalled. And we have made progress. Or, well, I have."

A notification flashed on my phone, laying on the polished table, and I stood. "Can we put that on hold for a moment or two? Our guest has arrived."

CHAPTER 9

I WAS ABLE TO maintain a stoic, emotionless expression, but honestly, it was difficult not to laugh outright at the agape look on Deputy Assistant Director Bradford Macallister's face.

Dressed in a dark gray, lightly pinstriped suit, he was shaking his head in wonderment as he examined the *Almaz* situation room. "This place is stunning," was all that he could verbalize as he took in the horseshoe-shaped table, the screens, the consoles, and the utter impressiveness of it all.

Selecting what would have been Rourke's seat to the left of Lockwood, Macallister settled into the black, executive-style chair. Slowly and deliberately, he swiveled left and then right, studying the situation room before locking eyes with me and chiding, "Porter, you've got it made here. What the hell am I doing in some stuffy office in the Hoover building?"

"It's a privilege to finally welcome you aboard *Almaz*, sir," I said formally. "It's a versatile tool for any task at hand."

"Bullshit, Porter," Macallister guffawed. "Seems to me like your current mission is right here in Washington."

"Be that as it may, sir, perhaps we need to relocate. Perhaps we need to stay away from stuffy office buildings and the bureaucratic oversight.

We have everything we need on this boat. High-speed communications, a supercomputer, ground and air transportation, an armory, and space for additional personnel."

Macallister had been shaking his head back and forth. "Whatever, Porter. For now, you're on my turf."

Volkov thoughtfully propped an elbow on the table and put a thumb under her chin. "Are we, though? Are we acting as the FBI? Or are we acting independently of the FBI as Quadrant?"

"Smart question, Volkov," Macallister concurred. "It's the latter. I've cleared this with the Attorney General of the United States. He was shocked, of course, at the allegations that Genevieve Sullivan has made against Hazel Ginachere, but he agreed that an investigation was required. And he agreed that this investigation should take place quietly. He did, however, task me with overseeing you. To report back to him."

I asked, "To him and to the Director of the FBI?"

"No. Only to the AG. The Director is not in the need-to-know group. Nor is anyone else at the moment. You're on your own. Any thoughts how to proceed?"

I was shocked by that statement. Macallister had sidestepped the chain of command by going directly to the AG without looping in the Director. In previous missions, the lessons had accumulated, and I was briefly proud of myself when I countered, "Before we talk about proceeding, can we talk about the silo that you've put us inside? That seems a little rash. To not include the Director, that is."

"Coming from you, Porter, with your knack for not typically giving a shit about these leadership formalities, I'm surprised." He eyed me with suspicion before adding, "Listen, I've got your back. And I'll run it all up the flagpole when I think the time is right. Meanwhile, the Attorney General has given this his blessing. As has the Under Secretary, obviously. You've got approval from two branches of government plus my sign-off from the FBI. That's not good enough for you, Porter?"

His tone was mocking, and my ego got the better of me. Ignoring my own reservations, I shot back with bravado, "Plenty for me. Just wanted to make sure I understood the structure. Let's get going."

The boss nodded. "Tell me how you think we should proceed."

"Yessir," I replied. "First order of business is an interview with Sullivan herself. She says she has circumstantial evidence. We need to lay it all out, in one package, instead of piecemeal. She's dripped it out to me and to you. We need . . ." I paused, searching for the word.

"A data dump," suggested Volkov. "We need her sitting at this table, and then we will corroborate what she claims."

Macallister had crossed his arms over his chest, a signal of defiance and disagreement, but I overlooked that as I demanded, "Get Sullivan here. Can you do that? Tell her we need to meet with her in person."

"You're kidding, right, Porter?" Macallister sneered. "You want me to summon the Under Secretary of State for Political Affairs to your yacht for a meeting?"

I mimicked his posture and argued, "Yeah. If she wants Quadrant to do her bidding, I think she can grace us with her presence in person."

Macallister was shaking his head back-and-forth. "Okay. Ah, Porter, do you even know what the Under Secretary does at State?"

My eyes darted to Volkov and then back to Macallister.

Oops. He got me, I guess.

I took a deep breath and confessed, "No. Not really. She has an impressive title, though."

The smug grin that I received from Macallister was punishment enough. The lecture that followed was torture. "Porter, next time, get to know the cast. The Under Secretary for Political Affairs is the number four rank in the US Department of State. Sullivan reports only to the Secretary of State and two Deputy Secretaries. However, those are political appointments. The Under Secretary job is filled by a careerist, making Genevieve Sullivan the top-ranking person in all of the US Foreign Service staff."

"Okay," I conceded, "We already knew that she's a big deal. What does she actually do?"

By Macallister's initial silence, I thought, *Got him. He doesn't know. He focused on the rank, not the duties.*

I was wrong, again, and Macallister made it clear that he was simply organizing his recollection of what turned out to be a very involved set of responsibilities for the Under Secretary.

"Let's see," he began. "Sullivan oversees the State bureaus on every continent. Africa, Asia, Europe, and the Western Hemisphere. This role, by the way, puts her in contact with members of the IC—the Intelligence Community—including the CIA. On top of that, she manages the daily affairs relating to State's policies. In other words, while the politicians posture, she does real work."

"Well, then, sounds like she's accustomed to getting her hands dirty. Let's get a meeting," I said jauntily.

He stared me down and cautioned, "I'll speak with her. But make no mistake, Porter, by trying to call the shots, you're playing a dangerous game."

Sitting there, smug with my little victory, I had no idea just how dangerous the game would become.

CHAPTER 10

WEDNESDAY, MARCH 10, 2021

IT TOOK ABOUT a week-and-a-half to find a large enough hole in Genevieve Sullivan's schedule, which I thought was actually pretty fast, given the demands on the woman by the Secretary of State's office.

That time was not wasted, however. As the team—now including Macallister, who became a regular occupant of Rourke's former chair—waited for our audience with the Under Secretary, we built a dossier on our presumed target: CIA Director Hazel Ginachere.

Basic facts were straightforward enough to obtain. Despite the clandestine nature of much of the CIA's operations, the Agency's leadership was a matter of public knowledge. Ginachere, as a career civil servant, had assembled quite a record, and her photo—a pale face, partially obscured by large, black-framed eyeglasses that matched jet-black, shoulder-length hair—was featured prominently on the Agency's website.

Sixty-one years old, the Director had risen through the ranks of the CIA with what was generally regarded as ruthlessness. For example, media outlets claimed that Ginachere, then the Deputy Director of the National Clandestine Service, was the author of the so-called extraordinary rendition project, whereby terror detainees were transported to CIA-run overseas "black sites," thus beyond the reach of US law. She managed to keep her nose clean, however, and Ginachere was elevated to Deputy Director, finally taking the reins as Director in 2018. Immune to criticism, she hardly faltered during a messy divorce in 2019 that was gleefully—and admittedly somewhat meanly—chronicled by the gossip column "Page Six" in the New York *Post*, which reported all the titillating details, complete with pictures of her ex-husband, two children, and one cute puppy. Her stoicism in the face of conflict was perhaps her armor.

What we didn't need to research was Ginachere's participation in our previous operation aboard *Almaz*. Her pale face and oversized glasses graced the big flat screen in our situation room a handful of times.

One of those meetings, in particular, was possibly not my finest hour. She called me a "loose cannon." That was in response to me having snarled at her, saying, "Oh, so you answer to the Russians now, Director?"

Anyway, that's a long story. You should read it sometime.

Suffice it to say, Ginachere and I did not get along. In retrospect, my going toe-to-toe with her, even virtually, was probably not wise on my part. Accusing her of colluding with a foreign government—also not smart.

Ironic, huh? Now that Sullivan was tasking me to research just that. Sullivan, and also Macallister.

With his constant presence in Rourke's seat, it became obvious that Macallister had every intention to work this operation alongside us aboard *Almaz*, as he counseled me from atop the gangway to the dock. "I gotta caution you, Porter. You gotta be on your best behavior."

"Understood," I replied, watching as a black Chevrolet Suburban rolled to a stop in the parking lot at the head of the dock. Those Suburbans were ubiquitously common in D.C., but the tiny, white-haired figure that clambered down to the pavement from the rear passenger door was unmistakable: Genevieve Sullivan.

The Under Secretary of Political Affairs hadn't traveled in a motorcade. Though, honestly, I wasn't sure if her position ranked a multi-vehicle escort. I was, however, certain that an aide or two would accompany her, and I was wrong. She left behind her driver, a bald-headed white man, as best as I could discern through the rain-streaked glass of the Suburban, and Sullivan stood alone as she popped open a cheery yellow umbrella to ward off the late afternoon chilly drizzle.

She climbed the aluminum gangway, her sensible low, navy-blue heels making a ringing sound on the cold, wet metal, and she extended a navy-blue gloved hand to me. "Mister Porter. It's very nice to meet you in person, finally. I've come to terribly dislike all these virtual meetings."

"Likewise, Madame Under Secretary. On both fronts, that is," I stammered. "On, ah, meeting you and not enjoying Zoom, I guess."

Her laugh was as squeaky as her voice, and her grin appeared quite genuine. "I think we're going to have a lot to agree on, Ben. And remember, the first time we spoke privately, we agreed on first names. My title is a mouthful."

I smiled in return as Macallister suggested, "Ma'am, let's get out of the rain."

"Deputy Assistant Director Macallister. How nice of you. Please, lead the way."

Now familiar with *Almaz*, Macallister did just that as Sullivan followed him into the superstructure of the yacht. Taking up the tail, I followed, wondering if my gut was telling me the truth: *Macallister is now in charge of Quadrant. Not me.*

I'd find out shortly.

CHAPTER 11

OUTSIDE THE TALL WINDOWS in the *Almaz* situation room, behind my seat at the head of the table, the overcast and drizzly gray skies gradually darkened to dusk, a marked contrast to Genevieve Sullivan's bright personality. The energy from her diminutive physique seemed boundless. She took in the big screens and high-tech feel of the situation room without comment; instead, she immediately focused in on what mattered more: the people.

Eying Lockwood, Volkov, and Hamid, she started, "Deputy Assistant Director Macallister provided bios on you three already. He has also asserted that you have passed the security checks and are cleared for this conference. Despite, I might mention, some questionable decisions that you've made in the past."

With that last comment, she looked at Volkov, who dropped her gaze in a gesture of submissiveness. Sullivan didn't wait for a verbal answer as she continued, "Our mission—and make no mistake, this is *our* mutual task—is to expose Hazel Ginachere. We are up against a formidable foe. It's obvious that Ginachere runs the world's largest international intelligence organization. It's obvious that this task cannot be sanctioned by the usual powers-that-be. It's obvious that it must remain strictly and totally confidential."

Sullivan inhaled and concluded, "What's not obvious is how we go about this. After all, how does one build a case against someone so powerful, who has so many resources, and who is virtually inaccessible and untouchable?"

The Under Secretary paused, intertwining her fingers together, resting her wrists on the edge of the horseshoe-shaped table. Turning her head carefully to look each of us in the eye, she asked, "Thoughts?"

No one breathed for a moment until, naturally, I blurted, "Hang on, ma'am." I couldn't bring myself to use her first name yet. "You've got more intel. You wouldn't be making these charges without something. We need that *something*. We need to know what you know. We need to know how you know. We need to know what you don't think you know."

"You sound like Donald Rumsfeld," she said with a smirk. "He was much more eloquent, though. But that is correct." She leaned to her left side and fished into her navy-blue blazer's inside breast pocket, withdrawing a shiny, metal-looking object. Holding it up for us to examine and inclining her head toward the massive, dark flat screen, she explained, "Flash drive. I have some visual aids."

Sullivan placed the USB stick on the table and slid it to me. I pushed it toward Volkov, who accepted it and inserted the drive into a port at her station. Volkov purred evenly, "One moment, please. I'll run a virus scan and will examine the contents first. I hope you don't mind."

"I would expect nothing less," Sullivan sniffed.

Whatever security checks Volkov did took a few moments of awkward silence, as I thought, *It would never have occurred to me to check for a virus or whatever. Ugh, stupid . . . focus and get yourself back in the game.*

Volkov's lilt interrupted my inner monologue. "We're good. I see nothing but a numbered series of four image files."

"That's all there is. No fancy PowerPoint. No circles and arrows and paragraphs. Just me to explain what each one is." Sullivan's face showed a hint of a wry smile as Volkov clicked and tapped to bring up the first image, and the stern, black-eyeglassed, black-haired visage of Hazel Ginachere filled the screen. Sullivan announced, "Hazel Ginachere. The Director of the Central Intelligence Agency, colloquially known as the

D/CIA. You know who she is, of course, because I know you've dealt with her before. Next image, please."

Volkov clicked once, and Ginachere's face was replaced with a sepia-skinned, black-mustachioed man, wearing a white *thawb*, with a red and white *keffiyeh* held in place by a black *agal* encircling his skull.

"That is Salman bin Abdulaziz Al Saud. He is pictured in his typical garb: a white robe, the traditional desert headdress with a cord to hold it in place. He is—"

"The King of Saudi Arabia." Abdul Hamid interrupted the Under Secretary somewhat abruptly, and I shot him a censuring glance.

Sullivan was unperturbed. "That is correct, Agent Hamid. He has been the King since January 2015. He is eighty-five years old. And this—next image, please—is his son."

King Salman's face was replaced with a younger-looking facsimile. The same eyes, the same headdress, but this face with a full beard. Sullivan narrated, "Crown Prince Mohammed bin Salman Al Saud. We refer to him as MBS. He is thirty-six years old. And at that ripe age, he is the de facto leader of the Saudi Arabian government. He runs an authoritarian regime at the behest of his father, the King. Indeed, all that stands in the way of his total power is, well, his father."

Sullivan leaned back in her chair. "And do you know who is a dear friend of MBS? Who has supported his every decision with enthusiasm? Without consultation or without political strategy?" The Under Secretary smiled an unsmiling grin before proclaiming, "Hazel Ginachere. Next image, please."

To no one's surprise, the fourth and final image on the USB stick was one of MBS and Ginachere, deep in conversation. Ginachere was standing just slightly behind the taller Saudi, her face and her large, black eyeglasses tilted up to his right ear, his head angled slightly to his right. They were not making eye contact, nor were they touching each other. Sullivan elaborated, "This is not only a rare photo of Ginachere with MBS, but it is also a rare photo of MBS with a woman. Despite his outward claims to champion women's rights, Crown Prince Mohammed bin Salman does not stray far from the male-dominated Saudi culture."

"What's his deal?" Macallister asked.

Sullivan scoffed in response. "Where do I start? When he appeared on the scene, so to speak, in about 2017, MBS was hailed as the next generation of enlightened Saudi leaders. He was called a gamechanger. He was also referred to as a psycho. A complicated man, to be sure. But one trait remains consistent: his attraction to power and his drive for nothing less. Not unlike that of Hazel Ginachere."

Having our full attention, Sullivan casually rested her left elbow on the table and made small hand gestures as she spoke. "Our government recently declassified a report that accused MBS of complicity in the murder of the dissident journalist Jamal Khashoggi. And, MBS has been implicated in the public release of photos that exposed that the chair and founder of Amazon, Jeff Bezos, had a mistress. The list goes on and on. I can and will provide far more background."

Recalling that Macallister told me to be on my best behavior, I asked, "May I comment?" Sullivan nodded, and I said, "Okay, that's all interesting. But is it that big of a deal that a high-ranking US government official has a speaking relationship with a high-ranking foreign official? I mean, what's the problem?"

"Oh dear, Ben, you're getting ahead of me," Sullivan responded kindly. "I'm afraid I can provide only definitive proof of impropriety on only one of the issues. You see, the D/CIA wanted to protect MBS from the Khashoggi accusations, and to do so, Ginachere attempted to bury a Turkish intelligence report. I will pass on the evidence to you and to your team. Your role will be not only verification but also exhaustive substantiation. And in doing so, I believe that it will become apparent that Ginachere was complicit in the whole nasty affair. In fact, she may have known that MBS was responsible for the murder of the journalist within days after it happened. It's quite possible that Ginachere had prior knowledge. By itself, if proven without a shadow of a doubt, those accusations are damning for anybody. They are certainly unbecoming and unlawful coming from the Director of the Central Intelligence Agency."

I raised my eyebrows. Now *that* was certainly a big deal. I was wholly unprepared for what came next when I asked, "You said, 'only one of the issues.' That infers that there's another, um, issue."

"That is correct, Ben," Sullivan confirmed. "The second item, which I cannot prove, but which I hope you and your team will establish during the course of your investigation, is that Ginachere and MBS are colluding on a different, forward-looking front." The Under Secretary licked her lips and inhaled deeply. "They're planning to assassinate King Salman."

CHAPTER 12

BEFORE I COULD REACT to Sullivan's allegation, Macallister blurted out a question—one that I would guess we were all wondering. "The head of the CIA is planning to assassinate the King? With Mohammed bin Salman? His own father?"

"That is correct, Deputy Assistant Director," Sullivan repeated.

I got the feeling that maybe *that is correct* was her catchphrase. Frivolity aside, what Sullivan alleged was an almost-incomprehensible national security concern, and it was as if she were reading my mind as she elaborated, "Now, think it through. Who would be better at orchestrating this than the CIA? Who has the black site experience that Ginachere has? Who is equally fearless? Who is feared around the globe? Again, Ginachere."

"Nah," Macallister grunted. "What does she have to gain?"

"Think broadly, Deputy Assistant Director. Think payback. Ginachere takes out the elderly king, thus elevating the king's son on a predetermined schedule. No more waiting around for natural death, with all the complications of a transfer of power from one leader to the heir. Of course, it speeds things up for MBS. And thusly, simplistically, MBS owes Ginachere."

I wondered, "What does she do with that IOU?"

"She controls Western political influence in the Middle East," Sullivan said firmly. "With Saudi cooperation—no, with the blessing and enthusiastic endorsement of MBS, her new king, the CIA director can assure herself of a solid foothold in the Middle East. Ginachere would be untouchable in the United States and extremely powerful politically. Give her a handful of years, and she would have the ability to run for public office and elevate her career immensely. Indeed, with a resumé that could potentially include widespread support from the Middle East, Ginachere might even consider the presidency. That, however, would come at a grave cost to the United States of America. Imagine if our president were so deeply intertwined with an assassination? Imagine the future favors that would be expected. She'd be setting herself up for extortion."

I raised a hand. "Whoa. But what if she fails? Or what if she succeeds, and she is exposed?"

"Exactly, Ben. Those are the outcomes with which we wrestle. If she is exposed now in the planning stage, she goes down now. We avert a crisis. That's the best case. But let's say she succeeds. She must be exposed as soon as possible while she remains Director of the CIA. She'll have some level of accountability, even if she tries to pass off responsibility. However, the worst case is that she succeeds, and time passes. Then she'll have the opportunity to successfully execute her continued rise in power. She'll be able to insulate herself. The CIA will take the fall. Therefore, the United States government will take the blame. Imagine if that happened. The United States would be persona non grata on the world stage for orchestrating a coup by assassination to elevate a despot—an alleged murderer—to power as a king. US influence would be eviscerated in the conference rooms of the United Nations. In the statehouses of the European Union. And in the Middle East? Outright war for retaliation. We're talking World War Three."

Macallister stepped in. "We're going over there. We gotta get to the Middle East. Get boots on the ground. We cannot let this happen."

"No, we cannot. The urgency is undeniable. We've already lost months. You had to deal with wrapping up your prior investigation, and since Ginachere was involved with that, I knew I had no option but to remain in the background. There's nothing that could have been done then. But when I learned that Quadrant was being shut down back in December, I was greatly disappointed. I didn't know where to turn." Sullivan looked directly at me and added softly, "And then, I heard about the poisoning. That's when I knew I had to intervene."

"I get the first part," I started, before saying with confusion evident in my voice, "but the second part? What does the poisoning have to do with all of this?"

"Because you were targeted." She cast her eyes down to the polished tabletop. "As I was becoming aware of Ginachere's treachery, I shared my suspicions with my team. I trusted them, of course, and I wanted their feedback. I wanted their opinion as to whether I could task the Quadrant group for this investigation ... and for the potential apprehension of a high-ranking American official. That was during the course of last summer and into the fall. As of January, my suspicions deepened because you and your colleague were poisoned. It's circumstantial, to be sure, but I think it is possible that I have a leak in my group." Finally, Sullivan lifted her gaze to meet my stare. "Hazel Ginachere's most-often chosen method of silencing her opposition is by poison."

There was a beat of silence at the table until Macallister blurted, "That's preposterous." Before I had a chance to be impressed by Macallister's utilization of a four-syllable word, he continued, "That has to be the most circumstantial link I've ever heard. You're attempting to convince us to take on this assignment based on that?"

Sullivan stared at Macallister; her brow furrowed. Squinting and speaking softly, she offered, "It seems you'd like another example of Ginachere's methods." She paused and considered each of us individually before saying, slowly and distinctly, "What I am about to relay to you is classified at the highest levels. Beyond top secret. Indeed, so classified that the CIA, I believe, has made a concerted effort to erase any records in any government database. Of course, the CIA is well-equipped for such a task. And, I have no doubt that Ginachere is behind the purge."

Macallister grunted, "Okay. We're all cleared for classified intel here."

"That is correct," replied Sullivan. "I am well aware of the level of sophistication and discretion that Quadrant has demonstrated. But before I go on, I'll remind you that this intelligence may not leave this room. It is highly damaging to the United States." She inhaled deeply. "However, you need to know because it is also critical of Hazel Ginachere, and therefore I will disclose to you what happened in Damascus in 2014 . . ."

CHAPTER
13

IN DAMASCUS, IN 2014

A SYRIAN AIR AIRBUS A320—one of only six of this type of aircraft currently being operated by the once-proud state airline—roared into the sky, departing Damascus International Airport on runway 23L, headed southwest. About one mile from the tip of the runway, the wheels of the Airbus were fully retracted as the plane commenced an arcing, elevating turn toward the north and to its destination of Aleppo.

On the ground below, inside a non-descript grouping of wooden structures, a woman with a pale face, partially obscured by large, black-framed eyeglasses that matched her jet-black, shoulder-length hair, apprised a desert-skinned Syrian, with unwashed, straggly black hair and an unruly beard flecked with gray hairs and spittle. Once the noise of the departing Airbus's twin turbofan engines died off outside and above, the woman spoke in English, "Mister Abbas, this is becoming tiresome. Despite the rather creative methods that have been employed to persuade you to tell the truth, I'm informed that you have refused to divulge the information that has been requested. To wit, the names of your accomplices and associates in Jerusalem."

From an involuntarily seated position atop a metal chair, his arms bound behind his back and his ankles tied to the legs of the chair, the man replied in perfectly enunciated, British-accented English, "As I have stated many, many times before, I have never been to Jerusalem." His eyes focused upward on the standing woman's glasses; he ignored the squalid surroundings of the dark, dirt-floored space. Cavernous in height, with exposed wooden rafters supporting a metal roof, the area was lit only by a single, bare light bulb in a portable painter's lamp. Beyond the lamp was a black curtain. The positioning of the lamp and the glare of the bulb made it difficult to discern what, if anything, the curtain obscured.

The woman was shaking her head. "No. This is so repetitious," she sighed. "Are you not Fouad Abbas?"

"Yes."

"Are you not an expert in chemicals?"

"Yes. I am a scientist."

"With the Syrian Scientific Studies and Research Center? The SSRC?"

"Yes."

"With your work with the SSRC, are you not an expert in the assembly of detonation devices? Those used, for example, in the creation of improvised explosive devices? Those used, specifically, in a bombing in Jerusalem three years ago?"

The man sighed and cast his eyes downward. "For the twentieth or perhaps the hundredth time, no."

The woman grunted. "I believe it is time to change your mind." She motioned to the only other occupant of the room, a tall, white man with darkly tanned skin and thinning, graying hair. Clad in desert camouflage fatigue cargo pants and a black, short-sleeved t-shirt, the man turned on his heels smartly and stepped toward the black curtain. With an out-of-place flourish, given the surroundings, he swished the curtain open as if he were on stage in a Broadway theater.

A glinting mass was revealed. The man stepped toward it and manipulated a switch. Sophisticated LED lamps illuminated gradually, brightening the entire space but focused on the interior of a glass box, its footprint about six feet by six feet, and its height approximately eight feet tall. A pair of hoses, each about the diameter of the man's biceps, curved from the top of the box and disappeared through imprecisely drilled holes in the side of the wooden structure. Sunlight peeked through the gaps between the edges of the holes and the hoses, creating a series of irregular bright spots on the woman ensconced in the box.

Abbas gasped and tried to stand against the constraints, but his weakened body was no match for the heavy metal chair. "Gamila!" His voice choked as he spat toward the standing woman, "How dare you?"

Ignoring the captive woman, dressed in rags and bearing a terrified expression, who was seated on the shiny floor of the clear enclosure near a clean, black box-like container of some type, Hazel Ginachere spoke evenly, "Typically, this apparatus is used for suffocation or for, ah, atmospheric experiments. Those hoses lead to an air pump which can create a vacuum by sucking air out or, by pushing air in, can increase the air pressure in the box to untenable levels. Either way, the outcome can be messy, but we won't hear the screaming since the box is soundproof." She grinned evilly. "Today, we shall conduct a new type of test using your bride as our subject. Shall we proceed?"

"I've told you a thousand times. I am a scientist. I am not a terrorist," the man protested, his voice cracking and his eyes tearing. "Don't harm her," he pled, whispering.

"I said before; your denials are repetitive and exhausting. But perhaps as a scientist, you'll understand better before we begin. You see, within the black box adjacent to your seated bride is an Indian cobra snake. Because this creature has been confined for quite some time, without sustenance, it will be agitated. And since I doubt very much that your Gamila will sit still, I expect that she'll react to the sight of the snake, and she will provoke it. With your scientific background, I'd also expect that you know that the venom of this species contains a neurotoxin and a cardiotoxin. That venom is very deadly to the human brain and heart. Shall we continue with the experiment to see what happens?"

"No. Don't!"

She ignored the protestation and talked over it. "Fortuitously, and probably as you know, Mister Abbas, your colleagues at the SSRC have developed a polyvalent anti-serum. Now, this alone is indicative of your tendencies toward treachery because the Indian cobra is not native to Syria. Be that as it may, that's a discussion for another time. At present, that antiserum is your wife's only defense against certain paralysis and near-certain death." She turned to the assistant and nodded.

With yet another theatrical flourish and with biceps bulging unnecessarily, perhaps for show, he withdrew a small device from the large pouch affixed to the right leg of his cargo pants. Waving the device once as if it were a magic wand, he depressed a button, and both sides of the black box flopped open.

Nothing happened.

Then, slowly, the mottled brown-and-grey head of a snake poked out of the right side of the box, the light glinting dully from its scales and from its small, round, black eyes. A forked tongue flicked and, as the cobra sensed the other occupant of its space, the snake's hood expanded majestically.

Outside the box, there was no sound, but it was obvious that Gamila was screaming as the bound, helpless woman thrashed and tried to wiggle away from the snake. Extending its body from the box further, the cobra twisted its head and lunged at the threat that had presented itself in the snake's unfamiliar environment.

"She is innocent!" screamed Abbas. "Let her go!" Tears streamed down both of his cheeks, creating rivulets of cleansed skin amidst the accumulated grime.

"I see," said Ginachere. "Therefore, if she is innocent, you must not be."

"No!"

The agitated snake buried its fangs deep within the prisoner's bare left leg, and yet true to Ginachere's explanation, the victim's screams were unheard.

Abbas, on the other hand, was burbling, repeating "*la*," Arabic for no, over and over, his head hung low, and his eyes closed to the terror.

"The venom works extraordinarily quickly," Ginachere hummed. "I give Gamila twenty minutes, given her weakened physique. Thirty minutes tops."

"I have nothing to tell you," Abbas cried. "She is innocent. I am innocent. I swear." His voice trailed off to an almost childish whine.

Ginachere withdrew a glass vial from her pocket and waved it under

Abbas's nose. "Look—the anti-serum. One final chance, Mister Abbas. There's still time."

"I can't tell you anything," Abbas whispered weakly.

"Very well," Ginachere hissed. Making certain that Abbas's eyes were open, she tapped his nose with the vial, and then with a grunt, hurled the small container at the larger, thick-sided glass enclosure. The vial shattered instantly on contact, shards of glass dropping soundlessly on the dirt floor as the liquid contents dribbled down the box, leaving a smeary trail.

Turning to her accomplice, Ginachere growled, "After she dies, shoot him and leave the bodies in the desert for the predators."

The man spoke for the first time in Boston-accented American English. "What about that snake?"

"Bring the handler back in to deal with the snake. Perhaps it might be useful soon. I wouldn't want to waste such a valuable asset."

With that, the CIA operative strode from the room without a backward glance and disappeared into the hot, dry Damascus afternoon.

CHAPTER 14

CAPTIVATED BY Genevieve Sullivan's story, not one person seated at the horseshoe-shaped table in the *Almaz* situation room spoke. I, for one, was spellbound.

Sullivan primly steepled her hands on the polished table as she scanned the faces of her audience. "Not a pleasant way for Gamila Abbas to perish. Would you agree?"

Like attentive schoolchildren, we nodded as one.

Sullivan, however, hadn't concluded her story. "Using a suspect's wife as coercion is nasty business, I think. It crosses ethical lines, humanitarian lines, and certainly diplomatic lines. That's not the worst of it, though."

I exclaimed, "There's more?"

"Oh, yes. Sadly, yes. For it turns out that Fouad Abbas was, indeed, innocent. A case of mistaken identity, I'm told. One that was not vetted properly but could have been. No, Ginachere wanted a confession, and she was convinced Abbas was her target. Her bias against the threat overcame any sort of restraint. To ask more questions. To confirm her sources."

Macallister asked, "Were there any repercussions when someone discovered that she had the wrong guy?"

"Eventually, the Syrians got word that Abbas and his wife, both well respected in Damascus, disappeared. Inquiries were made. The cover-up began and continues to this day. You used the word *repercussions*. Imagine the global outcome if it became known that an operative acting on behalf of the United States not only tortured a suspect who was wrongly accused but also included that suspect's wholly innocent spouse in the interrogation—and killed her." With her eyes downcast, Sullivan muttered, "It would be a disaster for diplomacy."

Macallister spoke again. "What about Ginachere? How did she wiggle out of the mess?"

Sullivan snorted. "She's wily. She figured it out. And, of course, Ginachere would never dare to come clean. That's not her style. Obviously."

With her gaze remaining settled in Macallister's direction, Sullivan wondered, "Deputy Assistant Director, has the FBI made any ground in your investigation on the Porter and Rourke incident?"

Macallister shook his head. "No. Unfortunately not. We know the chemicals and the application method. But we don't have a perp."

Volkov spoke up for the first time since accepting Sullivan's flash drive. "I pulled every camera image from the surrounding three-block radius. The FBI got me the warrants. But nothing matches up. And we have a robust exterior camera system here on *Almaz*, but only one of our cameras faces the lot where the Jeep was parked. While, unfortunately, the Jeep itself is blocked from view by other vehicles, we can see the perimeter of the area. We isolated eleven people in that lot that morning."

"Why only morning? What about overnight?" Sullivan asked.

"Well, two reasons," Volkov explained. "First, and most importantly, our lab techs indicated that the carrier of the poison—it was mixed into a hand moisturizer product—was going to dry and become inefficient as a transmission method. They worked backward and found an application time of about two hours max before the mixture was rendered ineffective. Even an hour of wait time reduced the potency. Therefore, we didn't feel that it was necessary to expand a search time beyond two hours. And what we found—"

"Wait. What was the second reason?" Sullivan was sharp. She paid attention to every word, obviously.

"Right," Volkov said. "The second issue was merely overnight darkness. The lot is lit by overhead pole lighting, but that particular camera doesn't have night vision capabilities. Civil twilight on that morning wasn't until 6:58 A.M. Porter and Rourke departed the yacht at 7:19 A.M. and got into the Jeep at 7:22 A.M."

"That's a short window of time," Sullivan offered.

Volkov shrugged. "Yes. Anyway, we pulled nine images starting at 5:00 A.M. We had seven people pass through the lot before natural light, and while those images required manipulation and enhancement to be useful, we eliminated those seven as either employees in the area or liveaboards, like us. After twilight, we saw four people pass by. One of them was also eliminated, leaving us three UNSUBs. Um, sorry, unknown subjects."

Sullivan smiled gently. "Yes, dear, I know what an UNSUB is. Please go on."

"Right. Anyway, for what it's worth, here they are." Volkov manipulated the keyboard and mouse at her station, and the on-screen photo of Ginachere and bin Salman was replaced with an image of an overcoated, hatted, and pale-skinned woman, hands in her pockets, trudging head down. "That's suspect one. Here's number two." Volkov clicked, and a photo appeared of a tall white man with thinning gray hair combed over his temples, dressed in a camel-colored overcoat and carrying a briefcase. "And finally, here's three." The screen changed to show a Black man, wearing a hoodie with stripes on the sleeves and baggy jeans—as Sullivan gasped.

"Wait. Wait. *Wait.*" Sullivan's hand covered her mouth daintily. Her eyes were wide open in surprise. "Go back," she demanded. "Go back to number two."

Volkov clicked as she commented, "The accountant? That guy? He's like, a banker or something."

The tall man's photo had refilled the giant screen. He *did* look like an accountant or a banker. Some sort of office type perhaps headed for his morning coffee before entering the halls of a government building. Probably, I'd guess, the Internal Revenue Service.

Sullivan had slowly dropped her hand from her mouth to the table as she breathed, "You're mistaken. But you would not be the first to make that assumption."

Macallister grunted, "You know him?"

"From his dossier only, yes," confirmed the Under Secretary. "And quite a dossier it is. It is Top Secret and then restricted beyond that. I'm surprised that I had access." She paused, examining the screen, and continued, "Yes, yes. I'm sure of it. His name is JJ Gansett. And his appearance—his appearance which caused you to dismiss him as a suspect—is literally the perfect cover. He's unassuming. He doesn't look threatening. He can pass invisibly through any crowd."

Sullivan sat forward in the black executive-style chair, raising her body as tall as she could and straightening her shoulders and neck. "I offer that this is a definitive link to Ginachere, for a younger Mister Gansett played a significant supporting role in the story I just told you about, in Damascus. You see, Gansett is the CIA's most deadly contract assassin."

CHAPTER
15

THE WASHINGTON SKIES were dark outside the tall windows of the *Almaz* situation room. Genevieve Sullivan had departed an hour ago, vanishing into the D.C. dusk. For a moment, I considered the benefits of vanishing, too; I'd be out of reach of Hazel Ginachere and of her assassin. *I was targeted by the CIA,* I thought with a mixture of fear, confusion, and, yeah, a tiny bit of pride.

I was a nobody less than five years ago. Way to go. Way to make a name for yourself.

I wasn't so thrilled that my apparent notoriety came with a target on my back, but then again, any publicity, even bad publicity, is good. Right? Wasn't that attributed to P.T. Barnum? *Appropriate,* I thought, *because now I'm a star in a CIA circus?*

Cautioning myself to think realistically and prudently, I tried to focus on the conversation as an agitated Macallister repeated his suggestion, "We're going there. We're goin' to the Middle East. Saudi Arabia. Gotta be on the ground. Intercept this thing. We can't do a damn thing from here."

Lockwood was saying, "We take *Almaz* trans-Atlantic. To the far eastern reaches of the Mediterranean Sea. South through the Suez Canal. Into the Red Sea. We could dock at Jeddah or at any number of the smaller ports on the Saudi west coast. Call it 5,500 nautical miles."

He shrugged his shoulders. "At our cruising speed of fifteen knots, call it fifteen days. Twenty days tops. Not too bad and well within our range. And I bet the price of diesel there is pretty good to refuel for the trip back home," he concluded with a chuckle.

"The capital of Saudi Arabia is Riyadh," Volkov offered. She pulled up a chart and cast it to the big center screen, and she populated the smaller flanking screens with Sullivan's four pictures and our camera capture of the alleged assassin. Motioning to the center screen, Volkov explained, "Riyadh is landlocked. Obviously, we're not getting there directly by boat. The closest port is Jeddah. However, I fear that *Almaz* would be anything but low profile in that harbor; it's mostly commercial ships and hosts very little in the superyacht sense. On the other hand, *Almaz* would blend in nicely in Dubai, but Dubai is substantially farther away."

"Yeah, I think Dubai is a good call," Macallister agreed as he looked in Lockwood's direction.

Our captain shrugged again. "Another 2,500 miles. Add a week. Still doable."

"That's it, then," Macallister barked. "For planning, we'll call it twenty-one days. Volkov, put a calendar on screen." With the briefest of glances toward me, Volkov did just that, and Macallister pointed at the dates displayed and said, "Monday, April 5th. That's the date we need to be in Dubai. Working backward with the transit time, that means we leave this coming Monday, March 15th. We have four days to prepare. I'm gonna find us a new chopper pilot. Lockwood, you get the crew you need signed up. Get me their passport info so that I can do background checks and obtain the necessary immigration visas. Not a lot of time, so let's get cracking."

Listening to Macallister, my boss, I was stunned. My instincts, when Macallister had led Sullivan into the superstructure of *Almaz* just hours ago, were correct. Macallister was taking charge. I didn't like it. "Hang on, sir. Let's talk this through. There are some holes in your plan. Dare I say, it's like Swiss cheese."

Macallister did not take kindly to me using a phrase that he once used when criticizing one of my previous plans, and he was quick with a rebuttal. "Bullshit, Porter. We gotta get going. Then I got three weeks, at least, while the boat is underway, which gives me time to fill in the blanks. To set up an operations plan for when we get there. To pull in additional evidence. We sit here on our asses doing that first, and we waste that time," he huffed.

"You heard Sullivan," I countered. "Even she used the word 'circumstantial' when linking Ginachere to poisoning Rourke and me."

"Uh, Porter, how about that assassin guy? In the parking lot? Near your Jeep? You think that's a coincidence? No way is a CIA bag man wandering in this neighborhood by accident."

Mimicking Lockwood, it was my turn to shrug. "Yeah, it's possible. It's probable, even. But here's what you haven't answered—what's Ginachere's motive? Why take *me* out? Why am I a threat to her?"

"You heard Sullivan on that, too," Macallister retorted. "Sullivan said that her office leaked it. Ginachere got wind of Quadrant being tasked to hunt down her duplicity. Ginachere can't target Sullivan. That would leave Quadrant still tasked, now with additional potential evidence against Ginachere. Better for her to cut the head off the snake before it strikes, no?" Smug with his analysis, Macallister crossed his arms over his chest.

"I guess," I mumbled. "I mean, I guess that's plausible. You're saying that I'm the head of the snake?"

Hamid had been uncharacteristically quiet, but when he joined the discussion, I couldn't help but agree with his observation. "I tend to side with Macallister. Remember, Porter, if we're en-route on the open sea, we—and you, personally—are out of the assassin's reach. It not only buys time, but it also buys safety. With the data capabilities on this boat, we can get a great deal of information without worrying about our perimeter." Turning his eyes to Volkov, Hamid suggested, "What would it take to make this boat disappear? Like, I mean, Lockwood was going to put it on the market. Can you fabricate an imaginary buyer overseas so that when the boat departs Washington, Ginachere will conclude it was sold?"

"Sure, I can do that," Volkov confirmed. "I'll set something up in, I dunno—"

"Greece," Lockwood suggested. "A country with a proud maritime history. *Almaz* would certainly be suited for cruising the Greek Islands."

"Get it done," Macallister ordered. "Any other questions?" He paused for a half-second, not nearly enough time for questions to be raised, in my opinion, before adding, "I'll brief the Attorney General. He'll cover me for my leave of absence, or whatever we'll call it. Then I'll pack my bags and be on board for good on Sunday afternoon. There's no way I'll get the people we need for a mission on the ground in Saudi Arabia in only a few days, so I'll assemble the team once we are underway. But we will be on our way, and therefore, we got the beginnings of a mission outline. Right? We good?"

Hamid, Lockwood, and Volkov all muttered some sort of affirmation. I didn't say anything. I couldn't decide if I was pissed off that Macallister was calling the shots, or if I was mad at myself for not being more proactive and taking the lead.

Come Sunday, I'd learn that it didn't matter.

CHAPTER 16

SEATED AT A KITCHEN ISLAND, wearing a maroon apron to protect his pressed white oxford shirt, striped tie, and pleated, gray dress pants, the gray-haired man arranged items beside the yellow legal pad that lay on the white quartz countertop before him. First, a plastic mat. Next, a small, buff-colored paper bag, perhaps eight inches high, carefully folded across the top opening and very much appearing like it contained a child's packed sandwich lunch. Then, a clear plastic tray, divided into equal compartments, something that might be on the shelves at a Bed, Bath and Beyond box store, containing a variety of plastic objects. Finally, a small stack of folded paper towels pulled from the wall-mounted metal dispenser located in the men's room adjacent to the gym in the basement of the building.

To the man's left, massive, floor-to-ceiling windows, cut with horizontally-running, charcoal-colored muntin bars offered picturesque views of dawn breaking over the Washington Navy Yard neighborhood, arguably one of the trendiest residential communities in the District, a perch made even more dramatic should the man have ventured outside to the rooftop terrace.

To his right, a comfortable sitting area, with mid-century modernist furnishings, with their angled, spindly legs and nickel-wrapped feet contrasting a substantially overstuffed sofa—all to be ignored at the present moment but promising a comfortable retreat upon conclusion of his task.

Above, discrete speakers in the ceiling vibrated with the melody of a Broadway soundtrack. The man cocked his head to listen, and he sang along softly, *"Five hundred, twenty-five thousand, six hundred minutes . . ."*

Within the one-million-dollar-plus penthouse condominium, with his background music playing, the man extracted a brown, glass bottle with a white, childproof cap from the paper bag and placed it on the plastic mat. Examining the label glued to the side of the bottle, he confirmed that the medication matched with his notes on the yellow pad: Digoxin Oral Solution, USP.

As he unscrewed the cap, he smiled. Few people would know what those three letters meant, though they commonly appeared appended to the names on many medications. "United States Pharmacopeia," the man recited softly.

The USP mark confirmed that a product conformed to quality, potency, and purity standards. His intent, as he carefully poured a 40cc amount of the bottle's liquid contents into a plastic measuring cup, was for a purpose unintended by the manufacturer, yet he too relied on those very standards.

Ensuring that the amount matched his notes, he added a touch more liquid to the cup before removing a McKesson 60 cc piston irrigation syringe from the divided compartment tray. Dipping the snout of the syringe into the measuring cup, he pulled the plunger, sucking 40 ccs of Digoxin into the device; as planned, only a trace amount of the liquid remained in the measuring cup.

Lips barely moving, he whisper-sang along to the music. *"How do you measure. . ."*

He placed the cap on the syringe and stood, removing the unblotched apron and replacing it with a blue blazer. Sliding the syringe into his left blazer pocket, he took his leave of the exquisite condo. He'd return later and tidy up, wiping the surfaces with a paper towel before burning it on the hearth of his fireplace. Indeed, the towel would absorb nothing, so exacting was his work.

His movements were calculated and thoughtful—almost prim. Unthreatening and unassuming—just like his appearance and his demeanor.

"In times that he cried," he whispered as he stood in the elevator vestibule. He had not shut off the "Rent" soundtrack in the condo, and though the music played to no audience, the man had no trouble reciting the lyrics. *"In bridges he burned, or the way that she died . . ."*

This operation was unlike any one previous, and he hesitated at the elevator for a split second.

No, he thought. *You're imagining things.*

As the man boarded the elevator, he reassured himself. He had every reason to expect that his next operation would be conducted with his usual grace and precision, and it would proceed completely unnoticeably.

CHAPTER
17

AS SUNDAY MORNING DAWNED, I knew that Macallister's planned departure for tomorrow, Monday, March 15, just wasn't gonna happen.

Really, I knew that when he blurted out that date. The timeline was too aggressive. Too short. Too much work to do.

But I had to admit, I was impressed. He got a lot accomplished in those four days since our conference with Sullivan. For starters, Macallister informed us that our new pilot would be arriving Monday, returning our Eurocopter EC155B1 to its home on the teak-decked helicopter pad aboard *Almaz*. Lockwood hired three new crewmembers, all of whom I would meet Monday, and he'd successfully convinced our former chef, the Paris-born Julienne Jacquard, to rejoin the yacht. All told, we'd be able to fly the chopper and navigate the vessel while eating well.

The only downside, I considered, was that Macallister would be moving into the stateroom once occupied by Heather Rourke. That disturbed me on two levels: first, and most obviously because my boss would now be on board, clearly running the show, and second, because I had spent more than a few nights in that stateroom, curled up with

Rourke. It made me a little sick to my stomach to imagine Macallister sleeping there.

I had to let it go.

Besides, I begrudgingly was forced to concede that Macallister's excuse for disappearing for an extended period of time from the Hoover building was downright brilliant: on paper, Macallister was assigned to the FBI's new campus in the 38,000-acre Redstone Arsenal in Huntsville, Alabama, already the home of the FBI's Hazardous Devices School and the Terrorist Explosive Device Analytical Center. Macallister's appointment would be seen as a prerequisite stepping-stone to an even bigger promotion in Washington, D.C., something that I'm certain that Macallister would have welcomed. In the meantime, though he'd be aboard *Almaz*, the risk of him not being at Redstone was minimal—no one there knew him.

It was exactly the kind of complicated, double-blind web that Macallister wove for me at one time, and I figured he was envious of the lack of oversight aboard the yacht. I, however, was not thrilled, obviously, to have him infringe on what I considered as my domain.

"Sunday morning coffee run, Benny boy! You want some? You in?" Hamid's voice interrupted my brooding, and I looked at him as he hopped from one foot to the other.

"You're awfully jittery for someone *before* getting a caffeine hit."

"Nah, man, just stoked. Ready to get rockin'. Time for adventure. Let's go!" He was halfway out the door when he turned and repeated, "You want some?"

"Yeah, sure, man. The usual."

"You got it, bro. Hey, I'm lookin' forward to having Jacquard back. I don't know how she did it, but her coffee was the bomb."

"Yep. Totally agree on that." I withdrew a Jackson from my wallet and offered it to Hamid. With a fast hand gesture, he waved off my magnanimous gesture and made for the gangway.

I gave that a couple of minutes of thought before deciding to follow him. I could use the exercise. I had tried out the fancy Peloton bike that Volkov purchased; I set up my profile name—beerhunter, if you must know—and I even figured out the fancy shoes with the clips that snapped into the pedals. *I got this,* I thought, until I started my first spin class. The on-screen instructor, a super fit woman named Jenn Sherman, who I learned was about twenty years my senior and could clearly kick my ass, barked orders at me, telling me to pedal harder and to keep my head up and my shoulders down and to rise out of the saddle and jog and to increase the resistance ... I was panting and dripping gallons of sweat while she was barely perspiring, laughing that the faint sheen on her arms gave her a "glazed donut" look. So, my first ride summary: demoralizing and intimidating—although I did enjoy Sherman's colorful language.

Maybe I'll give it another try during the trans-Atlantic trip. But first, I need a glazed donut, I thought as I trotted to catch up with Hamid with a renewed sense of energy.

Daylight saving time had begun overnight, the famous Washington cherry blossoms would soon be in full bloom, and spring was in the air. We'd miss that, at sea, but it was a good feeling nonetheless, and now with a planned Wednesday departure, we'd get to relish it for a few days.

Finally spotting Hamid, nine minutes into the eleven-minute walk to our favorite coffee-and-donut shop on the Potomac waterfront, I also felt like I could avoid that Peloton machine for a few more days as I huffed alongside him. "Hey, man, wait up. You walk fast."

"Bro! What are you up to?"

"Figured I'd walk with you. Hell, we're gonna be at sea for weeks. Might as well feel the ground below our feet."

Hamid grinned as we pulled the doors open to the District Donut shop. His nostrils flared as he inhaled the smells of coffee and freshly baked goods. "I love D.C., man. What a city, eh?"

"Sure," I agreed, as we placed our orders, me requesting not only a dozen donuts but also coffees for Lockwood and Volkov, too; we couldn't return to *Almaz* empty-handed.

Passing a cardboard carry tray with three large to-go cups to me and accepting a single cup for himself, Hamid grunted, "Whoa. I know you're doing the healthy, all-black these days. Not gonna lie, pal. That donut is your problem. Not a little sugar in your coffee." He made a face at me and added, "Gotta doctor up mine. Me, I gotta have a little more sweetness."

As he made his way to the self-serve condiment bar, I turned to take in the view across the river. Soon, the barren trees on the opposite bank would show shoots of green, and the jackets that folks wore would be replaced with t-shirts and tank tops. Summer was coming, and I hoped we'd be back from the Middle East in time to enjoy a bit of it.

"'Scuse me! Sorry, pal," I heard Hamid say as he shouldered by a blue-blazered man who happened to be standing between the condiment bar and the exit. Hamid possessed that charisma; he could simultaneously barge past someone while charming them at the same time, and the latest victim of Hamid's complete disregard for personal space didn't seem to be bothered as we made for the doors and began the walk back to *Almaz*.

And in those eleven minutes, everything would change.

CHAPTER 18

BEARING NOT ONLY our coffees but also our treats for Lockwood and Volkov, Hamid and I climbed the gangway to board *Almaz*.

Immediately, I sensed something was wrong. Hamid was clutching the top of the gangway railing, breathing heavily.

As was typical for him, he brushed it off. "Phew. Winded. I really needed the caffeine, apparently." He slugged a big gulp from the coffee, licked his lips, and then popped the travel lid from the wax paper cup container so that he could suck down an even bigger slurp. "*Much better,*" he panted after he drank. "Wow. Winded from the walk. Must be dehydrated or something."

I wasn't so sure. His breathing was uneven, and he appeared pale. "Let's get you inside. Sit down. Put your feet up. You don't look so good, bud."

"Nah, I'm fine, man." But despite putting on a brave face, he followed me to the living area, where he sank into a couch, lethargically pulling the coffee cup to his lips and swallowing the last of the liquid.

This is wrong, I thought. *The caffeine should have the opposite effect.*

I picked up the nearest intercom handset and pressed the numbers for the bridge, Lockwood's usual hangout, hoping that Volkov would be at his side as usual. Lockwood picked up on the third ring. "Yeah?"

"Hello Miles. Abdul and I brought Anastasia and you some coffee. Would you come down to the third deck, please? Right away, please. Before your coffee cools off." Using first names, I tried to get a message of intimate insistence to Lockwood while keeping the alarm out of my voice; I didn't want Hamid to hear it. He had closed his eyes.

"Ah, sure," Lockwood replied. I guessed he picked up my intent when he added, "We're both on our way now."

At 235 feet long, *Almaz* was big, but not that big, and it was a matter of less than a minute for Lockwood, dressed in a fleece quarter-zip top and track pants, and Volkov, also similarly casually attired in leggings and a sweatshirt, to appear in the living area. Volkov, not having heard my brief conversation with Lockwood, exclaimed, "You brought coffee!" Her enthusiasm waned immediately, though, when she caught sight of Hamid, slumped on the sofa. Her tone trailed off as she whispered, "What's up with . . ."

Hamid's eyes snapped open at the sound of Volkov's voice. "Who? What? Wait." He frantically looked left, then right, and then his head swayed back. "I'm gonna be sick."

Always the offshore sailor, and therefore always on the lookout for any anomaly, Lockwood sprang into action. He lifted Hamid from the seat and half-carried him, half-walked him to the outer deck. Coffees forgotten, Volkov and I watched helplessly as Lockwood leaned Hamid over the varnished teak-capped rail, and Hamid vomited into the Potomac River.

Still propping Hamid's body upward, Lockwood turned to Volkov and me, and he mouthed three words. I can't read lips, but I know a *'what the fuck'* when I see one. I could only shake my head in confusion.

Lockwood barked, "Get me the medical kit! And towels. Lotsa towels."

Almaz was stocked with medical supplies, and I knew that Lockwood had a fair amount of basic training. "I'll get the kit!" I yelled at Volkov as I dashed toward the stair to the bridge. "You grab the towels." Volkov disappeared in my wake, presumably to the galley.

By the time we reconvened, perhaps ninety seconds later, me bearing a red soft-sided case marked with a white cross, Volkov with a stack of dishcloths and two folded tablecloths, Lockwood had moved Hamid aft to the larger, covered *al fresco* dining area where the table and chairs were covered with fitted canvas wraps to protect them from the off-season weather. Hamid lay atop the teak decking, panting. Lockwood had a forefinger and a middle finger resting lightly on Hamid's inner wrist. "His pulse races. Then slows. Then races again."

Lockwood's tone was deeply concerned, and I caught his eye. He rarely, if ever, showed fear in his eyes, but I saw something else—an urgency.

Hamid shivered violently as if he was experiencing a seizure. Even as his body stopped shaking, his left hand quivered. His mouth moved, but he did not speak. As Hamid's head rolled involuntarily to face me, his tongue peeked between his lips.

"I'm calling a bus," I stated decisively. Lockwood quickly nodded his agreement as I whipped out my phone and dialed 9-1-1.

CHAPTER
19

MONDAY, MARCH 15, 2021

FBI SPECIAL AGENT Abdullatif al-Hamid passed away on Monday, March 15, 2021, at 4:20 A.M., at the George Washington University Hospital.

Despite its size—some 35,000 agents and staffers—the FBI moves remarkably quickly when one of our own is down. Emergency medical technicians were on-site aboard *Almaz* seven minutes after my call to emergency dispatch, but it was Volkov's call, made while I was still on the phone with the 9-1-1 operator, that truly triggered the response. The wheels of the Bureau began to move as soon as Volkov called Macallister, who also had quickly decided to call our ally Doctor Curtis.

Sadly, nothing moved fast enough for Abdul Hamid.

I had ridden the ambulance with Hamid to the GW Hospital, where the patient was greeted with a swelling cadre of doctors, courtesy of Macallister and his associates at the Bureau, who grabbed mobile phones and swiped through contact lists for their go-to doctors and surgeons. Cardiac, vascular, neuro, ortho, uro, gastro—they took their turns in the ER, ready to lend their specific expertise to the sickened agent.

Hamid's symptoms were terrifying. He was incoherent and confused, unable to walk or even control his gross motor skills. His skin was clammy and pale, and during the fourteen-and-a-half-minute ambulance ride, the attending EMT told me that Hamid's irregular heartbeat raced to well over one hundred beats per minute and then dropped, precipitously, to under forty, before shooting back up to the eighty range and then plummeting again.

Lockwood and Volkov trailed the ambulance in the brand-new Mercedes G-550 AMG SUV that we had sourced to replace the totaled Jeep. The luxurious vehicle was commonplace in Dubai and Riyadh, and should the team require ground transport upon arrival in the Middle East, it was a simple matter to use the aft deck crane aboard *Almaz* to lower the vehicle to a pier. The white sun-reflective exterior paint, the central tire inflation system (should the SUV need to be driven in sand with tires deflated and then back onto tarmac), and the quilted leather seats were all over-the-top—but they wouldn't do a damn thing for Hamid.

Nor could I do anything for my friend. The doctors raced in and out of the curtained areas, intent on treating their patients. Hamid himself was deep inside the Emergency Room area, inaccessible to visitors. I was shut out, with nothing to do but to hover at the nurse's station near the entry of the ER, much to the annoyance of the mid-forty-ish year old woman seated at the desk, her attention distracted from the various monitors that she oversaw by my repeated demands for an update on Hamid's condition. "We gotta do our work. Get outta here. Enough with your questions," she growled at me. Her nametag read *Raven*, and her demeanor was as dark as her name.

"Look, *nurse*, I *need* to talk to a doctor." I wrinkled my nose as I said, "nurse," using a snobby inflection to signify that only a doctor could give me the answers that I wanted. "I'm an FBI agent. I need to talk to someone who is accountable."

She did not take that well. "I don't care who you are or what you do. Nor do I care for your shit. Back off and get outta here."

"I just need to know what's going on with him," I begged. "Can't you tell me something?"

Nurse Raven glowered, eyes narrowed to bird-like slits as she snarled, "I ain't a doctor. And apparently, I ain't good enough for you. I said back off. Get out. You're in the way."

I retreated.

Eventually, Macallister arrived, and then we were joined by Doctor Curtis.

It quickly became obvious that Curtis was outnumbered and, frankly, outclassed by the specialists who had gathered, so Curtis became the messenger to Macallister, Lockwood, Volkov, and me as we waited for a prognosis.

"It's not good," Curtis announced somberly. "They're not sure what's going on. Respiration, temperature, and oxygen saturation levels are all over the place. They've run the usual gamut of tests, and nothing ominous was present in the standard hospital toxicology screen."

Volkov asked, "A tox screen is standard procedure?"

"Yes, certainly, of course. However, one of the specialist doctors—a cardiologist—observed an arrhythmia on the electrocardiogram plot. There are discrepancies with the t-wave. A second, more sophisticated tox screen has been ordered—but those results won't be available for some time. The sample must be sent to an outside lab, but I can assure you, that second tox screen is being expedited."

Macallister offered, "Let me know what I can do, if anything. I've got some pull, you know."

The doctor placed his palms together, fingers up as if he was praying, and as he did so, he bowed slightly toward Macallister. "Thank you, sir. I'll be seeing to it personally."

The doctor's slow diction and exaggerated formality annoyed me, and I moaned, "So, basically, doc, you're saying they're not doing anything for Hamid?"

"Oh, no, no, no," Curtis replied, with offense obvious in his tone. "There's a very solid team on his case. Currently, they're hydrating and sedating him, but his body is in shock. We must be patient." He shook his head. "There's nothing you all can do here other than be in the way. There's really nothing I can do except try and oversee it. I'm not going to second-guess the experts."

Eventually, helpless and ineffective at the hospital, we trundled back to *Almaz*, cocooned in the G-wagon. No words were spoken during the short ride.

Curtis's humble demeanor was admirable, and I knew first-hand that he would have Hamid's best interests at heart, but with dismay, I figured that his lack of positivity was certainly intentional. He did not want to imply false hope.

At the crack of dawn on Monday, Curtis called, and the team gathered around the coffee table in the living area aboard *Almaz*. Curtis's voice rang tinnily from Macallister's iPhone set to speaker mode. "He passed away early this morning. The doctors made a valiant effort, but his heart just gave out. He would not have felt any pain. There's nothing that we could have done."

I asked, "Were you there? By his bedside?"

There was a short pause before Curtis replied, "In a way, I suppose. I'm not an attending doctor at GW, as you know. My work is done in a lab, not in an ICU. But they were kind enough to let me stay. I dozed off in one of the chairs by the nurse's station." He cleared his throat and said bluntly, "I was woken by a Code Blue emergency. Hamid was in distress, and it was only a matter of time. A heart just cannot take that kind of strain."

"He was too young to go," I mumbled. I'd known Hamid for only about three years, but we had quickly become close friends, relishing our shared experiences at Quantico and beyond. Hamid's energy, good-natured bluster, and absolute loyalty were traits that come dear, that should not be taken for granted.

First Rourke, and now just over two months later, Hamid. I was deflated. But—wait—Rourke? "Doc," I called out to the iPhone, "what ever happened to that other test that was ordered? The one the specialist did that was more sophisticated?"

"Yeah," he said, drawing the word out slowly and causing the four of us to physically lean in toward the device on the table, "I was getting to that. I reviewed that report. It was clear except for one thing that should not have been there. Digoxin."

Macallister demanded, "What the hell is Digoxin?"

"It's a very common medication used to treat heart failure. But, if it's dosed too highly, it can trigger the exact problem that it's meant to solve." Curtis paused again, audibly inhaling, and announced, "Digoxin doesn't show up in a standard, quick-response tox screen, but the second blood test showed such a high concentration of the drug that there can be no question. Hamid overdosed."

CHAPTER
20

LISTENING TO Doctor Curtis's explanation of Hamid's cause of death, I felt my own heart speed up, and I placed my right pointer finger and middle finger gently on the inside of my left wrist. I think I was imagining things; my pulse felt okay. It was little consolation until I realized that I should be grateful that I still had a pulse.

Unlike Hamid. Unlike Rourke.

Volkov was apparently thinking the same thing, and she was pointing at me while mouthing something to Macallister, who was nodding at her even as he picked up the conversation with Doctor Curtis. "Hamid overdosed? Therefore, can I assume that there are no parallels to Porter's case? Or Rourke's case?"

"Medically, no. In a manner of speaking, a qualified yes, however, because both patients presented with foreign substances in their systems. Other than that, totally unrelated."

"What about cause? Anything on Hamid's hands, like Porter and Rourke?"

"No, and there wouldn't be," the doctor said quickly and firmly. "These cases are absolutely dissimilar. We establish that fact from the rarity of the chemical utilized with Porter and Rourke. That had to be intentional. However, with Hamid's case, you must consider the prevalence and accessibility of the drug. Digoxin is commonplace. It's used everywhere."

"I don't understand," I complained. "Why would Hamid overdose on this Digoxin?"

"It's an ordinary medication. Prescribed all the time. He must have overdosed himself. In pill form, that would be relatively easy to do; the pills are tiny, and you could easily swallow way more than you should."

"I don't think so," Macallister guessed, glancing at the three of us for any objection. "We're, ah, preparing for some work, and I reviewed the medical histories of the, um, workers. Hamid was not on any medications."

Clearly, Macallister was reluctant to read Curtis in on our planned overseas journey, and fortunately, the doctor didn't press the question. He did, however, make an accusation that I did not appreciate. "What about recreational drugs? Was Hamid a user?"

"No way," I shot back quickly. "He's clean. He's an active FBI agent, for fuck's sake."

"Easy, Porter," whispered Macallister.

"Routine question, I guess," Curtis stated, presumably without offense. In a clinical tone, he suggested, "Really, the only way to establish more is to do a full workup. An autopsy. I'll order the morgue to look for everything. Needle scars, bruising, stomach contents, or at least what's left of them. What I'd like to do is move Hamid to my lab over at Walter Reed. Macallister, you'll have to sign off on that."

"Consider it done," the Deputy Assistant Director affirmed. "Email me what you need. I'll turn it around immediately. And—let me know how long that will take. For a report, that is."

"A week perhaps. Maybe more."

"Alright. I'll be out of town but still in touch by phone, email, all the regular ways. You good with that, Doc?"

I was staring narrow eyed at Macallister as Curtis replied, "Yes," and disconnected the call.

Without blinking, I demanded, "Out of town? Whaddya mean, out of town? We got a man down. We're not going anywhere."

Macallister picked up his iPhone and slipped it into a pocket. "What are you talking about? We got a mission."

"No, we got an investigation."

"The Bureau will cover it. We got more important things to do."

I stood, crossing my arms over my chest. "Bullshit. We must work this case. Hamid is one of us."

From the corner of my eye, I caught Lockwood's and Volkov's heads swiveling in unison, back and forth as Macallister and I argued. Their gazes lifted as one as Macallister slowly rose to his feet. "Don't do this, Porter. Not now. We—"

"Don't do what? Do our jobs? Figure out why Hamid died? He didn't OD, obviously. He was drugged."

Macallister scoffed. "How do you jump to that conclusion?"

I huffed, "Easy. Someone targeted me. And Rourke. And now Hamid dies? Don't you think that it's all too coincidental that—"

Macallister's face reddened. "You're fucking joking, right? Now, I'll agree that it might appear, by circumstantial connection only, that Hazel Ginachere targeted you and Rourke. Yes, I'll admit that's possible. But anything is possible, Porter. We don't have a shred of proof other than Sullivan's word that Ginachere's favorite wet-work guy was spotted in the area. We don't have a positive ID on that person yet, and we definitely don't have a motive."

"Motive? Let's talk about motive," I spat back. "Ginachere targets Rourke and me. To get us off her tail. She gets Rourke. She misses me. Who's to say that she didn't just try again, only this time, Hamid was the collateral damage." I uncrossed my arms and jammed my hands into my pockets, partially because I was starting to shake in anger and partially because I wanted to look defiant. "No, we're not going anywhere until we figure this out."

Macallister, to my surprise, sat down, and he crossed one leg over the other, making himself comfortable. I thought he was backing down until he said smugly, "No, Porter, we've been assigned a mission. That mission is a matter of national security. A mission endorsed by the Secretary of State's office and by the office of the Attorney General. And I'm sorry to say, that takes precedence over an overdose investigation or even Rourke's investigation."

"I'm not going."

"What?"

"You heard me. I'm not going," I repeated, with as much venom in my voice as I could muster. "I'm staying here, and I am investigating this so-called overdose. And I will continue to investigate what happened to Rourke. These were my teammates, Macallister. They are my priority."

Macallister called my bluff, snarling, "With what resources? I'll remind you that you are not an active Special Agent."

Shit.

I mumbled, "I'll figure it out."

"How?"

"I'll figure it out," I stubbornly repeated.

"Figure this out, Porter. We depart on Wednesday for the Middle East. For a mission of national fucking security. How many hours away is that departure?"

I blinked rapidly, worried. "Um, like forty-eight, I guess."

Macallister uncrossed his legs and planted both elbows on his knees, clasping his hands together below his chin. In a soft but dangerous tone, he hissed, "Well, then, Porter, you got forty-eight hours to change your mind."

CHAPTER 21

WEDNESDAY, MARCH 17, 2021

SAINT PATRICK'S DAY.

I'm not Irish, but as we've established, I like a beer or two every now and again. And I should be looking forward to this evening, when I could be sipping a Guinness stout and devouring a heaping plate of fresh corned beef, perhaps up on the bridge of *Almaz*, watching the compass as it rotated to show the yacht's eastward course, leaving the mainland United States behind. Off on another adventure, on the yacht that I had purposed for this very type of mission, with the team I had assembled, under the cover that I had fabricated.

Instead, I stood morosely on the dock, under a gloomy gray Washington D.C. sky, shivering in the forty-degree moist air. I caught my reflection in the dark water where *Almaz* laid for months, as *Almaz* herself showed me her wide and low fantail. The aft garage door was closed, keeping the salt spray off the remaining Jeep and the brand-new Mercedes. Above, the Eurocopter was lashed to the teak-decked helipad, rotor blades drooping and tied off. *Almaz* was prepared and shipshape for the open sea.

Without me.

Snap out of it, I chided myself, even as I shivered. It just didn't feel right to watch *Almaz* depart.

I pulled my jacket tightly to ward off the chill. I was correct to be chastising myself. It was time to move on. To get to work.

After all, I struck what I thought was a very good deal with Macallister. He gave me about two weeks—the time for *Almaz* to cross the Atlantic and the Med—for me to investigate Hamid's death. When my time was up, on the last day of March, I'd fly to Egypt, taking commercial flights to Cairo, and then I would travel by car about three hours to the northern terminus of the Suez Canal, where I'd meet the yacht and the team in Port Said.

Volkov set me up with a credit card and a local bank account. She also equipped me with an encrypted phone which looked much like an ordinary iPhone; she loaded our case file onto the phone and promised that she would keep the file up to date with any new research that they developed during the trans-Atlantic journey. I could use the phone to remain in contact with the team. Lockwood found and purchased a car for me to drive, an older, tan 2005 Chevrolet Tahoe, which we figured would be innocuous enough for my use. It was up to me to find a place to stay; I'd grab an extended-stay hotel room.

Most importantly, Macallister's attitude softened. Ultimately, he agreed with my argument that my time might be better spent on the ground in D.C. than on the waves for a long Atlantic crossing. I buttered him up, a little, too, by offering, "Sir, I'm intimately familiar with the capabilities we have onboard *Almaz*, but you are not. You can spend a couple of weeks getting up to speed with Volkov and learning the vessel."

Obviously, he agreed, but to my surprise, he took my two-week leave of absence to heart as if it was his idea. Critically, he arranged for my FBI badge to be reissued. He lectured, "I pulled some strings, Porter, to give this assignment for you a better chance of success. As you recall, I'm sure, on the record, you were terminated, and to protect the cover of the mission, we're not going to undo that."

"Sorry, sir, I'm not sure I understand." I decided to take a much more deferential tone with Macallister, and it appeared to me that our argument, fresh off the raw news of Hamid's death, was in the past and would not affect our ongoing working relationship. "Why would issuing my badge compromise the mission?"

Macallister scratched his chin. "Because I left out a detail. I'm not informing Sullivan or the AG that you're staying in D.C. for a couple of weeks. They're gonna think you're on the boat with me. However, I told the AG you might need a badge, like a movie prop, in case you needed to show it in my company when we're on the ground in the Middle East. This, therefore, is not a real badge. Only the Attorney General and two of my assistants know about it. It won't show up in the system. Use it sparingly, if at all."

I raised my eyebrows. "Is this legal?"

"No," he replied, quite simply.

The badge was necessary, though, for it gave me the authority to carry a weapon, the usual FBI-issued Glock Model 22. "I'm not gonna leave you unprotected. Unarmed. But—don't use it unless you have to, obviously," Macallister warned. "If the D.C. cops or someone else catches you with the gun, the badge should give you a bit of cover. Unless they check it out and run it down with the Bureau, which will then show them it's a fake badge, and you're carrying a real gun. And then you're screwed. Got it?"

That was small comfort. I'd be on my own.

But I had a plan, and I knew exactly what to do next.

CHAPTER 22

WITH THE ONGOING PRESSURES of the Covid-19 pandemic, finding a place to stay for a couple of weeks was no problem, and I booked myself into a room at the Hyatt House. After all, if my squad was on a luxury yacht, why should I have to skimp on an extended stay hotel miles outside of the city, when instead space was plentiful in a swank hotel which was only a six-minute walk to the northwest of the marina where *Almaz* had docked. It was familiar territory, and I thought of Hamid both yesterday morning and earlier today when I grabbed a coffee at the District Donut shop—the last place where I had been able to joke around with my fallen friend.

The promenade along the Potomac River waterfront was also a decent spot for a late afternoon meeting, though I would have preferred a more private location. At least here, I would not have to clear security, and that was a real plus—I was reluctant to put my not-quite-legit FBI badge to work at the front desk of the Walter Reed National Military Medical Center.

"Nice spot you picked, Porter," said Doctor Curtis, as he settled into a chair opposite me on the patio outside of the Hyatt. There were a handful of these two-top metal, outdoor tables scattered about, and other than the one I selected, none were occupied. We had the place to ourselves.

"Nice Friday afternoon, too. Mid-fifties and sunny. Must be better than a morgue at Reed, I hope," I replied as I shook Curtis's hand. "Thanks for coming all the way downtown to meet with me."

Curtis smiled. "No worries. And apologies again for not being able to do this sooner. I know it's important to you, but I couldn't pull myself away."

"I understand, of course. And, honestly, this sure seems soon enough to me. After all, I called you, what, Wednesday afternoon? Two days is a very reasonable turnaround," I gushed, worrying a bit that I was laying it on too thick.

Curtis didn't seem to notice or care as his gaze wandered out to the river. "Well, it's always difficult to discuss these things with someone who was close to the, um, subject." He was certainly avoiding eye contact, and I couldn't blame him, as he continued, "It's unusual to review an autopsy with a friend of the deceased. With an agent, obviously, it happens all the time. It's when those lines cross that it is, ah, awkward."

"I get it," I replied softly. "But I have to know what happened to Hamid."

The doctor turned his head toward me, his eyes meeting mine. "He overdosed. I know from our phone call with Macallister on Monday that you want a different answer. But that is the answer. Hamid had no signs of any puncture wounds, so he was not stabbed surreptitiously with a syringe or something. He had no bruising. He had nothing foreign in his stomach. His brain was fine. Really, all systems normal." He paused a beat and cast his eyes downward to the black mesh tabletop. "Except for an extremely high concentration of Digoxin in his blood."

I demanded, "Well, where did it come from?"

Curtis sighed. "If he wasn't injected, it had to be oral."

"Pills?"

"That's most likely. Though Digoxin is available as an oral suspension, in that form, it does not taste very good. It's quite unlikely that he would have swigged enough on purpose. You'd need to fill a small medication cup. An ounce and a half, perhaps."

"How many pills?"

Curtis shrugged and returned his gaze to the waterfront, doing the math, I guessed. Finally, he announced, "The tablets are an eighth of a milligram. They're tiny. Twenty of those isn't even a handful. Dump a bunch into your hand, and you could swallow them without water. It would take less than a half-hour for the Digoxin to permeate your system."

I thought back to Sunday morning and muttered, "Even before we left for the coffee shop, he was jittery. I mean, he's always pretty hyper, but more so than usual, maybe."

Putting an elbow on the table, Curtis looked again at me, nodding. "You know, we see this occasionally. Let's say Hamid's doctor in Albany saw some heart rate irregularities, and that doc prescribed him meds. Hamid doesn't want that on his fitness report at the Bureau. And he knows that something that is irregular might not show up when he's in for a physical, or maybe he's on the drug so that he passes the physical. He keeps it all to himself." He cocked his head to the side and suggested, "It's unfortunate, but it does happen."

"I take it you've seen this type of thing before?"

"I can't divulge specifics, of course. But I can say that assisting law enforcement and taking the Hippocratic oath does present a conflict at times. Look, I don't question Hamid; for all I know, he's a good agent. He's on a good track. It's possible that he thought that he could manage this."

It all made sense, but I couldn't believe it. Or, perhaps, I didn't want to believe it, and I verbalized my confusion. "I don't get it. Why would he OD on his meds? To get a fix?"

"No, I don't think so," replied Curtis, speaking softly and gently. "I think it was a mistake. Like I said, the pills are tiny. Maybe he wasn't paying attention when he took a morning dose. Just tilted the bottle and didn't even look." He looked carefully at me. "I've never said that it was an *intentional* overdose. This may well have been an accident."

I sat quietly for a moment, and despite the hum of the Friday afternoon traffic, I could hear birds chirping—a sure sign of spring. It was a hopeful sound, and I was not ready to give up on Hamid. "There's no other way?"

"I'm afraid not, Ben. I'm afraid this was all a tragic accident."

"Okay," I replied in defeat.

Curtis stood and placed a comforting hand on my shoulder. "Call me at my office at Walter Reed if you need anything. If you have any more questions." He paused before adding, "I'm sorry, Ben."

I'm not certain how long I sat there, but it was long enough for the skies to darken and for the streetlights to illuminate. Headlights and taillights mingled in a blurry pattern of white and red as vehicles sped across the Dwight D. Eisenhower freeway bridge, only a quarter-mile north, suspended across the Potomac River on blocky piers.

Wait. Suspended?

I considered the bridge and then turned to see if I could find Curtis. I had, indeed, more questions for him, but he had long since departed.

No need to wait for Curtis, I realized. I could investigate that myself, as early as tomorrow morning.

CHAPTER 23

WITH THE TWINKLE of the Washington, D.C. skyline outside and, inside, the flicker of orange glow from the merrily-dancing flames in the natural-gas-fueled fireplace, the atmosphere was serene.

Reluctantly, the gray-haired man tapped at an app on his smartphone to mute the ceiling speakers—this time, it had been classic rock, not showtunes.

The steady beat of the music was replaced by the pops and crackle of the connection initiation sequence, and instead of sounding from the discrete speakers above, the noise emanated from the tiny speakers on a laptop computer.

On the computer screen, the active connection indicator switched from red to green, and the speakers snapped with the usual one-word opening demand.

"Report?"

Like stepping on—and breaking through—an ice-topped puddle, the man thought. *Not completely unexpected, but still, abrupt, and cold.*

He sighed and began. "Porter and Curtis met this afternoon at a promenade along the Potomac."

"What?" The one-word question screeched through the computer speakers, and the gray-haired man winced, but he said nothing. He would remain professional, as always. He gave his reports in clear and concise words. He did not feel the need to repeat them for dramatic effect. Instead, he turned his gaze to the floor-to-ceiling windows and to a late, dark, D.C. night.

There was a three-second pause before the speaker broadcast the squeaky, software-altered voice. "Why is Porter in Washington? The yacht departed on Wednesday."

"I don't know. My task was to shadow Curtis, not Porter. And Curtis has not altered his routine this week. He has been at Walter Reed as usual. Until this afternoon."

"Porter isn't on the yacht? He's meeting with Curtis? Why? You need to find out."

"Are you retasking me? Or is this a parallel assignment?"

"The latter."

"I see." The man absently rubbed an invisible smudge from the perfectly white, perfectly clean island countertop, thinking, *I should have cleansed myself of this assignment. But . . .*

Erasing any doubt from his mind, his prideful exactitude compelled his reply. "Fine. I'll need that in writing. And . . . shall I attempt to determine the topic of today's conversation?"

"I'll amend the contract. But no, I am perfectly capable of guessing what they talked about. What I need to know is two-fold: what is Porter up to? Where is he? Who is he talking to?"

"That's three-fold."

"You know what I mean." The words were spoken precisely and slowly, such that the software did a reasonably effective job in transmitting emotion, and the voice was harsh. Uncompromising. Unfriendly.

"No. I do not infer."

To the man's trained ear, accustomed to the vagaries of the software, the noise that came from the speaker was a sigh, though it sounded more like a long scratch, prefacing the instructions. "By this time on Monday, I want to know where Porter is sleeping. I want to know what he did over the weekend. Who he spoke with. What he wore. What he ate. Where he ate. How he travels. Every detail. Is that clear enough?"

"Perfectly."

"Thank you." There was a brief pause as if the speaker was considering word choice. "I must also thank you, Mister Gansett, for a successful operation with Agent Hamid. Both facets went exactly to plan."

As usual, JJ Gansett would accept no accolades. He did not gush or reply in kind, instead replying evenly, "Yes. And onwards. I will report, as instructed, at this time on Monday."

Clicking the appropriate icons, the man exited the communications program, switching to an application that displayed a street map of the District and the surrounding area. Scrolling past a menu entry for "Curtis," he selected "Porter."

As he clicked, he allowed himself a moment of self-satisfaction. *This is my calling. This is where my expertise shines.*

Gansett was, as always, superbly prepared. He had anticipated this very assignment as soon as he spotted Porter with Curtis. When their discussion concluded, Gansett detoured to the parking area of the Hyatt House, scanning the paper permits that were displayed on dashboards. There was only one that included a check-in date of Wednesday, March 17, and none thereafter. Gansett reasonably concluded the vehicle could belong to Porter, and the gray-haired man concealed a tracking device inside the maw of the trailer hitch receptacle mounted under the rear bumper. Upon his return to the condo, and prior to making the call to his superior to report, Gansett confirmed his suspicions by employing his clandestine access to the Washington, D.C. Department of Motor Vehicle database. The vehicle had been registered only on Tuesday to Quadrant Procurement Group.

The 2005 Chevrolet Tahoe remained where it had been parked earlier, on the grounds of the Hyatt House.

Any second thoughts vanished with the realization that, once again, he would outsmart and outmaneuver any opponent. *I'll pick up Porter's trail in the morning. Let's see what Mister Porter is up to.*

CHAPTER
24

SATURDAY, MARCH 20, 2021

ARRIVING AT District Donut at 7:52 am on a brisk but sunny, thirty-nine-degree, Saturday morning, I was ready for my mission. I'd duplicate my visit with Abdul Hamid.

I ordered exactly the same thing: four to-go large coffees and a dozen glazed donuts.

Watching the barista prepare the order, I identified my first suspect. Easy enough to spike a coffee, right?

Except—not precise. Four cups; she doesn't know who gets which cup. Eliminates that suspect.

Hamid didn't eat a donut. Eliminates that angle.

Taking my cardboard tray to the condiments station, I examined the offerings. *What the hell. A little milk and sugar won't hurt,* I decided, taking a leave of absence from my self-imposed black coffee diet. Besides, I needed to emulate Hamid's actions.

It hit me as soon as I popped the lid off the to-go cup. My coffee sat on the condiments bar, uncapped and unprotected. Straightforward to drop in something, right?

Returning to the service counter, which was fortunately devoid of other customers, I whispered to the barista, quickly reading her nametag, "Jolene. Hi. Sorry to bother, but do you guys have security cameras in here?"

She hesitated, adjusting her baseball cap and fiddling with a brown ponytail that stuck out the back of the hat. "Who's asking?"

"Well," I smiled, "I'm asking for myself. My name is Ben. My friend got, um, sick after visiting this shop last weekend. I'm not, like, trying to point fingers, and I'm not working a case." With that, I slid the Macallister-provided FBI badge from my pocket and slyly angled it toward the barista.

"Oh," was her blasé response. Jolene was clearly unimpressed by my creds. She shrugged. "Well, we don't have cameras."

"Oh," was my disappointed reply.

"But," she added with a slightly perkier tone, "I do remember you. I remember your friend. I remember lots of customers. You were in last Sunday. I took your order."

Behind me, I heard the door swish open. I was running out of alone time with my new friend Jolene, and I blurted, "Do you remember anyone else? Anything odd? Any customers lurking and not buying?"

She frowned in my direction and said, "Not really." Turning to the new customers who approached the counter, she chirped brightly, a big smile on her face, "Hi! What can I get you this morning?"

Picking up my tray and donut bag, I headed outside, dejected.

A dead end.

The outside patio was empty; it remained too cold for most patrons, I guessed, as I took one of the tables, instinctively pulling my phone from my pocket and setting it face-up on the table next to the carry tray of way more coffee than even I could drink. Catching the reflection of the sky on the dark screen of the phone, I heard Jolene's voice: "I remember lots of customers."

Leaving my coffees and donuts outside on the table, I rushed back inside the shop, bringing up the photos that Volkov had copied for me from Sullivan's flash drive and from our investigation. Selecting the picture of parking lot UNSUB number two, the man that Sullivan had claimed was the CIA assassin, I waved at Jolene. "Hey, quick question. You said you remember customers. Any chance this guy looks familiar?"

She appeared annoyed, and I couldn't blame her; the cadence of a job interrupted by a pesky patron would irk anyone, but nevertheless, she examined the phone. "Yeah. He was in last Sunday, too."

"Are you sure?"

Tipping her chin up, she confirmed, "Yeah, sure. Blue blazer guy. Definitely. He came in a little before you, ordered a hot tea. Plain Earl Grey."

"Thank you so much," I mumbled.

"Sure," she replied, returning to her tasks as I walked outside, almost in a daze.

Someone had stolen my bag of donuts, but I didn't care as I tossed the carry tray of full coffees in a garbage bin. I nabbed a lead. I also needed to find Doctor Curtis.

CHAPTER
25

WITH THE MOUTH of the Chesapeake Bay some seven hundred nautical miles to the west, *Almaz* had been on the open Atlantic Ocean for two days, as the yacht trundled east at fifteen knots toward her waypoint at the Straits of Gibraltar, over 2,500 nautical miles away. Deputy Assistant Director Bradford Macallister got himself comfortable in what would normally be Ben Porter's seat at the head of the horseshoe-shaped table in the situation room as he awaited his Secure Video Teleconference (SVTC) with Genevieve Sullivan.

Indeed, Macallister felt *quite* comfortable in that chair. It was a commanding position; he could swivel around and see the ocean through the big, forward-facing windows or turn to the screens that tracked the vessel's progress eastward. Macallister touched the button to close the shades on the windows; the glare of the Saturday morning sun would be distracting on the video call.

As the shades descended silently, Anastasia Volkov announced to Macallister, "She's connecting."

The giant center screen lit, only partially filling with Sullivan's petite face. Her camera angle caught her just above the chin, making it appear that she was straining and stretching to be seen on-screen. "Good day, Deputy Assistant Director," she chirped. "Miss Volkov. Captain

Lockwood." She paused, and her eyes darted left, then right. "Where is Mister Porter? Macallister, you're in his seat, I do believe."

Macallister grunted. "Yes, Madam Under Secretary. Porter remained in Washington. I'm having him run down what he can on Abdul Hamid's death. Porter will meet up with the rest of the team that I'm building. They'll meet us in Egypt."

Macallister noticed as Volkov rolled her eyes imperceptibly, but he did not comment. He knew she would be annoyed that he took credit—as if he assigned Porter's task. *I need to show my authority,* Macallister thought.

Despite Macallister's self-assurance, Sullivan appeared perturbed. "I wish I'd been made aware, Deputy Assistant Director. I want Porter on this team. And I am surprised that you didn't inform me earlier." Her tone was stern and dripped with annoyance.

Macallister remained firm. "Ma'am, with all due respect, you scheduled these sitrep calls Saturdays—as you explained it, so that you'd have less activity in your office. Fewer eyes and ears. Anyway, I did not feel it was necessary to let you know. After all, Porter will be onboard well before we arrive in Saudi Arabia."

"The FBI doesn't have the personnel to investigate what happened to Hamid?" Sullivan's voice took on a sarcastic edge.

"Plenty, ma'am. But he was a close personal friend of Porter's. Frankly, it was the least I could do. I think he'd be very ineffective here, right now. He'd be distracted."

"Very well. Your location?"

Lockwood consulted the data screen on the curved aft bulkhead and read off the numbers. "Forty degrees, forty-two minutes north, zero-six-one degrees, twenty minutes west."

"Thank you, Captain Lockwood," Sullivan said formally. "Are you on schedule?"

"Yes," Macallister replied, reestablishing his dominance of the conversation. "Do you have anything new for us?

Sullivan nodded. "I do. I have a timeline, and you'll just make it, I think. I've been overseeing diplomatic travel arrangements, which is quite customary for me, and Hazel Ginachere's office has requested that the Secretary of State's office coordinate high-level visits for her. Turkey, Austria, and the United Kingdom. A ten-day itinerary. And, perhaps you might guess what nation was added, as of yesterday, at the last minute, to extend the trip to eleven days?"

Macallister grinned. "Saudi Arabia?"

"That is correct," replied Sullivan, no trace of emotion on her face. "The Director of the Central Intelligence Agency—the D/CIA herself—will be in Riyadh for a one-day visit. In and out on Monday, April 12."

Though the conference was being recorded by the *Almaz* supercomputer, as a matter of practice for future reference and retrieval, Volkov took notes, typing at a lightning pace. A fraction of a second after Sullivan verbalized the date of the D/CIA's visit to the Saudi capital city, Volkov gasped. "The twelfth? That cannot be a coincidence."

"I don't think so, either. It's not a quote, last minute, unquote, change to the plan. It's structured to appear that way. After all, we are dealing with the CIA."

"I don't get it," Macallister grumbled. "What's with the date?"

Volkov waved her hand toward the screen, and, accepting Volkov's non-verbal cue, Sullivan explained, "The next day, April 13, is the first day of Ramadan. This would be the ninth—and most sacred—month of the Islamic calendar. It is believed that the Quran was revealed during this month, and Muslims fast by day, from sunup to sunset, as one sign of respect. In addition to abstaining from food and drink, they should abstain from anger and from immorality. They will pray. It is a most holy time in the Muslim world."

Sullivan adjusted her body in her seat, sitting up straighter, and concluded, "As Miss Volkov noted, this cannot be a coincidence— the day before Ramadan, Ginachere will be meeting with both King Salman and his son, Mohammed bin Salman, in a private audience. It won't be completely private, of course, as the King and MBS will have their private security details, and Ginachere will have hers. However, there will be no press present, no aides, nothing. A conference of principals."

Macallister was nodding. "And you think this is an opportunity for an assassination? In Ginachere's presence? Wouldn't that implicate her?"

"That would be a risk, but it might also provide an alibi. The Director would never be accused of a direct hit. She's more of a politician than an operative. But—imagine the circumstances. The King, surrounded by various security personnel, some from his son's squad, some from the CIA. Palace guards, too. It's a recipe for finger-pointing and blame games. Add in, for discussion purposes, a poison like one that was employed on Mister Porter. Cap it off with the pending religious month. Perhaps the perpetrator was anti-Muslim. Anti-Saudi. Anti-CIA or United States. All these things add up to decoys and layers of deception. Having Ginachere present might actually make her look more sympathetic, as if she could have been a victim, too."

"True, I suppose," offered Macallister. "But, again, with no disrespect, ma'am, it's a theory. And a bit of a stretch at that."

"That is correct, sir. Except for two points. First, to have two heads of state—the King and the Crown Prince—both agree to a last-minute schedule change is unprecedented. Circumstantially, that indicates that this is being premeditated by two of the three parties involved. Would you agree?"

"Sure," Macallister hummed.

"And two," Sullivan continued, "is the punchline that I've saved for last. I'm sending a file to Miss Volkov shortly. It will be encrypted, of course. It is a dossier of the D/CIA's security people, planned aides, and the medical team that travels with them during the tour. My office is responsible for visas, weapons clearances, that sort of thing, in the normal course of international affairs and cooperation. And—pay attention here—traveling under a pseudonym, you'll take notice of entry number three. JJ Gansett."

Volkov asked sharply, "You're certain?"

"Oh, yes," replied the Under Secretary. "His image is unmistakable."

Macallister stepped in. "Can you get us other details on the itinerary? For Ginachere's entire trip?

Sullivan smiled coldly. "You'll see that I am very thorough, Deputy Assistant Director. The file that Miss Volkov will receive contains a duplicate of the dossier that my office will be using, and it includes all of the details of the trip. Any changes that come our way, I will be sure to transmit to you. I should expect that you will have enough information to construct a plan."

Tilting her tiny nose closer to the camera, Sullivan squeaked, "And I don't need to remind you that you may not fail. You must not allow this to happen. I don't know how you insert yourself, and I wish Mister Porter was there to lend his creativity. Can I trust you to succeed?"

Macallister pursed his lips, making himself look serious and thoughtful. "Oh, certainly, Madam Under Secretary. We got this."

As Volkov terminated the connection, Macallister pressed the button to raise the window shades as he rotated his chair to look forward to the featureless seas that lay ahead of the towering bow of *Almaz*. With his back to Volkov, she would not have heard Macallister whisper, "I wish Porter was here."

CHAPTER
26

THOUGH I WOULD HAVE preferred to visit Doctor Curtis in person, I got cold feet.

Or, maybe, to give myself some credit, maybe I was smart. Risking my fake badge with Jolene the barista was one thing; flashing that badge at the security gate of the Walter Reed National Military Medical Center was a completely different level of stupidity.

Anyway, that's how I found myself driving aimlessly around the Chevy Chase, Maryland neighborhood that surrounded Reed, hoping that the doctor would return the three messages that I had left on his office voicemail.

Finally, at four in the afternoon on Saturday, a ringtone warbled through the Bose speakers in my Tahoe, top of the line back in '05, with this particular car sporting an aftermarket Bluetooth setup courtesy of a previous owner. The disembodied voice of Curtis protested, "Ben, come on. It's a weekend. A Saturday. I don't check my office voicemail box all that often."

I noted he didn't offer to give me his mobile phone number. I wasn't surprised. Frankly, I'd been a pest. I wouldn't have given my number to me, either.

That doesn't make sense, but you catch my drift. Fortunately, I was much clearer laying out my theory to the doctor, leaving no room for the doctor to misunderstand me. "I've been doing field work, Doctor Curtis." I explained my visit to the donut shop and my interactions with Jolene.

When I concluded, Curtis was immediately skeptical. "You're claiming that someone could have spiked his coffee at the shop, right? That Hamid took the top off to, what, doctor it up? Isn't that the phrase you used? That you said he used?"

"Yeah, exactly. Is it possible?"

"It's possible, Ben, but you're grasping at straws. For one thing, you'd need to pour a healthy amount of an oral suspension dose of Digoxin into that cup of coffee. How do you do that without being noticed?"

Drumming my fingers on the steering wheel, stopped at a red light, I stammered, "It's doable, I think. A physical distraction. A little bump. Move the target's attention elsewhere for only a second and *plop*! Drop it in."

"It sounds like you've gamed it out."

"Yeah," I admitted. "Like I explained earlier, I went to the donut shop this morning. Walked the scene. I think the tradecraft is feasible. What I need to know is whether the delivery method—a liquid version of the drug—would cause this. Would cause . . ."

Curtis picked up my sentence after the briefest of pauses. "Would cause death. Hamid's death." He sighed, perhaps in sympathy, but perhaps, I had to assume, in exasperation. "Look, yes, it is feasible. Call it 40cc's, which isn't that much, poured into a coffee. Sure. I mean, it wouldn't taste all that good, but if you had enough cream or sugar, maybe you wouldn't notice."

"I was afraid you'd say that. But at the same time, relieved. Now I've got a lead on methodology."

"It's thin, Ben. You must admit that to yourself. You can't make assumptions. You must rely on fact. And the fact here is that this would have been a very inefficient method of targeting someone. In quantity, in speed of consumption, of absorption. Not to mention the significant medical attention that Hamid received at the GW Hospital. There was a solid team of doctors on that case. I was there all night. Someone would have noticed if anything was amiss."

"There's no other explanation," I argued.

"That's incorrect, Porter," the doctor said sharply, replacing his cooperative tone with one far sterner. "I stand by my initial diagnosis. Hamid overdosed. Whether you like it or not, that is what happened."

For the benefit of future questions with the doctor, I backed down. "Right. I know. I want to be thorough, however. I owe that to Hamid."

"I understand," Curtis said, his imperious attitude immediately mollified. "I can respect that, Ben."

"Right. Thanks for the intel." I swiped the call off, and the Tahoe's tired Bose speakers clicked before resuming the Sirius XM feed of Alt Nation, my ninety-day free trial of the satellite radio service courtesy of the used car dealer.

"Courtesy," I mumbled to myself. "I hope it still counts for something. For someone."

The doctor's words had piqued my interest, and I knew who that someone was.

I've been in exciting situations before. Fast boats, helicopters, gun battles, extraditions, and car crashes, but this upcoming task . . . I dreaded immediately.

CHAPTER 27

SUNDAY, MARCH 21, 2021

HOPING THAT THE STAFF rotation remained the same as a week ago, I figured that late morning Sunday would be a good time to face my fears. Standing outside the GW Hospital Emergency Department entrance, I pushed my shoulders back, straightened my posture, and strode inside—where I was immediately stopped by a gruff security guard.

"Regular visiting entrance around that side," he grumbled, pointing.

I pulled my badge and put on my big boy voice. "Special Agent Porter. FBI. I was here last weekend. I'm here on a follow-up."

The guard stepped aside, suitably cowed by my introduction. I had dressed for success, too; dark suit, white shirt, striped tie, aviator sunglasses, which of course I had kept on, even once inside. The general public sees what they want to see, and I wanted to look the part.

I was permitted entry, naturally, and past that thin layer of security, I removed the glasses and loosened my tie, unfastening my top collar button. I had considered bearing a gift, perhaps a coffee, but I felt that went too far—until I heard a familiar voice rumble, "Damn, honey, it's almost noon. I could use a cup of coffee."

Crap. Missed opportunity.

Then, a new voice. "I gotcha, babe. BRB."

Ah! An opening!

A female nurse, perhaps in her late twenties, with ebony skin and black, curly hair sauntered away from the front desk in the ER, embarking on the promised coffee run. My target sat alone with her monitors. I soft-soled it and sidled up to the counter.

"Hi," I enthused, keeping my tone light and friendly. "You're Raven. I'm Ben Porter."

"Who?" She narrowed her eyelids, her plump, dark cheeks ballooning, her eyes cold and black. I felt a chill.

Seriously? Shake it off.

"I'm Ben. I was here a week ago. Last Sunday. It was much busier, then."

Raven leaned back slightly in her chair, her straightened, medium-length black hair cascading behind her ears. She apprised me with an icy stare. "Yeah. That was the morning of the time change. That day is always a mess, for some reason. And, yeah, I remember you." She drew out the last word in a mean manner.

"I was hoping you could help me with a few questions."

She jeered, "Oh, so now I'm good enough to assist you?"

"I'm sorry. I really am. It was a difficult day, and I was rude." I did my best to make eye contact. To make a connection. "I apologize."

The nurse rolled her eyes. "Oh, honey, not so fast. I've been here for twenty years. I've seen it all, so don't think for a second that you get to you stroll in here all nicey-nice to ask all your questions. What the hell do you want now?" She made a show of looking around the space as she asked, "Your friend still here?"

"No," I replied, shaking my head back and forth but holding her gaze. "My friend died."

That got her, and her eyes widened. Without the glare, she began to look softer. Dare I say, pleasant. "Sorry to hear that. He had quite a crew of docs lookin' after him."

I nodded. "Yeah. Which makes it all the more strange that he didn't make it."

"Whaddya sayin'?" Defensive. Less pleasant.

"Here's what I wonder. What I hope you can help me understand. He was in this ICU. Can I assume he stayed here all night? Until he, um, passed?"

"No. You can't assume that. This is emergency only. Active cases. We get a lot of turnover." She looked at one of her monitors, then at me. "You're not just a friend, are you?"

I smiled gently. "Oh, first and foremost, I was his friend. He was my roommate when we trained at Quantico." I pulled out the badge as I said that, letting it catch the light.

"Right. I forgot. You said you're a Fed." It was a statement, not a question.

"So was he."

Raven scanned the area and whispered, "My brother is in the Secret Service. I get it. You take care of your own." Her attitude became conspiratorial as she asked, "What was his name?"

"His ID would have shown Al-Hamid. First name Abdullatif."

She nodded as she clacked the keys. "He was moved to the fifth floor ICU. At about three in the afternoon."

"Is that typical?"

"Yeah." Peering at the screen, she elaborated, "He was admitted as a Level One case. Highest priority. That's like a resuscitation case. Immediate life-saving procedures. His condition was marked as 'critical.' Someone changed it to 'serious.' That's why they moved him upstairs. Must have figured he was doin' okay."

"Can you see who made that decision?"

"No. It would have been a doctor, and the doc's name would be on your boy's chart, but I ain't opening that file. My supervisor will wonder why and will bug me with stupid questions."

"I get it. No problem. Last question," I promised, as I caught sight of Raven's curly-haired compatriot returning unhurriedly, bearing two cups of coffee. "You see a lot happen here, obviously. Did what happened to Hamid look peculiar to you? Odd? Out of place?"

Raven merely shrugged, but her face told a different story. "You got a phone number?"

I scribbled my encrypted mobile phone number on the Post-it note that she handed me, and I obeyed her head jerk that clearly signaled it was time for me to leave. As I slipped away, I heard curly ask, "Who was that dude?"

Raven answered, just loudly enough for me to hear, "A cop checking up on a patient. We sent the patient upstairs. Hey, that coffee smells delicious."

Ten minutes later, as I sat in the driver's seat of the Tahoe, wondering how to un-parallel park the big SUV thanks to a blue BMW sedan that had wedged itself closely to my rear bumper, my phone chirped with a text notification.

It's raven - the docs name was Curtis

CHAPTER

28

MONDAY, MARCH 22, 2021

I SHOULD HAVE KNOWN BETTER. That lesson, repeated time and again: don't blindly accept the false assurances that because something appears, say, foreboding, that it is foreboding. Or, like they taught me in elementary school, don't judge a book by its cover.

I'm alluding to, of course, Raven.

A week ago yesterday, I was whiny. Underfoot. Demanding. Don't forget demeaning. And Raven had every right to treat me with disdain. Make no mistake; I was kicking myself for my lack of respect.

And also, my lack of foresight.

What if I had been more polite? Maybe Raven would have let me go in. To Hamid's bedside. Could I have changed the outcome?

I couldn't bear to mope about that, and therefore I plowed ahead with my one-man investigation, continuing to follow Hamid's path from the donut shop to the GW Hospital emergency room, and today, on a Monday morning, to the hospital's fifth-floor ICU.

Back in January, my room was also located on the fifth floor, but of course, not in the intensive care suite. Nevertheless, I exercised in these halls, understood the general layout, and dearly hoped that I would bump into a recognizable face as I stepped off the elevator.

Much to my immediate shock, that face belonged to Raven.

From her expression, I got the sense that she was just as surprised as I was, but true to form, she didn't let on. "You again?" The words were not friendly.

This time, I knew better. Raven's workday was demanding. Like, life or death demanding. She had every right to be curt. And therefore, I tried to respond with a non-adversarial, self-deprecating tone. "I'm afraid so. What can I say? Except maybe that I'm persistent."

"Honey, you're a stubborn fool."

"Probably." I smiled. "I'm happy to see a familiar face, though."

She wasn't buying it. "Whaddya want? I gotta go, anyway. Only ran up here to bring a file from downstairs."

"Yeah, yeah, sure. Don't let me hold you up. But in case you're wondering, I wanted to see where my friend Hamid ended up after being transferred upstairs." I spoke quickly, trying to keep Raven's attention before she hopped on an elevator. "I was on this floor too, after my accident in January."

The nurse cocked her head at me. "Your accident?"

"Uh-huh. I was in a car accident in January. With another friend. I had a rough go of it. She, um, died."

Raven's eyes widened. "Sounds like being a friend of yours is deadly. Count me out."

I nodded and said seriously, "I know. It's not been a good few months for that. That's why I'm here. That's why I'm so stubborn, I guess. I need answers."

It was Raven's turn to nod solemnly, and she ordered, "Follow me."

I trailed Raven through the double doors to the ICU, my former room now behind me in another wing. And, unlike the area where I resided, which was busy and sometimes noisy, the unit was quiet and still.

Approaching a central monitoring station, I took note of a handful of big chairs at the perimeter of the space. Only one of those seats was occupied by a white-coated doctor, who was writing in a file. At the station, numbered overhead displays showed the vitals of the patients in the enclosed rooms that comprised the unit. It was efficient but sterile, not a welcoming place.

At the desk, Raven chirped, "Hey, Bea."

The plump, matronly and middle-aged, pale-and-freckled-skinned, bleach-blonde nurse smiled tiredly. "You're back." She motioned at a file to her right, on the desk surface. "Forget something?"

"Nah. Got sidetracked."

Raven glanced at me. Since I couldn't know if she remembered my name, I offered, "I'm Ben Porter. Nice to meet you, Bea."

"It's Bethany," the plump nurse corrected me.

The B is for Bethany, I thought. *Now, how the hell was I supposed to know that?*

Hoping to unoffend her, I tried, "Apologies, Bethany. It's still nice to meet you, though."

The two nurses made eye contact; Bethany clearly peeved until Raven bailed me out of the awkward moment. "He's a cop. A Fed. Looking into a patient we had last weekend who passed."

"A cop?" Bethany's expression indicated displeasure. "Don't you need some paperwork?"

"The patient was a friend," Raven explained, greatly helping my case. "I looked him up, too. Last name Al-Hamid." She spelled it out.

Bethany only shrugged. "So what?"

Raven leaned closer to the nurse's ear, and I barely caught the sentence. "He was a Level One downstairs and got moved up here." She shook her head back and forth. "Wrong move. Look it up."

This is my lucky day, I thought.

If I had tried this on my own, I would have struck out. Raven was making it happen as Bethany tapped keys and narrated, "The patient died overnight, a week ago. Um, 4:20 A.M. last Monday. Oh, sure, now I remember that patient. I was on duty that night." She continued scanning the electronic file until she huffed, "And . . . huh. That's peculiar."

I caught Raven's eye. I used that exact word, "peculiar," yesterday. She dipped her chin a bit, signaling that she recognized the word, too.

Meanwhile, Bethany continued, in a questioning tone, "Lemme go back to the start of the chart. He was admitted at 10:13 A.M. as Level One. He was sent up here, what, only four or five hours later? Who ordered that?" Bethany's interest was triggered. Her tapping and her words picked up pace. "Curtis? I don't recognize that name. Specialist, maybe?"

"Right," Raven muttered. "I opened the file and saw that name, too. I don't recognize it, either."

I did, of course, but I wisely asked a different question. "What happened once the patient was brought up here?"

Bethany turned to her screen. "Looks like he was stable but still exhibited distress. Issues with blood pressure and heart rate. Then, at about 3:30 A.M., he coded with an abnormal u-wave, dropping heartbeats, and displaying rapid atrial fibrillation."

I thought back to my stay on the fifth floor, and to confirm my recollection, I asked, "In the middle of the night, he's obviously not being watched every minute, so how would they know that he was in distress?"

Bethany pointed to the screens above. "Those monitors. The nurse on duty would have been alerted by an audio alarm and by the change on the screen. The nurse would have called for a crash cart." She traced the electronic record on her screen with a finger, eventually announcing, "The chart shows that the resuscitation effort was unsuccessful. That's what I meant when I said it was *peculiar*, before. They treated him with a drug that we don't use much anymore because it requires constant monitoring—but of course, we can do that monitoring here. Anyway, I guess Digoxin didn't work this time."

"Wait," I demanded. "Digoxin? I was told that's why he ended up in the ER—because he OD'd on Digoxin."

Both nurses stared at me, and it was Raven who spoke first. "That's not in the chart. They wouldn't have treated the patient with that drug if they knew that. It's called Digoxin toxicity, and it would be fatal."

"This doesn't add up to me," I complained. "Let's say Hamid was prescribed Digoxin and took too much of it. Would that explain his symptoms when he was admitted to the ER?"

I looked at Raven as I asked my question, and she agreed, "Yeah, could be."

"And then," I continued, "he's stabilized and moved up here, to the fifth floor, and then goes into distress overnight. He's treated with Digoxin. You're saying that second dose would kill him?"

"Maybe, maybe not," Bethany waffled. "But they wouldn't have risked it. They'd use a beta-blocker or Captopril or something else. Otherwise, yeah, they'd be doubling down on Digoxin, and that's not ideal."

"Look, we do our best," Raven added quietly. "The doctors and nurses need to make instant decisions. Sometimes stuff just happens. You just never know." I immediately sensed that my welcome was wearing thin when Raven announced, "I gotta get back downstairs." She turned to me. "I should walk you out."

"This has been really helpful, I think. I mean, inconclusive. But all the same, helpful to know that maybe I'm not totally off base," I stammered. "Thanks, Bethany. Really appreciate it. Really." I smiled my most ingratiating smile; Bethany rewarded me with a thin grin of her own.

As Raven and I exited the ICU, I took one last glance at Hamid's final stop. The seated and scribbling doctor that I had seen when we came in had disappeared, but the sight of the empty chairs elicited a memory: Doctor Curtis reporting, on Macallister's speakerphone, that he had dozed off in a chair near the nurse's station.

I wonder whether it was one of those chairs.

As I gushed my thank-you's to Raven during our elevator ride down to the first floor, I clutched my phone in my pocket, ready to dial as soon as I was outside.

Let's ask him.

CHAPTER
29

I DIDN'T THINK it was appropriate to call Doctor Curtis and force him to listen to my labored breathing as I trotted the quarter-mile walk to my parallel-parked Tahoe. In retrospect, the walk gave me time to strategize and to cool off.

My first instinct, as I set off from the GW Hospital, was to confront the doctor. By the time I climbed into the Tahoe and started it, thinking that I'd run the heater to warm up a bit, I decided to take a more circumspect approach.

He picked up his office line on the first ring. "Curtis."

"Porter. Ben Porter."

"You again? How ya doin', Ben?"

"Oh, man, I've been better, Doc."

"You must move on, Ben." The doctor's voice was friendly but insistent.

"I bet you'd like me to move on," I replied. "However, I have this habit of digging and digging until I find answers, and I feel like I owe that to my friend."

"That's an admirable trait, Ben." His tone contrasted his words; he signaled dismissiveness. Arrogance. "I'm certain that perseverance serves you well as an agent."

"It does," I said agreeably, not allowing myself to be baited by his haughtiness. "Will you humor me and walk the case back with me one more time?"

He hesitated before saying, "I suppose."

"Thank you. Okay, let's begin. Last Monday, when you called Macallister and me after Hamid died, you said that the second tox screen showed Digoxin. You said that Hamid overdosed on the drug. Right?"

"Yes."

"Right. You also said that you were at the hospital overnight and that you were dozing off when you were woken by Hamid's code blue. Right?"

"Yes. What's your point?" His tone was sharp.

I had to be careful. I wanted him to lead the conversation. "Sorry to be so pedantic. This is the last step in rehashing the sequence, I promise." I cleared my throat. "When we met last week on the promenade, you said that his autopsy showed a high concentration of Digoxin, and you indicated that the autopsy, therefore, verified your initial theory that he overdosed."

Curtis sighed. "Well, that is all correct, but what are you getting at?"

"I want to make sure I have my facts straight and that my recollection of the timeline matches yours."

"It does."

"Cool," I said, keeping my tone light as I prepped myself for the big question. "Here's what I don't understand, then. Hamid and I got coffee at about nine in the morning on Sunday. He died at about four in the morning on Monday. Let's round it off and call it eighteen hours. After that passage of time, wouldn't the autopsy show a minimal concentration of Digoxin, not a high concentration?"

"That would be a layperson's assumption, yes, of course. But naturally, each body is unique, and therefore each person will present differently." The doctor's voice had deepened; apparently, it was lecture time. He continued, "Absorption rates, processing times, waste disposal—all these things are variables. Frankly, given the prevalence of Digoxin in Hamid's system based on the second tox screen that was done after he was admitted, I wasn't surprised that the substance remained at the time of death."

He dodged the question, I thought, *with a circular answer.*

I reflected on what I'd discovered with Raven's assistance and lobbed a new question. "Right. That second tox screen. I assume that the doctors at GW reviewed that and then made the call to move Hamid to the fifth floor ICU?"

"The fifth floor? Where are you getting this information?"

"I was at the hospital today. I wanted to drop off thank-you notes to the team that treated him," I fibbed. "You know, as a courtesy. They sent me to the fifth floor."

"Ah, yes, how very considerate of you. And, yes, I'm sure the doctors at GW would have taken all steps in due care, including reviewing that tox screen, before transferring the patient from the Emergency Room to the ICU."

The doctor lied, I realized. *Twice.*

According to Raven, and then confirmed by Bethany, it was Curtis who signed the order to move Hamid to the ICU. In addition, and even more concerning, both nurses said that Hamid's chart did not show Digoxin—therefore, the GW doctors could not have possibly seen the tox screen.

Curtis told us that he saw that report. Why didn't anyone else see it?

I realized that I needed to cover my pause, so I hurriedly said, "Sorry. Just lost in my thoughts for a moment. I just can't imagine what happened during my friend's last hours."

Curtis spoke solemnly. "Hamid's condition was stable. Serious, but stable. The irregularity seemed under control. I thought he was out of the woods, so to speak, and I deferred to the expertise of the GW doctors. Really, I had no reason to be involved in his care, and therefore I remained a distant observer once he was within the ICU. It was a shock to me that he coded, but I'm confident that he was treated expertly by the hospital's doctors in their duty of care. But, Ben, dammit, sometimes it doesn't work out. It just doesn't. And I am so deeply sorry . . ." His tone had been softening until his words trailed off.

I didn't reply and, after a beat, the doctor began anew, this time thoughtfully. "Ben, I treated you. I was rooting for you. And I was rooting for Hamid. I am just so shocked by his outcome. It's so very sad."

"Yes, yes, I know. Thank you, Doctor."

"Of course, Ben. Was there anything else?"

I was relieved that the doctor offered a way to end the call, and I grabbed the opportunity. "No, nothing else. Thank you for taking my call. Thanks for your support. Have a good evening."

As the call was terminated, I switched off the ignition of the Chevy.

Curtis is dodging something. He was there. He should have known that Hamid was treated with the same drug that he claimed Hamid overdosed on.

I climbed out of the driver's seat, slammed the door closed, and locked the car, reflecting, *One more round of thanks, Doc—for reminding me that you treated me.*

I spun on my heels and began the quarter-mile trudge to the GW Hospital.

CHAPTER
30

"YOU AGAIN?"

"Second time today that someone has said that to me," I replied, grinning nicely. "First, it was Raven. I wanted to give you your turn, Bethany."

The plump nurse sighed; she was obviously more tired than when I'd seen her with Raven. That exhaustion, I suppose, drove her blunt question as she groaned, "What do you want?"

Without Raven by my side, I was nervous that I would have been stonewalled by the fifth-floor ICU nurse, but so far, so good. She wasn't overly friendly, but fortunately, she was playing along. I knew I had to be quick, though, before Bethany changed her mind.

"This didn't come up when Raven and you and I chatted earlier. But—I was here, at the hospital, back in January. Into February. On this floor, but not in the ICU. I was in a car accident."

"Sorry. About the accident. You look fine, though."

"Yeah. I think I'm okay." I paused, searching for the words. "Remember in the file, for my friend Hamid, you said the doctor that ordered him to be brought up to this floor was Curtis. Let's just confirm that first name, okay. Because the doctor who treated me was also Curtis. David Curtis."

I hoped that my explanation would inspire Bethany's curiosity. After all, I knew it was the same guy. But she didn't—yet. It took only seconds for her key-tapping to reveal to her that the doctor was one and the same. "Yeah. David Curtis. You know him?"

"Yes. He's a pathologist from Walter Reed."

Bethany grumbled with evident suspicion, "What's a government pathologist doing here at GW?"

"Here's the short story. I'm a federal agent, and I was poisoned. Curtis did the tox work, and therefore he was overseeing my recovery here. My friend Hamid is also an agent, and my superior called Curtis in to look after Hamid's care."

"I'm guessing you already know that's unusual."

"Yeah. And you said you didn't recognize the name, but do you remember him lurking around here the night Hamid died? Tall white guy, white hair, usually a white lab coat."

"That covers a lot of people around here," Bethany said dismissively, turning back to her screen.

"This one speaks, um, pompously," I added, trying to draw her out. I had my suspicions, but I wanted Bethany to connect to dots; I didn't want to lead my witness.

My patience was rewarded as Bethany resumed eye contact with me. "Oh, that doctor," she giggled. "Oh, that voice. Like he was auditioning for a movie every time he spoke. He was so tedious." Bethany poked her upper lip. "And that mustache? Perfectly white. I wonder how he kept it clean."

I grinned. "That's the guy."

"Yeah, for sure. When he wasn't pestering me, he mostly hung out over there." She pointed to the grouping of big visitor chairs that I had seen earlier.

"Yeah, napping, probably."

The nurse squinted at me. "No, I don't remember that. He wandered in and out constantly, checking on the patient, I guess. I even caught him poking around the main desk on a couple of occasions when I stepped away."

Another lie by the doctor, I thought. *Curtis said that he was a "distant observer." Doesn't sound that way from Bethany's description.*

"Hang on, though. This random guy has full access to the ICU?"

She shrugged. "I couldn't name all the doctors who circulate around here. We get specialists all the time. See 'em once or twice, and never see 'em again."

I considered that opening and charged in. "Well, he was hanging around when I was a patient, and now that you see the connection between Curtis, Hamid, and me, can you pull up my chart? Porter. Ben Porter."

She shook her head as she flatly denied me. "No."

"Please. I have a couple of hunches. It will take two seconds. Please," I begged.

Bethany grunted. "And then will you leave me alone?"

"I promise."

I've had quite a run today of people asking me to stop asking them questions, I thought.

To my relief, Bethany pulled up my chart.

Examining it, she pulled a pair of reading glasses that she had not used earlier from atop her skull, leaning in close to the screen. "You had quite a ride," she whistled. "Motor vehicle accident trauma? Diethyl phosphonate poisoning? A dozen hallucination episodes? Wow. I'm surprised you didn't rank a room here in my ICU."

One hunch, verified.

She continued, now with a tone of awe and possibly disbelief. "You almost died and had to be resuscitated. Twice!"

I held my breath. "Twice? Only twice?"

She snorted. "Coding twice isn't good enough for you? Sheesh, once is enough for most people."

"Do you have the dates?"

Chuckling, she asked, "What, for your diary?" Tracing a finger on the screen, she announced, "January 9 and January 15." Bethany sat back and pushed her reading glasses back to their home on her head.

"Yeah, something like that. My diary," I agreed, my thoughts elsewhere. "Bethany, thanks so much. I really appreciate your help."

"No problem. Slow night, anyway." She winked. "Take care of yourself, now. Maybe, uh, drive carefully. No more car accidents for you!"

Riding the elevator down for the second time that day and returning to open-air, I walked slowly back to the Tahoe, running it through my head.

The first date after the accident that I recognized was January 20. Inauguration Day. And I distinctly remember the beginning of that episode. I remember looking at the monitor; the data was going berserk before the ghosts appeared. But no one came. No doctors. No nurses. No help.

And yet, all the medical professionals showed up for Hamid, but he died.

Waiting for a crossing lamp, I bounced on one foot, then the other. *What's the common thread? Curtis was hanging around the GW Hospital. He was involved in both cases.*

I reached the Tahoe, climbed inside, and hesitated before I turned the key in the ignition, half expecting it to explode in a fiery blast. The aging V-8 turned over nicely, though, and as I headed back to the Hyatt, I knew I needed help.

I couldn't put it together. I needed someone to talk to, and I wished I was at my seat in the situation room aboard *Almaz*, able to spitball ideas and theories with my team.

Reaching the Hyatt, I parked the Tahoe and returned to the solitude of my room. Settling into the chair at the desk, I dialed the satellite telephone number for the situation room.

There was no answer.

I suffered a moment of panic until I recognized the time. Evening in D.C. would be a single-digit morning hour on *Almaz*. They'd be asleep, mostly, with only one watch stander on the bridge, keeping an eye on the various navigational instruments, displays, and engine monitoring systems as the yacht trundled eastward on autopilot.

Dashing off a short text to schedule a call for the morning, my time, I recalled my experience on *Almaz*. I stood many of those watches. It was lonely but exhilarating all at once—the majesty of the sea outside the slanted bridge windows never ceased to impress me, and commanding a 235-foot vessel solo felt, well, pretty good.

We took turns, rotating every four hours by day and doing three-hour shifts by night. I looked forward to the end of the watch, when

I'd get to see another face and exchange a few words of banter with my shipmates—Volkov, Lockwood, Hamid, or Rourke.

Reciting those names to myself, it hit me.

Abdul Hamid and Heather Rourke, both dead.

A close call for me. Actually, two close calls, by my chart. Three, by my memory.

My pulse accelerated.

Wait, I wondered with horror. *Could we all be targets?*

CHAPTER
31

"REPORT?"

Gansett sighed but inaudibly. No pleasantries, as usual. He shook his head and mused, *Common courtesy would be appreciated once in a while. A simple "good evening" would do nicely.*

He dismissed the thought and began. "On Saturday, Porter started his day at the same coffee shop. He lingered inside and then came outside with four coffee cups and a brown paper bag."

"Why four? Did he have accomplices?"

This time, Gansett's sigh was loud enough to be heard on the voice-altered connection. "Allow me to report as requested, please. He exited the shop with four cups in a tray, plus the brown paper bag. Then he returned inside, leaving his items on a patio table, which gave me an opportunity. I swiped the bag because I wanted to know what was in it—a dozen donuts. I sniffed the cups. I believe they contained coffee. It was as if he was duplicating the purchase from the previous Sunday."

"Why would he do that?"

Gansett ignored the question. "He spent the remainder of the day driving in the area of Chevy Chase, Maryland. I didn't understand why, at first. Porter called the doctor—Curtis—three times, dialing a number at Walter Reed. Later in the day, Porter received a single call from Curtis.

Perhaps Porter was hoping to meet with Curtis in person. But instead, in the evening, Porter returned to the city."

"What did they discuss?"

Gansett confessed, "I was able to only retrieve the connecting numbers as the device handshaked with the network. I was unable to intercept the content."

"It is encrypted, I suppose." The phrase was a brusque statement, not a question. "Continue," the voice demanded rudely.

Consulting his notes on a yellow legal pad, Gansett resumed his narrative. "On Sunday, late morning, he went to the George Washington University Hospital. He entered through the emergency room doors, not the regular entry. You'll recall this as the hospital where Agent Hamid was transported on the previous Sunday."

"Yes. Go on."

"Today, this morning, he returned to the hospital. His vehicle was parked on a side street, approximately a quarter-mile away. Perhaps he wanted to remain inconspicuous, or he didn't want to pay for the on-site parking. I note this because he returned to the vehicle, called Curtis, and then walked back to the hospital. It was almost dark by the time he left the hospital for the second time today and retrieved the vehicle. He returned to the hotel, where he made a very brief call to an unknown number—but based on the 011-8816 prefix, I know it is an Iridium satellite telephone. Then he sent a text to the same number. Porter is at the Hyatt currently."

"Give me the number."

Gansett read back the details.

"Remain on the line and keep it active," was the immediate reply. "I know who can trace that Iridium device."

The voice went silent, and Gansett remained rock-still, immobile at the kitchen counter, listening to the fizz of the open connection. The assassin was accustomed to inactivity; in his line of work, it was oftentimes necessary.

Nine minutes later, the voice-altering software crackled, "The number is assigned to that yacht. *Almaz*. I will deal with the yacht. In the meantime, this cannot continue to develop. You have nine days before you depart, and in that time, you must terminate Ben Porter's questioning."

"Understood."

The connection indicator switched to red, and the fizzles went silent.

Gansett remained seated and, with his near-perfect memory, mentally recited the order: *"You must terminate Ben Porter's questioning."*

He knew what the caller intended, but the phrasing—*The ambiguity*, he thought—could be opportunistic.

CHAPTER
32

FOR OBVIOUS REASONS, Washington, D.C. has excellent mobile phone coverage, including an extensive roll-out of the latest cell phone technology called 5G. Recalling Volkov's instructions, I did not connect my encrypted phone to the Hyatt's Wi-Fi; that would not be secure. Instead, Volkov assured me that the phone would remain encrypted on 5G while offering a very fast connection speed.

Fast enough, I hoped, for a video call to a yacht somewhere in the Atlantic.

Perhaps the prevalence of video calls during the Covid pandemic taught us two things: first, face-to-face is almost always better, but a video call is a reasonable, albeit dry, substitute. And second, if you must do a video call, you need to consider your background. Like, what's in it?

Imposing bookshelves or majestic views are good. Those same majestic views when you've called in sick, and you forgot to enable a virtual background—not good, possibly grounds for dismissal. A kitchen sink with dirty dishes—probably not a deal-breaker. Something illicit, illegal, or just in poor taste—not ideal. Anyway, in my case, I had none of the above, relying on a bland watercolor in my hotel room, with a coffee cup strategically placed on the small hotel desk in view of the camera. I knew that the other end of my call would have a far more impressive scene, and sure enough, when my little screen lit with a view of Macallister in my seat aboard *Almaz*, I was jealous. Trying not to let it show, I asked casually, "Where are you?"

Lockwood answered, "More than halfway across the Atlantic. About four days to Gibraltar."

"I forget," I confessed. "From there, how long to Port Said? The Suez Canal?"

"Another five days," Lockwood informed me.

"Which means you've got less than nine days to get your ass on a plane, Porter," Macallister grumbled. "I talked to Sullivan on Saturday. She was miffed, to say the least, that you weren't on the boat with us. She bought the explanation, though."

"We sorta expected that. So, okay. Did she say anything about the mission?"

"She gave us a date. April 13. Long story short, I'll have Volkov send you a file. We're working up logistics and plans. I'm almost done assembling a team, and I have a Bureau Citation X jet lined up to fly the team over to Egypt. Departing on March 31. You'll be on that jet, Porter," Macallister insisted.

"Please send the file. But I requested this call to report to you. I am making progress with my investigation," I said, wanting to change the subject from Macallister's travel plans that I had no intention of honoring until I figured out what happened to Hamid. I mean, Macallister is on a yacht in the Atlantic. He can't force me to get on a plane. Naturally, I didn't tell my boss that.

"Progress on the Hamid investigation? Really?" Macallister looked surprised.

His smug tone annoyed me, so I gave it right back to him. "What do you know about Doctor David Curtis?"

Silence. Finally, Macallister admitted, "That's not a question I was expecting. But okay. Not unlike many doctors who work at a government or military location, he has a 'secret' clearance. For example, he can access our facilities with an escort. That's how he got into the lab at Quantico to examine the wrecked Jeep, for example. He was assigned to Rourke's case at Walter Reed, and I figured if he was good enough for them, he's good enough for me."

"That's it?"

Volkov stepped in. "No, of course not. After your accident, and after we learned Curtis was doing the autopsy, Macallister asked me to check him out. Because he's at Reed, the Bureau has a file on him. It's impeccable. He's extremely well-respected at Reed. Their top pathologist on chemicals and toxins. Why? What's your line of inquiry about?"

"Do you know who assigned him to Rourke's case?"

Macallister and Volkov looked at each other, and Lockwood turned to stare directly at the camera. At me. Sometimes, it's the obvious questions that are never asked.

Volkov confessed, "No. I mean, I guess I thought it would be standard procedure, and after seeing the doctor's record and understanding that this was his area of expertise, it just made sense."

"That's the problem," I muttered while wondering, *How did we miss this?*

I kept that to myself, however, and explained, in a more reasonable, level-headed tone than I felt, "The problem is that no one knew that the substance on the Jeep's door handles was poisoned *before* Curtis was assigned to Rourke's case. The Jeep was already at Quantico. Curtis hadn't seen it. Hadn't examined the compound. Therefore, the question remains: how was he, their top toxins guy, assigned to Rourke's autopsy before anyone knew toxins were involved?"

"We need to find out how he got that case," Volkov confirmed, with a note of embarrassment in her voice.

"We should interview Curtis," Macallister proposed.

"Not yet," I cautioned. "I've spoken with Curtis three times, and—"

"Three times?" Macallister's voice was tinged with displeasure.

I didn't back down. "Yessir. Remember, I remained behind to investigate Hamid's death. That's what I'm doing, sir."

Macallister grunted. "Hmmph. I think you should have cleared that with me, first."

"Next time, I will," I agreed obsequiously, with no intention of doing so and not knowing that there would not be a next time.

The Deputy Assistant Director appeared mollified, and he invited me to resume my report. "Go on."

"Let's turn to Hamid's case," I suggested. "I first met with Curtis in person on Friday, and he explained to me that his autopsy made it unquestionable that Hamid died of a Digoxin overdose. Got it?" Three heads nodded, and I continued. "The most recent time I spoke with Curtis was yesterday, by phone. Recall that Hamid died in the wee hours of Monday morning. Curtis told me that he did not have a hand in Hamid's care. That was consistent with what he told us, earlier. He said was napping near the nurse's station at the GW Hospital ICU when he was woken by Hamid's Code Blue emergency. Remember that?"

There was a quiet chorus of "yes" from my small audience.

"Well," I said flatly, "Doctor Curtis lied. There are significant inconsistencies in his story."

Volkov raised a hand and asked, "How do you know that?"

"I went to the GW Hospital. A nurse remembered him, and she told me that Curtis didn't nap but instead wandered in and out of Hamid's area overnight. In fact, the nurse caught him poking around the central nursing station."

Macallister coughed. "That's lame, Porter. Maybe he dozed, maybe he didn't. So what?"

"There's more," I revealed. "I learned at the hospital that Curtis had a direct involvement Hamid's care. *Curtis* was the doctor who ordered that Hamid be moved out of the emergency room and up to the fifth floor ICU. Why would he do that?"

Not allowing enough time for my colleagues to try and answer my impossible question, I barreled onward. "On top of the pattern of inconsistency by the doctor, there appears to be a deadly omission. I convinced a nurse in the ICU to review Hamid's chart. When he coded, he was treated for atrial fibrillation with Digoxin. Yet, Curtis told us that the second tox screen that was done on Hamid showed the presence of that exact drug. That suggests two things, both concerning. First, if Curtis knew about the tox screen, why didn't the doctors at GW know? And second, where is that report? Remember, Curtis said he was expediting it. Did he bury it?"

"Remind me," Macallister requested, "Why does that report matter?"

"It matters because it showed that Hamid had Digoxin in his system when he was admitted to the ER. Treating him with the same drug when he coded would have induced potentially fatal Digoxin toxicity." I paused and added, "It *was* fatal."

Even through the video call, I could sense that Macallister was skeptical. My suspicion was confirmed when he commented, "Curtis is a lab doc, not an investigator. He may not have laid out the timeline properly, but that doesn't incriminate him for anything."

As usual, Macallister cut through the noise and delivered a salient critique. But I wasn't finished. "Stay with me, please. I convinced the nurse at GW to pull my chart because Curtis was attending to both Hamid's case and mine. I was on the same floor, at the same hospital. She examined the chart and said I coded twice. Two emergency resuscitations. That's what they told you, too, Macallister. Right?"

He confirmed with an exaggerated nod and a verbal, "Yes."

"Wrong. My chart showed two incidents. The ninth and fifteenth of January. And yet, I *distinctly* remember a third episode. I remember looking at the indicators on the screen in my room. They were going crazy, and I wondered why no one was coming to help, even though I felt fine. Then one of my hallucinations started, and I don't know what happened next."

"But Ben," Lockwood said, in a quiet and respectful tone, "if you were hallucinating, how do you know you didn't imagine that, um, episode?"

"Fair point," I admitted. "But that's how those things went. One moment, I'd be completely lucid, and the next, attacked by ghosts. There was always a prelude, like a kaleidoscope. It happened frequently. So, no, just because I hallucinated does not mean I don't remember. Because I recall the exact date. January 20. Inauguration day. Kinda a big deal, you know?"

"I don't follow," Macallister protested.

"Let me tie it together," I replied. "Why is a Walter Reed pathologist taking such interest in these cases? He's a common thread to Rourke, Hamid, and me. He performed both Rourke's and Hamid's autopsies.

Why is he hanging out overnight by Hamid's bedside? Why is he poking around the nurse's station?"

I noticed that Volkov was typing and clicking rapidly at her station, her eyes angled toward her computer screen, not to the video call camera. When I paused, she looked up and asked, "Can you describe that nurse's station?"

"Sure," I replied. "It's like the one in the emergency room where they first admitted Hamid. You were there, and the one on the fifth floor is similar. It's a central desk equipped with monitors that show each patient's vital signs so that the nurse on duty can oversee several patients at once without going room-to-room. Standard set-up, they told me."

"That's what I thought," Volkov said with raised eyebrows. "I have a theory."

CHAPTER
33

ANASTASIA VOLKOV WAS, without a doubt, the most tech-savvy person I knew. Her mind didn't work like mine. She lived in an interconnected world, and while I might see clues in facial expressions or in questions that should have been asked but weren't, she collected her observations from the massive amount of accumulated knowledge on the Internet and beyond—in the dark web and in the classified databases that the United States government maintained and continually updated.

Her typing and clicking slowed but did not stop as she outlined her theory. "Your description of the monitors at the nurse's station and that your room included a similar screen—that could be a link. Those are called vital signs monitors. And, just about every hospital does what GW does—they interconnect the patient vital signs monitors to a central location."

"Commonplace, right?" I asked.

"Absolutely. Dozens if not hundreds of commercial sources. Medicine is a big business. Tech and medicine together? If combined, those are the world's largest industries."

Macallister groused, "So what? What does this have to do with Doctor Curtis?"

Volkov's eyebrows lifted. "That the big question, isn't it? Here's what it has to do with Hamid and Porter, however. Because those central vitals monitoring systems are interconnected, they can be manipulated. Hacked."

"Here we go again," Macallister muttered. "Hacking. It's always hacking."

Volkov chuckled. "The entire world has gone digital, Macallister. Even you figured out how to use a smartphone."

"That's true. I struggled with technology," Macallister admitted. "I had to figure it out. Get with the times, ya know."

"But that's the point, isn't it?" Volkov said. "Connected computers are pervasive in everyday life. They can be tools of convenience, sure, but oftentimes, as we know, they can be used in nefarious ways." She paused to tap at her keyboard. "We are only just beginning to understand the risks of that interconnectivity. Can I offer some specific examples of risks within the hospital systems and, specifically, the medical devices that Porter referenced?"

Her question was obviously rhetorical. Volkov elaborated, "Back in 2018, cybersecurity specialists with a McAfee Security team bought a system on eBay and demonstrated that they could alter the vital signs sent from a remote patient monitor to a central station. A hacker could raise a patient's heart rate, for example, to trigger an unnecessary intervention, or the hacker could falsify that heart rate to appear that it is normal, even if it is not. And, indeed, a hacker could suppress a signal from the patient's room to the central station, and thus a medical condition requiring emergency intervention would go unnoticed."

I asked, "Has that ever happened as a documented case? As opposed to the McAfee test?"

"Not exactly," Volkov admitted. "But similar incidents have occurred. Back in September 2020, one of the nation's largest hospital systems, Universal Health Services, was targeted by ransomware. The hospital shut off their systems, and therefore a specific patient attack did not happen, but the collateral damage was extensive. Canceled surgeries, ambulances sent on wild goose chases, that sort of thing. Fortunately, no one was directly harmed. The next month, in October, a hospital in Oregon was targeted. They had to shut down their network and rebuild it from scratch, and in the meantime, there were no electronic records available for doctors or nurses. No charts, no imaging data from MRI or X-ray machines, nothing. Imagine how patient care gets affected in that scenario."

Ever the agent, Macallister was unconvinced. He preferred evidence to conjecture. "I'll concur that it's concerning that Curtis was present when Hamid died, and I'll concede that Porter has uncovered an unsettling number of inconsistencies in Curtis's interactions with us and with Hamid. But we don't know where Curtis was when Porter had his episode on January 20th. In my view, we need to find out, however, before making that link. He might have been at Walter Reed and nowhere near Porter."

"That's true," I agreed. "We also need to know who assigned him to Rourke's case."

Volkov volunteered, "I can run both of those things down."

With skepticism in his voice, Macallister demurred. "Sure, get a bead on those two items." He looked down at the table briefly before resuming eye contact with me, or, rather, with the camera. "Porter has been correct in the past, but lemme be the voice of reason here. I just don't see proof. I'm unconvinced. Your hacking examples, Volkov? If the desired outcome is to cause disruption or instill fear or even distrust in the medical systems, yeah, I get it. This is something that the Bureau has already warned about. It's big picture stuff. But you haven't established a link to Hamid or Porter. Or to Rourke. None of this is targeting. It's theory. It's not specific to a threat."

"I'm not done yet," I countered. "I've uncovered more. What's not theory is that Rourke and I were targeted. One suspect is Ginachere's alleged hitman, remember?"

Heads nodded, and I continued. "I won't bore you with details, and I'll send you my write-up, but I also revisited the coffee shop that Hamid and I went to that Sunday. I showed the barista the picture of the hitman. She swears that guy was in the shop when Hamid and I were there."

There was a beat of silence before Macallister scoffed. "That's thin, Porter. It's something, yes, but for this to stick, we're gonna need more than one eyewitness."

"I know, sir. We're not going to solve a case with that as evidence. But, consider this, too—I'm no doctor, but I researched Digoxin. In fact, Curtis helped me do so without knowing it. Curtis told me that Digoxin is available in an oral suspension. A liquid form. Watch."

I pushed my phone, propped up against a Mitch Rapp hardcover book that I was reading in the evenings, a little farther from me. Pulling the staged coffee cup to the center of the camera's field of view, I popped off the lid and narrated, "I bought this coffee a half-hour ago. And I bought this medicine dispensing cup at the CVS Pharmacy on the way back from the donut shop to the hotel. Remember I told you that I spoke to Curtis three times? Well, the second time, Curtis told me that 40ccs of liquid Digoxin might trigger Hamid's symptoms, and this dispensing cup is filled with 40ccs of water." I picked up the off-screen dispensing cup and held it next to the coffee cup, and for the benefit of my audience on *Almaz*, I poured the contents of the little cup into the bigger cup.

Tilting the coffee cup slightly toward the camera, I said, "You can barely tell the difference in volume." Then, I brought the coffee cup to my mouth and took a sip. "And I can barely taste a difference."

"Nice science experiment, Porter," Macallister said, but for once without a hint of sarcasm in his voice. "But what are you trying to prove?"

"Let's say the barista was correct. Let's say the hitman was in the shop that morning, and he dumped Digoxin into Hamid's cup. Plausible, right? Remember, this is the same guy who might have poisoned Rourke and me. Different scenarios, yes, but still poisoning. Meanwhile, Curtis oversees all three cases?" I shook my head sideways. "We're tripping over coincidences."

"Still, what are you trying to prove?"

"Sir, my theory is that Rourke and I were targeted. Curtis was there to ensure an outcome. He failed, obviously, because I'm still breathing. But then Hamid was targeted. Curtis was there and perhaps facilitated Hamid's death, perhaps by intercepting and burying the second tox screen report, or perhaps by manipulating the vitals

monitoring system. I don't know, exactly. I admit it's theory." I paused
to make sure they were paying attention before concluding, "However,
I conclude that if Hamid's death was no accidental overdose, I think
it's possible that I could still be an active target. And I think that you all
should consider that you are targets, too."

I watched as Macallister exchanged glances with Volkov and
Lockwood before Macallister placed his palms on the polished tabletop.
"On Saturday, when we conferenced with Sullivan, when she gave us the
April 13 date, she said that Ginachere would be in Saudi Arabia, with
the Crown Prince, with the King, and . . . with your hitman. Gansett is
going to be there, Porter. Sullivan gave us a dossier, a few more photos,
and a pseudonym."

"You're headed right toward him," I blurted. "It could be a trap."

Macallister was unfazed. "Except Ginachere doesn't know we are
headed there. Remember, we set up a cover story for the boat leaving
the States."

"So?"

With concern in his eyes, Macallister suggested, "I think we are safe
aboard *Almaz* for now, and I'd feel better if you were here with us. In the
meantime, I tend to agree; you are a target. Stay away from Curtis and
keep yourself outta sight until you can get on that Bureau jet. You gotta
weigh your safety against your investigation. My advice . . . no, my order
is for you to lay low, Porter, for the next eight days."

As the team prepared to disconnect the call, Volkov reminded me that
she would send me the itinerary and the Gansett dossier that Sullivan
had provided. Volkov also assured me that she would immediately employ
her incomparable digital sleuthing methods to track down our two open
questions—first, how and who assigned Rourke's case to Doctor Curtis,
and second, what were the doctor's whereabouts on January 20.

Eight days.

I couldn't sit in this hotel room for that long. I had to keep moving
and at least get out of Washington.

I didn't know it then, but wherever I went, it wouldn't matter—nor
did I have anywhere close to those eight days.

CHAPTER
34

WEDNESDAY, MARCH 24, 2021

SAVE FOR A STOP on the New Jersey Turnpike to refill the thirsty Tahoe's gas tank and to empty my, uh, tank, my butt had been stuck to the cracked leather seat for over six-and-a-half hours. After checking out of the Hyatt at about 8:30 A.M. on the second-to-last Wednesday in March, I piloted the SUV northbound on Interstate 95 under ominous, rainy skies.

Not an ideal day for a road trip, but all the same, I was pleased to think that I was leaving my hitman behind in the rear-view mirror. I took Macallister's advice literally. Instead of laying low in D.C., I figured I'd get out of sight. Get out of town. And therefore, I decided to head to Boston, where I knew I could find a safe house, so to speak. Off the radar, no hotel check-in, and good security; all ideal for eluding a shadow, if indeed I was being targeted.

Because I did not want to broadcast my movements, I'd wait until I neared Boston to make a call to see if I'd be welcomed. If not, I'd come up with an alternate plan. In any case, I would no longer be in Washington. With about an hour-and-a-half remaining on the road, I figured I'd call my host in thirty minutes.

Carving the Tahoe off I-84 and onto the Massachusetts Turnpike, I felt a renewed sense of energy. This was my highway to home, and I knew this road like the back of my hand.

Actually, that's not exactly true. I'm not sure what that phrase really means because I closed my eyes briefly and tried to imagine what the back of my hand looked like. I got nothing.

But I did know that this would be the final leg of the eight-hour drive. Eager to finish the trip, I touched the gas pedal, and I shrugged off the click that I heard before the big V-8 responded to push the SUV up a slight incline. The aging chassis made all sorts of strange noises that I learned to ignore. It was impossible to overlook, however, the message that flashed onto my phone screen, clipped into a suction-cup mount on the windshield: *Slowdown Ahead*.

Examining the map display, I groaned. The road ahead was painted red, indicating slow or stopped traffic. It would be only a matter of a few minutes before my speedy progress toward Boston would be delayed.

Reaching the crest of the big hill in Charlton and passing beneath the bridge at Center Depot Road, the highest point on this section of the Pike, I saw the westbound service station across the median, which prompted me to check the fuel gauge. I didn't want to stop again, and fortunately, the needle aimed just below the halfway mark. *Plenty of gas to get to Boston*, I thought, even as I eased off the accelerator to let the SUV coast down the four-mile decline toward Auburn and toward the red brake lights that began flashing sporadically ahead as vehicles reached the predicted slow-down.

Gravity and mass results in velocity, so it was no surprise that the heavy Chevy picked up speed, rolling downhill in the center lane of this three-lane stretch of the Pike—but it was very much a surprise when I tapped the brakes as I overtook a cautiously-driven sedan, already slowing for the upcoming traffic, and nothing happened. The Tahoe didn't decelerate the slightest.

I pushed the brake pedal harder, and I felt it smoosh to the floorboard.

I checked my mirrors. Clear left. I twitched the steering wheel to pass the sedan using the left lane, the speedometer at 62 miles per hour, and climbing.

The Tahoe slowed somewhat as I pumped the brake pedal furiously. I inhaled. I'd been holding my breath, I realized.

Relax. It's an old truck. It's a long drive. It's just a glitch.

Then I heard that clicking noise again. It was underneath me. And with my right foot resting on the brake pedal, not the accelerator pedal, I concluded the noise might have had nothing to do with me touching the gas earlier.

It had to be something else, and I realized, with horror, that the speed was ticking up again. 64. 65. 66 miles per hour.

The Tahoe began to wobble slightly, but worse, the lane ahead was also occupied.

Frantically checking my passenger-side mirror, I saw the sedan was well back, and I swerved into the center lane, still declining the hill and still accelerating. 67. 68.

Squinting, I peered ahead. Center lane, semi-truck, slowing, brake lights lit. Left lane, SUV, also slowing. Right lane, open. Fighting the pressure on the steering wheel, I coaxed the Tahoe to the right. 69. 70, all while pumping and pushing the brake pedal as hard as I could.

Nothing. There was no resistance. An orange warning light illuminated in the gauge cluster, and I realized, *I have no brakes. I can't stop this thing.*

Ahead of the semi, perhaps intimidated by the brawny snout of the tractor, a compact car that I had not seen before glided smoothly into the right lane, appearing directly in front of me. In my lane. *In my lane!*

72 miles per hour.

The breakdown lane was my last option, and with the tires growling on the uneven pavement, I flashed by the compact, its teen driver flipping me a middle finger as the old Tahoe shot past at 75 miles per hour, trembling violently as if it was going to shake itself to pieces.

I couldn't hold a line. The seventeen-year-old suspension in my vehicle was probably as old as the driver that I had just passed, and I knew it was a matter of time before I completely lost control or ran out of roadway before reaching the fully stopped traffic jam ahead. At this speed, I had little faith that I'd walk away.

Time for drastic measures. I yanked down on the steering-column mounted shifter, switching from Drive to 3rd gear. The engine howled in protest as the RPM gauge redlined, but the engine braking helped, and I could feel the truck slow slightly.

And then I spotted the cause of the traffic mess: a stopped police cruiser ahead in the breakdown lane, lights flashing and, beyond, the orange trucks of a roadway repair crew.

I have to stop this thing!

My mind raced, and with few options, I guided the Tahoe further to the edge of the road, right wheels now in the grass, and with a heart-rending screech of metal-on-metal, the truck's right side contacted the shiny surface of the steel road safety guardrail.

With the help of the squealing friction on the guardrail, I tried 2nd gear. Once again, the motor maxed itself out, screaming under load, warning lights flashing on one after another on the dash. I knew my actions would grievously damage the motor, but I'd rather kill the V-8 than me—or the cop ahead.

With my left foot, I tried the emergency brake, fortunately still pedal-activated in this vehicle as opposed to the commonplace e-brake button in more modern cars. One click in, then two, then three . . . and . . .

I can do it! It's working! I can stop this thing!

It wasn't to be. Despite one last downshift into 1st gear, and with the emergency brake fully applied, the Tahoe rear-ended the cruiser at about 20 miles per hour, and for the second time this year, my face smacked into an airbag blasting full in one-twentieth of a second.

CHAPTER
35

SWEEPING THE DEFLATED AIRBAG away from my face and chest, I sat for a moment, trying to settle my breathing.

As the semi-truck I had passed moments ago rushed by, I heard a loud horn blast. The driver was obviously unaware that my brakes failed and probably presumed that I was just a typical Masshole driver.

Once I pushed the air bag clear, I could see that the gauge cluster was lit with countless red and amber warning lights. I figured that the crash sensors shut the ignition off. And, given the steam that streamed from under the bent hood and from the front grill, I was quite certain that the engine was never going to function again. I realized that the Tahoe would take me no further.

The police car—a gray Ford Explorer—was probably fifty feet in front of the mangled snout of the Tahoe. The Explorer's rear window was gone, obviously shattered, and there was body damage on the cruiser's right side and rear; its rear bumper hung loosely and awkwardly.

Ahead, I could see two road construction workers running toward the crash, and to my left, all three lanes of the Pike were stopped, drivers ogling the mess in the breakdown lane.

I took another deep breath as I watched the driver's door of the Explorer swing open, and I prepared to greet the stone-faced Massachusetts State Trooper who exited the cruiser with his left hand cupping the back of his neck and with his right hand resting on the pistol in his belt-mounted holster.

He was clearly upset. Very upset. I didn't blame him in the slightest, and with the electronic windows inoperable due to the shut-down ignition, I pulled the door handle. Big mistake, and I was immediately reprimanded with a stentorian demand, "Remain in the vehicle!"

The trooper unholstered his weapon and paced slowly toward the front end of the still-smoking Tahoe, scowling at the steam and then at me. I tried to make it obvious that my hands were positioned exactly at the ten and two positions on the steering wheel, airbag draping over the bottom rim of the wheel.

"Get out of the vehicle," the officer barked, reaching the door and yanking it fully open "Out. Keep your hands behind your back where I can see them. Got it?"

I slowly and carefully complied, keeping my hands visible until I could stand erect by the side of the Tahoe, then clasping my hands behind my back as ordered.

The humorless trooper slammed the door closed and pushed me toward the front of the vehicle. "Hands on the hood," the cop ordered. "Spread your legs wider. Keep your head down."

I blurted, "What the hell? You're treating me like a criminal? I'm sorry I rear-ended your car, but my brakes failed and—"

"Shut up and comply," he spat, shoving me toward the hood of Tahoe.

As my palms connected with the metal, I thought, *Shit, that's hot!*

I yanked my hands off the hot hood, and the officer grabbed my right wrist, growling, "Don't move again, son. Don't move another muscle."

I couldn't believe it as I heard the sound of clanking metal—and he cuffed me.

Though pissed off by the unnecessary handcuffs and the outrageous behavior, I held my temper in check, and eventually, I got to tell my story. Officer Green, as I gleaned by squinting at his nametag, displayed obvious disdain. "Brakes don't just fail, son," he lectured sternly, his coffee-stained teeth occasionally visible through his distinct, slow enunciation of each word. "This here truck has got two braking systems. Front and rear. I doubt very much that they would both be compromised at the same moment." He shook his head negatively. "License, registration, and proof of insurance, please."

The final word was a formality, a reflex, perhaps. Officer Green was not being polite. He was reciting his lines.

"In the glovebox. And my license is in my wallet on the center console."

Fortunately, I thought, *my Glock and my somewhat false FBI badge were in a lockbox inside my backpack, sitting on the rear seat.*

The officer pulled open the driver's-side front door to retrieve the documents from the Tahoe, his right hand remaining on the grip of his now re-holstered pistol. I'd faced worse than a self-important police officer—except for the part about, you know, rear-ending a cop car.

With my documents in hand, the trooper demanded, "This way," and he pushed me to the partially crushed Explorer, showing me the back door.

"You're detaining me? It was an accident."

"Bullshit, son. Keep your head down."

He pushed my skull clear of the door frame and shoved me into the Explorer's backseat, fabricated from unforgiving, molded plastic—straightforward to sanitize after being occupied by criminals like me. He slammed the door shut in my face and pulled out a phone, clearly calling for assistance as he examined my driver's license.

I dearly wished I, too, had made my own phone call earlier.

CHAPTER
36

I SETTLED, with my hands uncomfortably manacled behind my back, to watch the shitshow that ensued.

Within ten minutes, a bevy of Explorers had screeched to a stop at the accident site. Three? Four? Five? I'm not sure how many a "bevy" totals, but the scene was crawling with troopers. Setting out cones, taking photos, talking on phones, examining my Tahoe, and ogling me—the caged criminal—cuffed in the backseat.

Perhaps after a half-hour of captivity, the door swung open. Officer Green motioned me out, a difficult task, actually, with my hands behind my back. Thankfully, he unlocked the cuffs and clipped them onto his utility belt. "Mister Porter," he grunted. "I ran your record. Former FBI agent, huh?"

"Yessir," I replied.

If only it was that simple . . . but I am not telling him that story right now.

"When I called it in, I got a response back awfully quick. Got a message that the Bureau would send a wrecker. Same message told me to let you go. You must be connected."

"Something like that," I muttered.

The Bureau was sending a tow truck? How?

Green didn't notice my confusion and continued, "You're damn lucky, you know. You're lucky that I was smart enough to see you approaching in my rearview, and I shifted my vehicle into gear and floored it so that when you impacted, I didn't get the brunt of the collision force. Could have messed me up pretty bad, you know."

That explains why his car was a distance ahead, I thought.

I smeared my words with awe and respect. "Great instincts, sir. It's obvious that you're very experienced. I am lucky that it was you that I ran into." I tried a grin to go along with my wordplay.

The Officer was unimpressed by my wit. "If you say so. You can wait in my vehicle until the tow arrives. It's not safe to sit in . . . in that wreck." He motioned at my smoldering Tahoe.

"I'll wait outside if you don't mind."

"Fine. My troopers and I will conclude our investigation."

An hour after my unexpected detour in the grassy verge alongside the Mass Pike and a forced stop against the backside of a cop car, I watched as the Tahoe was winched up the incline of a flatbed wrecker truck, the still-locked-up left rear tire squealing in protest. I winced at the high-pitched sound, rubbing absently on a raw spot on my wrist where the cuffs had abraded my skin.

I climbed up to the passenger side of the wrecker cab, and the driver mumbled, in a thick, Boston accent, "Normally, I don't let people ride with me. 'Specially with the Covid. But I got instructions. I gotta take you all the way to Salem?"

"That's right," I replied, fastening my seatbelt, not willing to admit that I didn't have a clue what his instructions were. Hearing that Salem was my destination, however, affirmed the hunch that I held. I examined my phone screen—Officer Green permitted me to retrieve it from the totaled SUV before it was loaded onto the flatbed. There was a single notification on the screen:

MISSED CALL - SAC

I couldn't return the call, given my present company, and as if he knew I was thinking about him, the driver shifted the big truck into gear.

A throaty diesel engine rumbled as the rig picked up speed and merged onto the Pike, resuming my journey to the east.

I closed my eyes, the stress of the runaway Tahoe and the arresting officer now catching up to me. I could rest for the remainder of the drive. Another mistake, and I missed catching a glimpse of a blue BMW sedan that doggedly followed the wrecker, keeping a four or five vehicle buffer between its front bumper and the lumbering flatbed.

I'd understand that error soon enough.

CHAPTER
37

"GOOD EVENING, PORTER," said Special Agent in Charge Jennifer Appleton, her lightly tanned, unlined face mottled by the flashing reflection of the flatbed wrecker's yellow rooftop lights as she stood outside in front of her impeccably restored, white-painted, Colonial-era home in Salem, a residential community about fifteen miles north of Boston.

"It's good to see you again. And I'm really grateful that you've still got my back," I replied, with as much true sincerity as I could muster in my tone.

As the highest-ranking official at the FBI's Boston Division Field Office, SAC Jennifer Appleton was generally feared; her demanding expectations and ice-chill composure made her a daunting SAC. I, however, had cracked that code and gained Appleton's respect, though I knew I was in for a heavy round of questioning. She dove right in. "Care to explain how I got a notice that you were in a traffic accident involving an officer of the law?"

Appleton had bailed out my ass before. More than once, in fact. To be fair, though, I'd done the same for her. Our history together was built on strength and common trust.

Because of our track record together, I was absolutely confident that I could count on Appleton in a case of need—and I figured having a black-book assassin on my heels qualified as one of those cases. However, I wasn't quite ready to get into that while standing on her lawn, so I replied, "Well, that's a long explanation, which I am happy to share. In fact, that story is why I'm here. I was going to call you in advance, but I ran into some trouble on the road, as you've obviously discovered. Before I get into my saga, can you tell me how you knew to intervene with Officer Green?"

Unlike Green, she allowed just a hint of a smile to show at my wordplay, my rhyme. "As you might recall, when you were off the books, it was my job to monitor all things that had to do with the undercover assignment of one Ben Porter. Officer Green's inquiry triggered a hit on your driver's license, which escalated to me in about sixty seconds. A little digging by our associates at the Bureau, and within minutes we had a good handle on what was going down on the side of the Mass Pike. We heard a story about failed brakes and a rear-end collision incident."

"Obviously, you called the wrecker. The driver had instructions to take me here."

She absently brushed at a loose strand of her conservatively styled, shoulder-length auburn hair. "Brakes don't just fail, Porter."

"Funny. I've heard that line before. From Officer Green as he cuffed me."

She glanced at me; her left eyebrow raised slightly. "Cuffed, huh? You didn't behave?"

"I thought I did. Just not my day, I guess. Anyway, why the white-glove treatment with a tow truck driver who is obviously friendly with the Bureau?"

"Well, Porter, I thought it prudent to have our people have a look. The car will be taken to one of our shops. They'll look it over. And while they do that, you've got a lot more to explain. Let's go inside."

I retrieved my possessions from the Tahoe and followed SAC Appleton into her home as a blue BMW rolled by slowly.

CHAPTER 38

IT TOOK A WHILE, but I told Appleton everything.

We sat in Appleton's first floor living room on matching, white-upholstered club chairs. I'd not only been in this room before, but I also knew that the space was wired with hidden cameras and microphones, and that it functioned as a home office for the SAC. The setting was tranquil, which to me was a stark contrast to the roadside terror I'd experienced hours before.

The SAC was read in on my prior escapades, so I didn't have to dive deep into the backstory. I picked up the thread in Washington and brought her current: starting from the accident on the sixth of January, to the allegations by Genevieve Sullivan, to *Almaz* making the trip across the pond to the Med and the Middle East with Macallister in charge, to my D.C. investigation on Hamid's death, and to Macallister's directive that I should lay low—that I could possibly be a target.

Appleton sipped from a glass of water and took a moment to think. "Let's unpack this. Sullivan claims that the man spotted in the parking lot prior to your accident is an assassin who the CIA has employed before. Thus, the link she's proposing is that the CIA is using this guy again to target you and your team. Correct?"

"Yeah, that about covers it."

"Let me poke two holes in that theory. First, that presumes the CIA is operating on domestic soil. That is a direct violation of their charter."

"So what?" I argued. "Assassination attempts are, by definition, unsanctioned. And yet they happen. The world of espionage and counterspies is not covered in some manual. Some charter. It's the very opposite of being clearly defined."

"True. What the public doesn't know and what the public expects are two vastly different things. I can accept, perhaps, that the CIA is operating locally. Certainly, the FBI has, on occasion, been active overseas. One can always claim exigent circumstances, or an extension of a task, or an opportunity. But," Appleton paused for another sip of water, "what does the CIA have to gain? What does Hazel Ginachere have to gain by eliminating you? Rourke? Hamid?"

"It seems drastic, right?" I said as I nodded my agreement. "Let me theorize. Sullivan's explanation was that was that her office had a leak, and Ginachere found out that Sullivan was planning to task Quadrant to expose Ginachere. Therefore, Ginachere needed to shut down that inquiry. She could scare us so we would reconsider engaging in that task. Or she could kill us, which would guarantee we didn't, well, do anything further."

Appleton was shaking her head. "I can imagine that is possible, but without more evidence, it strains plausibility." Her face showed obvious skepticism, but before she could continue, her mobile phone chirped. Accepting the call and bringing the device to her ear, she said, "Good evening, Agent Havens."

I know that name, I realized.

I watched as Appleton's expression morphed from disbelief to disturbed. She spoke rapidly. "Wait. Stop there. Let me put you on speaker and then start over." Appleton put the phone on the coffee table next to her water glass, and she tapped an icon on the screen. "Okay, repeat that, please. Porter is listening in."

A deep voice sounded from the phone. "Porter. You gettin' yourself in trouble again? And I gotta ride in and save the day?"

"Yeah, man, that about covers it," I replied with the familiar, slightly sarcastic tone that Special Agent Leroy Havens and I used together. We enjoyed a long history; Havens was assigned to the Critical Incident Response Group, the FBI equivalent to, say, the Navy SEALs or the Army's Delta Force, and as a CIRG agent, he happened to be assigned in the field during my first case. Since then, I had several opportunities to rely on his expertise and skill, not to mention his loyalty and friendship. I asked, "You still with CIRG?"

"Yeah. I'm on a specialist CIRG team in the northeast, reporting to SAC Appleton. I'm based in Boston. And when the SAC called, naturally, I jumped."

I mouthed *thank you* to Appleton; having Havens as an ally was a step in a positive direction.

Appleton ordered, "Let's move on. Repeat what you told me, please."

I leaned closer to the coffee table as the baritone began anew, "As I said, I met the flatbed over at the shop in Peabody. You know, Mauer's place. He does good work and keeps his mouth shut. Anyway, he put the Tahoe on one of his lifts and . . . bam! I took one look underneath and knew right away that was no accident."

My eyes met Appleton. She nodded. I assumed she heard this part before putting Havens on speaker, and Appleton said, "Explain in-depth, please."

The voice boomed, "Both the front and the rear brake lines were cut. Really clever, and really easy to miss—unless you had prior training. We've looked into this type of operation before, but to my knowledge, we never used it. Though, that means nothin', doesn't it?" He chuckled. Hearing no response from his listeners, Havens cleared his throat. "Um, right. Anyway. Like I said, we've experimented with a device that can be triggered remotely. I'd say something like that was used here. What it does is to create a sudden charge to a cutting element that makes a nick at the brake line—which is a solid, pre-bent hose, stainless steel, if I recall correctly—where the line meets the swage at the end, entering the cylinder."

"A nick? Clarify that, please," I requested.

"Yeah. Doesn't need to cut it, only damage it, so it bleeds. Any pressure in the hydraulic braking system takes care of the rest. The hydraulic pump activates when the pedal is pushed, and it will force brake fluid out of the system. No fluid, no brakes."

"And the device is still present?" Appleton asked. "Perhaps you can examine it. Trace it."

Another chuckle from Havens. "That's the nifty part. These things can be set up with a two-stage charge. First stage nicks the brake line, second stage not only destroys the device into a hundred little bits but also releases the magnet that attaches the device to the chassis. The fragments drop to the road, and it's gone. If you got lucky and knew where to look, you'd find pieces no bigger than peas of gravel alongside the roadway. In the case of the Mass Pike, where you told me it happened, you'd have to close the road and inspect several miles of it leading up to the actual accident site with a microscope."

"A fool's errand," whispered Appleton, with an absent-minded expression. Her eyes refocused, and she spoke firmly. "Thank you, Havens. Let me know if you discover anything further."

"Oh, there's more. May I continue?"

Appleton's eyebrows raised slightly as she said in an incredulous tone, "There's more?"

"Porter was being tracked," Havens stated. "I found a white disc, about the size of a large coat button, hidden in the trailer hitch receiver that's located under the rear bumper of the Tahoe. Another nifty device. It's been in development for a while, and I believe it's being released to the public next month. It's called an Apple Air Tag."

"Never heard of it," I said. "What does it do?"

"It's a little gizmo that sends a Bluetooth signal to any Apple device that can receive it, and therefore it's a crowdsourced receiver network. There are billions of Apple devices out there. If the Tag gets in range of one of them, the Apple device relays the Tag's location via an encrypted message to the owner of the Tag. Therefore, it's not functioning as an always-on tracking device. But if a Tag is left in one place for long enough, chances are excellent that an Apple device will be in the Tag's vicinity soon enough."

Appleton scowled. "I have two questions. First, if it's not always-on, why use it? There are far more sophisticated devices that any run-of-the-mill private investigator could get their hands on. Second, if this has not been released to the public yet, how did Porter's stalker get one?"

"I'll take those questions in reverse order," Havens replied. "There are a few governmental agencies, including the FBI, who have prior knowledge of the product. This one is probably a prototype."

I asked the obvious question. "How about the CIA? Would they have access to this?"

Havens grunted. "I wouldn't know, but I wouldn't doubt it."

Appleton leaned toward her device as I held up a hand, signaling another question. "Do you know anything about battery life on these things? Like, when could it have been planted? Hours or days?"

"That's the answer to Appleton's second question. An always-on device has a limited battery life. However, this Air Tag battery lasts about a year. But I also heard that Apple didn't want these things to be used as tracking devices for this kind of scenario, I suppose, so when the product is launched, it's going to beep or something if it has not made contact with its host in a while. Three days or something. That's probably irrelevant with a prototype, though."

Appleton rolled her eyes. "Another tech device which can be used for evil purposes, unintended by its developer. Job security for us, I guess."

"And job security for car thieves," Havens suggested. "That's one of the scenarios that the Bureau has gamed out with these things. Say a thief sees a high-value Porsche sports car in a parking lot. Said thief affixes a Tag and waits. The Tag eventually pings when the Porsche is parked overnight. The thief gets a static target location from that ping, and therefore enjoys the advantage of time and stealth. If for some reason the heist doesn't work out, the thief removes the Tag and moves onto the next target."

"Wonderful," Appleton commented sarcastically. "Something new to look forward to. Any more surprises?"

"Not at this time, ma'am."

"Thank you, Havens. That's enough for now." Without waiting for a reply, Appleton ended the call, turned to me, and said, "I had a hunch. Brakes don't fail like that, and I knew the Bureau did some work on that sort of scenario as well as fabricating test devices. Add in the fact that your car was being tracked—with that evidence, I am far more convinced that you were targeted."

As usual, Appleton's decisions were quick and decisive. And, as she demonstrated again, she played multiple angles, considering one situation while dismissing it at the same time and then backing off a previous assumption in light of newly revealed facts. It was no wonder that the SAC was so well-respected in the Bureau.

However, none of that knowledge would have prepared me for her final comment, which took me by surprise and scared the shit out of me at the same time. Considering me carefully, Appleton spoke slowly, "Unfortunately, the only real way to prove you are a target is to draw out an attack while being prepared for it. Otherwise, you're trapped in a waiting game, fearful of a strike."

I shook my head and said, "What's wrong with waiting? All I need is a few more days. Hide out and then hop the Bureau jet to Egypt."

Appleton scoffed. "Porter, you have no clue how these people operate. Bugs, multiple tracking devices, database access. You can't hide from an assassin. In fact, you're already exposed. Because you were targeted during your drive from D.C., it's obvious that your stalker knew where you were with that tracking device. Knew that you departed the capital. Knew when to trigger the devices. For all you know, your foe was driving in a car, tailing you. Knew that the Tahoe stopped here since the wrecker driver dropped you off in front before heading to the shop where Havens examined the vehicle. Therefore, it's quite possible that the assassin has driven by this house and is waiting to pick up your tail outside."

She stood and examined the windows. "The glass here is resistant to bullets, thanks to my role with the Bureau. But there are other ways to find entrance and, consequently, it's not secure here in the long run. Get your things."

"Not secure?" I asked as I dutifully complied, rising and shouldering my backpack while lifting my duffel bag from the pristine white rug in the SAC's perfectly appointed living room.

As Appleton strode toward a stairway, I peeked into the kitchen—to no surprise, it appeared photo-worthy for a shiny magazine, with stainless steel appliances, white cabinetry offset by a blue-painted island topped with quartz. Appleton's voice interrupted my snooping as she called, "Follow me."

I hurried along.

As Appleton climbed the stairs, naturally tastefully carpeted in a blue-and-white hexagonal patterned runner, she advised, "Porter, there comes a time when your only option is to turn the tables." She stopped mid-tread and turned to face me, looking down at me from her higher perch on the stair. "Now is one of those times."

CHAPTER 39

AT THE TOP of the stair, I found myself at a second-floor landing. Framed paintings hung on white-painted walls. It seemed more like an art gallery than a home.

Before I could take it all in, Appleton spoke. "Let me show you to a room where you can stay, but also where you can change." She glanced at my bags. "Are you armed?"

"A Glock."

She rolled her eyes. "That's all? We'll need to do better than that. But—how did you obtain the piece?"

"Macallister. He also arranged for me to carry an FBI badge."

"Hmmm. That could be helpful," Appleton mused. In a stronger voice, she said, "Macallister has no business being in Washington. He's a field agent, and he is out of his depth at the Hoover building. Furthermore, I have reservations about how he has structured this current plan."

"Other than taking my boat across the Atlantic, I'm not sure he had much of a choice," I replied. "Sullivan made it very clear that we were on our own. Unless Macallister did more than he said, our authority comes from the Department of Justice and the Attorney General."

"I suppose."

"You don't sound very convinced."

"Not really," Appleton confessed. "I would have done things differently. But that can't be helped, now, can it?" We reached what was obviously a spare bedroom, well-appointed with a queen-sized bed, a deep-looking chair adjacent to stocked bookshelves, and an antique writing desk. "Feel free to charge your devices. En-suite bathroom with shower through that door," she said, pointing. "Dress nicely. Loose-fitting garments, if possible. Say, one hour? We're going out for dinner."

"Terrific. Can't wait," I effervesced falsely, thinking, *A beer and a pizza delivery would be more my speed than a dress-up dinner date with the SAC.*

"Oh," she called over her shoulder as she began to close the door to the room behind her, "don't put that nasty duffel bag on my comforter when you unpack."

"Okay," I said flatly in the direction of the door as it latched shut.

Great. I'm moving in with my mother.

I couldn't have been more wrong.

I didn't bother unpacking, instead leaving my bags on the polished fir floor that was exposed around the perimeter of the room, making sure that my "nasty" duffel wasn't sullying the Persian-looking rug. When I returned to the room from a hot shower in the Carrara marble-tiled, polished-nickel-accented bathroom, I saw that several surprises awaited me.

My duffel was placed on a folding luggage rack at the foot of the bed, and next to it, on the bed itself, were two garments which I recognized immediately from my training at Quantico: a three-quarter sleeve, black shirt and slim, black, knee-length pants. Short pants, or long shorts.

Or, more precisely, tactical gear.

Clad in a puffy white towel wrapped around my waist, I poked at the fabric. It was vaguely rough with a slight sheen. Kevlar. It would stop a knife, and it would slow down a bullet. No wonder Appleton instructed that I wear something loose-fitting. Fortunately, March in Boston isn't exactly beach weather, so an extra layer wouldn't matter, at least outside.

To go with my tac gear, Appleton left three harnesses: a standard shoulder harness in nylon webbing, a hip harness in the same material, and an ankle holster. Truly the height of fashion for a dinner out in suburban Beantown.

I was shaking my head in wonderment, trying to envision what Appleton was planning, when my encrypted phone dinged with a notification of an incoming email.

Standing there in my towel, considering my outfit choices, I swiped the phone to read the short note from Anastasia Volkov, dryly composed in her usual, matter-of-fact style:

> My tasks from yesterday are complete. Doctor Curtis was not assigned to Rourke's case at Reed. He opened the file. Macallister and I think that means that somehow he knew she was being brought to Reed. Almost as if he expected her.
>
> Also Curtis swiped in at GW Hospital at 9:08 AM on January 20 and swiped out at 6:22 PM. He was at the hospital the day you said you thought you were going into distress, on Inauguration Day.
>
> He's obviously involved. -AV

"Curtis is involved," I repeated out loud as I dressed. "But with who?" Remembering the pompous doctor's admonition, I corrected myself. "With whom?"

I heard Appleton's voice from beyond the door. "Did you say something? Are you ready?"

"Yeah, gimme a sec," I called. "Be right out."

"Good. 'Bout time."

I heard her footfalls—sounded like boots clomping on the carpeted runner atop the wood floor— and her voice rang out again, "Come down to the kitchen so you can select some weaponry. Let's go hunting."

CHAPTER
40

"TARGETING COMPLETE."

"Target verification?"

"Affirmative. Three positive identifications."

"I don't like this," Captain Logan Roberts murmured. "XO, run it by me one more time."

The executive officer, Lieutenant Commander Amy Schmidt, on a track to be promoted as the first female captain in the undersea Navy, apprised Roberts and spoke softly so as not to be overhead in the quiet, red-light illuminated control room/attack center of the USS *Ezra Lee*, a Los Angeles 688-class submarine. "Sir, it's not our job to do the homework," Schmidt cautioned. "It's our job to follow orders."

The captain briefly removed his customary baseball cap and rubbed his bare scalp, snorting almost soundlessly before he whispered, with a slight drawl—Gulf Coast Florida, perhaps, "I know, I know. All the same, XO, I've never seen orders like these. We're not at war. We're not being attacked. We're stalking prey. We are to sink a defenseless vessel?"

With her Midwest twang remaining soft to remain unheard by the crew in the attack center, Schmidt looked at the captain and replied, "Sir, the orders were clear. Locate and sink the target vessel. She is carrying a large quantity of weaponry destined for Syria, with a skeleton crew aboard, and the paperwork indicated that the vessel was bought and

resold at least three times in the past two years. The vessel was sighted a
year ago in Europe and then returned to the United States. The Central
Intelligence Agency believes this to be a high-value smuggling target,
and resolution via diplomatic effort is no longer feasible. Covert action
was authorized under Title 10 by the Department of Defense under the
Operational Preparation of the Environment framework."

"Very well recited, XO. It's also apparent that you remember your
classes from the Naval Academy on the chain of command," the
captain observed with genuine admiration. His tone changed to be
more somber as her added, "However, there are sailors aboard that boat.
Sailors just like us."

"Agreed, sir. But . . . our orders, sir."

The captain exhaled, shaking his head, removing any doubts,
as he mentally reaffirmed the oaths he took to his command. He
cleared his throat and addressed the bridge in his usual, definitive
tone. "WEPS, report."

In accordance with protocol, a Weapons Officer replied smartly, "Fire
Control reports that tubes one and three are loaded and flooded, sir."

"Very well," Roberts said.

Continuing in the normal, precise, clearly spoken cadence of voice
that was practiced time and again on the submarine, Roberts addressed
the Chief of the Boat, sitting at the helm position and who also served as
the Diving Officer. "Chief, make for a depth of sixty-two feet and then
raise periscope one."

Schmidt watched as the depth indicator leveled at sixty-two feet
even as a new voice said, "Scope active. Commencing three-hundred-
and-sixty-degree visual and infrared sweep."

The digital bridge aboard *Ezra Lee* alleviated the requirement to
have a single sailor stand at the eyepiece of a traditional periscope;
instead, cameras on the photonics mast broadcast the surrounding seas
to monitors. As a ghostly white image appeared on-screen, Captain
Roberts stated, "Mark. Target position acquired visually. WEPS, confirm
you have a valid firing solution."

"WEPS confirms a firing solution," another voice rang out.

Schmidt knew that, given the 688's technological abilities, the

visual surface sweep ranging was unnecessary, but it remained a
formality. The XO was pleased that Captain Roberts would execute
his orders by the book.

Roberts, focused on the task and the procedures, ordered, "Scope
down. Diving officer, take the boat to one hundred feet."

As the sub's deck declined toward the bow, driving her deeper under
the surface, Roberts spoke again in a serious, slow voice. "Navigator,
record this for the ship's log. Position. Forty degrees, forty-nine point
four nine north, twenty-five degrees, twenty-one point four three west.
Time. Oh-one-three-two Zulu hours. Target was verified via visual
identification at periscope depth approximately seven hours ago, during
the last hour of daylight, and has been tracked continuously since. Target
was also confirmed via Automatic Identification System and cross-
checked with the satellite images provided with the orders received. The
validity of those orders was examined and cleared as per the operations
manuals and security codes."

The captain eyed Schmidt and ordered, "XO, prepare to fire."

Schmidt repeated, "Combat, prepare to fire. Open doors."

A sailor at the combat station replied, "XO, aye." After a short pause,
she stated, "Doors open."

The XO turned to face the captain. Roberts pursed his lips, dipped
his head, and closed his eyes briefly as if he was saying a short, silent
prayer. Snapping his skull up and his eyes open, Captain Roberts spoke
clearly and decisively. "Shoot tube one. Shoot tube three."

The sub shuddered only slightly as the air-powered rams in each
torpedo tube forced seawater into the tubes, launching two wire-guided
Mk-48 torpedoes. The guidance was redundant; it was an uncomplicated
shot to a straight-moving, constant-speed target, and the acoustic homing
systems built into each weapon would be adequate to locate the target
even without guidance from the attack center. Nevertheless, protocol
dictated that each fish would run by wire for one mile before resorting to
their onboard systems. The Weapons Officer reported, "Normal launch.
Torpedoes are away and running smoothly."

Splitting the water at well over thirty knots, the high-pitched whine
of their swashplate piston engines was masked by the white noise of

wind and waves as the weapons rose from their firing depth to a running depth of thirty-five feet below the surface. The dual torpedoes took just over eight minutes to reach their target. Each detonated just under the keel of the plodding vessel, the accuracy of their Common Broadband Advanced Sonar Systems pinpointing the exact moment of ignition with precision.

"Command, sonar. Two hits at the target. Almost simultaneous."

Captain Roberts grimaced. "Put it on speaker," he commanded.

The noises were almost indescribable as the steel-hulled target was split along her backbone, the wrenching of metal-on-metal combining with the thunder of the vessel's fuel tanks combusting, and the clatter of collapsing frames and shifting contents as the wreck slipped, slowly at first, but then with increasing velocity, below the waves, fragmented into hundreds of pieces.

Roberts sighed. "Take her up," he said absently.

Schmidt nodded and ordered, "Diving Officer, make the depth sixty-two feet, please." The sub shivered slightly as the water pressure decreased with the water depth, and Schmidt requested, "Raise periscope one. Forward optical scope image on the main monitor."

By the time the periscope was fully extended, the flames from the burning, sinking wreck were gradually being extinguished by the unending onslaught of salt water.

Roberts stood and paced closer to the screen, asking, "Any distress beacons? Radio calls? Strobes?"

Schmidt shook her head. "Negative, sir."

The XO and the bridge crew continued studying the displays, examining them for any sign of survivors. A moment or two passed before Schmidt's shoulders straightened. "Sir, it appears that a life raft auto-inflated, but infrared does not show any persons aboard the raft."

"Monitor it."

"Yessir. We will remain on station."

"Affirmative," agreed the captain. "However, put us below the surface before dawn so that the sunlight doesn't reflect off the periscope."

"Aye, sir," confirmed the XO.

"Make certain that the log includes the pertinent details of the mission and concludes that the target was destroyed."

"Aye, sir." Then, departing from the usual custom while submerged, the XO raised her right hand to salute the captain.

Respecting the gravity of the moment at hand, Roberts removed his baseball cap. The captain returned the salute snappily and formally as he said, "Continue the watch for survivors until the last possible moment. Notify me immediately if anything changes." With that final command, the captain departed the control/attack center, calling, "XO has the conn," as he disappeared.

Lieutenant Commander Schmidt turned her gaze to the screen and watched as the starboard side nameboard affixed to the target vessel's topmost deck was briefly illuminated by a last flicker of a lingering flame before slipping below the surface, and she whispered, "Godspeed to those souls aboard *Almaz*."

CHAPTER
41

YOU KNOW, it's damn difficult to truly enjoy a fine meal while wearing Kevlar and packing heat. Distracting, to say the least.

Appleton, of course, remained perfectly composed and impeccably coiffed, wearing a long, dark-colored skirt over tall black boots and a loose blouse under a shawl—I think it's called a pashmina. Yet, hidden beneath that finery, she was equally if not better armed than I. Certainly, she was better dressed; I resorted to the roomiest pair of khaki pants I possessed plus a button-down shirt and blue blazer, the extent of the garb in my duffel that might qualify me to "dress nicely."

We arrived about ninety minutes ago at what she said was one of Salem's best restaurants—a dignified establishment called The Register located in a red brick building with a red brick interior, off a red brick sidewalk. The abundance of brick, I imagined, would stop a bullet.

But no assassins, apparently, were dining with us.

Our time was productive, though. I continued to brief Appleton, elaborating on the details that I hurried over when we first discussed my predicament in her living room. Our conversation turned to Doctor Curtis by the time coffees were set down for us on the dark wood tabletop. I took a moment to scan the restaurant; even in the dim lighting, under bulky, hewn-wood beams and amidst more brick, I could tell that the staff of the restaurant had thinned out as the night advanced. I glanced around; other than a table for two in a far corner and three people sitting at the bar, we were alone.

Good thing, too, because my throat was sore from whispering, and I was desperate for a beer—definitely out of the question given my usual Glock 22 in my shoulder holster and a backup, .25 ACP Beretta Jetfire mouse pistol holstered on my right calf. Oh, and a K-bar knife at my left calf. Club soda with a lime was my drink of choice for the evening until I took a sip of the hot coffee, soothing my rasp and allowing me to say, "I can't imagine how Curtis fits in."

"Did you run a background on him?"

"Yes," I replied, recalling research that Volkov had sent me. "All we dug up was medical stuff. Harvard med, a career at Walter Reed and elsewhere, all plain vanilla stuff. Of course, if the guy was CIA, one would expect that his records were sanitized."

"Exactly," agreed Appleton. She examined her coffee with disdain. "I could do with a whiskey, neat. It can wait. Let's wrap up soon and go for a walk."

"Loose plan," I commented. Appleton had filled me in on her ideas to draw out the assassin during the drive to the restaurant in her Bureau-issued Tahoe—miles nicer than the one that I totaled—and I wasn't convinced. "We're going to walk around downtown Salem and hope for the best?"

She nodded. "Exactly. And while it's possible that your assassin may attempt a hit from long range, what I think is more likely is that we may pick up surveillance. I'd like to see if anyone pays attention to us."

"You'd think that an assassin would know how to stay out of sight."

"You'd think that I'm well trained to anticipate that eventuality," Appleton chided.

I proposed, "Let's get back to Curtis, shall we?" Appleton shrugged in response, and I continued, "We think he had something to do with Hamid's death. But he couldn't possibly have poisoned Hamid at the coffee shop—I would have recognized him there— so let's assume the drop was made not by Curtis but by our assassin. Perhaps that makes Curtis the failsafe? The clean-up guy?"

Appleton snorted with derision. "An assassin that requires a clean-up is not a very effective assassin."

I felt my eyes widen involuntarily. "What if that's the point? What if..." I let my voice trail off as I tried to compose my thoughts. Appleton waited patiently; her cool composure was well-suited for thoughtfulness.

Finally, I managed to verbalize my theory, and I spoke slowly, "Look at the parallels and the sequencing. We have data that this Gansett dude was stalking our parking lot on the morning of the sixth of January. We can't prove it, but to game this out, let's say he's the guy smearing the poison on the Jeep's door handles. Rourke, not me, gets the bigger dose and crashes the car. Curtis is on standby. Rourke gets sent to Reed, which is perfect for Curtis, but I end up at GW. Curtis gets himself into GW. And—"

"And he makes a hit on you, at GW, via the vitals monitoring systems, during one of your hallucinations," Appleton exclaimed.

"Exactly. And, *exactly* as it played out with Hamid. Gansett does the field work and the poisoning, and Curtis is ready to make the final hit." I sipped my almost-cold coffee but, so caught up in the theory, I didn't notice the lack of taste or heat.

"What did Volkov say about the vitals systems?" Appleton asked.

"She said that it's not new news—but imagine this angle. Imagine using that system to mask a final attempt. I mean, who knows what happened to Hamid that night."

"No," Appleton said, shaking her head. "Not mask the final attempt."

"Of course—like my accident on the Mass Pike!" I blurted. "Let's say that was the assassin, somehow triggering the device that Havens explained. Remotely operated gizmos severed the brake lines on my Tahoe—but—think about that. It's sloppy. It's not guaranteed to kill me. However, it pretty much guaranteed that I'm gonna crash."

"And if you crash the car, maybe you get sent to the hospital."

"And if I'm in the hospital, Curtis waits for his opportunity and uses the vitals system as cover if something's going wrong and I'm coding—"

"Or, as Volkov outlined to you," countered Appleton, "he uses the vitals system to falsely justify a dose of a lethal medication."

I looked at my coffee cup but pushed it away as I elaborated. "Exactly. And either way, you'd never know that the person was targeted because it will appear that the victim dies in a hospital while under medical care."

I paused for a bit of dramatic effect before closing, "I've just described the perfect assassination."

Appleton had been nodding her understanding as I reached my conclusion. Her eyes were bright, and the faint grin on her face spread widely. "I'm in agreement with your theory, Porter. The methodology is quite clever and obviously very dangerous. I think it's time to widen the scope of the need-to-know circle, but before we do that, let's brief Macallister and Volkov as soon as possible. Tonight, or at the latest, first thing tomorrow morning."

I didn't know it at the time, but briefing the team on *Almaz* would prove impossible, and not only for the reason that you're assuming.

CHAPTER 42

APPLETON PAID THE TAB and stood. She picked up her overcoat and draped it on her shoulders, purposely keeping her arms out of the sleeves so that she would have better access to her weapons. I noticed that she subtly adjusted her hidden armaments, so I followed suit, albeit more clumsily. Together, we walked through the mostly deserted, dimly lit restaurant.

I was first to the door, a single sheet of obviously thick glass in a hefty, distressed wood frame, and I stepped slightly to the side as I pushed the door ajar for Appleton. I paused inside the restaurant as she ambled into the chilly, March evening, planning to show me the pedestrian-only, red-brick, center square of Salem, lined with witchy-type places like museums, themed shops, and touristy destinations. We'd linger, taking our time as we walked back to Appleton's Tahoe, parked three blocks away in a municipal lot.

The genesis of the plan was Appleton's insistence that we'd put ourselves in plain sight, but because we were suitably aware and armed, we would have the upper hand on reconnaissance and, if needed, defense.

Unfortunately, the plan was doomed, and we didn't make it far.

As soon as Appleton cleared the threshold, with me just slightly behind her, she grunted, and a split-second later, the wood-framed door, still in my hand, splintered above me.

Thwack! Thwack!

It was the unmistakable sound of two supersonic rifle shots; the bullet impacts being heard before the report from the gun.

I grabbed the SAC's shoulder and levered her to the ground, trying to pull her back over the threshold and behind the safety of the red-brick walls.

Thwack!

The glass in the door shattered with a crash as tiny tempered shards rained on our heads.

Thwack!

Another impact smacked the brick above, adding little red chips and bits of gray mortar to the mess.

I heard screams from the waitstaff and remaining patrons inside as I pulled Appleton around the corner of the entry, noticing that the sounds of the bullet impacts ceased. In the brief moment of quiet, I heard Appleton groan, "Roof. Diagonally across the street."

As I yanked my Glock from inside my blue blazer, I glanced at her; she was pale, and I exclaimed, "Are you hit?"

"Yeah."

"Shit."

Leading with the muzzle of my pistol, I dared a peek around the door jamb. The street was silent, and as I cautiously elevated my view, I could see a shape moving behind the bulwark of the flat-topped, three-story building directly across from The Register. I aimed high and squeezed the trigger three times.

Pop—pop—pop!

I knew that my aim was imperfect and that I wouldn't have the time or the opportunity to target properly. All I wanted to do was send a message.

"Shooter is gone," Appleton croaked. "Making escape."

I couldn't believe it. The SAC continued to imagine opposing tactics and maneuvers, even when down. I turned my attention to her, knowing that trying to chase the suspect was futile. "I know," I replied. "I saw a shadow, but there's no way I'm gonna track it."

Through the mangled door, I could hear a distant siren, and seconds later, a second siren joined in dissonantly. Kneeling next to Appleton, I mumbled, "Where are you hit?"

"Shoulder."

I probed her coat gently, and she winced.

Strange, I thought, *there's blood on her cheek and*—I realized that was *my* blood, dripping from my head. I passed a hand across my scalp; it was sticky.

I don't feel hit . . .

The wail of the sirens was directly outside The Register, and amidst that cacophony, I heard tires screech and car doors slam. Blue-and-red lights strobed through the front windows of the restaurant and dazzled on the piles of glass and brick beside us. A uniformed, local police officer cautiously peeked inside. Holding my badge in view, I barked, "I'm a federal agent. FBI. My partner is down and injured. Call a bus!"

The officer reached for his lapel-mounted radio microphone. As he began speaking orders to his dispatch, and as more and more officers began arriving on the scene, I figured it would be only minutes before medical help arrived.

Instead, it was only the beginning of what would become a very long night.

CHAPTER 43

JENNIFER APPLETON was a total badass. Riding in the ambulance with her, I felt equal measures of shock and awe.

I already knew of the SAC's fearsome reputation. She was known to be cold, calculating, and fearless. But I wrongly figured that was within the confines of the office bureaucracy; I had no idea that her stone-like, stoic composure was also evident in the field, even when under fire.

As soon as the green-scrubs-clad, dirty-blonde-haired Emergency Medical Technician cut away Appleton's coat and blouse, revealing the damaged Kevlar undershirt, the EMT muttered, "Oh, no, I can't deal with that right here. I'm just out of training. I think we need to get special tools to get that off."

"Don't worry about it," Appleton said through clenched teeth. "Do what you can to triage and clean it. And give me my phone. Left coat pocket."

The EMT's eyebrows raised as she stuttered, "You . . . you . . . want your phone?"

"I got it," I snapped. "You deal with the wound."

"You're bleeding, too," protested the EMT.

"It's nothing—some scratches on my scalp from bricks and glass, I think. Her bullet wound is far more pressing," I decided as I began to awkwardly dig around Appleton's overcoat pocket.

After I found the device and held it up for Appleton to see, she commanded, "Tap it and angle it at my face." The phone screen lit, and, when the facial recognition process unlocked the device, Appleton spoke again, "Good. Open contacts. Find Mary Miller, dial, and put it on speaker."

I did as she ordered. After two rings, we heard a stressed-sounding female voice answer directly, "I'm a little busy, Jennifer."

"I know," Appleton groaned. "The shooting at The Register. That was me, Chief Miller. I was involved. Can't explain right now, but here's what you gotta do—"

"You? You were there? One of my officers reported that FBI was on-scene. I had no idea it was—"

"Yeah, me. And one of my agents. His name is Porter. Listen, you know me. You know I stay out of your business. Right?" Appleton inhaled; I could tell that the conversation was an effort, but she soldiered on. "Listen, Mary, for now, I'm asking that you keep this quiet as best you can. Obviously, the press is gonna be all over it. Keep my name out. Make up something like it was one of those witch nutjobs, firing at shadows. I don't care."

There was a short pause before the woman, the Salem Police Chief, as I could discern from the description under the name on Appleton's phone screen, replied, "Yeah, sure, Jennifer, I guess so. Where are you now?"

"Pulling into Salem Hospital."

"Yes, I heard there were injuries. Are you with the victim?"

Appleton croaked out a dry laugh. "Not exactly. I am the victim. Help me out on this one, Mary. I'll owe you one. Gotta go." She caught my eye and sliced her finger across her throat, and I tapped the *End Call* icon as the ambulance began a three-point turn to back into the emergency bay. Turning her head to the EMT who was busy sanitizing the impact site, Appleton grunted, "Don't unload me yet. One more call."

"Ma'am, we gotta get you into the operating room. There's infection potential, possible nerve damage and paralysis, and—"

"Not yet. Don't open those doors," Appleton demanded. Looking at me, her eyes ablaze with decisiveness, she requested, "Porter. Contacts again. Havens. Dial. Speaker."

I understood the shorthand instantly and swiped the screen to locate the contact card for the CIRG agent we had spoken with earlier, who had investigated my Tahoe. He accepted the call after a half-ring, which, of course, you and I would both do if we saw an incoming from our boss. "Havens."

"Get to Salem Hospital and find Porter. Got it?" I could tell from her brevity that Appleton was exhausting herself.

Fortunately, Havens was quick on the take. "Yes, ma'am. What's up?"

"Porter will explain. I'll be indisposed. Do what he tells you to do."

"Yes, ma'am. I'll be there in twenty minutes."

Appleton exhaled and, once again, signaled for me to end the call. The EMT opened the side door, and I could hear the back doors of the bus unlatch. Appleton crooked her finger at me, and I leaned toward her face. She whispered, "Listen carefully. Here's what we're gonna do . . ."

CHAPTER
44

AFTER JENNIFER APPLETON, badass extraordinaire, was wheeled away on a gurney as a priority procedure, befitting the Special Agent in Charge of the area's FBI Field Office, I was escorted to an exam room. While waiting for a nurse to arrive and clean the wounds on my scalp, I pulled out my encrypted phone to dial the team on *Almaz*. There was no answer, which was surprising to me until I realized that I had made the same miscalculation of time that I did back in Washington. The yacht was well across the Atlantic, and about five or six hours ahead, timewise, so, therefore, ten-ish in the evening in Salem meant something like three or four in the morning for them.

Briefly imagining my nights in Rourke's stateroom on the opulent vessel, I shook myself from my reverie. Right now, it would be Macallister nestled in those Italian-made, 100% Egyptian cotton sheets.

Eek. Put your head back in the game, I chided myself.

The door to the exam room swung open. I was expecting scrubs but got a towering, ebony-skinned man wearing dark jeans and a black leather jacket, his skull polished and shiny under the harsh glare of the hospital room lighting. "Hey, Porter."

I recognized the face that went with that deep voice immediately. "Havens!" After the chaos of the night, it was a welcome relief to greet my former accomplice in the flesh. "You made good time."

Havens smiled, and he absently tugged at a perfectly trimmed goatee. "The boss calls, and I move with alacrity. But we're not here to talk about travel arrangements."

"Lemme bring you up to speed," I replied as the door opened again. This time, it was scrubs, a petite, dark haired woman with pearly white teeth. "Um, nurse, can you give us a few minutes?"

She looked at me quizzically. "I was sent in to examine bullet and shrapnel wounds. I'm not sure you should be putting that off."

"'Tis but a scratch. Just a flesh wound. I've had worse," I countered. "I need fifteen minutes."

Havens flipped his jacket open, exposing a shiny FBI badge on his black leather belt. "I'll come find you when we're ready," he said quietly but with a commanding tone.

The nurse backed out, and as soon as the door latched, I explained the background to Havens, closing with my requirements. "I don't know the hospital layout, but I'm guessing we need six men. If we can ID our assassin, those six start the tail on him."

"I can get ten agents. Fifteen, maybe. They won't be all CIRG, though," Havens offered.

"I don't think we need CIRG. And fifteen is too many people. Appleton wants this on the down-low. You gotta get the assets in person. We've got to assume that we're compromised somewhere, somehow. I mean, lemme back up and lay out the chain of events."

"Explain," Havens demanded.

"Okay, so we know that my Tahoe was both targeted and tracked. Right? I have a suspect who is also qualified to be a shooter. The working theory is that the person who is tracking me is likely to be, or to be an accomplice of, the person who shot Appleton."

"Maybe that bullet was intended for you," Havens suggested.

"Sure. Possibly," I agreed.

"But why there? If you're being tailed, why not make a hit when Appleton and you were together earlier?"

"Yeah, at her house, before we went to the restaurant. Frankly, I don't know. Maybe the shooter didn't have time to set up or couldn't find a suitable shooting platform."

"Appleton's house would have been a more low-profile location."

I squinted at Havens as he strategized a better way to kill me. "Well, maybe if you catch the guy, you can explain to him what he did wrong."

Havens scoffed. "I'd like that. But, you know, you could have been tailed to this place. The hospital. Not difficult to follow an ambulance with flashing lights or to pick up chatter on the police radio nets."

"That's exactly what Appleton said," I confirmed, adding, "So, it's our turn to track him, especially if we think that this hospital will be a good starting point to pick up the scent." Fiddling with my smartphone, I opened the Gansett dossier file that Sullivan sent to the team and that Volkov transmitted to me. "Here's the target. JJ Gansett."

As I shared Gansett's photos with Havens, the CIRG agent confirmed, "I'll distribute the pictures to my team. We'll find him if he's prowling in the area. We'll go with six men, plus you and me. But I'll have to run back to Boston to get comms gear, and if you really want this on the sly, to recruit agents in person. It's getting late, so the office won't be fully staffed. That could work to our advantage since I can grab gear without too many questions, and I'll make some calls while driving."

"How long are we talking?"

"A half-hour there, a half-hour at the field office, and then back. Ninety minutes tops."

I considered the timeline. "Yeah, that'll work. Appleton will be in surgery for a while, I guess. Not sure if she'll still be in when you get back, but there's no way she's being discharged in an hour-and-a-half. Appleton and I figure that the assassin will be waiting for her to leave the hospital. That's when we strike."

"Got it. We've got time, but I ain't gonna waste it. See you shortly."

Havens turned to leave, but as he pulled the door open, I called, "Hey, two more things. One, send in that nurse, please. And two, can you bring me a fresh magazine for my Glock?"

"No problem," Havens boomed as he disappeared.

Yeah, it would have been no problem . . . if only I hadn't needed that mag sooner.

CHAPTER
45

FORTY MINUTES LATER, I imagined Havens rounding up agents, cars, guns, and comms gear at the Chelsea Field Office. Certainly, more action-packed than what I'd been doing: sitting on a paper-covered exam table. And more dignified, too—my clothes removed and replaced with a sterile dressing gown, as the dark haired nurse cleaned and dressed my wounds. I objected, weakly, when she requested that I disrobe, thinking that taking my shirt off would suffice, but she insisted. "You've put this off, so at least let's get you cleaned up correctly and thoroughly. Put on the gown. You can keep your socks on, but take your shoes off too, please."

I valued her professionalism and learned to appreciate her efficiency; her work was complete in short order. Gathering her instruments and dropping them onto a plastic tray for sterilization later, she showed me the fruits of her efforts: a second plastic tray with an assortment of brick fragments, glass bits, some of my hair, and the cast-offs of the bloodied gauze pads that she used to clean my head. "That's an impressive collection," I said. "Can I keep it to show my colleague?"

"Gross, but sure," the nurse laughed.

"Do you know where she is? I'd like to check on her."

"Operating Room number one. Quiet night. It's the only operating table in use. You can speak with the nurses outside the room."

"Thanks," I replied, as sincerely as I could. "For that, and for this." I pointed at the trays.

She grinned. "That's what I'm here for. You can get dressed now."

Carrying the tray of instruments and leaving the tray of souvenirs behind, she departed the little examination room as I contemplated my pile of clothes, reluctant to drag on the uncomfortable Kevlar garments again but knowing I'd want them once Havens returned.

My moment of indecision was interrupted by the blare of a buzzer and a strident voice that announced, "Code Blue. Code Blue. O.R. One."

It took me a second to process the words.

O.R. One? That's . . . Appleton!

I tugged on my pants, grabbed my shirt and my Glock, and bolted.

In the hallway, I realized I didn't know which way to turn. Jabbing one arm then another into the sleeves of my shirt, I saw a big digital clock on the wall. 11:35 P.M. *Bottom half of the hour,* I thought. *To the right.*

As I ran, hoping I was headed the correct direction, I stuffed the Glock into my waistband and managed to fasten a few buttons on my shirt. My guess was correct, and I stumbled into the throat of the first-floor ICU and emergency operating rooms.

Contrary to the urgency of the message on the public address system, the place was eerily quiet. There was one nurse at the central station, and a handful of nurses and perhaps doctors gathered at an opening labeled *ONE*.

I shoved through the group to sounds of protesting voices.

"Hey!"

"You can't go in there!"

"Stop!"

Appleton lay atop the operating table, her left shoulder clearly a work in progress, and with modesty sheets stripped back, leaving her torso and breasts on display. My focus, however, was on the screen above Appleton's figure.

The SAC appeared to be flatlining, the monotony of the lines on the display complimented by an incessant, non-ending beep from the vitals monitoring system.

A masked and scrubs-suited doctor, her hair pulled up and hidden under a surgical cap, stood over Appleton, holding the paddles of the crash cart defibrillator. I heard the doctor's voice. "Prepare the epinephrine, and clear."

"*No!*" I shouted at the top of my lungs.

As two doctors or nurses or someones tried to pull me away, I forced my way to the bedside and grabbed Appleton's left wrist. Sure enough, I could immediately feel a pulse.

"She's fine!" I barked, spinning to face the doctor. "It's a false reading."

"She crashed!" the doctor retorted, but with a look of hesitation on her face.

"Ignore the machines," I demanded.

I acquiesced to the protesting O.R. staffers who shoved me to the side because that gave the doctor room to reach Appleton. The doctor handed the paddles to someone I couldn't see and followed my lead, checking Appleton's vitals manually—first pulse, then respiration, then, perhaps as a parent might do, laying the back side of a hand on Appleton's forehead to feel her temperature.

The doctor looked at me quizzically. "But . . . but, how did you know?"

"I don't have time to explain. Take care of her. And don't trust those machines."

I bolted from the O.R.

I knew that one of two people must be inside the building. And I'd be damned if I wasn't going to track them down.

Curtis or Gansett, I thought with conviction. *Has to be one of them.*

CHAPTER 46

RUNNING FROM the operating room on the first floor of the Salem Hospital, I found the duty nurse who I saw before at the station inside the emergency entrance, and I called, "Hey! Have you seen anyone come through here who shouldn't be here?"

I can only imagine what the nurse saw—exactly that. I fit my own description perfectly: a crazed guy, shoeless, a black pistol stuffed into the unbelted waistband of boring, roomy khaki pants, the pistol grip of the gun intermittently visible as a shirt, half-buttoned and untucked, flapped about.

The nurse didn't respond and instead ducked below the desk and probably, if I could guess, pressed a hidden emergency button to summon help.

I figured if my hunch was correct, my target would not be hanging around, so I darted to the exit doors. Reaching the wide, covered bay reserved for ambulances, I looked right and then left, and finally got a break.

Sure enough, about to disappear out of my line of sight was a tall man with gray hair clad in a knee-length white lab-type jacket. Something a doctor might wear, for sure.

I sprinted and tripped over a curb.

Shit!

Picking myself up, I realized that I was in no state to be outside—the humid, cold, perhaps forty-degree night air was whipping through my unbuttoned shirt, and I wasn't wearing shoes. It didn't matter.

Move!

I lost sight of my target, but I could see the regularly spaced light poles of a parking lot off to the side of the building.

Logical, right? He's probably got a car.

At this late hour, the lot was sparsely populated. As soon as I reached the perimeter, I saw lights flash, and I heard the distinctive trill of a BMW being unlocked remotely. Angling toward the sound, now more slowly to try and keep out of sight, I listened as a car was started. A pair of headlights flared to full intensity.

A car pulled out of a spot, perhaps one hundred feet from me, and began to turn left toward the street. It was, indeed, a BMW. Blue. Sedan.

For a brief moment, I could see through the windshield as the car passed under one of the light poles. A white coat, thinning gray hair, and—

Gansett!

I'd studied that face. I memorized it. I was one hundred percent positive it was Gansett.

I pulled my Glock, clicked off the safety, and squeezed the trigger four times at the turning, accelerating vehicle.

Pop—pop—pop—pop!

The assassin hit the gas as bullets connected, shattering the right-side rear passenger window, the rear window glass, and pinging into the metal.

Aiming at the back end of the fleeing sedan, I fired two more shots.

Pop—pop!

The BMW gained speed as it neared the street.

Now running as fast as I could in my socks—not ideal for sprinting, but with adrenaline, good enough—I watched in frustration as the BMW turned left onto the street with tires squealing, making its escape.

Wait. Left turn. It would turn *toward* me.

My opening!

I stopped, froze, and steadied my aim. With deliberate motion, tracking the left-moving car in the gunsight as best I could, I pulled the trigger five times.

Pop—pop—pop—pop—pop!

Both left windows exploded. And, better yet, I could hear the distinct sound of metal impact, and the BMW's engine whined raggedly.

In the imperfect lighting of streetlights under gray, cloudy night skies, I was convinced I saw the BMW smoking as it rumbled away, a finely tuned German motor now stuttering and the car no longer gaining velocity. Gansett was not going to make it far, I guessed, and my socks and I picked up the chase as the BMW vanished round a bend in the roadway.

Hustling on the asphalt, it was easy enough to follow the traces of fluids and little bits of shiny glass that must have shaken free from the wounded sedan. Gansett made it only a few hundred feet before pulling the car over to the side of the road.

I hesitated. I tried to recount my shots, tallying them against the fifteen-round magazine in my Glock, all while being furious at myself for leaving the backup pistol that Appleton armed me with behind— now uselessly sitting in the pile of gear back in that little exam room.

And then I spotted the lab coat.

Perhaps one hundred feet from the steaming BMW, the coat lay in an untidy heap at the doorstep of a home that was clearly under construction, a dumpster and portable toilet unit in the vacant driveway, and stacks of lumber on a dirt yard.

Using the metal-sided dumpster for cover, I peeked at the scene, and I concluded the lab coat was a trick.

He wants me to rush in. No way.

I went the other direction, tiptoeing around the far side of the dumpster, looking for a different way into the house.

Either he's inside, or he's gone into the darkness—and there's only one way to find out.

CHAPTER
47

IN A CROUCHED walk-shuffle, I snuck through a half-completed breezeway to nowhere, or at least to the raw foundation of an unconstructed detached garage, and I found the back door. Or, more precisely, I found the back door frame gaping open. No door, no problem, and I slipped inside, now grateful for my soundless socks.

The residence was dim and depressing. Gutted to the studs, and then some, it was obviously in the beginning phases of reconstruction work, and my enthusiasm waned because it was also totally silent.

The coat was a decoy, I thought. *Dammit.*

Settling back on my haunches, I caught my breath, trying to breathe slowly and evenly, and that's when I heard it. A creak. From the floor above.

I dropped to my knees, conserving my energy, and I checked my weapon. The extractor didn't feel like it was in the depressed position, signaling that there was a round in the chamber. As silently as I could, I pressed the magazine catch and slid the mag from the grip.

The magazine was empty.

Fuck.

That meant that my only round remaining was the one in the chamber.

Fuck.

Me versus an assassin with a single bullet.

Fuck!

I couldn't help myself. I recalled an acquaintance, a woman who objected to profanity. *Well, Betty,* I thought, *sometimes "golly gosh" just doesn't fucking cut it.*

And then a grimmer thought.

What kind of weaponry does an assassin carry?

I heard the floor above creak again. He was on the move. And if I could guess, toward the stair.

I heard a siren in the distance.

Busy night for the Salem PD.

The stair creaked, and I desperately looked for cover, but among the forest of studs, there was nothing.

I soft-socked it back the way I came, my eyes focused on the bottom of the temporary stair that creaked again, and I almost tripped on a snake.

A snake?

No, an air hose. A hose for compressed air. Attached to a framing nail gun.

I saw feet on the stair, and a red dot tracking slowly side-to-side, up-and-down.

A laser sight. Shit.

I crouched, and I could see the nail gun clearly—a Porter-Cable brand framing gun. Perhaps that was a sign. About a year ago, I moonlighted as a carpenter at a shipyard as part of my undercover legend, and I recalled building crude racks for supplies with a similar tool. I laid my Glock gently on the floor and picked up the nail gun. It was loaded with three-inch nails, spikes, as they were called in the trade.

I focused. Legs became visible on the stair and then, as the sound of sirens got louder and louder, a body, and then hands, and then a head.

Gansett!

Using my left pointer and middle fingers spread on either side of the nail gun's orifice, I pulled back on the safety stop and bump-trigger, used when a framer has the gun in the auto-fire position, which allowed the carpenter to drive nails just by bumping the gun against material. I could defeat that safety ... but the nail would fire within just a few millimeters of my fingers.

Gansett was fully in sight as I held my breath, hoping that the carpenter was lazy and had left the gun's air hose attached to a compressor. Even if the air compressor was off, if it was charged, it would have enough pressure to fire.

And fire it did.

A nail gun like this fires a nail at about one hundred feet per second, but it's intended to fire into a directly contacted material, like a board, not into the air. This makes it wildly inaccurate as a weapon, not the least because a nail isn't a projectile.

Therefore, I chose quantity over precision, and I peppered Gansett with three-inch spikes.

I knew I made contact because the tall man dropped, howling in pain, his screams louder than the now-nearby sirens which converged at the house, attracted, no doubt, to the bullet-peppered, smoking, and glassless BMW outside.

Knowing that my opportunity to use any cached air in the compressor was limited, I ceased my spray of nails and called, "Gansett! Don't move. I've still got one round left in my Glock!"

The assassin was collapsed in a pile at the bottom of the stair, groaning. In the dim light, I couldn't discern if he was bleeding or determine how extensive his injuries were. Cautiously, I tiptoed toward him, nail gun in one hand, Glock in the other, noticing that a pistol with a laser sight lay on the plywood floor well out of Gansett's reach.

Without knowing if he had any other weapons or, conversely, if there was any air remaining in the compressor tank, I decided to favor my luck with the Glock, and I picked it up even as I let the nail gun drop to the floor, using the air hose to control its descent.

As the tool plunked onto the plywood, the front door smashed open.

CHAPTER 48

"DROP YOUR WEAPON!" ordered the uniformed police officer who burst through the front door.

"Drop it!" rang a second voice behind me. "Get down on the floor!"

Nice pincer approach, I thought with admiration. *Well-timed with two separate angles of attack.*

"Yessir," I called out as I began to kneel, my Glock held high in an outstretched hand, my forefinger through the trigger guard such that with the weapon dangled upside-down. "I'm a federal agent. Ben Porter. FBI." Holding eye contact with the officer in my field of vision, I slowly placed the Glock on the plywood. I shoved it out of reach with a slight push. "Call the chief. Mary. Chief Mary. I work with Jennifer Appleton."

"Who? I don't care who you work with," grumbled the officer. "Hands where I can see them."

Hearing a footfall behind me, I felt, for the second time in short order, the cold steel of a handcuff on my right hand as I said, "Miller! Sorry. It's Chief Miller," recalling the identifier on Appleton's phone screen.

"What the hell is going on tonight?" A new voice, female, one that I could place but couldn't identify. A plain-clothed, stocky, slightly plump woman with a pale face and gray hair appeared through the open front door. "Did I hear that correctly, from outside? You're Porter?"

"Yeah. I'm Ben Porter."

"Mary Miller. Chief Mary Miller."

That was the voice, heard on Appleton's speakerphone hours earlier.

I spoke quickly. "Chief. The victim is over there at the base of the stair. He needs to be in custody, but he needs medical attention. Right away. And I need to get back to the hospital."

Miller crouched at Gansett's unmoving form. "He's still breathing. Call for an ambulance." She looked up at her officer and then at me skeptically. Angling a pudgy nose in my direction, she ordered, "Cuff that one. You got a lot of explaining to do."

"Absolutely, Chief. The cuffs aren't necessary, but I get it. But I gotta ask a favor."

"You're in no position to ask for anything, son," she snarled. "Shooting up my town? Was that you earlier?"

"Yes, Chief. Well, not the first shots, over at The Register. But I returned fire there, and I fired at his car," I replied, jutting my chin in Gansett's direction, not risking a hand movement. "And," I hurried on, "we got into a situation over at the hospital. You'll find my identification and my phone there, and another weapon. You need to secure it. And we need to secure Appleton."

"Appleton?"

"Yeah, when she called you earlier, I was with her in the ambulance. Now she's in surgery. Or was, last time I saw, and when this guy—" now on a roll, and having the chief's undivided attention, I pointed at the assassin— "tried to kill her."

The chief rose and whistled. "Long night's gonna get longer." She looked around. "We gotta secure this scene, we gotta—"

"We got reinforcements coming. One of our colleagues, Special Agent Havens, is bringing five or six agents up from Boston. We're all yours," I offered, but having absolutely zero authority to do so. I figured, given our history, Havens would play along.

Miller was shaking her head as more sirens approached and vehicle doors slammed outside. "The ambulance is here," she stated emotionlessly as two officers led two EMTs into the now crowded space. "Load him up," she commanded, pointing at Gansett.

"And watch him, please, with an armed presence at all times," I requested. "He's dangerous."

Miller snapped, "You have no business issuing orders."

My adrenaline was waning, and I shivered in the unheated, under construction, drafty house. I realized that I was physically and emotionally exhausted, and I snarled in a decisive tone as I rose to my feet, "Listen, Chief, here's the deal. You're gonna uncuff me."

"Not so fast, sport," Miller retorted. "Who the hell do you think you are?"

I inhaled deeply and spoke evenly. "Let me remind you. My name is Ben Porter. I'm a Special Agent of the FBI. My creds are back at the Salem Hospital, where I was being treated after being in a gunfight alongside SAC Appleton. *Your* personal friend, Jennifer Appleton."

Miller's face softened, and her eyes darted left and right. I took on a conciliatory tone. "I'd like to suggest that we escort this victim to the hospital, but under guard. He's no victim. He's a dangerous criminal. In fact, I'd shoot the fucker if he made even the slightest move."

"I see," replied Miller. She wore the faintest of grins.

"Then," I added, "we should check on Jennifer Appleton and make sure she's in stable condition. And finally, you and I should sit down, and I'm gonna brief you. Does that work?"

Chief Miller took an unconscious step backward. I'd won her over. She said, "Yeah, Agent. Sure. Anything else?"

"I'd like to get my shoes. And, if you don't mind, a cup of coffee." Crossing the space, a single cuff dangling and clanking at my right wrist, I knelt at Gansett's form. I could see his chest moving as he breathed, but his eyes were closed. I whispered, "I'm not done with you yet, Gansett."

I stood. "Let's roll."

CHAPTER
49

CHIEF MILLER WAS CORRECT about one thing—a long night would get longer. But having left my watch with the rest of my clothes back at the hospital, for a while, at least, I was along for the ride, getting more and more tired by the minute as the exhilaration wore off.

That's not to say that it was monotonous.

I rode to the hospital with Chief Miller in her unmarked car, and we arrived almost simultaneously with the ambulance bearing Gansett. Moments later, Havens returned.

Havens was accompanied by six other agents, who piled out of two Suburbans and a Dodge Charger. Together with Havens's vehicle, yet another Tahoe, the parking apron at the Salem Hospital emergency entrance resembled, briefly, a government convention.

You can have any color vehicle that you want, as long as it's black, I thought.

With the benefit of Appleton's order, made verbally to Havens hours ago as her ambulance arrived at this very spot, I was in charge. I directed Havens to send four agents to the house where my showdown with Gansett occurred. Salem police would also be there, checking it out as well as inspecting the parking lot for bits and pieces of the BMW. Those investigations, really evidence-gathering missions, would last well into the daytime hours.

In the meantime, two of Havens's associates would assume responsibility for Gansett, whom I obliquely referred to as "a person of interest," figuring that calling him "the CIA assassin" would probably not be in our best interests. Good call, eh?

I'm learning.

I begged for a fresh pair of socks from the hospital staff, adding the socks that I wore during the chase to the plastic tray of bricks, glass, and gauze in my exam room. Gratefully, I slipped shoes onto my battered feet and finally buttoned my shirt properly. Threading a belt around my waist and tucking the shirt in loosely, I put on the chest harness and slipped in the .25 ACP Beretta Jetfire backup that I would have been very grateful for earlier. The little pistol fit loosely in the holster, but better there than loose in the hospital, and for the moment, Miller's men still had custody of my Glock. Finally, I shrugged on my blue blazer and clipped the bogus-but-serviceable badge that Macallister gave me to my belt.

Macallister.

Leaving the exam room, I fastened my watch around my wrist and checked the time. 2:34 A.M. They'd be awake, now, aboard *Almaz*, but as I knew all too well, at a cruising speed of fifteen knots, they weren't going far. I'd call them later.

Appleton was the priority, and fortunately, it was reported that she was doing well, a partially impacted bullet removed cleanly from her shoulder. The Kevlar gear did its job and, while not preventing the penetration of the projectile, limited the depth of the wound. Appleton's left shoulder would be tightly wrapped for some time, but otherwise, she was expected to make a full recovery.

Instead of turning right in the hall, now having my bearings, I turned left, making my way to a corner of the hospital cafeteria which Miller had commandeered. I was happy to see her sitting alone, her men assigned to various tasks. She'd even gotten me a coffee, which I accepted gratefully. "Thank you," I breathed, taking a sip.

The chief nodded. "No problem."

"Appleton is in recovery," I reported.

"I heard. She'll be out of the anesthesia shortly. Then what?"

"I could use a few more favors."

"You're pushing it, you know." Miller sighed. "Tell me."

I smiled, trying to show my appreciation. Once Havens's team arrived, my bona fides became obvious to Miller, even if she didn't need to know the full background. I didn't hesitate to request what I needed. "First off, I'm certain that Appleton's purse or bag or whatever is back at The Register. I'm guessing her key fob is in the bag. Her car, a Tahoe, is parked in a municipal lot around the corner, but I'm afraid I can't tell you exactly where. I don't know the area that well."

"We'll find it. Anything else?"

"One more item, please. Can you arrange accommodations for Havens's team? You know, like a staging room or something. Get them access and clearance here at the hospital. Once they're done with evidence collection over at the house, I'm going to put them on a rotating watch on Gansett. Our person of interest. Who, going forward, should be referred to as John Doe, an unidentified victim."

"I can do that, sure," Miller agreed. She rose. "I'll get on this. Enjoy your coffee."

"Thank you," I replied, my words directed to her back as she walked away.

As soon as the chief was out of sight, I stood, picked up my half-full coffee, and sought out Havens.

Pulling him aside in a corridor, I whispered, "Listen, as soon as Appleton can travel, I want an unmarked car to transport her back to her residence. I'll need your help to arrange for additional medical care there."

"You're not comfortable keeping her here in the hospital? Why? Your suspect is down, and I have plenty of well-trained, very qualified people here on-site to keep Appleton secure," Havens protested.

"That's not the point."

"Oh?"

I exhaled. "I'm sorry to say this, but . . . Appleton must die."

CHAPTER
50

THURSDAY, MARCH 25, 2021

AT SUNSET ON THURSDAY, about twenty-four hours after a flatbed wrecker truck dropped me off at Jennifer Appleton's pristine, perfectly restored Salem colonial, I took stock in the previous day-and-a-half.

I'd made quite a mess.

Let's see. I survived a sneaky, intentional brake failure in my now-totaled Tahoe. I rear-ended a cop car. I participated in a shoot-out in historic downtown Salem and partially destroyed the entrance to a very well-heeled restaurant. I shot at and grossly damaged a now unserviceable BMW sedan. I took out what I'd been told was the CIA's most deadly contract assassin with a framing nail gun. And I caused the death of the FBI Boston Division's Special Agent in Charge.

That's quite a rap sheet.

I lifted a glass of whiskey from the table to my left and swirled the brown liquid around inside a crystal rocks glass before touching it to my lips. "This is smooooooth," I murmured, drawing out the word. "What'd you say this stuff was called again?"

"Jameson Eighteen."

"Eighteen as in eighteen years old?"

"Yes, but that was when it was bottled. This particular batch is more like twenty-five years old. It should be smooth. It's like a couple hundred bucks a bottle. And it's super difficult to obtain," Jennifer Appleton replied calmly, lifting her own glass to her lips with her usable right hand, her left shoulder bandaged and encased in a bulky, temporary sling. "I figured I'd treat us to the finest bottle in my stash. To celebrate my death."

"Yeah," I chuckled. "I think you earned the honor."

Appleton set her glass down gently on the table between our white, upholstered armchairs in her beautiful Salem living room. "I was taken aback at first, but that was a creative move, Porter," she offered, with a note of admiration in her voice.

"Thanks," I replied. "I think faking your death is key. It keeps you off the radar."

"You have a plan for me?"

"I do," I confirmed. "Let's talk out some scenarios, first. Gansett was sent to Salem, or more likely, given what Havens discovered on my wrecked Tahoe, Gansett followed me here. Let's say, for argument's sake, Ginachere dispatched Gansett."

"Okay."

"What happens next?" It was meant to be a rhetorical question, and I continued, "Gansett kills me and reports a successful mission to whoever is tasking him. Or—"

"Or he doesn't report because he can't. Because he's unconscious in the hospital," Appleton offered. "What does that have to do with me?"

"Well, I hope that whoever is behind this does the math, so to speak. Word gets out in the intelligence circles that the Boston SAC is dead from a gunfight in Salem. Whoever is behind Gansett must know that Gansett tracked me to Salem. They put two and two together, and perhaps they'll conclude that I was involved. But—Gansett is incommunicado. They can't confirm anything, and meanwhile, we've created a smokescreen. I think this buys us some time. Not much, but a day, maybe two, before someone goes looking for Gansett. They wouldn't want to compromise him by exposing him. They'll let him stay in the shadows."

Clearly, Appleton was not convinced as she sipped her whiskey before scolding, "Chasing theories, I'm afraid. You know I don't like to do that."

"Understood. But hear me out. We have a second suspect, our Doctor Curtis, who must be connected to whatever this is. I'm well aware you don't like theories—but hear me out. Let's say that Gansett and Curtis were both part of Ginachere's plan in Saudi Arabia. Ginachere uses Gansett to poison the King; Curtis takes over and makes it look like a medical issue. An accident, not an assassination. MBS is cleared, Ginachere has clean hands, and they're good."

"Or Gansett does it himself, as he proved he can do here in Salem, by hacking the vitals monitoring system on me," Appleton observed. "You said I would have been hit with a defibrillator and with epinephrine. I don't know if my heart would have survived."

"Exactly. And exactly as we discussed earlier. It's the perfect assassination ploy. Terrifying, really."

"True," Appleton murmured. "But let me point out something. Say we're correct. Say Gansett and Curtis are collaborating. They've just demonstrated, I'd assume inadvertently, that they can work solo. Unless Curtis is here in Salem."

"That's possible," I admitted. "Consider, however, Hamid's death. Gansett drops the poison, and Curtis completes the hit in the hospital."

"It fooled everyone but you," Appleton said in a complimentary tone. "Macallister, Volkov, even me, when I read the report that Hamid died of a self-inflicted overdose of Digoxin. It now appears that it was a double dose that killed him, orchestrated to make it look like he died in a hospital under care. It would have worked, too, except for your investigation and perseverance."

"Thanks, I guess. Doesn't help Hamid now," I said bitterly. Putting that dreadful thought aside and restoring my focus, I added, "Speaking of Curtis, who's to say that he needs Gansett? Who's to say that Curtis couldn't stand in for Gansett in Saudi Arabia?"

I raised my glass to my lips as Appleton offered, "That's absolutely plausible. But I still think we've got some holes in our theories."

"I know. And when Sullivan calls—which should be any minute now, because I sent her an emergency message so I could bring her up to date—maybe I can infill those holes."

Appleton took another sip of whiskey. "Speaking of calls, you still can't reach Macallister and the team on the yacht?"

I shook my head. "No. I've called three times. At sunrise, at noon, and an hour ago. It's really strange. Maybe a weather event or something is messing with the satellite connections," I surmised. "Perhaps Sullivan can help with that, too."

At that, my phone buzzed, and I said, "Perfect timing. Let's ask her." As I reached for the device, I reminded Appleton, "Don't forget, you died. Don't speak from the grave."

"I hope you don't talk ill of the dead," Appleton smirked.

"Don't tempt me," I replied with a wide grin, and I swiped the face of the phone to accept the call.

CHAPTER
51

"GOOD EVENING, Madam Under Secretary."

Perched on the drinks table between the white armchairs in Appleton's living room, my phone crackled with Genevieve Sullivan's squeaky voice on speaker. "Mister Porter," she began in a stern tone. "I do say I had fair warning that your methods are unconventional. I confess I wasn't expecting this level of disruption and surprise. I was quite disappointed to learn from Macallister that you chose to remain in Washington to investigate the death of your friend. That's not your job, and I do not appreciate your deception by not bothering to inform me in advance."

I heard a *tsk-tsk, tsk-tsk* sound as if I was being admonished like a child.

Shaking off Sullivan's obvious disapproval, I kept my voice balanced. "Be that as it may, Madam, Macallister and I made an agreement—which I didn't think required your approval. Furthermore, I've made significant headway."

"Oh?" The word was drawn out, and her inflection was skeptical.

"Abdul Hamid was murdered."

"Oh?" This time, the word sounded like a surprised inhale. It was sharp.

"Let me explain. It is my working theory that Gansett poisoned Hamid with the desired effect of hospitalizing him. Once in the hospital, a doctor named David Curtis—the same pathologist who did the autopsy on Heather Rourke and who consulted on my case when I was hospitalized in January—stepped in so that he could quote, oversee, unquote, Hamid's care. Within hours, Hamid was dead."

"You believe that Gansett and this Curtis are working in concert?"

"Yes, ma'am. Furthermore, I believe that they've developed a very effective method of assassination. They poison their targets with the goal of introducing them to medical care, and then they somehow gain control of the vitals monitoring system in the medical facility so that they can kill the target while under care—all while making it look like the target succumbed to a medical issue. It never registers that it's really an assassination."

"Ohhhh." And this time, a long exhale. I glanced at Appleton; her face was as non-committal as Sullivan's response, until the Under Secretary queried in her warbling voice, "This is a compelling theory, I grant you, and if you are correct, this assassination method by medical means is a wicked ploy. Have you reviewed this theory with Macallister?"

"Partially, ma'am. I spoke with the team two days ago. Then, yesterday, Volkov sent a text message and confirmed two clues that would seem to implicate Doctor Curtis. However, I've tried to call the yacht several times, with no success. When was the last time you were in contact with them?"

"Oh, days, I suppose," Sullivan quavered. "Saturday, I recall. Five or so days ago."

Appleton pointed to the ceiling, and I picked up on her intent. "It's unlike *Almaz* to be unreachable, not with the communications gear aboard. She's not showing up on any of the marine tracking sites. Do you have any maritime channels to employ? Satellite images, for example?"

"Certainly, I can make inquiries," Sullivan offered in a high-pitched tone. "This is quite a development, Mister Porter." Her voice was friendly and almost conspiratorial. "Is there anything else?"

"Yes, ma'am. There's another matter that will be of interest to you," I said, choosing my words carefully. "Last I spoke with Macallister, we agreed that I should lay low and hide from Gansett until next week, when I'd fly to Egypt to meet *Almaz*. I chose to leave D.C., and I traveled to Boston, thinking I'd be safer there—because I could find refuge at Jennifer Appleton's home."

"Ah, yes," Sullivan chirped. "The Boston SAC. I don't know her personally, but, oh, dear, I don't think I'd like to know her. I've heard she's effective, but quite cold. Ill disposed. She doesn't have too many friends, I'm afraid."

Appleton raised her glass and toasted toward my phone, hiding her sneer as she sipped her whiskey. I stifled a chuckle and resumed my update. "Well, in any case, Gansett shadowed me to Appleton's home in Salem, Massachusetts."

Sullivan was uncharacteristically slow to respond, which I thought was odd. "How do you know that?"

"Because, last night, he tried to kill me. He missed—but, sadly, he shot Appleton. She's dead."

"*What?*" Sullivan's voice rang out so high-pitched it might have shattered a wine glass. "First Rourke, then Hamid, now Appleton? This is outrageous. Ben, these people around you, they're all dying!"

"I like to keep things spicy."

"I'm certain that now is *not* the appropriate time for frivolity, Mister Porter."

"Perhaps. However, I'm certain that a tiny bit of humor might temper what's been a really long day, ma'am," I protested.

"I am terribly sorry to hear about Jennifer Appleton. I'm sorry for what I said about her before. She was a distinguished asset to the Bureau, I'm told."

I turned to face Appleton as I replied, "Yes, she was. A true hero in many respects." I paused before adding ponderously, "A great woman, with fearsome composure and grit. She will be sorely missed." Appleton rolled her eyes and sipped her drink.

After a respectful moment of silence, I picked up the narrative. "The Salem police responded to the incident with Appleton, which of course also involved me. This led to a series of events that concluded with a John Doe in critical but stable condition at the Salem Hospital."

Sullivan clucked her tongue. "May I assume this John Doe was involved in the shooting? The murder of Appleton?"

"Yes," I confirmed. "However, I am aware of that person's identity. It was Gansett."

Appleton and I both leaned, perhaps inadvertently, toward the phone as we heard Sullivan inhale sharply before stuttering, "That's— that's quite a development. That means . . ." Her voice trailed off.

I pulled on the thread. "That means that the immediate threat to me has been extinguished. It also changes the mission parameters. Based on the intel you provided to Macallister and Volkov on Saturday, which indeed was the day you spoke to them, and which they passed onto me, Gansett was going to accompany Ginachere to Saudi Arabia. That's obviously not going to happen, now, with Gansett laid up in the hospital. Therefore, I'm wondering if there is, well, still a mission?"

"Yes, of course."

"That was fast," I observed, glancing at Appleton. She was focused carefully on the phone. I wondered what she was thinking.

But before I could signal her, Sullivan restarted. "Ben, while to my knowledge, Gansett was one of Ginachere's go-to's, he is of course not the only arrow in the CIA's quiver. Ginachere is quite resourceful."

"Then the plan stands," I commented. "I'm on a plane to meet *Almaz* in less than a week. We're scheduled to fly on March 31. Next Wednesday. That gives us plenty of time to transit the Suez Canal and get to Dubai."

"That is correct," Sullivan said dryly. "However, there is one problem, as you must have realized. You've made our task far more difficult. Before, we had intel that Gansett was going to be with Ginachere, and therefore we had a target. Now, we've lost that advantage. This is all complicated by the short notice. I myself will be on a diplomatic trip to the southern hemisphere next week, allowing me only a small window of opportunity to extract information on Ginachere's travel companions from one of the world's most preeminent intelligence agencies. I'll do what I can to find out who Ginachere will be employing in Saudi Arabia, but that will be a monumental task. I'm afraid this is a significant setback. I'm terribly disappointed in you and your recklessness."

Are you kidding me? I thought angrily. *I took down a CIA assassin who had targeted Hamid, Rourke, and me, and who for all Sullivan knows killed an FBI Special Agent in Charge—but I'm getting reprimanded?*

Sullivan's croak interrupted my thoughts. "Are you still there, Ben?"

"Yes, ma'am," I snapped.

"Onwards we go," Sullivan continued evenly. "It can't be helped, now, can it?" Apparently, that was a rhetorical question, made perhaps to humiliate me further, because she didn't wait for an answer. "I'll do my research, you'll get in position, and maybe we can still prevent this terrible thing from happening in Saudi Arabia on the eve of Ramadan. We cannot fail. And, therefore, Mister Porter, I do hope that you've learned that your preference to keep things spicy is akin to being impetuous and irresponsible. Every action has a reaction. You must be more mindful."

The call log flashed off my phone's screen, indicating that the Under Secretary finished her lecture and was not going to offer me a chance for rebuttal.

Appleton, finally free to speak, commented with a sarcastic edge to her voice, "Next time you're shot at, Ben, and next time someone tries to kill me in a hospital bed, take a moment to be more mindful."

I chuckled, but I didn't dare say what I was thinking: *Appleton and Sullivan are more alike than not. Both are cold and calculating.*

Not wanting to insult my host, I said instead, "Sullivan is playing a game of three-dimensional chess. She's always a few moves ahead, and in this case, also thinking halfway around the world." Deciding to float a compliment, I added, "Much like you, in fact, during your career."

"The career that recently ended with my death?" Appleton gulped the last of the whiskey in her glass. "Unfortunately, if I'm thinking like Sullivan, perhaps making me appear to be dead wasn't the best of moves. Because now what good am I to you?"

"Well, for that matter, that's one area where I am thinking ahead." I examined my empty glass and pointed my chin at Appleton's, asking, "You got any more of this stuff?"

"I do," Appleton replied.

"How 'bout another?"

Appleton stood. "Sure. Why do I get the sense that you're stalling? Or setting me up for something?"

"Remember, earlier, I said that there was a plan for you?"

"Uh-huh," Appleton replied, her head cocked to the side in amusement.

"Well, pour some more whiskey, please. Because you might need it."

CHAPTER
52

THE TALL, WHITE-HAIRED, white-mustachioed, white lab-coated white man examined the ringing smartphone device. Typically, the small screen would show a caller identification; instead, it displayed one word: "BLOCKED." He shrugged and picked it up with his right hand, announcing, "Curtis."

"I have a report. Are you free to speak?" The voice was obviously computer altered; scratchy, with an irregular and unnatural cadence.

The doctor's shoulders jolted upright. "This is unusual."

"Circumstances have changed," replied the voice. "I need you to take care of someone."

"Oh? Who?"

"Gansett."

"Gansett?" Doctor David Curtis leaned forward in his chair. Placing his right elbow on the wood desk in his office at the Walter Reed National Military Medical Center, he pushed the device tighter to his ear. "Pardon?"

"You heard me. There's been a development. Gansett was on an assignment. He erred and eliminated the wrong target."

"The wrong target?"

"Gansett was assigned to terminate Porter. Instead, Gansett killed the Boston Field Office SAC, a woman named Jennifer Appleton. Porter and Appleton worked together at one time, and I believe that Porter retreated to what he felt he knew best. In a way, Gansett failed successfully; if Porter told anything to Appleton, that breach has been closed."

"I see," mumbled Curtis, though clearly he did not. "I—um—Gansett?"

The connection crackled with what might have been a snort. "You're well equipped for this task. You see, my sources indicate that Gansett is injured. He is being treated as a John Doe in the Salem Hospital in Salem, Massachusetts. You'll be comfortable operating there."

"Yes, yes, yes," Curtis said with more conviction. "A static target. In a medical setting. That I can handle. But what of Porter?"

A humming noise might have indicated latency, or possibly admiration. "Excellent question. Porter is at large, but with Appleton down, and with Porter's resources on the yacht unavailable to him, he is isolated. He can wait. However, we cannot take the risk that Gansett recovers from his injuries, and therefore he is the immediate priority. Time is of the essence. And clear your schedule. You'll be substituting for Gansett's next assignment. In Riyadh."

"This is very concerning on a number of levels."

"Agreed, I'm afraid," admitted the voice. "However, nothing changes. I'll explain more when I can brief you in person."

Curtis straightened in his chair and then leaned back, the white charging cord of the device tethering his movements. He yanked the cord out of the port on the device and asked, "And when will that be?"

"I suppose in a matter of days. Departure is April first. Eliminate Mister Gansett as soon as possible, and when you report your success, we will arrange a time to meet."

"Understood. Anything else?"

There was a pause, punctuated by staccato crackles of the voice-altering software. "Mister Gansett has apparently lost his touch. He's been quite a disappointment. I see this to our advantage, though; he would have been the only loose end. However, this circumstance does put some pressure on you."

Curtis chuckled softly. "Not really. Gansett was trained on a method that has been shown to be inferior. I've refined the protocol. It's quite effective if in the proper hands. In fact, this gives me a valuable opportunity to test it on Gansett himself."

"I value your confidence. And your hands."

The connection went silent, and the display on Curtis's device reverted to a darkened screen as the doctor slowly replaced the device onto his desk surface with a delicate touch.

CHAPTER
53

FRIDAY, MARCH 26, 2021

APPLETON AND I SPENT a good portion of the night sharing her bottle of Jameson Eighteen. At roughly six in the morning on Friday, too early, I thought, given the throb in my head from too much whiskey, and too early for even the sun to rise, Appleton packed a couple of bags as I downed a couple of Advil.

It wasn't much of a farewell party.

Appleton drove off in one of the Suburbans that Havens and his team brought to Salem on Wednesday night, or rather, very early on Thursday morning. I wanted Appleton to use a car that couldn't be linked back to her; that particular Chevy was signed out by a member of the team Havens brought to Salem. While, indeed, that Bureau Suburban could be tracked, no one except Havens and me knew that it was Appleton behind the wheel.

Jennifer Appleton effectively vanished from the grid.

In the meantime, I'd commandeered Appleton's Tahoe for wheels, and Havens and I regrouped at the Salem Hospital.

I wanted to talk to our John Doe, but he wasn't in any shape for conversation, given the sixteen puncture wounds from three-inch spikes that he sustained. The assassin lost a great deal of blood, and one spike managed to penetrate his cheek, another lodged dangerously close to his spine, and critically, one punctured a lung. The doctors in Salem were impressed that he was alive.

Havens was impressed with my ad-hoc weapon.

CIRG Special Agent Leroy Havens was a man that I trusted with my life, and since I couldn't interview the assassin, I chose to tell Havens the *full* story, beginning with Sullivan's call to me aboard *Almaz* last summer. Havens spent considerable time on the vessel; he knew Macallister, Lockwood, Volkov, and the crew of the yacht well. Bringing him under the tent was an easy decision for me.

And I needed a local ally.

Well, any ally, I suppose, since I still couldn't reach *Almaz* by phone. Havens shared my growing concern as he asked in his baritone, "You got any leads? It's real unusual for Volkov to have an ongoing technical problem."

"Sullivan said that she was going to check it out, too. Hopefully, she can get access to satellite images. Or possibly she's got better gear than this," I said, waving my smartphone.

"A phone call is a phone call," Havens retorted. "You should come up with a backup plan."

That was one of the many lessons I'd learned from Havens: always have a contingency plan. I was therefore pleased to inform him, "That's part of Appleton's assignment."

"I hope she drives with a heavy foot," Havens observed.

"I expect nothing less from the indomitable SAC. She should be in Washington, D.C., sometime this afternoon. Cutting it close, I think, for a pre-weekend, Friday quitting time."

"Hmmm," Havens grumbled. I could tell he was unimpressed.

"She'll make it," I said wearily. "Listen, I'm tired. I've been mostly on my feet since I departed Washington on Tuesday morning, and as you know, those hours were, um, eventful."

Havens patted my shoulder as I read concern in his eye. "You need to catch a nap. Chief Miller reserved a couple of hospital rooms for my team to use to facilitate their rotating watch on Gansett. I'll cover the assassin, and if he wakes up, I'll wake you up."

"Thank you," I replied gratefully. Getting some rest would be important; if Appleton was successful, I'd need to be sharp.

I looked at my watch. I'd know in six hours.

CHAPTER
54

LEAVING HIS TEAM BEHIND to guard the nail-riddled assassin, Havens and I departed Salem at 2:00 P.M. and drove to Boston in Jennifer Appleton's Bureau-issued Tahoe.

Well, he drove; I gratefully gobbled the sandwich that he'd thoughtfully grabbed for me. And, admittedly, we didn't go to Boston. We headed for the Field Office in Chelsea.

That kind of exactitude would be good practice for the Secure Video Teleconference (SVTC, in FBI jargon) that Appleton booked for us at three in the afternoon. Her drive to D.C. was uneventful and ahead of schedule. She reported that she used the time productively; not only did she manage to get the meeting scheduled, but she also found a secure, out-of-sight location to keep her footprint in D.C. as invisible as possible.

Our shorter ride was also uneventful—functional brakes, no sirens, and no gunshots, for a welcome change.

Upon arrival at the eight-story, 286,000 square foot, concrete-and-glass sheathed Boston Division Field Office at 201 Maple Avenue in Chelsea, Havens and I were shown to the cavernous operations center, where I'd spent many, many hours several years ago. Most of the faces were new to me, save one, as a swivel chair rotated to reveal fuchsia and green eyeglass frames, spiky, blond hair, and a purple Twenty-One

Pilots concert t-shirt paired with a blue-and-red diagonally striped tie—the familiar and always color-agnostic get-up of Intelligence Analyst Louis Lewis.

"Hey, Havens. Hey! Porter!" Lewis called, rising from his perch. "This way. Got you set up this way." He strode our direction, carrying and absently clicking at the trigger of a ball-point pen, before leading Havens and me to a secure, windowless conference room, equipped with a screen, camera, and two chairs. Honestly, it looked more like an interrogation room. Government hospitality was a far cry from my former digs on *Almaz*.

"It's good to see you, Lewis," I gushed. Then, remembering that he didn't know the truth, I added in a somber tone, "I'm sorry about Appleton. She's going to be dearly missed."

His face fell. "I know." He turned to Havens. "I assume this has something to do with . . . that? With Appleton?"

Havens nodded. "Porter may not be with the FBI, but he does have a history with Appleton. That's why I asked you to set this call up for me."

"Yeah, yeah, sure. No problem. Happy to help CIRG," Lewis said.

I shot Havens a glance. I couldn't make the ask, given my status. It had to come from Havens, and the CIRG agent served the request that we rehearsed during the drive. "I appreciate that, Lewis. And, say, while we're on the SVTC, can you do me a favor?"

"Sure, man, what's up?"

"See if you can track down a 235-foot yacht named *Almaz*. She departed Washington, D.C. on March 17th. Dig beyond the usual sources, if you know what I mean."

"Sure, man," Lewis repeated. "Are you and Porter in the market for a yacht?" He was grinning.

"I need to contact that vessel, so find it, please," I replied directly, staring into Lewis's eyes. We once sat side-by-side, on the same team, in the adjacent Operations Center, and I hoped he would comprehend my intensity. Lewis was not in the need-to-know circle for the *Almaz* operation, but I didn't have the time to explain, and I was counting on his innate curiosity and technological prowess to go further than my simplistic attempts to dial a phone number.

I settled into one of the chairs as Lewis closed the door behind him. Havens locked the door and sat next to me as the screen lit, showing a wood-paneled library-like setting as a background and two faces in the foreground. One was Appleton. The other head belonged to the Attorney General of the United States, Bart Williams, the Black man seated to Appleton's left.

Williams ran a hand through his short, gray hair and began in his deep voice, "Mister Porter. As I recall, this is the second time that I've had the opportunity to conference with you. You have a knack for inserting yourself into these things, wouldn't you say?"

"It would appear so, sir. Somehow these plots keep ending up on my lap."

"Indeed," rumbled Williams. "And somehow, your plots keep involving the Department of Justice. Typically, as the AG, I prosecute crimes. And yet here we are, attempting to prevent a crime, and I am in slightly unfamiliar territory."

"Sir, it's my understanding that you authorized Deputy Assistant Director Macallister to run this operation. To pursue the tip from Under Secretary Sullivan that the Director of the CIA is plotting an assassination for political and personal gains. We've made significant progress. But there are a few open items," I explained.

"Understood," the AG said. "That's the history. SAC Appleton confirmed that before we met in a concise briefing. What I don't understand is your ploy to declare Appleton dead when, by all rights, she's quite lively, seeing as she's sitting beside me. Nor do I comprehend your insistence to meet with me." He paused and then commanded, "Report."

I cleared my throat and dove in. "Very well, sir. As I'm sure Appleton explained, I arranged that Appleton, as a patient being treated for a gunshot wound in the Salem hospital, be recorded as deceased. We've got a way to reverse that in a couple of days because continuing that lie will be unsustainable. In short, it will be revealed as a record-keeping mix-up; for a short while, the ruse will be protected by health privacy laws."

The AG grunted, "Why?"

"I wanted Appleton to set up a meeting with you under the radar. Sullivan disclosed that her office was compromised; we must assume that Ginachere also planted sources within the Department of Justice. But here's my intent: because we know Sullivan has a leak, I did not tell her that Appleton is actually alive. In fact, Appleton listened in on that conversation. Therefore, we've created an opportunity that will give us a short-term advantage over Ginachere."

"How?"

Though I didn't know the Attorney General well, I was appreciative of him and his short, to-the-point questions, a far cry from Sullivan's pontificating and posturing. But I needed to confirm one more detail. "I suggested to Appleton that you meet off-site. Where are you, anyway?"

Appleton spoke for the first time. "A safe house in Georgetown."

I demanded, "How safe? Who knows about it?"

Appleton leaned toward the camera. "It's a pied-a-terre owned by a Georgetown University law professor whose cousin lives in Los Angeles. The Californian is originally from Texas and was next-door neighbors with the woman who eventually moved to Salem and now owns my favorite liquor store. It's an oblique connection."

"How did you manage to pull that off so quickly?"

"It was an eight-hour drive, Porter. And I have a number of these bolt holes ready to trigger at a moment's notice," Appleton replied smugly. Out of the corner of my eye, I caught sight of Havens nodding appreciatively.

"Sounds good," I agreed. "Let's get on with it. Here's Appleton's task, which she can do completely out of sight of Ginachere and, frankly, of Sullivan. Appleton is to track down the assassin's co-conspirator. We have Gansett in custody in Salem; Appleton is going to get Curtis in custody in Washington. And with that, we will have Ginachere's two operatives in hand."

"And then what?" I could tell from his tone that Williams was skeptical.

"You're going to arrest and charge Ginachere." I hoped I sounded confident. I had no business giving orders to the Attorney General of the United States.

Williams scowled. "Charge her with what?"

"Ginachere's two associates—Gansett the assassin and Curtis the doctor—have been doing wet work on United States soil. What I'd like you to do is to charge Ginachere before she leaves on her trip. Why even give her the opportunity to leave the country? Or to make the hit attempt that we believe that she will make in Saudi Arabia?"

Now Williams squinted, his expression becoming almost angry. "That's ridiculous. I can't do that. You don't have a shred of evidence. You have allegations."

"I will get you that evidence," I said with more calm than I felt. "I have four days before I need to be on a plane to meet *Almaz*. We have five days before Ginachere departs on her trip, and Appleton has a couple of days before we need to reverse the ruse about her death. But I need to know that you'll be ready to go. That you'll have the case built and ready to go."

Williams's expression softened. "You want me to charge the Director of the CIA now? Prior to her trip? That's actually quite interesting, as you're right—it would prevent Ginachere from doing anything and, as importantly, keep this entire mess on American soil. No jurisdiction issues." He scratched his scalp again. "What evidence will you get?"

"I'm going to make Gansett confess," I replied, with as much confidence as I could muster. "Gansett will talk. He'll pin Ginachere. And he'll give us Doctor Curtis as a co-conspirator as well. Meanwhile, Appleton will get Curtis to do the same. A classic pincer move, if you will."

"All right," Williams grumbled. "We need to put this thing to bed. I'll agree. I'll begin the work to prepare charges, assuming that you'll bring me that evidence. I won't be able to prove intent of a planned assassination attempt in the Middle East, but I will be able to charge Ginachere with operating on American soil, with the murders of Rourke and Hamid, and with the attempted murder of Appleton."

Williams leaned back in the old-fashioned, leather-wrapped wingback chair in a law professor's Georgetown home. *Imagine if the professor knew who was in his library,* I thought unnecessarily, until I realized that the AG was waiting for me to reply.

I stammered, "Ex—exactly, sir. That's the plan. But there's one other item we could use help with."

He raised his eyebrows, clearly annoyed. "Oh?"

"You authorized Macallister to run point on this operation, and therefore you also know that Anastasia Volkov is with him on *Almaz* doing the tech work."

"Yes. So?"

"I've been trying to reach *Almaz* but with no success. Sullivan said she'd try as well. In the meantime, maybe you can help. As we were putting together Gansett and Curtis's method of attack—send the victim to a hospital, then use the hospital systems to make it look like the patient died naturally—Volkov told me about several hospital hacks. Surely, the Department of Justice has evidence. Someone working on that investigation. Who?"

"I don't know," Williams admitted. "But yes, that material has crossed my desk. I'll make inquiries and get you a name."

"Thank you. I think that will become helpful," I purred.

However, Williams was shaking his head negatively. "Perhaps. However, in the short term, I don't think it is of much value. As I see it, bringing charges against Ginachere would prevent future attempts, and therefore building evidence must be your top priority. Don't let the mechanics of Gansett's and Curtis's actions be a distraction to you. Your task is to get the assassin to talk, and you also need to find Curtis. If you can do both those things, I agree. Let's do this before Ginachere departs on her trip on April first. But if you don't have the evidence, we will have tipped our hand. It's all or nothing, Porter. Time is of the essence. Don't blow it."

"Yessir," I replied, thinking, *We're a go.*

I wouldn't have been nearly as confident if I had known who I was up against.

CHAPTER
55

IN THE WINDOWLESS ROOM within the FBI Boston Division Field Office, Havens turned to me as the SVTC with Williams and Appleton concluded, and the screen went dark. "You seem too confident, Porter. Your plan is solid but relies on two separate angles, as even you said to the Attorney General. Both must succeed. Otherwise, you're screwed."

"Yeah," I agreed, my thoughts elsewhere as I thought about the next move.

"You're not listening," Havens growled, quite correctly. I blinked and focused on his face, forcing myself to pay attention. "You think you're gonna waltz in on a CIA assassin and just get him to talk? It's a long shot?"

"Let's come back to that in a sec," I suggested. "What about Appleton and Curtis? You think she can get him to talk?"

Havens shrugged. "Appleton can be very persuasive, and Curtis— though I don't know him, obviously—is a doctor, not a field work guy. My guess is that he's gotten a little ahead of himself. From what you've told me, the doctor has trouble keeping his story straight. He's not accustomed to this game. I give Appleton better chances with her task than I give you with yours."

"Thanks for the vote of confidence, man."

"Sorry. You gotta be realistic, though."

I clasped my hands behind my head. "I know. But you have to be creative. And here's what you're missing. What you're forgetting. We've got one of the best resources for finding stuff out. And so far, we have not deployed that. We've been so focused on Ginachere that we have been overlooking Gansett and Curtis."

"I don't follow." Havens did not look the least bit impressed.

I pulled my hands away from my head and planted them on the table, steepling my fingers as Macallister might have done. "We're going to task Macallister and, more specifically, Volkov. They're gonna do a data dump on Gansett."

"A what?"

"A deep dive." I pointed at the satchel that Havens had carried from Salem, which I asked him to pack before retreating for my nap. "Inside that bag that you packed are Gansett's effects. I asked you to take them to keep them secure, which is true. But there was another reason. You see, unlike before, now we have his DNA. We have his fingerprints. We have close-up photos so we can build a perfect facial recognition match. We have the phone that he carried. We didn't have any of that before. We're gonna send all that stuff to Volkov digitally, with Lewis's help here in Boston. And then we're gonna find something that we can use as leverage, and we'll get him to talk."

Havens finally grinned. "Now that sounds promising."

"Bring Lewis in here, would you?"

Havens stood, unlocked the door, and leaned out of the jamb, calling, "Lewis. Can you join us, please?"

I began to feel uncomfortable as Havens stood motionlessly, scowling, at the door. It took far too long for Lewis to appear. Finally, the techie entered the small room, but he didn't sit in the chair that Havens had occupied. He stood, fidgeting, clicking at the trigger on his ballpoint pen almost frantically.

My unease was justified when Lewis announced, "I can't find that boat."

Shit. If anyone could find Almaz, *it would be Lewis.*

I tried to remain composed as I said, "Tell me what you found, and tell me where you looked."

"There's more to this boat, isn't there?"

"You could say that," I confirmed.

"What are you up to, Porter?" His eyes narrowed behind the eyeglass frames.

I sighed. "I'll explain. I promise. But I'm sensing hesitancy." I repeated, "What did you find, and where did you search?"

"Well, I started with what you gave me—a name, which I matched with the vessel's length and departure date from Washington. A target named *Almaz* was tracked transiting the Potomac River, then the Chesapeake Bay, and then heading east across the Atlantic with a steady course that pointed to Gibraltar. Makes sense, you know, since I also found sales and registration documentation showing a transaction to a buyer in Greece. Looks like a delivery to me."

"So far, so good. That's the boat I'm looking for," I confirmed.

"Well, not so good, actually," Lewis sighed. "The tracking signal from *Almaz* disappeared on Wednesday evening."

"Where?"

"About 175 miles north of Ponta Delgada. That's the capital of the island archipelago of the Azores, a territory of Portugal," he explained as he removed his eyeglasses and polished them with his tie.

"Yeah," I countered, "I looked at the usual tracking sources too. Maybe the AIS signal isn't being repeated or picked up for some reason. Weather, glitch, whatever. That happens all the time, I've learned. But— you've got more access than me going on the internet."

Lewis slipped his glasses back onto his head. "Right. But here's the problem: the last signal pip received was at 1:40 A.M. Zulu, or Greenwich Mean Time, on Thursday morning. That would be Wednesday evening for us, and like the middle of the night where the *Almaz* was located. Therefore, I pulled satellite images from the day before, and from every day since, from the National Reconnaissance Office. They operate the birds that can be tasked by the Department of Defense, the CIA, or whatever, and of course, we have some access here at The Bureau."

"I know what the NRO does," I said with impatience, and as I watched him squirm, I got the sense he was stalling.

He shifted in the seat. "The weather was fair on Wednesday and on Thursday. On Wednesday, I could easily match up the shape of the yacht with the tracking signal. The vessel was making fifteen knots on a steady course. Therefore, it would be equally easy to figure out where it should have been on Thursday when daylight returned." He shook his head. "It's nowhere to be found. At its previous course and speed, by now, it should be only three hundred miles from Gibraltar. It's not. And even if it changed course in any direction, it's not a big search circumference. It's nowhere."

Havens and I exchanged glances, and I stammered, "But . . . but how could it disappear?"

Lewis hesitated. "Um, there's more. There were two nighttime satellites that tracked that position in two distinct passes. They've got infrared sensors. You know, heat-seeking, so that they can see at night, or through the clouds, or whatever."

I spat, "What do they show?" I felt badly for my sharp tone, but my patience was exhausted.

"The data is blocked."

I threw my hands up in the air, exasperated, and I hissed, "By who?"

Lewis inhaled deeply. "The CIA." I opened my mouth to speak, but this time, Lewis held his own hand up to stop me so that he could finish. "It's a blanket block. I can't see who authorized it. All I can see is that the Agency initiated the block. What may be concerning, though, is that I think I set off an alarm or something. My searches on those images seemed to trigger an identification protocol. In other words, I hope you don't care that whoever blocked those images now knows that an analyst named Lewis at FBI Boston tried to get access."

Havens, still standing in near the closed door of the little room, crossed his arms tightly and narrowed his eyes. "Nothing good ever comes from something like that."

I felt my blood pressure rising even as I sensed sweat on my palms. I knew Havens was correct. Lewis could obviously tell that Havens and

I were both disconsolate, and in a soft voice, the techie asked, "What's your interest in that boat, Porter? What's the deal?"

I met his eyes. "I'm breaching national security confidentiality by disclosing this to you, Lewis." His eyes widened as I continued, "That boat is my operation. And on it are Bradford Macallister, Anastasia Volkov, Miles Lockwood, and a crew."

Lewis, usually pale, gasped and blanched. He knew those names. He worked with those people.

My gut churned as I spoke, verbalizing what I dreaded. "Could the boat be gone? Could Ginachere have discovered that it wasn't really sold to a buyer in Greece? And could she have authorized an operation to sink it?"

"That's jumping to a conclusion, man," Havens counseled. "She's the Director of the CIA, so yeah, she's probably got the assets. But that's murder."

Remembering the story that Sullivan told, while aboard *Almaz*, about Ginachere in Damascus, I groaned, "She's done it before. Ginachere is capable of doing it again. Hell, this whole thing is about her planning to assassinate the King of Saudi Arabia. Taking out a boat with a handful of no-name intelligence operatives aboard is nothing compared to that."

Havens leaned in. "Lewis, you gotta figure out what's going on."

I closed my eyes briefly and then snapped them open to say, "Not only that, but also you gotta do what I wanted Volkov to do since obviously, I can't reach her. I hope you don't have plans for the weekend, Lewis. 'Cuz you're not going home tonight."

The Intelligence Analyst's blond hair got even spikier when he became emotional or excited, and he offered quietly, "Whatever you need, I'm in."

I nodded. "Let's get to work."

Not being able to locate *Almaz* was bad enough. But it was going to get worse.

CHAPTER
56

TRUTHFULLY, I WAS AMAZED that I was yet to be kicked out of the Boston Field Office building. I mean, I was a Special Agent—emphasis on the past tense—with a proper badge, authorized and expected to carry a weapon at all times while on duty. But those days were gone, and while there was good reason, very few people were privy to the circumstances.

Therefore, to the current personnel staffing the Field Office, I was only Ben Porter, former Special Agent, fired for insubordination. *Disgraced.*

Heads turned, and lips tittered as Havens, Lewis, and I emerged from the confines of the little interrogation room. While the former two were welcome in the Operations Center, I was not. And, with Appleton presumed dead, and because I was known to have worked under the deceased SAC, my presence was certain to bring unwanted attention.

We needed a place to go. A place to get our shit together. A place for Lewis to work.

My thoughts raced. I felt desperation, a level of angst that I'd never before experienced. I could not fathom what happened to my team aboard *Almaz*. I had to get to the bottom of that, and yet at the same time, urgency pressed at me to find some fact to use as leverage on Gansett—so that I could find out for sure if it was Ginachere targeting me. Targeting us.

But I was stuck at a loss. I didn't see how it would be feasible to run that two-pronged investigation from here in the Field Office.

Lewis returned to his workstation, and Havens and I shadowed his movements. Lewis sat down at his desk while Havens and I stood behind him. I whispered, "This is ridiculous. This isn't a movie. Lewis isn't gonna push a few buttons and magically reveal everything we need. We can't just stand here."

Havens nodded, and in a sonorous, low tone, he concurred, "Too many eyes staring us down. Who knows if Ginachere has spies here, too. And Porter, you're attracting attention."

Without turning his head away from his computer monitors, Lewis whined, "I'm not gonna be able to concentrate with you two whispering behind my back. We need to go someplace more private. And quieter, please."

Quiet and private, I thought.

I turned to Havens. "Let's go to Appleton's house."

"No," he protested. "We can't show traffic or occupancy there, if you know what I mean."

I did, but Lewis obviously did not. "That's offensive, Porter. You can't go hang out in the deceased's living room. Have some respect, dude." His voice, still directed at his screens, clearly sounded his contempt for my idea.

After a second, though, Lewis said contemplatively, "I wish Appleton were alive. She could get us inside her bunker. *That's* the perfect place."

I side-eyed Havens. Dumbfounded, I whispered, "Appleton has a bunker?"

Not having eyes in the back of his head, Lewis missed the exchange of glances between Havens and me, and Lewis answered softly, "Yes. There's a smaller version of this ops center hidden under her house. Unfortunately, with Appleton gone, there's no way we could sneak in."

"Why not?" I kept my tone innocent. It was an innocent enough question, right?

"It's really secure. There's a timed protocol which changes the access codes, but then there's another layer, which would prevent someone from stealing Appleton's device or even coercing her to disclose the code."

"What's that?" My two-word questions would impress Attorney General Williams.

Lewis rotated his chair to come face-to-face with Havens and me, leaning uncomfortably and conspiratorially close. Facing away from his screens, Lewis could see the stares from his colleagues. "We're not being real . . . subtle, here."

I grimaced and repeated my earlier question. "What's the other layer?"

Lewis shrugged. "Well, I guess she's gone, so what does it matter? You can't get into the bunker through Appleton's house itself. It can only be done from a secret entry, accessed through the backyard neighbor's garage. Once you're at the entry, you must pass four tests at once. First, you need in your possession two physical items: Appleton's house key as well as her car key fob—which, by the way, is not just an ordinary fob. Then, you need her phone, which receives a randomly generated, fifteen-character, alphanumeric security code every hour. And finally, you need to know where to look on Instagram for the most current access phrase. Actually, that's the easy part, because I know where to look. It's an account which posts a photo every week, accompanied by a quote, some well-known, some obscure. But—that quote must be spoken by her voice." Lewis grinned. "Pretty cool, eh? I designed it myself. And even I couldn't defeat it."

Havens dug into his jeans pocket, extracted his fist, and opened his hand, palm up. "You mean like this house key, and like this key fob?"

Lewis's hair stood on end. "How'd you get those keys?"

"Doesn't matter," I said. "Get what you need from here, leave your phone behind, and let's go."

Lewis shook his head. "I don't need anything from here. Everything I could possibly need is already there. But didn't you hear me? Security code from her phone and access phrase spoken in her voice? I can't fake those."

It was my turn to grin. "We can. Wanna find out how?"

CHAPTER 57

TO KEEP MY EMOTIONS in check, and to keep me from worrying about *Almaz*, I worked up rudimentary tradecraft to cover our departure from the Chelsea Field Office. Assuming my suspicions proved correct, Ginachere's arms were long and could possibly reach into the FBI.

Therefore, I wanted to stay under the radar, so to speak.

Havens escorted me from the Field Office firmly to the relieved expressions of the staff. Assuming that Appleton's Tahoe was trackable, we left it behind in the Bureau's employee parking garage, and we walked three long blocks to a suburban mall. Taking positions on opposing ends of a bank parking lot, we waited, examining the cars that passed through the drive-up teller portal one-by-one, presumably depositing or cashing their Friday paychecks.

Havens moved first, intercepting an old but clean, red Toyota Camry sedan as it pulled from the portal to the exit. Watching Havens, I was relieved he beat me to the ask; his smooth delivery was certainly going to be more persuasive than my awkward pleading. Sure enough, he waved me over as he climbed into the front passenger seat of the car.

I trotted over and clicked open the rear passenger door, only to find an empty child's car seat. "Other side," Havens ordered, and after I closed one door, opened the other, and slung myself into the backseat, the car pulled forward. "Say hello to Eladio."

"A pleasure to meet you," I said to our driver, a thirty-something Hispanic man with close-cropped hair and a wisp of a beard. "Thanks for the lift."

"Um, this is really kinda weird," Eladio replied. I could tell he was nervous.

"Look, my friend, like I explained, it's cool. Cash for a ride for me and my two friends," Havens offered smoothly.

Eladio was clearly having second thoughts. "You're not, like, trying to avoid the government or something?"

The guy is a quick study, I thought. *If only he knew . . .*

Havens laughed. "Nah, man, nothing like that. My car broke down." He flashed Appleton's key fob before adding, "We gotta get to a surprise party. I got the gift right here." Havens patted the satchel on his lap; obviously Eladio couldn't have known that the bag contained the belongings of the CIA's most deadly contract assassin. Without missing a beat, Havens continued his sales pitch, "It's a quick trip. You'll drop us off down the street, we walk the rest of the way, and you get three hundred bucks in cash."

"You could take an Uber, you know." Eladio was definitely getting cold feet.

Havens leaned toward Eladio conspiratorially. "I ain't getting one of those cell phones, man, and I don't trust credit cards. Cash, amigo. Cash is king." Havens scratched his chin. "Except now, I guess, is one of those rare times when that stuff would come in handy." He chuckled and sold it, "But that's why I got you, my friend. Help me out?"

Eladio hesitated but then wavered. "Where's the cash?"

Fortunately, Havens was prepared. He counted out the money in twenties, tens, and a one-hundred-dollar bill.

"You're not, like, a dealer or something?"

Havens patted Eladio on the shoulder. "Nope." There was something charismatic about Havens; he could almost always get his way.

A moment later, Lewis showed up, searched the area, and finally spotted my wave from the Camry. The techie boarded and shoved me to the middle seat. My ribs squeezed against the hard plastic sides of the car seat.

We rode in awkward silence toward Salem.

Up in the shotgun seat, Havens directed Eladio as I thought, They don't show this kind of glamour in the spy movies.

My attempt to amuse myself backfired, though, because thinking of glamour caused me to remember the plush luxury of the white Mercedes SUV that was loaded onto the fantail of an expedition-style yacht only weeks ago. I whispered to Lewis, "*Almaz*. It's gone, isn't it?"

Lewis leaned close, his hair brushing my face as he nodded. It wasn't spiky; it was actually quite soft, as was his voice. "Visible by day, not visible the next morning, and overnight footage blocked. That's no coincidence."

"You think it sunk?"

"What else could have happened?"

I couldn't think of any other scenarios. Phone contact unsuccessful, visual contact disappeared, and infrared images blocked.

Before I could dwell further, we reached Salem and took our leave of our driver on a side street, with Havens giving him an extra hundred. It wasn't the perfect cover, but it would be close; a cab or the Uber that Eladio suggested could be tracked. A cooperative driver picked at random would be much more difficult to find. As Havens and I had discussed, Ginachere could be tracking us with satellites, and paranoia took precedent to convenience.

We walked the final two blocks to Appleton's backyard neighbor's house. There, Lewis instructed us to unlock the side door to the detached garage with Appleton's house key. I could see Appleton's white colonial beyond a six-foot-tall cedar fence. Lewis caught my look and winked. "That's not a wood fence. It's steel. Set in concrete."

We slipped inside the garage, and Lewis led us toward the rear to a trap door, disguised under a collection of yard and gardening implements scattered at the front end of an older, dusty, maroon-colored pickup truck. Havens asked, "How'd you get the neighbor to agree to this?"

"They're renters," Lewis explained. "They don't have access to the garage. The Bureau owns the house through a shell company. When it's not rented, it's used as a safe house."

Descending the stairs and closing the trap door over our heads, Lewis found a light switch. A clean, well-lit tunnel was revealed ahead, and I commented, "I hope my phone works underground."

"Oh, sure, it will," Lewis said confidently. "There's a cell repeater here just for that purpose. But who you gonna call?"

I tapped an icon, and as we walked closer to a solid-looking metal door, Appleton's voice rang from my phone's speaker. "Hey, Porter. It's good that you called." Her voice was somber.

"What?" Lewis's voice notched up an octave. "Appleton? Ma'am?"

"Oh, hello, Lewis," Appleton replied. "As Mister Twain may have said, reports of my death are greatly exaggerated."

Lewis's eyes went wide, and his mouth dropped as I clarified, "Lewis, we'll explain more when we're inside. Ma'am, we have a lot to discuss— but first, I'm with Havens and Lewis. We're at the tunnel door to what Lewis tells us is your bunker. Can you give us the current access code from your phone?"

"My bunker? With Lewis? That means—never mind, you'll tell me. Hang on."

Lewis motioned to Havens, who handed Lewis the key fob and house key. Lewis cracked the fob open, removed the valet key, handed the fob back to Havens, and inserted the valet key into a slot to the right of the door. He inserted the house key into a second slot and turned both keys to the right simultaneously. A glossy area above the two keys lit with a digital touch keyboard. Lewis asked, "Code?"

Appleton read the alphanumeric code as Lewis tapped key icons. "L-t-t-a-p-m-l-2-f-g-q-4-u-0-m."

Lewis tapped an icon, which turned from red to yellow, and said, "Phrase?"

Appleton's voice was clear through the speaker on my device. "The source of wisdom is whatever is going to happen to us today. Pema Chödrön."

Nothing happened.

Then Lewis, his eyes frantic as he held a finger to his lips, poked Havens. Lewis mouthed a single, one-syllable word and stretched out his hand, palm open and up.

Havens saved the moment by understanding Lewis's non-verbal message, and he handed the techie the key fob. Lewis simultaneously squeezed the *Lock* and *Unlock* buttons once, then again, and again, and again.

The icon became green, and I heard a click. Lewis exhaled. "Almost forget that last step. Key fob. Number of syllables in the name that the quote is attributed to."

Havens pulled the door open, straining slightly from its weight. I reported to Appleton, "Great. Deep thoughts and a four-syllable name. We're in."

As Havens closed the tunnel door behind our little trio, Appleton replied, "Well, you might be in, but . . ."

She paused and sighed, and the firmness in her tone was replaced with one of exhaustion. "But I struck out."

CHAPTER
58

JENNIFER APPLETON'S underground bunker in Salem was fit for a villain. I mean, seriously, who comes up with this stuff? Who paid for it? I was jealous.

From the exterior, Appleton's place appeared to be a restored Colonial-era home, like many of the residences in Salem. It was a simple design; two stories fenestrated with two-over-two double-hung windows, the wavy glass of the windowpanes as immaculately spotless as the perfectly manicured surrounding yard. In short, it was storybook perfect.

While I knew that the living room of the house was wired with hidden cameras, microphones, and speakers, giving the SAC a comfortable place to conduct Secure Video Teleconferences and interviews, and just earlier this week, I learned that Appleton stored a small armory somewhere in the house, I had absolutely zero clue about the basement bunker. Whoa.

Hidden below the white-clapboard-sided home, Appleton's bunker rivaled anything I could imagine. Lewis prattled on and on about its features. "Eighteen hundred square feet with a blast-proof concrete and steel ceiling and outer shell. Geothermal heating and cooling which is invisible from the surface. Air purification as well as air ducting to the surface, with the snorkels located several hundred feet away, hidden within a small cemetery. If the electrical power is interrupted, the generator at the neighbor's house services the bunker, and there's a battery bank which can run all the equipment for seven days and which is kept charged by the solar panels at the neighbor's place or can be charged by the grid or by the generator. Water and provisions for thirty days. And, of course, high-speed connectivity to the terrestrial data networks plus a direct satellite upload and download capability."

"I assume the dish is at the neighbor's house, too," Havens said.

"No, certainly not." Lewis appeared offended. "The dish is on top of the local library. A block or so away."

As he spoke, Lewis was powering up the various computers in the bunker and, using an Internet Protocol address that Appleton provided, he initiated a SVTC to Appleton's Georgetown safe house. I ended the phone call, and we all took comfortable seats in the bunker. With the carpeted floor, maple-paneled walls, and contemporary light fixtures, we might as well have been back in the Field Office ops center, just at a smaller scale.

On the big flat screen in the bunker, Appleton's grim expression, however, forced me back to the reality of our case. I offered a quick precis of our findings, concluding with a four-sentence summary: "No offense to Lewis and to his capabilities, but I was counting on being able to have Volkov not only analyze the phone that Gansett carried but also, and more importantly, to dig up something that I could use to compel Gansett to disclose Ginachere's involvement and future plans. Yet Volkov, not to mention Macallister, Lockwood, and everyone else aboard *Almaz*, are nowhere to be found. We fear the worst. We believe that the yacht disappeared under suspicious circumstances, which appear to have a CIA fingerprint. And it's possible that Lewis's search also triggered a link to Lewis at the Boston office."

"It's demoralizing," Appleton agreed. "It's as if Ginachere is a step ahead. I'd expect nothing less from the Director of the CIA, but still . . ."

I suggested, "It's like she has inside knowledge."

Appleton nodded. "Exactly. It was a good call to leave the Field Office. You're isolated at my place. The investigation work on Gansett that Volkov was going to do, Lewis can do in my bunker. He'll be fine. He may not be as fast as Volkov, but I have full confidence that he's as talented as she is." Lewis beamed as Appleton continued with less enthusiasm, "However, Porter and Havens, I'm open to your suggestions. Because I've completely struck out on locating Curtis. Like *Almaz*, he's nowhere to be found."

I shrugged and tried to look nonchalant. "We disconnected with the Attorney General what, almost four hours ago? That call was at 3:00 P.M. It's now 6:45. You searched the city?"

Appleton scoffed. "I didn't have to. I have contacts here, contacts that I can trust not to reveal my involvement. They know how to keep a secret. Anyway, my source at Walter Reed told me that Curtis signed out of the building last night and was not on-premises today. And remember when Macallister initially hooked up with Curtis at the outset of this mess, after Rourke's body was brought to Reed for autopsy, Macallister ran a dossier on the doctor. I got that file. Utilizing the data within it as well as a handful of Bureau and Secret Service agents that I trust, I coordinated a canvas of Curtis's usual locations: home, hospitals, a dining club, that sort of thing. Like most people, he lived according to a pattern. And suddenly, today, he deviates from the pattern?"

"Something's up," Havens grumbled.

Lewis was tapping away at a keyboard, and I incorrectly assumed that he was beginning the work that would have been done by Volkov. Indeed, Lewis had unpacked the satchel that Havens had carried, and Gansett's phone was tethered beside Lewis's keyboard with a white cord. However, Lewis was working on a different device, which became obvious when he stated, "I tracked the doctor's cell phone. It's at his home address in Chevy Chase, Maryland. Also, his personal vehicle is a Land Rover Discovery. Those cars are app-enabled, so I could locate it, and it's at his home address, too."

Appleton was shaking her head. "I arranged for eyes and boots at that site two hours ago, and that individual was going to keep watch. I have full faith, and if there's been no report, Curtis is not at his home. Hang on." As Lewis continued to click and type, Havens and I watched Appleton do the same on a smartphone. After a couple of moments, Appleton looked at the camera. "My agent reports that the Discovery is in the garage."

"Maybe Curtis is dead inside the house," Havens suggested with a tinge of enthusiasm.

I looked at Havens and then at Appleton via our camera. "Only one way to find out."

The SAC sighed. "In for a penny, in for a pound." She tapped again at her device as she mumbled, "We've got no warrant. We're gonna do an unauthorized entry on my order. This better work out."

Lewis turned his attention to Gansett's phone as Appleton, Havens, and I twiddled our thumbs, removed from the action in Maryland.

Seven minutes later, Appleton shook her head back and forth. "Nope. He's not there. Curtis is gone. Either he's been kidnapped, or he's gone intentionally. Given what we know of him, and since he executed basic tradecraft by leaving his phone, car, and possessions behind, I'm with Havens. Curtis is up to something."

"Yup," Havens and I chorused.

"Speaking of stuff we don't know," I added after a pause, considering a thought that was bouncing around in my head and finally coalescing into an idea, "if Curtis is attempting to go off-grid, do we have any idea where Hazel Ginachere is currently? We've been operating under the assumption that she's going overseas on April first. Where is she now?"

"I'll get on that," Appleton offered. "What about Sullivan? Last you left it with her, Porter, she was going to look into *Almaz*. Do you want to bring her up to date on what you guys discovered about the boat?"

I scratched my chin, thinking that over. "Not yet. We spoke with her about twenty-four hours ago. Let's see what intel she gathers independently. We can wait on that. But in the meantime, here's what we're gonna do. Appleton, you're on Ginachere. Where is she?"

"Agreed," Appleton said simply.

I turned to the techie. "Lewis. Get into Gansett's background. Find us leverage."

"Will do," Lewis replied.

Facing the CIRG agent, I ordered, "Havens, find us transportation. We're gonna need wheels."

"Actually, I can help with that," Appleton announced on-screen. "The pickup truck in the neighbor's garage belongs to me. It's yours to use. It looks nasty, but it's in perfect mechanical condition."

"Good," Havens said. "In that case, I'd like to run over to the Salem hospital and check on my team there. They would have reported if there was any change in Gansett's condition, but I'll get a firsthand look, and it's what, only a three- or four-minute drive from here to the hospital?"

"Yeah, go for it," I agreed. Having an actionable plan always seemed to improve morale, and I tried to remain upbeat as I presented my role. "As for me, I'm calling the AG. I want that contact in his department that he promised. Justice's research into these hospital hacks might be another piece in our puzzle."

We ended the SVTC with an agreement to check back together in five hours, at midnight, before turning in for rest.

Little did I know that I'd have another sleepless night.

CHAPTER
59

APPLETON'S BUNKER WAS EQUIPPED with everything a spy might need. Havens grabbed a burner phone as well as the keys to the old pickup truck and took off toward the hospital. Lewis made himself comfortable with caffeine and keyboards at the primary workstation. Seeing as it was just after 8:00 P.M. and dinner time, I set myself up in a small kitchenette with a microwaved meal, a spare laptop, superfast Wi-Fi, and my encrypted phone.

Turns out I could have done without the mystery meal, which was purportedly frozen fish sticks with an unidentifiable side dish—to stay away from *that* menu would have been self-evident to a real spy, I suppose—but everything else proved essential. In short order, I had indigestion, as well as a series of texts that started with Appleton, escalated to the Attorney General himself, and led me to a woman named Sara Lin. The AG texted that Attorney Lin would be expecting my call.

The voice that answered was difficult to describe, but I'll try: a touch of a Japanese accent combined with a little Northeast US privileged lockjaw interspersed with a Southern California drawl. I was captivated. I couldn't help myself when I asked, "Miss Lin, where are you from?"

"Oh, please, call me Sara." But she said the name not like an American would, but with a Japanese pronunciation, with a rolled *R*. Sensing my silence, she explained, "My name is spelled like the American one, but it's native to my country of birth, and it means vivid blossom." She laughed softly. "Americans, as usual, simply assume it's an American name."

"Maybe I should stick with Miss Lin," I suggested. "Is it 'miss'?"

She laughed. "Yes. Miss. I'm single. And I'm comfortable with whatever you're comfortable with, Mister Porter."

I wasn't quite ready to fire questions at her, so I continued the small talk. "How long have you been at the Department of Justice? And in the States? Oh, and please feel free to call me Ben."

"Thanks, Ben. About five years. At the DOJ, that is. In the States since boarding school. Hotchkiss, then Stanford, then the Law School at Columbia University."

"Quite a résumé."

"Oh, just say it," Lin laughed. "Quite pretentious. But I'd rather get it out of the way than pretend to ignore it."

I grinned and then realized that she could not see me through the phone. "Ha," I began awkwardly, "it's all quite impressive, as is your gig with the Attorney General. But technically, you are in the National Security Division and report to the Assistant Attorney General. No offense, but why did Williams connect me with you, not with the Assistant AG?"

"I've been leading the coordination effort of the IC—um, the Intelligence Community—as we work to better understand and prosecute the cyber threats that have been perpetrated against our nation's hospitals. In a way, because that system is very fragmented and decentralized, it's intrinsically more difficult to crack. To hack. However, that also means that we're dealing with multiple bad actors, from fringe elements to foreign groups."

"Foreign groups?"

Lin sighed. "Primarily Russian, in fact. A group—no, a gang—known as Ryuk has originated over two hundred ransomware attacks on US hospitals. The investigation is ongoing, but the target is elusive."

"What's the typical ransomware attack methodology?"

"The attackers hack into the system of a particular hospital, freeze it, and demand payment to reopen it. Payment in the hundreds of thousands of dollars, so enough to make a hospital, especially a smaller, independent one, think twice, but not enough to be impossible to pay. Really, it varies per case, and the amount is, dare I say, appropriate to the hospital's publicly known resources."

I considered that and asked, "What if the hospital refuses to pay?"

Lin clucked her tongue and replied, "It becomes a stalemate. A standoff. The hospital would scramble to build a new system, or they would raise the money."

"The hospitals pay?" There was a real note of incredulity in my voice.

"Oh, yes. Usually. It's easier and significantly faster to pay than to stonewall or to build a new system. And they need these critical systems for patient care. The tally last year to Ryuk alone was at least one hundred million dollars."

"Whoa," I whistled. "I had no idea of the scope. Is this commonly known?"

"Not really. It's been picked up occasionally by the mainstream press, but there are always juicer stories to report. Not to mention with incessant Covid news, there's plenty of pressure on hospitals at the moment. It would be a public confidence disaster if people knew just how tenuous these patient care systems really are."

I wanted to direct the discussion toward my case, so I tried to hint at my ultimate question. "Those are hospital-wide systems, right? This Ryuk group is targeting, essentially, a randomized patient group or those who are in the care of a single hospital. They're not targeting a specific patient, are they?"

Lin hummed. "Not to my knowledge or that I've seen. The patients in care are collateral damage. So yes, I'd agree these targets are randomized, not specific. That's only a matter of time, though."

I jumped on that. "What do you mean?"

"When hospital systems are down, administrators and record keepers and nurses and doctors can't communicate effectively. Furthermore, even within the confines of, say, a floor or suite, the flow of information ceases. We've seen instances where patient care has had tragic outcomes because data from vitals monitoring systems or patient records were unavailable.

In our view, these attacks could become less random and more focused. The technology seems to be available."

Oh, it is already, I thought.

But I asked Lin to clarify, "Can you elaborate on 'seems to be available'? Is it, or isn't it?"

"Good question. It is available. Hospital systems. Vitals monitoring systems, record-keeping systems, diagnostic systems—they have been hacked from the inside. We just haven't seen a specific case where an individual person was deliberately targeted and suffered an adverse medical outcome." She paused and added, "Yet."

"Sara," I said, trying to pronounce the beautiful name correctly as best I could, "let's say such a case existed. What would you need for evidence in order to prosecute the case?"

Silence. Lin's answers were complex, and I took the downtime as her thinking, not stalling. She rewarded my patience. "I'd never thought about this scenario from that angle before. I'd have to imagine the sequence. I'd need patient records—admittance, symptoms, treatments, procedures. I'd need patient location and supervision. I'd need a detailed list of every patient and staff interaction because any holes or gaps would be used by a defense team to create reasonable doubt. And I'd need the electronic records, too. I'd have to show that the electronic records didn't match the actual outcomes or vice versa. Because if the intent was a hack to kill, those electronic records—or gaps within them because of a hack—would have to be compared to manual records, if those even existed."

Lin paused and sighed. "Phew. That's a really long list. I'd have to depose who knows how many individuals. The evidence gathering and testimony would be extensive and exhausting. I'm shaking my head, Ben, because the magnitude of such a case is immense when you examine it from that perspective."

"Complicated, to say the least, I guess."

She chuckled. "I hate to sound dark, Ben, but let's say you wanted to commit a crime. Say, murder. It would be a lot more efficient and easier to just hire a hitman than to pull off that hospital stunt."

I laughed, too, but hollowly. Clearing my throat, I prompted, "Let's play it out from the opposite side. Any upside?"

Lin's voice turned somber. "Yeah, sure. The upside for the perpetrator is the stuff I outlined before. If the perp were really talented, and they knew that proving malice and successfully prosecuting a case would be a Herculean effort, our hypothetical perp would get away with murder."

"And what if the perp attempted this stunt, as you called it, but failed? Could our perp be prosecuted for attempted murder?"

"Sure. Listen, if the evidence is there, I could build the case. I said it's difficult. Not impossible. But you need one other element," Lin said in a cautionary tone.

"What's that?"

"Motive."

"I can provide that, too."

The silence now was, certainly, Lin stalling. Finally, she choked out a sentence. "I don't follow. Er, actually, I think I do. Your questions have been very specific. Are you insinuating that you know of such a case? Such an incident actually happening? And you have details?"

"You catch on quick, Sara," I said in an equally complimentary and serious tone. "I'll confirm with Bart Williams, but I'm afraid I'm about to ruin your weekend."

Lin groaned. "Wonderful."

"You don't mean that."

She giggled. Her laugh was contagious and broke the tension, but Lin steered the conversation to professional territory by confirming, "Okay. Williams will approve it, I'm sure. Your specificity should be more persuasive toward a conviction than attempting to prosecute a vague hacking group for what's really a financial crime. Can you give me a name? A plaintiff? I'll get started right away."

I replied to Lin, "Actually, I'll give you two names. The first is a murder case. The second is attempted murder."

"Okay. Murder. Who's our victim?"

"FBI Special Agent Abdullatif al-Hamid." I spelled the name for her.

"Got it," Lin confirmed. "And the second case? The attempted murder target?"

"Ben Porter."

"No . . . shit? Really?" Her voice was soft and gentle.

"I'm afraid so. There will be a third case, too, another attempted murder. I can't go into those details yet. And possibly a fourth, another murder. That one is more complicated. Hell, the whole thing is byzantine, so let's start with Hamid and me. Both of those cases will be located in Washington."

"Local to me and to the AG," Lin quickly observed.

"Yeah. Williams already has the outline. There's only a minor hitch, though."

Lin giggled again. "After all that, why am I not surprised? What's the hitch?"

"We're gonna need all that work completed in five days. No later than the morning of April first."

"Shit. You're gonna owe me a drink, Ben. Maybe dinner."

I smiled. "I'd like that. You're on."

It's amazing how a voice and an attitude can be so captivating, and I truly looked forward to meeting Sara Lin in person. But first, I'd have to survive.

CHAPTER
60

I DISCONNECTED THE CALL and allowed myself a moment to stare at my laptop screen, where I'd Googled Sara Lin and found her LinkedIn page, complete with photo. The DOJ attorney's face—dark, subtly wavy hair, flawless light brown skin, and soft, dark eyes that somehow managed to meet mine through the screen and static picture—was as alluring to me as her voice. And the way that she strung together my disjointed narrative and immediately homed in on the case? Clever and intuitively smart, too.

My reverie was rudely interrupted by Lewis. "Porter! I got somethin'."

Returning my focus to the underground bunker in Salem, I closed the laptop screen and stood. "Be right there," I called back.

In the main room, Lewis was agitated, frantically clicking at the trigger of his ballpoint pen as he updated me on his inquiry into Gansett's past. "This guy is complex. Check this out." He pointed at the screens in front of him. "Gansett's phone is going to take time. It has security layers that I've never seen before. However, thanks to having this guy in custody at the Salem Hospital, we've got all the identifiers that we need. Fingerprints, DNA, facial images, dental records, blood type—you name it, we got it. Even a guy like him can't hide from me."

Lewis chuckled, but I didn't. "Get to the point, please."

"Right. Right. Okay, subject name is JJ Gansett. Born in Boston. Local guy, eh? He's fifty-three years old. He's a widower. That's really important?"

"Really? Our assassin was married? That doesn't fit the usual profile."

Nodding, Lewis confirmed, "Exactly correct. Typically, we see these guys as lone wolf types. But this one is different. He didn't start out on that path."

'What happened?"

"Lemme give you the background. Gansett went to college in Maine and then served a three-year tour in the Army, probably to get payment assistance on student debt, or maybe because he just wanted to get out of Maine. Anyway, he ranked as a Specialist—nothing noteworthy, really, except for his expert marksmanship badges."

"Oh, yeah? *Expert* marksmanship? That's the highest grade. Interesting choice for someone who would become an assassin."

Lewis aimed his pen in my direction and clicked it once. "Yep. He consistently scored perfect scores in the qualification competitions across a range of weapons and disciplines. He's a natural shooter."

"Really?" I scratched my chin in disbelief. "And yet, he missed the shot at Appleton. At The Register."

"Well, like I said before, he's in his fifties. Maybe he's not as good as he once was," Lewis countered.

That seemed off to me, but I couldn't pinpoint why. Instead, I urged Lewis to continue, "Okay, so our suspect starts off as a shooter. You obviously have more."

Lewis flashed a thumbs-up at me. "Right. Gansett completed his service and got married to his college sweetheart. Within three years, there's two kids, a boy and a girl. Gansett worked at a financial services firm in Boston, and the young family lived in Dedham, a wealthy suburb. The guy did very well for himself; this was in the dot-com era on Wall Street, and Gansett made a killing. Um, financially. We'll get to the actual killing part in a bit."

Lewis paused to sip from a bottled water, and I settled into one of the office-type chairs next to him and repeated my question. "Sounds like he had it made. So, what happened?"

"Remember that college sweetheart? She was Israeli. Summer vacation, August 2001, she took her kids to Jerusalem to visit their grandparents, and they were killed in a terror attack at a pizza place."

"Was Gansett there? Did he survive or see it happen?"

Lewis shook his head. "No. Gansett was in Boston but must have flown over there as soon as he learned of the tragedy. Because this is where it gets interesting. I don't have actual evidence yet, but there's a very strong circumstantial link. Guess who the CIA station chief in Tel Aviv was at the time?"

I raised an eyebrow. "I'm betting all my chips, and I'm going all-in on Hazel Ginachere."

"That's an aggressive bet. You must be really confident."

"This all happened in Jerusalem? In 2001?"

"Uh, yeah," Lewis confirmed. "September 11th happened only a month later, so here in the States, that attack didn't get much press. But obviously, it got Gansett's attention."

"That's not my point," I said, correcting Lewis.

I looked at him carefully. He was in deep with me on this case, and I couldn't think of a reason not to reveal the connection that he'd just established. "Sullivan told us a story about Ginachere running an op in Damascus sometime in 2014, which I think had to do with that bombing in Jerusalem three years prior. Ginachere erred badly, though. She had the wrong target, a case of mistaken identity. There was a cover-up afterward, of course, but it was Ginachere's hand that resulted in the murder of an innocent man and woman. Spouses. Or, rather, Ginachere ordered the hit. It was Gansett who did the wet work."

The Intelligence Analyst whistled.

I leaned back in the office chair and crossed my legs. "Let me summarize. The working theory is that Gansett crosses paths with Ginachere in Israel back in '01. The CIA chief realizes that this guy mourning his family is an Army vet and an expert sharpshooter of independent means. His life as he knew it is ruined. He's angry and bitter, disconsolate. She recruits him. She used him three years later, and—guess what—he used snake venom to poison a target. Does that sound familiar?"

Lewis finally put his pen on the desk surface. "I think it's definitely plausible."

"It's difficult not to feel sorry for Gansett," I murmured. "Nor is it too far of a stretch to see why he would be loyal to Ginachere. Who knows what sort of other ops they've done over the last twenty years or thereabouts. That's a long relationship."

"Yeah," Lewis confirmed, somewhat unhelpfully interrupting my train of thought.

I continued, "It's going to be difficult to get Gansett to turn on two decades of loyalty. Except . . ."

Picking up his pen and clicking, Lewis asked, "Except what?"

"Why would Gansett, an Army veteran and presumably a patriot, agree to target American law enforcement? First Rourke and me, then Hamid, then Appleton, even if that shooting was intended for me?"

"Maybe he doesn't know those details? Maybe Ginachere withheld that info."

I was shaking my head back and forth even as Lewis verbalized his suggestion. "No, no, I don't think so. I mean, I'd think an assassin does research on his targets. Like, he knew where to target Hamid. He knew the pattern, and he knew Hamid's favorite coffee shop. Gansett did background work. There's no way he didn't dig into the target's history and profession."

"Uh-huh," Lewis murmured, also not helpfully.

"We gotta interview Gansett. Ask him these questions. Only he can tell us. I'm calling Havens for a status check."

I picked up my phone, and, to my immediate surprise, it began to vibrate with an incoming call notification. I glanced at the screen and was taken aback for a second, and I told Lewis as I tapped the speakerphone icon, "How 'bout that, Lewis? It's Havens. He's calling me."

CHAPTER
61

WHEN THE CALL CONNECTED, but before I could say a word, Leroy Havens's voice boomed from my phone. "Porter! I'm pulling up outside the neighbor's garage in two minutes. Get out there on the double!"

I shot to my feet. "What? Why? What's going on?"

"Gansett is in the ICU. I'm picking you up. We gotta get back over there." His tone was demanding, urgent, and yet perfectly clear. There was no invitation for discussion. It was an order.

"What? Why?" I realized I repeated myself as I ran for the tunnel.

Getting out of the bunker was a lot easier than getting in, and within ninety seconds, I pushed open the trap door in the neighbor's garage and found fresh air. Bolting outside, clutching my phone, I reached the driveway just as a pair of headlights turned into the street ahead.

An older, dusty, maroon-colored pickup truck chirped to a stop on the street; Havens didn't bother to pilot the truck into the driveway. I ran for the passenger side and slung myself aboard, and Havens hit the gas before I could close the door. He barked an update as street signs and houses flashed by. "Fifteen minutes ago." Left turn, no stop. "Gansett's vitals slowed." Right turn, then a quick left. "They called the doc." Long straightaway on Essex Street. "They brought in a crash cart, and they're running tests and triage now."

Squealing a left turn into the hospital's entrance, Havens slammed on the brakes under the Emergency portico. He clicked off the ignition key, and we ran inside.

Havens's massive form cleared a path for us to the ICU, two of his agents pointing the way for us. Reaching the obvious source of the action, a bay off the central emergency receiving area, I skidded to a stop and heard a voice say, "Congestive heart failure and atrial fibrillation."

This is all too familiar, I thought, trying to comprehend the scene.

Another voice replied, "Got it. Dosing for CHF and AFib." Then, "Five hundred micrograms Digoxin, intravenously."

I blurted, "What did you say?"

The scrubs-and-cap clad male doctor standing at the side of Gansett's gurney spun to me and snarled, "Who are you? Get outta here!" His words were said so forcefully that his surgical mask inflated and deflated.

Havens stiff-armed an orderly who was attempting to remove me as I barked at the doctor, "Did you say Digoxin?"

"Get out!"

I ignored the doctor's command as Havens kept the scrum at bay. Choosing a level and clear tone, I said clearly, "Doctor, I'm Agent Ben Porter. FBI Boston. I'm not a doctor, but this is my suspect, and I am working a case. Brief me on your diagnosis." I held the doctor's eye and added, "Please."

The doctor's face clouded for a moment, but the activity around us didn't slow. I heard the same voice from before say, "Dosing ready. Doctor? Proceed?"

"Please tell me what's going on," I urged the doctor, locking eyes with him.

He broke my stare to glance at the IV bag and at the waiting nurse who prepared to add the drug to the IV drip. To my relief, the doctor held up a hand, signaling the nurse to pause, and the doctor spoke in a fast but steady voice. "Vitals went berserk. I'm seeing signs of heart failure and arrhythmia in the EKG plot. We need to stabilize the patient."

I spun to Havens. "Was anyone at Gansett's side earlier?"

Havens eyed me. "You don't think—"

I turned to the doctor. "Were you in the patient's room?"

"No. I'm the only on-duty doctor at the moment. And you're wasting precious time."

Havens tapped his earpiece and said, "Vance. ICU. On the double."

I demanded, "Who's Vance?"

"The agent who was on duty in the room this evening."

"Did he see—"

"She," Havens corrected me.

"Whatever. Did she see anything that—"

Another figure joined the melee, and I remembered her from the duty rotation, a twenty-eight-ish-year old brunette agent. She spoke in a husky voice, "Havens, what's up?"

Havens snapped, "Vance. What was—"

"Tell me about the person in John Doe's room earlier," I interrupted. "Description. Actions."

Vance shrugged. "Tall guy. White. White hair. White mustache. White coat. Stethoscope. You know, a doctor. He flipped through the chart, examined the patient and the screens, and fiddled with the IV. Then he said something like, looks good, and he left."

"Whaddya mean, fiddled with the IV?"

"Like, I dunno. He put some more stuff in it and made sure it was flowing, I guess."

"What was in the IV bag?"

The doctor answered on behalf of Havens and Vance. "Normal drip. Fluids and electrolytes."

I stepped forward to the doctor and begged, "You gotta trust me. Hold off on the dose. Run another test or something. You'll find that he already has a high dose of Digoxin in him. More is gonna kill him."

"We already ran a tox screen," the doctor protested. "Nothing unusual."

"Yeah," I growled, "but you know that Digoxin doesn't show up in a typical, quick-response screen. Oh, and test that IV bag, too."

The monitor at Gansett's shoulder sounded with a long, steady beep, and his vitals flatlined. I ordered, "Seal this place up and find that doctor. Curtis must be here. And ignore that fucking machine."

CHAPTER
62

TWO HOURS LATER, two facts became apparent. After a locked-down, whole-building search, Doctor Curtis was nowhere to be found inside Salem Hospital. However, he left behind a clue—an inconspicuous, normal-looking, big-box-store-branded flash drive plugged into a computer at the central nurse's station.

I dearly wished that Volkov was at my side so that I could hand her the USB stick for analysis. However, we'd get it to Louis Lewis soon enough.

Havens asked, "Want me to have my team run a fingerprint scan on the flash drive?"

I shrugged. "Can't hurt, but I'm certain Curtis would be smart enough to wear gloves, which wouldn't be out of place in a setting like this hospital. You must have a fingerprint kit in your team's gear. Let's do that and then get the drive to Lewis."

A sample of Gansett's blood and the IV bag was rushed by an FBI vehicle to a lab that served Mass General Hospital in Boston. Both the blood sample and bag tested positive for Digoxin.

Gansett's condition moderated and returned to stable.

This crisis was over, but our suspect perpetrator remained at large. Havens and I commandeered two chairs in the hospital's security office in order to examine the replays of the hospital's pertinent camera footage.

It was easy to spot the tall, white-haired doctor as he sauntered into the building three hours earlier, carrying himself with the confidence of someone who was not only comfortable in his surroundings but also who would have been assumed to have every right to stroll the halls.

I commented to Havens, "I'm kicking myself for not anticipating this. I should have seen it coming. But everything happened so quickly. My accident, meeting up with Appleton, the shooting at the restaurant." My voice trailed off.

Havens attempted to console me. "The fog of war, my friend. When the hits keep coming at you, sometimes you miss something."

"Yeah, I suppose. Another lesson to learn." I shook my head, annoyed at myself, and whined, "When I gave you the picture of Gansett, it never occurred to me to include a photo of Curtis. You could have put that out to your team, Curtis would have been spotted on the security cameras, and there would have been an excellent chance we'd be face-to-face with the doctor right now."

"Don't Monday-morning-quarterback it, man," Havens advised.

I barely heard him as I thought about what I had just said. *Face-to-face. Wait!*

I bolted out of my chair in front of the security monitors. Quizzically, Havens rose slowly, wondering, "Porter?"

"Follow me," I demanded.

At a brisk pace, I stepped outside into the unseasonably warm, end-of-March night air and found Appleton's pickup truck where Havens had left it. I climbed into the driver's seat. Havens took the shotgun side and asked, "Where are we going?"

"Nowhere, yet. I wanted a secure place to talk," I responded, fumbling with the encrypted phone that Volkov gave me. I placed my device between Havens and me on the middle of the bench seat, screen up, speakerphone icon lit, and we waited for the call to be answered.

"Appleton." *That must be a habit,* I thought, as she quickly added, seeing the contact information that we had programmed the night before, "Hey, Porter."

"Are you clear to talk? Where are you?"

"I'm an hour out of D.C. in Churchton, Maryland."

Havens and I, momentarily distracted, together sang, "Where?"

"I'm in my Suburban, and I'm canvassing the area around Ginachere's house on the Maryland waterfront just south of Annapolis. What's going on?"

"I'm with Havens. You're on speaker. Take me off that Suburban's Bluetooth."

We heard rustling, and then Appleton's tinnier voice said, "That's quite a security precaution."

"Everything has changed," I replied, with a knot in my throat. "We can't trust anyone."

Havens leaned toward me, his eyebrows raised and his squint obvious as Appleton murmured, "That's ominous, but you'll have to be more specific."

I began. "A couple of hours ago, there was an attempt on Gansett. It followed almost exactly the same scenario as what happened to Hamid. Gansett was given an illicit dose of Digoxin in his IV bag, the vitals monitor freaked out, and they were going to give him more Digoxin—the killing dose—when I intervened." I pursed my lips and concluded, "It was Curtis. Doctor Curtis is in Salem."

I heard Appleton's voice whisper, "But . . ." before her voice trailed off, leaving only silence.

Shaking my head morosely, I spoke again. "Other than the three of us on this call, only two other individuals know that the John Doe patient in Salem is really JJ Gansett. One of those people is the woman we are working for: Genevieve Sullivan. And the other is our Attorney General, Bart Williams."

CHAPTER

63

"REPORT?"

"The operation failed."

There was silence on the scratchy connection. Not only did the voice-altering software create latency, but also the circuitous route the packets made as they bounced around the world from one internet node to another resulted in lags. This delay, however, was too long to be computer-generated.

Finally, the voice boomed, "Explain."

"My revised and updated protocol proceeded flawlessly. I dosed the patient. The hospital staff reacted they should have been expected to react. It was perfect, until there was an intervention that could not have been foreseen."

"An intervention?"

"Yes. Porter showed up. He's clearly figured it out. He stopped the final dose, even though I triggered the vitals machine to report the patient in severe distress."

"Outrageous. This is outrageous," the voice repeated angrily. "This is going to fall apart. There's too much time to kill before the real strike, and there's not enough killing happening. First, Gansett failed. Then you. It's time to escalate this to the professionals."

"To whom?"

The voice spat, "That's not your concern. I have vast resources, and perhaps I should have used them—instead of relying on you. It's obvious to me now that it was my error for keeping the circle tight. However, make no mistake, Doctor Curtis. I will not hesitate to employ those professionals to assure your demise, should you disappoint me again."

Curtis fidgeted in the driver's seat of the rented car, involuntarily beginning to sweat but gathering strength from the view out the windshield. "I have just as much to gain—and to lose—as you. And I assure you; not only is my loyalty to our collaboration uncompromised, but also that this was my protocol and my design, and I will see it through. Furthermore, recall that with Gansett out, it is only I who has the expertise to deliver the final strike in Riyadh, and I am committed to that course."

"Porter needs to be removed, first. Otherwise, we're not going to make it to Riyadh."

Curtis scoffed. "We planned for that eventuality. Not, specifically, for Porter, but for a scenario to dispose of the protocol."

"Don't you dare," seethed the voice. "I'm beginning to doubt your effectiveness."

Wiping his brow with a sleeve, Curtis regained his composure. Sitting erect in the motionless vehicle, he spat, "Don't underestimate me. We're partners on this, and I'll pretend that you didn't say that. For now, I'll also pretend that you didn't threaten me a moment ago."

There was a soft crack of static. "That's better, Doctor. Some courage."

Reminding himself of the dual end games, Curtis replied, "All is not lost. I'm sending you a link."

"To what?"

"I borrowed a method from Gansett. I saw Porter and a Black man arrive at the hospital in a red pickup truck. When I took my leave of the place, I planted an Air Tag on the truck. We'll be able to track the truck."

"A pleasant surprise. Finally."

"I'm not finished. I've got a disguise, and since it's dark, I'm comfortable that even if Porter has asked for help in locating me, assuming he's watched the hospital's security footage, I'm safe for now. In fact, I'm parked across from the hospital now. Porter and the

Black man are sitting in the truck at this very moment. I'll keep an eye on them."

"Send me a photo along with the link, please."

"Will do," Curtis replied, relieved to have the tone of the conversation move from conflict to cooperation. "Anything else?"

"No. I'll assemble a team to target Porter and his accomplice. If that fails for whatever reason, we activate the alternate plan. Monday morning. Agreed?"

"Yes," Curtis replied.

"We need to move quickly. Time is of the essence." The connection went silent, and Curtis realized that it was not a delay in transmission but that the call disconnected.

The doctor balanced an iPhone on the steering wheel of the rental and stabilized it for a low-light photo, aiming the lens at the maroon-colored pickup truck. He tapped the shutter icon not a moment too soon, as the headlights of the truck blinked on, the brake lights flared, and the truck began to move.

CHAPTER
64

SINCE IT WAS ME sitting behind the wheel of the maroon pickup, I figured I'd begin the drive. I started the truck, switched on the headlights, and Havens and I set off to Washington.

The truck purred. Its automatic transmission cycled through the gears smoothly, and there was not a rattle to be heard. I called to Appleton, still on speakerphone, "This truck rides beautifully. What is it, again?"

Appleton's voice replied, "A 2002 Ford F-250. Don't let the age or exterior condition confuse you. It is literally perfect mechanically. No expense spared."

"Nice toy," Havens said.

Appleton chuckled. "It's my bug-out truck. You know, in case of the apocalypse or whatever. Or if I need to be incognito. Oddly, a big ole truck is a pretty good disguise. No one takes any notice of it."

Havens asked, "How long is the drive?"

"Usually a bit over eight hours," Appleton said. "But it's what, after eleven at night? You won't hit any traffic. You should be in D.C. by seven in the morning."

Havens grumbled, "And then what?" I could sense that he didn't like the plan, what little of it there was. Havens preferred contingencies and backup plans.

Appleton chuckled dryly, and then she said in a mean voice. "And then we have a decision to make. How do we unravel this thing? Because we're being double-crossed by either Genevieve Sullivan or by Bart Williams. I don't know about you, but I don't like being a pawn in someone's game."

Don't mess with Jennifer Appleton, I thought. *No one, ever, has gotten away with that for any length of time.*

Wait. *Time.*

Trying to do the math in my head while also driving the unfamiliar truck, I asked the windshield, "Can we conference in Lewis?"

"I can," Appleton replied. "Why?"

"Just do it, please," I begged in a distracted voice.

Eight hours.

I heard rustling from Appleton's connection and then the sharp voice of Louis Lewis. "What's going on? Porter? Havens?"

Remembering that Lewis was in the dark, so to speak, inside the underground bunker, I rattled off a situation report. "Here's a quick sitrep. Curtis made an attempt on Gansett a couple of hours ago. Havens and I caught on and intervened. Gansett will survive. Curtis is on the lam."

"Curtis?" Lewis sounded incredulous.

"Yeah," I shot back. "Here's what I need you to do, Lewis. Get the manifest of every shuttle flight out of D.C. this afternoon. Make Logan in Boston your priority, but also check flights to New York, Providence, and Hartford. See if Curtis was on any of those flights."

"I can do that," the techie confirmed. "It'll take a couple of hours, though."

"That's fine. You'll have to dig deeper, though. Run a facial recognition scan at those airports, too, in the event Curtis has another identity."

"That will take considerably longer. Six hours, probably."

"Porter," Appleton interrupted, "I'm not following. Why?"

"Hang on," I requested. "Lewis, two hours plus six hours, or you can do both tasks in six hours?"

I heard the analyst's nasally laugh. "You don't think I can run two investigations at once? With the computing power in this bunker, no problem. Six hours total and I'm already getting started."

"Good. Because you've got no more than eight hours."

"Porter!" Appleton exclaimed, her voice stern and cold.

Don't mess with Appleton, I reminded myself.

"Sorry, ma'am. Lewis needs to get going. You see, you said it earlier. The drive to Washington is around eight hours. Let's work backward. The first hit on Gansett, the dose in the IV bag, was between roughly 8:15 P.M. and 8:45 P.M. or so. Havens called me at 8:50. I was just off a call with Sara Lin, the attorney that the AG recommended."

"What'd she say?" Appleton interrupted again.

"Not important right now. I'll come back to that. Anyway, think through the timing. We talked to Bart Williams at 3:00 P.M. and told him who the John Doe really was. If he hung up and dispatched Curtis, there's no way Curtis could have driven to Salem in that amount of time. It's impossible. And, honestly, I think it's really unlikely that he managed to grab a flight that lined up with that window. But we need to know whether to eliminate that as a possibility."

"You've already shortened my work time," Lewis called. "I can narrow down the commercial flights to those departing later than 3:00 P.M., and I can also track private flights from the D.C. area to the Boston area. Even those planes have to declare their passenger manifests, and the FBOs—Fixed Base Operations—where they come and go to will have cameras. In short, if Curtis flew, I'll find him."

"Good work, Porter," Appleton said, the edge gone from her voice. "If that's the case, and Curtis did not travel from D.C. to the Boston area this afternoon, we can eliminate the Attorney General as our suspect."

"Exactly," I confirmed, "leaving Genevieve Sullivan. You listened in as I talked to her last night. Plenty of time to dispatch Curtis from D.C. to Salem."

"Hmm," Appleton murmured. "Still, it's too circumstantial. We need a way to actually pin Sullivan. Gansett is out for the count, and

Curtis is no doubt hiding in the shadows. We'll find him, I suppose, but eventually. And I don't get the sense that eventually is going to cut it."

"I know," I mumbled. I felt that the pieces were slowly coming into focus, but we weren't there yet.

In investigation work, you never know where the next clue comes from. I was about to find it in a place that would become obvious.

CHAPTER
65

AFTER DISCONNECTING THE CALL with Appleton, Havens and I rode in silence in the big F-250. I knew, and I think that Havens knew, that the enormity of our task was looming. Cruising at 70 mph on the mostly deserted Mass Pike at midnight, I felt . . . lonely.

I missed my team. Don't get me wrong, Appleton and Havens were fantastic partners. But Lockwood I counted as a true friend, a mentor. Macallister, who at one time was my office nemesis, became a trusted and reliable colleague, and I think he felt the same about me. And Volkov may have been a traitor to me and to my family, but with humility and perseverance, she redeemed herself.

Perseverance.

That was a word Curtis used to describe my investigation.

There's a fine line between perseverance and stubbornness. The former trait is often lauded as admirable. The latter is seen more negatively.

As the mile markers flashed by, reflected in the Ford's headlights, I realized that my perseverance to prove myself often manifested itself as stubbornness.

Rourke was the first victim of my stubbornness to prove myself—to solve the next case. She was a victim of my hubris when I agreed to Genevieve Sullivan's task, last August.

Then it was Hamid who paid the price for my drive.

And then—*Almaz*. My team.

All gone, because, if we were correct in our assumption, we had been duped.

No, rewind that. *I* had been played. By Genevieve Sullivan.

That not only saddened me to the point of guilty heartbreak, but it also pissed me off.

The little woman was so eager, so energetic . . . so righteous. I believed every word that she said, but now I questioned it all.

But why? What the hell was this all about?

Stealing a glance at Havens, I saw his eyes were closed. Based on our prior missions together, I figured he wasn't asleep, but instead possibly meditating. He calmed himself as he thought through strengths, weaknesses, opportunities, and threats. I needed his counsel, and I dared to interrupt the motionless giant. "Havens?"

"Yeah, man?"

"Thoughts?"

Havens guffawed from deep in his belly. "Where do I start in to unpack this shitshow?"

It was my turn to laugh. "Let's dive in. Sullivan. What the hell?"

"Nah, man, I'm the ops guy. You're the thinker. That's on you. I'm working on a way outta this. Like Appleton said, we gotta figure out how to get evidence. Facts. The why of it all is less important to me at the moment. I'm working on the how."

I thought that over. Good advice as always from Leroy Havens. I was rushing to the end game; he was conceptualizing the plays that needed to happen before we got that far. I needed to slow down. *One foot, then the other,* I chastised myself.

Havens closed his eyes again. I got the message; he wanted to think, not talk.

I-90, I-84, I-91, I-95. The interstate highway emblems blurred through my heavy eyelids. I drove the reverse of this route less than a week ago. I didn't need navigation on a phone or a paper map. I knew where I was going—on the roadways, at least.

The Ford, which didn't have a full tank of fuel when we departed Salem, was nearing empty. I found a rest stop on the New Jersey Turnpike and pulled up to a pump.

"I'll take over the driving," Havens offered.

"Thanks," I replied with relief. I was also running on empty, so to speak, so I suggested to Havens, "Can you run inside and grab us some coffees and snacks? I'll fill the truck."

"Sure," he said as he swung open the passenger door and disappeared.

I stood just behind the open driver's door, dispensing fuel into the truck's fill receptacle recessed into the Ford's dirty left side flank. My mind went blank with the monotonous but entirely instinctive task.

Turns out that was fortuitous. I stopped thinking about the case and began to observe my surroundings. I idly watched the numbers tick up on the pump's display, and my thoughts, once jumbled, began to feel more orderly. My brain had been bogged down with dead ends. The simple act of filling that fuel tank reset me.

Havens appeared, hefting two coffee cups and pinching the top of a brown paper bag between two fingers. He gracefully perched himself in the driver's seat as I dropped the fuel fill nozzle back in the pump, calling to Havens, "I'm gonna hit the head. Be right back."

He mouthed an acknowledgement as he slammed his door shut while I trotted around the backside of the Ford—and in my newly-found state of awareness, a synapse in my brain jolted. I looked down.

Down at the truck's trailer hitch receiver.

Sure enough, I saw a glint of white.

I knelt. I saw a clean, white disc, somehow affixed to the inside bottom ledge of the metal box-shaped hitch receiver.

I straightened and made for the passenger door, pulling it open to Havens's surprise. "That was too fast. You change your mind?"

"We're being tracked, I think. Just like you discovered on my Tahoe. Have a look to confirm, please. I'm going inside," I replied calmly.

Seven minutes later, we rolled onto the southbound Jersey Turnpike, Havens saying, "I'm no fool. I checked over the truck before I took it from that garage. That thing wasn't there in the hitch."

"Therefore, it was planted after you arrived at the hospital and before we departed Salem. That window of time was three hours. Four hours tops."

"Curtis," we chorused.

"Has to be," Havens said.

"Not necessarily," I proposed. "He could have an accomplice."

Havens grumbled, "Maybe. But does it matter? Game it out."

I nodded. "Gansett tracked me from D.C. to Salem. To Appleton's house. Maybe Gansett tracked me around D.C. and knew what I did there. But in whatever case, he made an attempted hit on me, or Appleton, in Salem. I told Sullivan on Thursday night that it was Gansett in the hospital and that his hit failed. Sullivan sends Curtis to Salem. In the hours after his attempt on Gansett, he could have planted the tracker on this truck." I re-thought the sequence and added, "Hell, when you picked me up, and we raced back to the hospital, the truck was sitting right in front of the emergency entrance. Curtis could have seen us get out of it."

"Plausible," agreed Havens. "Which means that Curtis—or Sullivan, I guess—is going to know that we just stopped on the Turnpike, and they'll locate the truck in D.C. eventually. We need to ditch this truck."

My mind was no longer blank. Just the opposite. A plan inspired by Appleton was coming together. I mumbled, "Hold that thought. Just keep driving."

Havens turned his entire head to me, taking his eyes off the road. "What are you up to, Porter?"

"Honestly, I'm not sure yet. But I do know this: when Appleton suggested that we draw out the assassin, she said something like, 'our only option is to turn the tables.' We might have just gotten that opportunity. All I need is a little time to figure it out."

There it was again.

Time.

I hoped I'd have enough.

CHAPTER
66

SATURDAY, MARCH 27, 2021

WITH A DEFT, expert touch, Havens parallel-parked the maroon F-250 a block north and east from Appleton's Georgetown hideaway on 28th Street Northwest. Maneuvering the big truck through the narrow D.C. streets was challenging enough; slotting the beast against the curb was a notable achievement, in my mind.

We dismounted and stretched our legs, having made the drive from Salem in just about eight hours, including the hiatus of our one brief stop on the Jersey Turnpike and accounting for a handful of roadwork slowdowns during the overnight drive. Havens checked his watch. "It's 7:30 in the morning. Appleton said she'd be back from her recon run at Ginachere's place by 8:00. Let's get some breakfast."

I checked the map on my phone. "Three blocks south and one west, and we'll find M Street Northwest. We'll find something to eat there."

It was shaping up to be a beautiful, early spring day in Washington, with fair skies and with the air temperature already exceeding fifty degrees at this hour. A balmy, seventy-degree Saturday was forecast. As we strolled south, with the greening lawns and budding trees of Rose Creek Park to our left, it was difficult not to be in a good mood.

That is, until a white van, traveling north on 27th Street Northwest, screeched to a stop beside us. The van's right-side cargo door slid open, and four big men wearing balaclavas leapt to the pavement.

Three of them aimed for Havens.

One ran toward me, and I bolted, spinning on the balls of my feet. As I sprinted into the park, I almost nosedived onto a brick-paved pathway as I caught a toe on the curb, costing me valuable seconds that wouldn't matter.

Arms pumping and legs churning, I made for the stand of trees at the opposite perimeter of the park's lawn area. Behind me, in between my huffs of breath, I heard panting.

Racing by a tree, I tripped on a root and stumbled. That was all it took.

Powerful hands lunged at my shoulders as I tried to regain my balance, and I was tackled from behind. I stretched my arms out just in time to break my fall into the dirt at the base of the tree. My head dropped, and I tried to turn my face, my left cheek dragging around the rough mulch. In the distance, I could just make out the commotion on the sidewalk; Havens and now five men, with two more running toward me.

I tried to fight back, but I was winded, out of shape, and exhausted from several sleepless nights. My efforts were weak as I tried to yank at the balaclava that shielded my foe's face. He—I'm certain it was a he, given the body shape and size—swatted my hand away without exerting any apparent effort.

With my head pressed into the dirt, I attempted to coil my legs and kick. Pathetic. I was overpowered.

The two reinforcements reached us, and I could see that one was dragging a sack of some sort while the other whipped out a small box from a cargo pant thigh pocket.

As I struggled, flailing and twisting and turning to no avail, hands and knees pressed me into on the soil, immobilizing my arms and legs. Out of the corner of my right eye, I saw the man with the box flip it open and withdraw a syringe.

Shit.

There was nothing I could do as a burlap-y feeling sack was drawn over my head and eyes, turning my world to a muddy, brown, featureless fuzz.

Then I felt the sting of a needle, driven through my pants into my right buttock.

My heart sank. In a prior operation, I oversaw an injection like this, and I guessed what was about to happen. I counted, desperately trying to keep my focus. *One... Two...*

Nothing.

CHAPTER 67

IT WAS DARK, but not burlap-bag dark, I realized. It was merely the absence of light—but as my eyes focused and adjusted to my dim surroundings, I pieced it together.

I'd been here before. Or, at least, a similar place.

The smells—faintly acrid. The sounds—hushed, except for a persistent *beep beep beep*. And the light, what little there was, came from a screen mounted on a gray arm just above my left shoulder—the familiar, multi-colored, oddly pulsating glow of a vitals monitoring machine.

A hospital.

That was the plan—the trap that I wanted to set. A lure for my foe, facilitated by my discovery of the tracking device on the Ford. If I was being followed electronically, I could lead them where I wanted. At least, that was the plan as Havens and I plotted it as we drove south to Washington and to our rendezvous with Appleton.

We'd take the upper hand. We'd take control. We'd bring them to us.

Until the attack. That was not anticipated. Which meant—

Sullivan was still ahead of me.

It doesn't matter. I'm still alive. For now.

I could still fight back. I needed to prepare.

I'd find out the truth soon enough.

CHAPTER

68

THE SHAPE MATERIALIZED like a ghost, white-clad and furtive, stealing into the room on soft soles, with a practiced confidence. The door closed with a muffled thump-click noise.

With nary a sound, the shape moved to my left.

My right eyelid remained closed, and through the fuzzy slit created by my left eyelashes, I watched the shape—a man—approach my bed.

This could be it.

I froze. I couldn't give up the advantage that had been given to me. I didn't know how, yet, but there were enough clues to know that the plan was in motion—

Stop. Focus. Don't overthink.

I held my breathing to slow, even breaths, but my heart was racing. I wouldn't be able to sustain the ruse much longer.

The white-clad shape loomed over me, and through the slit of my eyelids, through the blur of eyelashes and in the gloom of the room, I caught sight of a perfectly trimmed white mustache.

Doctor Curtis!

Apparently satisfied with his cursory exam of my still form, Curtis straightened and took a pace toward the stainless-steel tree at the head of the bed.

He tapped at the IV bag slung from a branch of the tree.

He withdrew a syringe. He tapped at the syringe.

Then, carefully, precisely, he injected the contents of the syringe into the port on the bag, his thumb making slow, steady pressure on the plunger.

Withdrawing the instrument, he snapped a protective cover on the needle and slipped the assembly into his pocket, tapping again on the bulbous IV bag and turning away slightly.

Now!

With a single motion, I ripped the bedsheet off my body with my right hand, casting the flimsy material to the side. Clad in athletic shorts and a white t-shirt, I sprang from the bed, the tube from the fake peripheral intravenous catheter that was adhered to my right arm whipping about like a snake.

With my left arm, I snagged Curtis around his neck, my sudden movement taking him utterly by surprise, and I dragged his frame down to the linoleum floor. He collapsed to his knees but began to struggle.

I had laid in the bed too long, and my muscles were slow to react. The taller doctor would soon have the physical advantage. I needed to create a diversion, and through gritted teeth, I hissed, "What's in the syringe, Doc?"

"*Oomph.*" The doctor grunted as he used the leverage of longer legs, torso, and arms to push me away. "You'll be dead too soon to care," he grunted.

He didn't notice that the IV was fake and unconnected, I realized. And then, I knew what to do.

"Oh, because of your injection?" My tone mocked him as I grabbed the tube of the fake IV line. "Because it's not connected, you fool!" I yanked the tape on my arm free, and in a split second I was able to whip the tube around his throat.

I pulled both ends of the tube, tightening it against his jugular and airway.

My improvised garrote wouldn't choke him, but it sure as hell spooked him. "*Echhh,*" he gasped, lifting a hand to pull the irritating tube clear.

That was what I needed. With his mind focused on his neck, I lunged my shoulders against his torso and drove him to the floor.

Finally, I enjoyed a benefit to being slightly overweight, and I used my mass to crush him to the floor. "You're done, Curtis. I know what you've been up to. I know about the Digoxin and spoofing the vitals monitoring systems."

I inadvertently released pressure on the tubular garrote, and Curtis sensed the opening. He squirmed as he rasped, "Not so fast, Porter!"

I lifted myself up and then allowed my entire mass to drop on his chest with a thump. My amateurish wrestling move would have been a joke on a mat, but here on the hard, slick, linoleum hospital floor, it created the desired effect as the air was driven from Curtis's lungs. "That was for Rourke." I did it again. "For Hamid." And again. "For *Almaz*."

The fire went out from Curtis's eyes, and they fluttered.

I needed to wrap this up. I knew the plan was in motion given the garb I was wearing, provided earlier by a stealthy Raven. I left Curtis wheezing on the floor and poked my head cautiously out the room's door. I risked calling loudly, "Havens? Raven?"

The massive form of a similarly clad Havens materialized from the adjoining room, and he barged past me. Curtis would prove to be no match for the giant CIRG agent, and within seconds, Havens lifted the doctor and twisted him to face the floor.

With Havens holding the doctor perfectly still, I felt for the offending syringe in the right pocket of the doctor's white lab coat. It seemed intact, and relieved, I called, in a quieter voice than the one I had just employed, "Raven?"

The nurse glided into the room and grinned widely, her white teeth almost glowing in the darkened confines of the room. "This is definitely going to be the most interesting day I've ever had at work," she whispered with a soft chuckle.

"I bet," I replied. "Pull this out and secure it," I requested, showing her the outline of the syringe in the coat. She knelt and extracted the syringe with a gloved hand. Standing, the nurse turned to the IV pole and twisted the valve atop the bag, stopping the drip of the liquid contents. Raven squatted to reach under the bed, where she retrieved the plastic bottle that had actually received the IV drip, ensuring that none of the liquid leaked to the shiny floor. "That's evidence," I said, pretty much unnecessarily. From her careful motions, I knew that Raven was not going to let anything happen to the tainted IV bag or syringe.

Before the nurse could speak, a fourth shape appeared in the doorway. From my position on the floor, straddling the unmoving doctor's legs, my eyes moved upward, taking in black boots, then trim black pants, then a black turtleneck, and then to auburn hair pulled back in a ponytail with a black elastic.

The woman knelt at the side of the prone doctor, and leaning close to his ear, she lilted in a clear voice, "Doctor Curtis, my name is Jennifer Appleton. Federal Bureau of Investigation, Special Agent in Charge, Boston Division Field Office. You're under arrest, Doctor."

CHAPTER
69

SPEED BECAME an absolute necessity. We needed a cleaner, our very own Winston Wolfe. Fortunately, Appleton thought of that, too. I couldn't wait to debrief with her; that opportunity would come soon.

After reciting—from memory, of course, no note cards required—the doctor's Miranda rights, Appleton lifted her right hand to her mouth and spoke into a tiny wrist-mounted microphone. "Paxton. Now, please. Porter's room." I noticed, then, that a tiny, coiled, black wire led from the inside of her turtleneck to her right ear. Appleton was wired for comms.

Curtis was wiggling under the combined hold of Havens and me, and I glanced at the big CIRG agent. He tilted his head to our captive. "You say one word, it's gonna be lights out. Got it?"

I could see the doctor attempt to nod in the affirmative, and I let go, trusting Havens to do whatever it was that he needed to do. Havens allowed Curtis to sit up; meanwhile, Raven retreated from the doctor, toward the closed door, still tugging on the IV pole and carrying the plastic bottle and syringe. She looked significantly less enthusiastic than she was a few moments ago, and I sensed that she was frightened. "Hang tight, Raven," I whispered.

She flinched at a tap on the door, but Appleton, cocking her head as if she was listening to her earpiece, said, "It's okay, Raven. It's my man. He's gonna open the door."

Swishing open, the door jamb revealed a red-headed pale man, tall
and skinny, with a spotty ginger beard, the unruliness of the facial hair
contrasted with a well-tailored gray suit, and a fastidiously Windsor-
knotted necktie patterned with American flags. It was his boots, though,
that were perhaps most remarkable, but now, I thought, was probably
not an appropriate time to talk about footwear. "Let's git goin'," he
drawled in a Southern accent, extracting zip ties and a roll of black duct
tape from the small, tan satchel that he carried. He passed the items
to Havens while instructing, "Pull the perp's arms out of his sleeves,
then zip 'em behind his back and drape that lab coat back on 'im. He a
talkative fellow?"

I decided to answer that question. "I don't know about that, but I do
know that he is not trustworthy."

"Fair nuff." The red head knelt on one knee and addressed Curtis.
"My name is Paxton Parr. My specialty is sanitation. As in, cleanin' up
somebody else's mess. Now, we can do this the hard, sticky way—" Parr
tapped at the roll of tape that he had handed to Havens— "or you can
decide to keep your trap closed on your own. Which one will it be?"

Curtis stammered, "I—I—I'll be quiet." His eyes, however, darted
down and away from Parr's gaze.

Parr clucked his tongue. "Now, see, ace, that was a trick question.
'Cuz you just opened your mouth. Shoulda just nodded or somethin'.
And I can sense that you're lyin' to me." Parr motioned his head at
Havens. "Secure his arms and tape his mouth." He stood. "But—change
of plan. We're gonna git him disrobed, first."

Disrobed? I thought.

It became clear in a few minutes, with Parr working efficiently,
first getting our names, and then ordering Appleton, Havens, Raven,
and me to accomplish various tasks, his drawl soft but direct. Once his
preparations were complete, he gave us our stage directions and then said,
"Miz Appleton, let's go borrow us an ambulance. Your badge may come
in handy. And you three—take our patient down the elevator and meet us
at the emergency entrance. Give us a three-minute head start."

Parr and Appleton exited. Three minutes later, we wheeled the
hospital bed through the door with Curtis mostly covered by the sheets.

His duct-taped mouth was snuggled almost invisibly in a mound of pillows. A strategically positioned blanket and sheets hid his limbs—because those legs and arms were zip-tied to the rails of the gurney.

I pulled at the foot of the gurney, leading the procession to the elevator. I was dressed in Curtis's pants and shirt, the pants rolled up at my ankles and taped in place, the shirt fitting loosely on my shoulders and tightly at my gut. Close enough. His shoes were two sizes too big for me, and my feet clomped on the shiny floors awkwardly.

At the opposite end, near the head of the bed, Raven wheeled the IV pole, the non-flowing IV tube itself taped to Curtis under the sheets.

With a hand on a rail, Havens guided the gurney from the side. He wore the doctor's white lab coat, complete with a stethoscope dangling around his neck. The only obvious fault in our rudimentary disguise was his legs, still, bare from the hem of the long coat to his bare feet, but we assumed that the bulk of the gurney would mask that discrepancy, and together we ensured that Havens was positioned close to a wall as much as possible.

Exiting the elevator on the ground floor, the layout of the GW Hospital now familiar to me, we wheeled Curtis to the maw of a waiting ambulance and slid the gurney inside. Parr was at the wheel and drawled, "Appleton is meeting us in Georgetown. Let's roll, folks."

With that, we kidnapped Doctor Curtis, soon to be our star witness.

Or so we thought.

CHAPTER 70

THE GEORGETOWN STREETS were dark and desolate as we pulled up at the address, a compact, red-brick, two-story, single-family home. Inside the back of the ambulance, Havens and Raven released Curtis from the zip ties that bound him to the gurney. Havens manhandled a shivering, underwear-clad Curtis to Appleton, waiting in the doorway of the home.

I turned to the nurse to shake her hand, but she responded with a hug. I said with as much sincerity as I could, "Thank you. I'm still not sure how Appleton pulled this off, but I'm so glad she found you. I'm certain one of us will be in touch."

Raven released the hug and looked me in the eye. "I take my job very seriously, as I think you know by now." She grinned wryly, but then her expression turned cold. "That guy, Curtis, does not deserve to be practicing medicine."

"I couldn't agree more." We said our goodbyes, and I circled the ambulance to join Parr, who was standing in the street outside of the open driver's side door of the ambulance. "Mister Parr, that was quite a show. Well done."

"Mah pleasure," drawled the red-headed Southerner.

I couldn't help myself. "I gotta ask you somethin'," I said, unconsciously slipping into a bit of a drawl myself. "Your boots. They're, ah, quite impressive."

Parr chuckled. "'Gator. Wrestled it mah-self." He lifted a foot and angled the boot to the side, catching the light on the shiny, patterned material. "Now, normally, I respect all creatures unless they've wronged me." Setting his foot back down on the pavement, he raised his left hand—it was missing its pinkie and ring fingers. "That particular alligator and I tussled due to a disagreement. I'd tell you the story, but it would take too much time, and we don't have the appropriate libations to properly enjoy it."

I laughed. "I look forward to that opportunity, Mister Parr."

"Miz Appleton told me that I'd enjoy your company, Porter. I dunno what you're up to, but if you ever need a paw . . ." He let that invitation hang for a moment as he waved his three-fingered hand gently.

I replied, "Well, Parr, something tells me that our paths will cross again."

He smiled as he hopped up into the ambulance and closed the door. I stepped back, and Parr drove away to return our borrowed ambulance, our borrowed gurney, and our borrowed Raven to the GW Hospital. I stepped inside the red-brick house and immediately recognized the wood-paneled library where I'd seen Appleton and the Attorney General on the video conference only days before.

Appleton was pacing, and she turned to face me as I closed the door behind me. "Porter."

"Care to catch me up?"

"Let's give Havens a bit more time to join us. He's getting Curtis settled upstairs," the SAC replied.

"Fine. Speaking of time, what time is it, anyway? What day?"

"It's Sunday night. Or, actually, about three in the morning on Monday."

Monday? Havens and I arrived in D.C. on Saturday morning, I thought.

"We've been out and off-grid for two days?" My voice was incredulous.

Appleton's response was succinct and direct. "Yes."

My shoulders sagged. Appleton pointed to a sofa, and I sank into it, asking, "Any news or progress on locating *Almaz*?"

"I'm afraid not. No news. Though, to be fair, I was immediately concerned when Havens and you were attacked. That became my priority."

Havens appeared and descended the stair before I could comment. "Curtis is out cold. Raven dosed him with a sedative before we got out of the bus. It's taken full effect. He's not going anywhere for several hours."

"Good," Appleton agreed. "I brewed coffee. We have a lot to discuss. Notably and most pressing, what our next steps will be."

Havens shook his head and repeated my sentiment. "Not yet. Why did you fast-forward our plan? It would have been nice to know about the hit instead of being surprised like that," he grumbled accusingly in an exasperated voice. "I thought we agreed to stage an attack in order to get Porter into a hospital and then leak that to Sullivan to draw her out with Curtis."

Appleton chuckled mirthlessly. "That was the plan, yes. Entrap Curtis."

"The attack on Saturday morning wasn't your doing?" I had my suspicions when I was in the hospital, and I hoped Appleton would clarify the situation.

She did, but not as I expected.

"No. I had nothing to do with it," Appleton confessed. "Therefore, it appears that Sullivan beat us to the punch. Um, no pun intended." Appleton paused. "I'll be right back with coffee."

Havens eyed me. "I'm not making this up, am I? After the stop on the Turnpike, when you realized we were being tracked, we called Appleton and came up with the scheme to try and trap Curtis. You gave Appleton Raven's number. You told Appleton that we'd meet her at eight in the morning on Saturday."

"Yeah," I confirmed, "and now it's 3:00 A.M. on Monday. That means—"

"That means you were out for almost two days." Appleton reappeared and set down a tray of three steaming coffee mugs as she began to fill in the blanks in the narrative. "You were drugged, presumably to allow Curtis time to get in position. Raven and the other nurse that Porter connected me with, Bethany, were awesome. They kept an eye on both of you and kept me updated in the event something had to be changed on the fly."

"But the attack?" Havens protested.

"I watched it happen," Appleton informed us. "White van at first, then a gray sedan. Eight men, Professionals, from what I could witness. There was nothing I could do but to follow the van which took you to a service entrance at the GW Hospital." She sipped her coffee. "From the car, I started making calls. First to the Field Office in Chelsea, to undo the ruse of my death, then to Lewis. He confirmed that Curtis was not on any flights from D.C. to the Boston or New England area during the window of time you suggested, Porter. I called the AG and told him what we were up to. He looped in the Director of the FBI and got me clearance."

"That's a lot of conversation," I observed. "Timeline?"

"Hmm. By the time all the pieces were in place, it was Saturday evening. You two were spirited away in the hospital, not on any records or charts. That's when Raven got involved and tracked you down. You'd been given a fast-acting drug which paralyzed you for twenty-four hours. Thus, I figured you'd be safe from Curtis until Sunday morning."

I nodded. "That's when Raven gave me a change of clothes."

"Me, too," Havens said. "And that's when I knew that our plan was a go, somehow."

"Sullivan did us a favor," I suggested. "By taking us out, she brought Curtis to us."

Appleton grimaced. "It could have gone wrong in so many ways. If I hadn't happened to watch the takedown, the outcome could have been very different."

Havens grumbled, "Luck. Dumb luck. I hate when that's a factor."

I gulped some coffee and announced, "I have more questions. First off, why didn't they just kill us? It's so clunky to drug us and then wait for Curtis. It's like the bad guys are literally making their work harder."

I watched as Havens's eyes brightened visibly. "Amateurs. I think you're onto something, Porter. It's a poorly conceived plan, and because of that, we got lucky, like I said. That meant the SAC was able to intervene."

"True," I quickly added, "and you know who's an amateur? Not an operator? Sullivan."

Appleton was nodding. "Agreed. However, Porter, we don't know that Sullivan was behind the attack. It's the logical assumption, but we can't prove it."

"I think we can," I replied. "We need to interview one more player."

"Who's that?" Appleton asked.

"Do you have any to-go cups? Let's take our coffees and go for a drive."

CHAPTER
71

MONDAY, MARCH 29, 2021

LEAVING HAVENS BEHIND to watch over the still-unconscious Doctor Curtis in Appleton's borrowed Georgetown pied-a-terre, armed with coffee, a phone, and a Glock—you know, the usual accouterments when you stay as a guest in someone's home—Appleton and I set off for a one-hour drive in her Suburban.

The SAC was reluctant at first but warmed quickly to the idea as I fleshed it out. She agreed, "The timing is actually pretty good. By the time we get there, it will be pre-dawn on a Monday morning and well before commuting time into the Washington area."

"Exactly," I confirmed. "You think you can talk your way in?"

"Yes," Appleton replied with confidence in her voice.

And that's how we found ourselves on the doorstep of a sprawling, light gray, one-story home, dotted with dormers and adorned with teal blue shutters in Churchton, on the Maryland waterfront, just south of Annapolis, at 4:30 A.M. on a Monday morning, waiting to be greeted by the Director of the Central Intelligence Agency.

That was a bold move, eh? I was betting the farm on this. I tried not to let my nervousness show as the door swung open.

Hazel Ginachere had been woken by her security team after Appleton, with the decisiveness and charisma that I'd become accustomed to, demanded access. She displayed her credentials and my driver's license, which the CIA security men took for verification. We left the Suburban behind at Ginachere's driveway gate after being frisked ourselves. Our phones, watches, and even Appleton's jewelry were appropriated.

Frankly, it was good security, and it didn't bother the SAC or me one bit.

It also allowed Ginachere time to wake and dress. From her doorway, two steps above the landing where we waited, and wearing a severe, dark-colored pantsuit that matched her dark eyeglass frames, Ginachere examined her uninvited guests. "A matter of national security, SAC Appleton? Given your reputation, I'll entertain the notion. However, seeing Mister Porter here gives me pause."

"Director, we obviously got off on the wrong foot," I stated evenly, putting my hands respectfully behind my back. No, actually, that was because I needed to furtively wipe the sweat off my palms. "However, I did what I had to do. And I did not mean disrespect."

Ginachere snorted. "Hmmph. Be that as it may, you've got a lot of nerve showing up here. While I'll admit, reluctantly, that you were correct, in the end, you acted like an ass."

"Point taken, ma'am. I don't disagree, and I apologize."

I thought that by being disarming and humble, accepting her scolding, I might trigger at least the hint of a smile from the D/CIA, but her face remained inscrutable. She stepped to the side, pointed, and called, "Come in. Your things are over there. Collect them, and then we'll talk."

Talk we did.

The skies lightened to a gray overcast monotone, with intermittent drizzle streaking the windows of Ginachere's conservatively styled living room. In fact, it was almost sparse, and then I recalled reading, during our research on the CIA Director, that Ginachere endured a difficult divorce. *Perhaps,* I thought, *she gave up some furnishings.*

As we sat, Appleton and I on a leather sofa, Ginachere on a busily patterned slipcovered armchair, the Director called for her security team to bring coffee and pastries from the kitchen; a good sign, I guessed, since it made it clear that she was to use her word, entertaining our story. When the foodstuffs were delivered, she whispered to one of her men, "Call Langley and cancel my morning meetings."

I knew that "Langley" was not a person such as an aide, but instead was shorthand for the George Bush Center for Intelligence, the CIA headquarters building in McLean, Virginia, located within the aforementioned community of Langley and less than ten miles as the crow flies from the White House and the United States Capitol building. Ginachere's orders made it clear that the D/CIA was taking Appleton and me—and our allegations against Genevieve Sullivan—seriously.

One big question remained, though. You know, the elephant-in-the-room question. Well, several, in fact. With the background out of the way, mostly as told by Appleton, it was my turn to speak. "Director, here's the rub. How do we know that you're not playing us, and this isn't one big 'ole double-cross?"

Ginachere didn't flinch. "You don't know. You can't know. But you're leaning to Sullivan as your suspect. You need to prove it. You need a motive. What motive do I have?"

"What's your relationship with MBS? The son of the King of Saudi Arabia?"

"I know him. I've met with him. He's green. A lightweight. But he doesn't know that, and he's cocky. Therefore, he's dangerous. The King is a stabilizing influence, and while I don't doubt that MBS wants unfettered power, certainly I'm in no rush to see that happen, though it's inevitable."

I asked, "What would Sullivan have to gain, then?"

Ginachere cackled, the first hint of emotion that I'd ever seen from her. "Oh, that's obvious, isn't it? Sullivan pins me for an assassination. I'll be disgraced, and Sullivan makes a move for my job. She's been angling for more visibility for years. Her ego knows no bounds. That demure attitude? Bullshit. She's a wily, tiny woman with a serious Napoleon complex. She's calculating and, I'll admit, smart, but she's also mean, devious, and dogged, and she'll stop at nothing to achieve her goals."

No bad blood between them, I thought sarcastically. *Can you think sarcastically? Never mind.*

I resumed my questioning and dared to reprimand Ginachere. "But neither will you. You'll do whatever it takes. Like you did in Damascus. In 2014."

Ginachere's eyes narrowed. "Damascus? So what?"

I returned her stare, my own eyes as slits. "You killed two innocent people."

"Hardly."

I spat back, "Whaddya mean, hardly? You murdered Fouad Abbas and his wife, Gamila. You poisoned her with a snake bite as he watched. *That's* not mean or devious? Where does that fit into humane behavior? How does that establish that you are trustworthy?"

I knew my face was flushed as I heard Appleton say, sotto voce, "Easy, Ben." The fact she used my first name reinforced the message; I had to find calm.

Ginachere, however, appeared undaunted, and her expression was cold. "Let me guess. Sullivan used that episode as an example of my treachery."

"I researched Damascus. The few records I could locate were sealed. Why'd you do that? Why the cover-up? And while we're on the topic of blocking records, why did the CIA sequester the satellite data just before and well after *Almaz* stopped transmitting her tracking location?"

"What?" Ginachere sat back in her chair. Either she was a master at a bluff, or she was genuinely confused. "Who is Almaz? I don't know anyone named Almaz."

Appleton intervened in her level, soft voice. "It's a yacht. The yacht's name is *Almaz*. That's the platform from which Porter ran his previous operation. The yacht was on her way to Saudi Arabia to be in position to intercept you, or whomever, prior to this assassination attempt. But the yacht disappeared in the Atlantic, near the Azores."

"I have no idea what you're referring to," Ginachere protested. "I can look into it. But what I don't need to look into are the records surrounding the event in Damascus. They were sealed in cooperation with the Israeli government. You see, Fouad Abbas developed the bomb that was used in the Jerusalem massacre in 2001, and Gamila Abbas recruited the terrorist who carried the suicide weapon that her husband imagined and built." Ginachere steepled her hands as if she was praying and added quietly, "They deserved their death, but they did not deserve the niceties and formalities of a trial. If we had allowed a system of justice to pursue its required trail of evidence, we would have compromised our sources, and in turn, that would have set our intelligence gathering network in the Middle East back years. Decades, perhaps. However, it was established that the Abbas pair were unequivocally guilty. And, Mister Porter, because our work takes us to a dangerous, messy place, sometimes it becomes necessary to employ extreme methods. This was one of those cases."

"Let's say I believe that speech," I countered. "I don't understand why you'd seal the records."

"Two reasons. First, as I just outlined: connecting the dots to Abbas would likely have exposed our operatives in the area. And second, the Israelis already had enough issues with the Syrians. Adding this to the mix was unproductive. The Abbas husband-and-wife pair were extremists. Justice was done, and those in the know—in the States, in Israel, and even in Syria—were satisfied with the outcome and complicit in burying it."

I glanced at Appleton, who suggested, "We can verify all this. In the meantime—"

"No," Ginachere corrected, "we're not done with this topic. You asked about Damascus. Gansett was there. He had every reason to—"

"We know that part," I interrupted. "We know his family was killed in the bombing."

Ginachere nodded. "Yes, that's right. Gansett became a very effective operator. I worked with him many times, and he was paid well for his discretion and his effectiveness."

"Exactly. Gansett is your guy. Doesn't that pin you in all of this?" I asked rhetorically.

Ginachere shook her head negatively. "These sorts of relationships are hardly exclusive, Mister Porter. To be candid, while I'm miffed that Gansett would work for Sullivan, the reality is that I have not employed Gansett for a while. Since before Covid, I suppose. Frankly, he's gotten too old to be effective. What he does is a younger person's game."

I cocked my shoulders in a slight shrug. "I'd say. He might be a CIA assassin, but I took him out with a nail gun. Furthermore, he can't even shoot straight; he missed Appleton with an easy shot on a small-town street."

"Exactly," Ginachere huffed, "his marksmanship is certainly not what it once was." She hesitated. "But you said earlier that he's still alive. Who's watching over him? Miller?"

"And Vance," I said. "One of our agents, and she has a team on-site. Gansett is not going anywhere, and he won't be conversing with anyone anytime soon."

"Good." She pursed her lips and scowled. "You know, it's possible that Sullivan may have figured out a way to pose as me. Perhaps Gansett thinks he is under contract with the CIA."

"You're asking us to make quite a leap of faith," I argued.

The D/CIA's eyes remained narrowed, drilling me. "You're hiding something. What did Gansett say? Did he say that he was working for me?"

I returned her stare. "Appleton and I have told you everything we know. I've been wanting to question Gansett all along. Unfortunately, he's still in no shape to talk."

Ginachere looked at me strangely. "How did you find out about Jerusalem, then, if you didn't speak with him?"

I tilted my head toward Appleton. "One of the SAC's most talented Intelligence Analysts did a deep dive on Gansett. After all, with him detained, we have his fingerprints, his DNA, his phone, his facial details, his—"

"Stop. You have his phone?" demanded Ginachere.

"Yeah."

"That's the key to all of this," the D/CIA said with a note of enthusiasm in her voice, and I could even see that, behind the reflection of her eyeglass lenses, Ginachere's eyes were bright. "Where is the phone?"

"Salem, Massachusetts," Appleton replied.

"We need to get it to Langley. If we can do that," Ginachere exclaimed, "we will find out who is behind this in a matter of minutes."

CHAPTER
72

HAVE YOU EVER felt enthusiasm and trepidation at the same exact time? It's an odd feeling, right? Two emotions that appear to be contradictory, and yet they work in harmony. I guess it's like strapping yourself into a roller coaster ride. If it's not your first ride ever on a coaster, you know what to expect, pretty much, but still . . . you wonder with nervous excitement about what lays ahead, as the gears under the coaster engage and the cart begins to move.

Sure, that's a long-winded way of trying to describe my mental state, sitting in the living room of an unfamiliar home on the Maryland shore, at 6:45 A.M. on a March Monday. Invisible beyond the overcast gloom, the sun would rise in a matter of minutes. And according to Hazel Ginachere, we could solve this case in that amount of time, too.

Turns out that was an optimistic projection. First, we needed to get JJ Gansett's phone to Langley. Even as Appleton disclosed, somewhat reluctantly, the capabilities of her bunker to Ginachere, it became evident that the CIA would require the actual device in hand. With a flurry of phone calls, a Bureau vehicle would be ready to whisk Louis Lewis to Logan Airport, where he would hand off the device to a waiting CIA jet that would be given a priority departure slot and direct flight plan to Dulles International Airport. The private plane would be met by a helicopter for the sixteen-mile flight to Langley.

"We can get this done in two hours," Ginachere stated, ending a call with an aide. Turning to Appleton, she asked, "You have your own personal ops center inside a bunker under your house?"

"It's not important," Appleton protested.

I could sense that Ginachere was jealous, and I decided to redirect. "Should we go to Langley and wait there so we're ready to move once your team analyzes the device?"

Ginachere thought for a moment and replied, "No, I don't think so. But I'll keep the chopper and plane on standby, and I'll arrange for additional crews, too, in the event that Gansett's phone sends us elsewhere."

"I don't understand," I admitted. "How does Gansett's device matter?"

"It's a specialized device," Ginachere explained. "It can create an encrypted, impossible-to-follow connection, using cut-outs on the Internet that will bounce the transmission packets around the world. It's faster when it's tethered to a computer since it will take advantage of a computer's wired Internet connection, but it can also be used as a stand-alone device utilizing cellular signals. For an additional layer of security, the device itself cannot connect to Wi-Fi or a similar network."

"I'm missing something," I protested.

"Getting there," Ginachere said. "There are log-in hurdles baked into the device, which can be defeated only at Langley, where it was initially programmed. Once past those gatekeepers, we will be able to see where the device has connected and therefore drill down and discover who Gansett has communicated with. Because it certainly wasn't me."

I was hung up on her phrase, *defeated only at Langley,* and I pressed, "As you might recall, one of my associates was an extremely talented programmer and, yes, hacker. Anastasia Volkov. She was aboard *Almaz* when it disappeared." I sighed.

Ginachere noticed my deflation and said complimentarily, "Yes, I remember Miss Volkov. I certainly know of her prodigious talents."

I blinked, driving the thoughts of loneliness and sorrow and guilt from my mind, forcing myself to focus on the CIA woman. "While we're waiting for Lewis to arrive with the phone, can you, uh, drill down into that topic? Like, why was that satellite data blocked? Perhaps the authorization for that is another clue."

Appleton raised her hand. "Not only that, but we also still don't know who attacked Porter and Havens on Saturday morning." She scrutinized Ginachere. "Let's utilize CIA assets for that task."

Ginachere groaned. "You know as well as I that I'm not authorized to deploy CIA assets on American soil."

I picked up on Appleton's line of inquiry, and I hinted, "I don't believe the SAC is proposing to put CIA boots on domestic ground. I think we're looking for something more, um, elevated."

CHAPTER

73

THE DIRECTOR OF THE CIA grinned mischievously when I said the word, "elevated." I was beginning to appreciate Ginachere's quick mind.

In turn, I think she was wooed by my subtle but dry humor, and she returned it in kind. "Very nice, Mister Porter. Let's do some satellite work. First, something more grounded? More coffee?"

As Ginachere bustled about, I reflected on my high school history lessons, recalling that while United States President Dwight D. Eisenhower is often rightly credited for the establishment of the interstate highway system, his influence is rarely mentioned in the creation of a very different network—indeed, one that is extraterrestrial. Eisenhower was instrumental in the formation of the National Reconnaissance Office (NRO) in 1960, a decision intended to streamline and coordinate the separate systems operated by the United States Air Force and by the CIA. Later, the US Navy and the National Security Agency would join the effort, and in 1982, after a decade of rumors, the NRO was declassified.

The operations of the NRO, however, remain a well-guarded secret. It's estimated that the Office manages a constellation of about 50 spy satellites, although there are almost 500 satellites termed as "military/civil" units. The capabilities of the NRO fleet are the subject of rumor and spy novels alike. I can disclose that optical imaging satellites can read a license plate easily and are capable of even more telephoto resolution. But I should also tell you that my security clearance is not high enough to be in the "need-to-know" circle as to what the NRO birds really can do.

The Director of the CIA, however, was granted that clearance. "Put it this way," Ginachere offered as she settled in with a topped-up cup of coffee, "the NRO donated two space telescopes to NASA—that's right, to NASA!—in 2012. The units were unused and had capabilities well beyond that of NASA's Hubble Space Telescope. Imagine how advanced the NRO technology was—and currently is—if they had stuff like that sitting in storage." She paused and looked at Appleton. "Let's start with Saturday morning. Time window and search radius, please."

Appleton didn't hesitate. "Start at 7:45 A.M. on 27th Street Northwest. Between Dumbarton and Olive, adjacent to the Rock Creek Park. You're looking for an unmarked white van that stops near that location."

As Appleton spoke, Ginachere was typing on a smartphone and added, "We'll zero in on the vehicle and then backtrack its route to that destination."

I wondered, "You'll have satellite coverage for that area at that time?"

Ginachere tapped her device with finality, and I assumed she sent her message because she looked up at me. "Yes. There's a dedicated imaging and infrared spacecraft in a geostationary orbit focused on the US East Coast. If I recall correctly, these geo sats are about 22,000 miles above the Earth, and therefore they have a very large range of view, but we maintain a focus on Washington as a priority surveillance target, for obvious reasons."

I considered my next question. I didn't want to appear foolish, but I chose curiosity over ego. "What about clouds? Or at night?"

"That's why we also utilize infrared. We can track discrete heat signatures. Not only vehicles but people and animals. Still, to make a positive ID, we must cross-reference the satellite data with terrestrial camera data, which we can also match to cell phone signals." Ginachere cackled. "No one can hide. Everyone can be tracked."

"That's quite a lot of data," Appleton groaned. "How long to run the search?"

"The target time in question enjoyed fair weather. A cloudless morning, I believe. That will expedite the task. Not long," Ginachere replied.

I leaned forward. "Let's run a second, concurrent search. Let's see if you have better access than Louis Lewis could get."

Ginachere understood instantly. "The boat?" She hefted her device a second time and eyed me, ready for my instructions.

"Yes. The vessel's name is *Almaz*," I confirmed. Scratching my head, I tried to remember the dates and times that Lewis found. "1:40 A.M. Zulu time, Greenwich Mean Time, on Thursday morning. Uh, call it two hundred miles north of the Azores. That data was blocked, as was image and infrared for the following day. Knowing who blocked it would also be helpful."

"Right," Ginachere said. "Stand by. An inquiry into the archival data should be quicker than running a search on a moving target like that van."

I entwined my fingers together behind my head and leaned back. "While we're waiting for a response, what I don't get is who was in that van. How does Sullivan get those assets? The Sec State's office doesn't have that kind of talent."

"That's a common misconception, Mister Porter. I'd expect you to be better informed," Ginachere scolded. "The Department of State has two military arms, and the Under Secretary is number four in the pecking order of power."

I bristled at her haughty tone, but uncharacteristically I bit my tongue and reserved a snarky comeback for later, instead asking in a normal voice, "What military arms, exactly?"

"State formed an Air Wing in the seventies for counter-narcotics operations. That mission evolved to include transport for diplomatic personnel. The Department also formed an entity called the Naval Support Unit, which partners with the Navy, Marines, and Seabees. They work on sensitive construction and security and often are plain-clothed even though they are military."

"Those guys could definitely have been military types," I recalled, thinking how they knew to split up and put three men initially on Havens and only one on me—the weaker, plumper target.

Weak, plump target? Like a defenseless . . . yacht?

"Wait," I said quickly. "You mentioned the Navy. The State Department can't direct naval action, can it?"

"Not to my knowledge, but that doesn't mean that it couldn't be done through the proper channels," Ginachere replied, as her phone chimed with a message. She scowled as she scrolled with a forefinger. "That's . . . troubling. Follow me."

We trailed Ginachere deeper into her home to a den, lined with half-filled wooden bookshelves, with pairs of French doors looking out to the gray and rain-streaked Chesapeake Bay. Ginachere sat at a simple wooden desk equipped with dual computer monitors, a keyboard, and a mouse. Appleton and I, with no place to sit, stood behind her at her shoulders.

I looked downward at the unadorned desk surface. Ginachere's mouse pad, to my surprise, was not plainly colored or even an image of the CIA logo—instead, the pad was printed with a photograph of a dog. "Cute puppy," I observed. "You have a dog?"

"Had. She died. Old age." Ginachere moved the mouse, and the screens lit, but her attention remained briefly on the printed pad. "I'd like another dog someday, but my current lifestyle is not exactly conducive to having a pet at home."

Her voice was weary and sad, the first sign of humanity that I saw in the blustery Director.

I'm cracking the code, I thought, *and getting through to Ginachere. Maybe she's not so bad after all.*

With Appleton and I hovering behind her simple, almost modernist upholstered chair, Ginachere turned her attention to the screens, typing at lightning-fast speed as she logged into her system. In seconds, she brought up images. "These links were sent to me a moment ago. You watched as I read the cover note. It's a video feed from the North Atlantic Ocean weather satellite, not a surveillance bird. My office told me that indeed, the images from the NRO sats are inaccessible, so while waiting for clearance, they ran this down." Ginachere looked over her left shoulder at Appleton. "Your man apparently didn't think to do this."

"No," Appleton admitted.

"Watch." Ginachere clicked on a *PLAY* arrow icon, and the grayscale image began to show motion. "Langley matched the Automatic Identification System data from *Almaz* to this vessel," she explained, pointing with her cursor at a light gray, ship-shaped mass moving from left to right on the screen. "The infrared picks up that the vessel is warmer than the ocean water, so you can see the shape of the vessel itself." We could have been watching paint dry; the image was almost static, so slow the boat was moving, as wisps of warm clouds and dots of wave tops came and went from the screen. Despite that, though, my throat was dry as I kept an eye on the marching time indicator, showing *0139 ZULU*.

A minute passed in silence, and then the gray mass bloomed in size, its color becoming whiter and whiter. "That's an explosion," Ginachere narrated. "The heat return got much hotter; that's why it gets brighter." Behind her chair, I sank to my knees.

There could be no question. Whatever happened to *Almaz* was catastrophic.

Ginachere continued, "Secondary explosion. Probably fuel. And then—look. The infrared returns are separating. It's breaking apart."

I couldn't speak as the clock ticked up by several minutes, the bright white blobs on the screen eventually fading to gray spots and then black. Only a handful of very light gray spots remained until most of them, too, faded into the randomness of clouds and wave tops. I swallowed, trying to contain the lump I felt in my throat, and I blinked rapidly. Honestly, I wanted to cry.

These were my friends, my colleagues, my confidants. Macallister. Lockwood. Volkov. Even our chef, Jacquard.

I couldn't deal with the enormity of the situation, and I felt Appleton place a comforting hand on my shoulder.

I couldn't deceive myself any longer. I'd seen the satellite footage with my own eyes. I knew, at that moment, that my worst fears were real and that they would haunt me forever.

I agreed to the operation. I was sucked into the deception of this case.

Now, however, was not the time for guilt. Time for that could come later. I knew I could close the case, but I wasn't there—yet.

No one spoke for several minutes until I composed myself and whispered, "We need to keep going. We need more data." In a stronger voice, now with anger creeping in, I added, "We need to make Sullivan accountable."

Ginachere twisted in her chair and spoke softly and respectfully. "I'll task Langley to get to the bottom of this right away. We'll get better images from the surveillance satellites at a much higher resolution"

I was studying the recorded images on her screen. One dot of light gray remained, persevering amidst the vast monotony of gray and black. "Higher resolution?" I pointed at the lingering dot. "See that? That tiny heat return? Could that be a survivor?"

"Be careful with false expectations," Ginachere warned. "It could just be debris. But, yes, the high-res images will clarify a great deal. If there is any remaining evidence or, we hope, survivors, we'll be able to track the human heat signatures. I'll also get a priority message about initiating a search-and-rescue mission to the Navy."

That one word refocused me. "Navy. I asked earlier if State could task the Navy. Dig deeper. *Almaz* was in impeccable condition. Her captain was experienced. She wouldn't have just, um, exploded." I gulped, and to neither woman in particular, I choked out, "*Almaz* couldn't have been targeted, could she? Sunk on purpose?"

Appleton's phone rang before anyone could theorize, and she lifted an eyebrow as she listened for ten seconds. "It's Havens. Curtis is awake. Havens wants to know what we want him to do."

My chest was thumping, and I felt sweat on my palms. "I've seen enough. I've heard enough. I've had it. Tell Havens to tell Curtis that I'm gonna be there in an hour, and I'm gonna wring the truth out of that fucking so-called doctor if it's the last thing I do."

Ginachere grinned wickedly. "I'm beginning to like your style, Porter. Let's go. We'll take my car with my people; we'll get there faster. I'll contact the Secretary of the Navy and the Director of the NRO from the car."

In moments, Appleton and I were seated in the back of Ginachere's armored Suburban. The Director rode shotgun and focused on her smartphone, ignoring her driver who occasionally squawked the siren to urge a slow-moving commuter out of the way of the big, black car with its emergency lights flashing. At this pace, we'd be in Georgetown in well under an hour, roughly the same time as the plane carrying Gansett's device would be landing at Dulles.

I felt tinges of confidence and of hope—that there might be a survivor out there on the open sea, and that I could crack this case. I'd persevere.

The problem, though, with perseverance is that there's no time limit—and at this point, I had no idea that I was racing a completely different kind of clock.

CHAPTER 74

FORTY-EIGHT MINUTES LATER, at 8:43 A.M. on a drizzly, gray Monday morning, Appleton and I shouldered the heavy doors of the armored Suburban open, dropped to the Georgetown pavement, and barged into the borrowed pied-a-terre to find Havens and Curtis in the wood-paneled library.

Curtis was pale, with an almost yellowish cast to his skin, and his white hair was disheveled. He looked scared. I hoped so.

The doctor tried to rise to greet me, but Havens shoved him roughly back down into his seat. Curtis pouted, "Porter. *Ben*. You gotta help me," he whined. "I never meant for it to go this far."

"Bullshit," I snarled as Appleton placed a cautionary hand between my shoulder blades. I shrugged off the gesture. "You murdered Abdul Hamid. You tried to kill Gansett. You've been complicit all along. The death of Heather Rourke. Attempted murder of Appleton and me. Actually, me, twice!"

I took a deep breath and steadied my tone. "Here's the deal," I offered evenly. "I just got off the phone with an attorney at the Department of Justice." That was true; I called Sara Lin from the CIA Suburban and confirmed the legality of what I wanted to say. "We've built a case. We're assembling the trail of evidence, and in a matter of hours, we'll be ready to charge you with murder. You have sixty seconds to decide what happens next. Because, in one minute, I'm outta here, and either you risk a murder rap backed up with the full weight of the power of the FBI and the DOJ, or you agree to turn State's witness for a negotiated sentence, and you testify against Genevieve Sullivan."

The doctor's eyes darted to and fro, and then he blinked rapidly before stammering, "Sull—Sullivan?"

"Priceless," I muttered. "Dumbass trying to deflect." Appleton's phone rang as I looked at my watch and spoke clearly. "Forty seconds, Doctor."

"Pause the countdown, Porter," Appleton said, but with a slight grin to her face. She subtly tilted her head in the direction of the waiting Suburban outside while she was holding her phone out to me.

I put the device to my ear, and I heard Ginachere's voice say, "Porter. Two updates. We got the high-res sat images of Georgetown on Saturday morning. The white van is registered to the Seabees as a civilian construction vehicle. The vehicle would be used in their line with work with the State Department. However, it is also indicative, to me and to my team at least, of a rushed operation. They should have rented or, better, stolen a vehicle. Amateurs," she snorted.

"Okay. What's the second update?"

"Gansett's device is at Langley. My team reverse-cracked the phone, seeing as it was originally our device. The IP address that Gansett used for communications is not CIA. In fact, I can give you a physical address. Foggy Bottom. The State Department building." Her voice notched up slightly as she repeated herself. "Did you hear me? Sullivan's office is at that location!"

"I heard you. Stay on the line and listen in," I said to Ginachere.

I stabbed the speakerphone icon and addressed Curtis. "Too bad, Doctor. I don't need you anymore."

"No—no—no," the doctor whined, his lower lip quivering. "I want the deal. Please. I can give you everything on Sullivan."

"Yeah," I taunted, "but like I said, I don't need your cooperation or testimony. We've got a separate, wholly credible link to Sullivan."

"There's more," Curtis protested. He ran a hand through his hair, attempting to smooth it in a vain attempt to appear, perhaps, more professional. Clearing his throat, he spoke evenly, without a quaver, "Give me two minutes. I'll explain it all, and I'll not only give you Sullivan, but I'll also prevent even more damage—however, I want your assurance that your deal stands."

I set Appleton's phone, still connected with Ginachere on speaker, onto the table in front of Curtis. "Record this," I said to Appleton, who leaned in to tap icons on her device. Making eye contact with the doctor, I scowled. "Fine. Two minutes. This better be substantive, though. Or no deal."

Curtis nodded and wiped his mustache with the back of his hand, which I took as a gesture to stall. He hung his head and addressed his knees but with an edge to his tone. "I wanted something bigger than Walter Reed. The monotony of it all, day in and day out, operating in the shadows, rarely getting credit for my work with toxins. No one cares about the scientists and the doctors in the labs, do they? Until there's a pandemic, maybe, and then it's the lab boss that gets the spotlight. The career bureaucrat, who's out of touch but still gets the Sunday morning talk shows and gets the press because of a fancy title and a degree that's fifty-five years stale."

Curtis looked up, finally, as I shook my head. "Okay, you're bitter. However, you're wasting your two minutes with your ranting. You'd be terrible on a talk show. The point, please."

With a haughty sniff, Curtis resumed, "In my lab, I developed a method to hack the vitals monitoring machines, and I experimented with various toxins and drugs. Initially, I expected to sell a package of security consultations to hospitals. With my body of research, I could show cause and effect. Now, this is not something you can patent, so I made some inquiries online, drumming up interest. I got nowhere."

"When was this going down?"

He looked at me briefly. "I started the research five, six years ago. Call it 2015. I was satisfied that the method worked by early 2018."

Smugly, he added, "Naturally, I've been refining and improving the protocol all along."

"The background is fascinating, Doctor, but thus far, all you've done is incriminate yourself. You're running out of time. Where's the tie-in to Sullivan?"

"I got an inquiry in early 2019. I did the dance, you know, online, to verify identities and so forth, and it checked out. It was Genevieve Sullivan, and she wanted to utilize the protocol for a very different outcome. She wanted to use it for an assassination. Ultimately, I agreed; the potential money was so much better than selling security to individual hospital networks, and there was an end game. But that was all Sullivan's idea," he concluded, his voice rising slightly in pitch.

I sat, finally, and offered, "Let's forego the two-minute limit because now you're getting somewhere. Tell me about your meetings with Sullivan. Do you have records? Times? Dates? Topics?"

Curtis dropped his head again and shook it back and forth. "No, no, not really. We agreed very early on never to meet face-to-face. She said that could be tracked by mobile phone location, by cameras, by the GPS systems in cars, and even by satellites. We communicated using a secure connection that even altered our voices. High-tech State Department stuff, you know, for messaging to embassies and ambassadors for the touchy political topics. Kind of an online version of the cigar smoke-filled, dark back room for deals that you'd think of from the movies." Curtis chuckled softly at his imagination.

I glanced at Appleton, who rolled her eyes and said, "The problem with that story, Doctor, is that it relies solely on your testimony. You've got nothing concrete or factual that links back to Sullivan, other than your allegations."

"There's one thing," Curtis offered. "We tried the protocol, and it worked."

Appleton spoke again. "What? Who? When?"

"Senator Abiaria. 2019. Sullivan hated him and his human rights bandwagon. She said he was always in the way, so he died. Heart attack." Curtis air-quoted the last two words.

"Continue," Appleton directed.

"Then the whole Covid thing came along, and it delayed us. With people gathering again, though, Sullivan looked for an opportunity. She read the tea leaves and decided to target Saudi Arabia. The King and his son."

"Whoa," I interrupted. "Both of them? Why?"

"Chaos," Curtis replied. "It would create a void of power and an awful lot of accusations. Sullivan would manage the elevation of the next King, loyal to her, naturally, and meanwhile, it would look like the sitting King died of a heart attack after his son was poisoned by the CIA. By that witch, Hazel Ginachere."

I gave credit to Ginachere for remaining quiet on the phone connection; after all, Curtis couldn't have known who was connected via the phone on the table in front of him. Curtis continued with barely a pause. "Then, Ginachere is disgraced for her role in the mess. Sullivan said that she'd even tie in a CIA bag man to make the association to Ginachere even stronger, so she brought in Gansett and trained him on the protocol. Meanwhile, when the dust settles, Sullivan rises above as the statesperson who can bring order to that chaos."

Shaking my head, I asked, "Then why did Sullivan bring me in to this mess?"

"You'd be the star witness to Ginachere's treachery. You'd have first-hand knowledge. Sullivan would take credit. She'd say that she put the FBI and the DOJ on the trail."

"But what if I succeeded in preventing the assassinations?"

Curtis raised an eyebrow. "That's a slightly different path to the same outcome. Ginachere is still pinned as the mastermind for the assassination attempt, and she takes the fall. Meanwhile, both the King and his son are indebted to Sullivan, and she's the hero."

I shrugged. "This is helpful, Curtis, but so far, I haven't heard anything that directly incriminates Sullivan. Like the SAC said earlier, it's all conjecture and unfounded accusations. You yourself said there are no records of your communications with Sullivan, so it's your word versus hers. That's not gonna work for us. No deal."

"I've rambled," argued Curtis. "One more minute. You see, you're forgetting my method. I said I'd considered selling it as a proactive security measure for hospitals and governments. But it's also marketable to the bad actors. I dunno, the Russians, the North Koreans, terrorists, you name it. Having the ability to target a victim in a hospital without really getting your hands dirty, and without a chain of evidence that is visible or even trackable, is a very valuable commodity."

"Not anymore," I grunted as I picked up the phone that lay on the coffee table. "Like I said, Curtis, no deal."

He held up a hand of caution. "It's being marketed right now, Porter. Here's my offer: I tell you where and when to stop the transaction, and my deal is back on."

That got my attention. "What do you mean, right now?"

Curtis bared his teeth wickedly. "Sullivan and I had a backup plan in the event that we couldn't pull off the stunt in Saudi Arabia. We tracked you to from Salem to D.C., as you obviously figured out, somehow. She was going to take you out, and I was to deliver the final blow. You'd die like Hamid. So, when I didn't report into Sullivan on Sunday night, Sullivan would have pulled the trigger to activate the backup plan first thing Monday morning."

"What's the backup plan?"

"Do we have a deal?"

I knew this was treading on dangerous ground; a Special Agent has no authority to offer deals to suspects. Certainly, my status as an undercover agent, off the books, clouded that even further. Appleton, however, as a Special Agent in Charge, did possess the authority to make the deal and to move the investigation along.

My mind raced. Appleton was sharp, but I wasn't sure the SAC was at the same point in the investigation as I was. I couldn't explain it now. I had to trust my gut and my instincts, and to trust the same of Appleton.

I looked at Appleton and repeated Curtis's question. "Ma'am, I recommend that we proceed. Does the doctor have a deal?"

Appleton hesitated. She wasn't with me yet.

The SAC bit her lip, and then said, "If that's your recommendation, Porter, then yes. We have a deal."

There was one more critical move to make. Angling the phone to my mouth, I asked, "Director Ginachere? Your thoughts?"

Curtis blanched as Ginachere's voice rang out from the tiny speakers on the phone, the volume control set at maximum. "I suppose I've been called things a lot worse than a witch," she cackled. "Mister Curtis," she added, and I could tell from the emphasis on "Mister" that she purposely omitted the "Doctor" honorific, "I'll agree to the deal with one proviso, and that is this: your information must be timely. No promises, no conjecture. Actionable intel. Agreed?"

Curtis nodded, but I demanded, "Say it out loud."

"Agreed," Curtis said. He wiped his mustache quickly and inhaled. "Sullivan is running an auction right now on the dark web. It will conclude with the highest bid at 10:00 A.M. Eastern Standard time, and a half-hour later, she'll be wheels-up on a private jet to Argentina."

I dared a peek at my watch. *Shit*. It was 9:32 A.M.

The plan in my head was one I made in haste. Macallister would have called it Swiss cheese, "full of holes." I wished he was with me now, with Volkov watching our six. I cleared my mind; I couldn't think that way.

I mashed the *END CALL* icon.

With Appleton in tow, I rushed outside the pied-a-terre and approached Ginachere's waiting Suburban. The rear passenger window slid down, and Ginachere spoke reluctantly. "I'm torn. I should go with you to the State Department to apprehend Sullivan. But if this manifests into the public eye, as the Director of the CIA, I absolutely cannot be seen participating in an operation on American soil. I'll do what I can in the background."

"Makes sense," Appleton agreed.

"We gotta go," I said urgently, adding, "Director, I will call you from my phone. We will link you in that way."

Ginachere indicated her agreement as the window glided upward and closed.

I ran back inside the pied-a-terre, calling out an order. "Appleton. Get the keys to the truck and pick me up." The SAC snagged the keyring and spun, bolting to the street.

I eyed Curtis, knowing full well that even the best plans rarely hold together once in motion. I would be improvising, and even as I sat down next to Curtis, I barked at Havens, "Call Lewis. Tell him to put everyone on this. He's gotta find that auction and win it at any cost, while making it look like he's in, ummm, Damascus—*not* in Boston!"

Havens hesitated. "That's our plan?"

"That's our back-up plan," I clarified. "My plan is to intercept that auction and stop it!"

CHAPTER
75

"WHERE HAVE YOU BEEN?" Even with the voice-altering software, exasperation and annoyance were evident through the scratchy connection as it bounced from one server to another, each transmission packet taking a circuitous route from transmitter to receiver.

"Dealing with our problem."

"I expected to hear from you sometime on Sunday."

"I was unavoidably unable to communicate." There was a pause, clicks, and faint chirps filling the dead space. "Have you commenced the auction?"

"Yes, of course. That was our agreement, as you surely remember. Monday morning."

"Good. Is the auction generating interest?"

There was a sound like a snort, or perhaps it was a transmission issue. "It's like any auction. eBay, for example. Annoying. The bidders start low, which is to be expected, and then wait, hoping to squeeze their competitors at the last minute."

"How many bidders?"

"Five. Wait—one new party indicated interest. I'm putting you on hold so I can register the bidder." The connection went silent, but the clicks and pops continued, indicating it remained active.

CHAPTER
76

BY THE TIME I slung myself into the passenger seat of the big Ford, I had already connected my device with the D/CIA. I set the phone on the console between Appleton and me, and I held on for dear life as Appleton punched the accelerator.

Ginachere, on speaker, briefed us on our destination. "The State headquarters building is named after Harry S. Truman, but everyone calls it Foggy Bottom. It's one-point-four million square feet of space housing about eight thousand people."

I stole a glance at Appleton, who was concentrating on the road, as I directed a question to Ginachere. "How are we gonna find Sullivan, then?"

"I told you that the IP address that Gansett's phone linked to is at Foggy Bottom. My techs at Langley are working on isolating that address within the building. In addition, we've got the NSA geo-locating Sullivan's personal cell phone. It's also at Foggy Bottom, but we are waiting on granular altitude data to determine a floor level. We'll have that data shortly."

Even Appleton's big Ford F-250 pickup couldn't magically make Monday morning traffic disappear. The seven-minute drive to the State Department Headquarters building dragged beyond ten minutes, each second ticking closer to 10:00 A.M. with excruciating, slow-motion agony.

Appleton wrestled the wheel to weave around a stopped bus even as she said, "I called the Hoover building as I ran to the truck. Two agents will meet us at the new public entrance, that steel-and-glass annex on 21ˢᵗ Street, not at the main entrance on C Street. We're two minutes out. We'll be allowed access without passing through security. Other than that, I don't want to go further in the event word gets back to Sullivan."

"Good call," Ginachere agreed.

Appleton swerved to cross the double yellow line and hit the gas again to pass slow-moving vehicles. I could see the outline of the giant State building through the windshield.

"I'm back. Seven bidders now."

At the sound of the scrambled voice in my left ear, I jabbed the mute icon on my phone and hefted the second device that was in my lap—a smartphone that Paxton Parr had confiscated from Doctor Curtis.

Before I bolted from the pied-a-terre, I had demanded that Curtis show me how to initiate a call to his co-conspirator, thinking I'd use that later. To my surprise, the call was answered, but I grabbed at the opportunity, remembering the doctor's words when he told us that he and Sullivan "communicated using a secure connection that even altered our voices."

So far, I was pleased. I handled the opening of the conversation well, and the fact that the connection remained enabled was a very good omen.

I adjusted the headset that I wore, and I clicked the cord-mounted mute button on the headset as I prepared myself. *Time for more improv,* I thought, before I spoke into the headset, "Locations of the seven bidders? Any indications of level of interest?"

"The dark web does not make it straightforward to determine location. From the financial data that accompanied each bidder's one-million-dollar deposit to enter the auction, I expect three are from the Middle East, two from the Asian continent, and two from Europe."

Trying to recall Curtis's confession, I asked, "Are there any specific questions on the protocol that I can answer?"

"None yet."

As the Ford braked to a hard stop, I realized that I needed an excuse to go back on mute. "Uh, I have to step away for a moment."

"Why?" The response was almost instant.

I grabbed Appleton's right hand before she could open the door to the faces of two burly-looking men wearing FBI-branded windbreakers, with pistols and badges in plain sight, who were waiting outside the F-250's dirty windows. I shoved my phone, still connected to Ginachere. in Appleton's direction so I could carry Curtis's device, and I blabbed into the headset, "Porter and the Black man—his name is—was— Leroy Havens, an FBI agent—are dead. I'm making arrangements to dispose of the bodies via the morgue at Reed. Gotta take this call. Be right back."

I squeezed the mute trigger, and Appleton and I piled out of the Ford from our separate sides.

"Let's go," grunted Appleton as we scampered to the entrance of the mammoth State building. For a woman who should have been recovering from a bullet wound, the SAC ran fast; her stamina and fortitude never ceased to impress me. While on the move, Appleton draped her badge, encased in a folio on a lanyard, around her neck, and she hefted her gun with her right hand.

I didn't dare extract my Glock; my right hand carried the doctor's device, and I needed my left hand free not only to steady the ungainly headset but also to operate the mute button. We shouldered our way past a team of State security guards who allowed us passage, presumably briefed by someone at the Bureau's Hoover building headquarters.

"We're inside," Appleton barked to my device in her left hand.

"Good," Ginachere's voice squawked. "Ignore any signage you see about Sullivan's office, which is in the newer State Department extension on the fifth floor, east wing. Her personal cell phone is pinging from a location inside the west wing of the original structure, known as the War Department. You're going to pass straight through the first section of the building and then through a west-to-east linking structure to the second section."

Suited State staffers and executives, maintenance workers wearing drab, brown-and-green uniforms, and security personnel dressed in blue scattered at the sight of armed FBI agents at full trot, trailed by two security officers from the entry. Vainly, I wondered what they thought of me—sporting an odd-looking headset and casually clad in athletic shorts and an oversized Georgetown University hoodie sweatshirt borrowed, of course, from the professor's pied-a-terre. Fortunately, the professor must have been huskier than me.

The voice in my headset interrupted my irrelevant thoughts. *"Are you back? What are you doing? The auction is closing shortly. And a question has arisen."*

Four seconds later, Ginachere's voice spat out, "Third floor. North side."

Appleton called, "Heading up a set of stairs. We need a room number or something."

"Silence," I yelped. Pressing the mute button, I tried to control my breathing as I paused on the second-floor stair landing. "Yes, I'm back. What's the question?"

"What's the operating range of the receiving USB device? In other words, how far from the central monitoring station can the operator be to trigger a simulation on a specific patient's vitals monitoring data throughput?"

I pinched the mute button. "Shit. How the hell do I answer that?"

"What?" Appleton snapped.

"Up," I spat, resuming my upwards climb on the stair. Curtis had informed me that the connection was frequently laggy, so I hoped this would be inferred as one of those moments.

No such luck. *"I require an answer. Curtis?"*

Halfway to the third floor, I stopped, clutching the handrail. I took two deep breaths, squashed the mute button, and recalling how Curtis sat in one of the chairs outside the GW ICU suite, waiting to kill Hamid, I guessed. "Ten meters."

I compressed the button yet again and mounted the last set of steps.

The speakerphone that Appleton carried broadcast Ginachere's hurried voice. "I can't get you a room number, but I have a high confidence fix on a northeast corner office on the third floor of that wing."

Our group veered to the right as we exited the stairwell, shoving our way to a corner where we could see the hallway disappear to the left. "Let's bust down some doors," Appleton sang, a glint in her eye.

"Ten meters is unacceptable to this bidder. There are four-and-a-half minutes remaining. The bid is at twenty-two million. The inquiring bidder will go to thirty, but they want longer range. Can you do it?"

I crushed the button and bullshitted, "Yes. I'll have to alter the frequency handshakes and simplify the encryption methodology to remove any undesirable latency. But I want fifty million."

Unfortunately, I didn't mute in time, and one of Appleton's men slammed an office door open and shouted, "FBI!"

"Curtis?!"

I suspected my deception had been played out, so I swapped Curtis's device into my left hand, not needing to mute any longer. As I pulled my Glock from the holster at the small of my back, under the sweatshirt, I said calmly, "No. Of course not. This is Ben Porter."

Connection latency or surprise, I couldn't tell, but the voice was silent.

Appleton tried a second door as I ran past her. I wanted to hear our target speak. "Hello? Hello? Genevieve? We're still on a first-name basis, right?"

I smashed an office door open—the last door in the north corridor. The diminutive figure at the desk inside literally jumped to her feet. From behind me, I heard Ginachere's voice scream, tinnily, from the speaker on my device, "Fourth floor! Fourth floor!"

Without a word to the hapless State staffer whose morning I rudely interrupted, I spun and led our group racing to the stairwell, as the voice sneered in my ear, *"You're too late, Porter. I'm closing the auction at twenty-six million, and I'm gone."*

"Nice try," I huffed in reply, spinning my body at the stair landing between the third and fourth floors. "You wouldn't dare end it early. Otherwise, you'll be tracked by the disgruntled bidders who you screwed over. I've got two minutes."

"So naïve, Porter."

I slammed the door of the stairwell open and turned to my right, catching a glimpse of a white-haired woman bolting from an office doorway at the head of the hallway. Sullivan!

A bald-headed white man tailed Sullivan out of the door, and to my shock, he raised a pistol.

Pop!

Shit! That's not part of the plan!

I skidded to a stop and dove for the safety of the stairwell, colliding with Appleton.

Pop!

Plaster and wood splintered on the door frame.

Appleton flipped her badge lanyard from her neck and flicked the credentials pack open, revealing a small mirror. She angled it to the hall as Ginachere blurted, "Was that gunfire?"

"Yes," I replied. "Sullivan has protection, and she is on the move. Northwest. And—you might not believe this, but the auction was closed early."

"I got the auction covered," Ginachere said, without elaborating. "Sullivan has a plane waiting at Reagan National airport. I'm still tracking her phone, and she's got it with her, it appears. I'll continue to coordinate with Langley, and I'll rendezvous with you at Reagan. We will require as many assets on this as we can get."

"That's a gift. Thank you." Turning my attention to the stairwell, I barked to one of our agents, "You hear that? Call in backup."

"Yessir," was the curt reply.

"Follow us," I ordered. "Back to the vehicles." I flew down the stairs, three at a time, Appleton and our two men close behind. Realizing that the connection on the doctor's device was no longer active, I yanked off the headset.

She was gone.

CHAPTER

77

DESPITE ITS OBVIOUS WEIGHT and bulk, Appleton's Ford was quick, especially in the hands of its Quantico-trained driver. As Appleton piloted the F-250, rocketing across the Arlington Memorial Bridge, Ginachere called out, "I'm conferencing in the ops center at Langley."

A new, second female voice stated, "The target is in a silver Chrysler 300 sedan with Washington diplomatic plates."

Ginachere asked, "Are we tracking her phone?"

"Yes," came the reply. "And we've got positive ID via visuals from terrestrial cameras. Sullivan is confirmed inside the sedan. We also have facial recognition on the man who escorted her from the building. It's her State bodyguard and driver. Name is Darian Cook. Infrared satellite data showed the outline of a hot pistol on Cook's body before they got in the car."

The D/CIA demanded, "Confidence in the surveillance mesh?"

"One hundred percent. Unbreakable coverage via ground and air assets, despite the overcast. The target will not slip the net. Stand by." There was a moment's silence as the Ford overtook one slow-moving vehicle and then another, squealing around a sharp corner to pick up South Washington Road. "There is a Dassault Falcon 8X jet with warm engines at Signature Flight Support at Reagan. Two pilots aboard, no passengers, which is unusual with hot engines. According to air traffic control, the pilots filed a flight plan to Buenos Aires."

"Don't permit that plane to depart," Appleton ordered.

"Understood. You are six minutes out and two minutes behind the Chrysler."

"Director," I called, "we've got those six minutes. What was with your comment on the auction?"

Holding onto the A-pillar mounted handle in the shotgun seat of Appleton's fast-moving truck, I heard Ginachere's wicked cackle—which, honestly, I was beginning to enjoy because it typically seemed to precede a pleasant surprise. "The winning bidder of Sullivan's dark web auction, at twenty-six million dollars, used a Syrian bank account and a Syrian IP address. Such a shame for Sullivan that I set up a CIA account, in Damascus, in 2014." Another cackle. "By the way, Porter, I was impressed by your obfuscation on the range question. You stalled Sullivan nicely with that line of nonsense."

"I don't even remember what I said, but I'm happy it worked," I admitted, watching as the view outside of the George Washington Memorial Parkway blurred by, with the acres of gray tarmac of Reagan National visible from the left side of the Ford.

"The target Chrysler is at the Signature Flight Support security gate," said the voice from Langley.

"We're not stopping at that gate," I warned. Directing my voice to Appleton, I confirmed, "Got that?"

Appleton's face was placid. "No problem," was her monotone response, her attention focused on the road as she guided the big vehicle off the highway and onto the switchback of the exit ramp, tires chirping and motor gunning as the pickup accelerated on the uncreatively named Airport Access Road.

Barely slowing, the Ford blew through a red light and screeched right to Abingdon Drive, flashed under an elevated train track, and again carved right on Thomas Avenue as our overwatch informed us, "Target sedan through the gate and pulling up to the plane. It's directly inside the gate."

Passing a long, low, two-story white building to our left, Appleton tapped the brakes and yanked the Ford left. Ahead, I could see a two-lane gated entry; the black chain link fence would be no match for the heavy F-250, and without even slowing, we blasted through the gate.

Appleton and I shouldered our doors open a split-second after the Ford skidded to a halt alongside a silver Chrysler 300 sedan, stopped at the base of the Falcon jet where a crew member was retracting the integrated stair-and-door assembly to the closed, in-flight position. Glock in hand, I screamed, my voice almost unheard over the whine of the three spinning jet turbines, "FBI! Drop that stair!"

At the sight of the guns brandished by Appleton and me, the crew member hesitated. Then, reinforcements called by the Bureau began to screech in through the security gate and raced onto the rain-soaked tarmac. Two, then five, then ten vehicles, lights flashing and sirens blaring, surrounded the aircraft, and men and women in FBI-branded gear took perimeter positions.

The airstair dropped, and the whine of the tri-jet engines decreased. "Pilots got the message," Appleton observed.

"Yeah, and look who showed up," I said, as the Suburban that I recognized as the one we rode in earlier today squealed to a stop. Hazel Ginachere, notable for those round, black eyeglasses, exited her Suburban's left rear passenger door.

I glanced over my shoulder at the Chrysler sedan. The bald-headed driver remained inside, and through the windshield, I recognized him as the man who shot at me in the fourth-floor corridor in Foggy Bottom. I also remembered that face from Sullivan's Suburban, back when the Under Secretary met with us aboard *Almaz*. "Sullivan's bodyguard," I called to Appleton and Ginachere, twisting my head in that direction. "She's probably alone on the plane. Let's go."

I climbed the short airstair and slipped inside the cavernous aircraft. Appleton and Ginachere followed on my heels. Turning right to the passenger cabin, I spotted Sullivan, her white hair barely visible behind a set of tall-backed seats.

Striding down the center aisle of the luxurious jet, I slipped into the four-person seating configuration to join Sullivan, Ginachere taking a seat beside me, and Appleton dropping into the open chair next to our target. Sullivan feigned surprise. "Mister Porter. Care to explain what's happening here?"

"Please don't insult my intelligence, ma'am. You know exactly what's happening." I leaned into the supple, tan leather of the very comfortable chair and placed the butt of my Glock on the highly polished, burled mahogany surface of the table between Sullivan and me, the muzzle of my pistol aiming at the Under Secretary. "Now, we can do this the easy way, and you can confess, or we can spend gobs and gobs of time going over the evidence. What will it be, ma'am?"

"Porter, as you've no doubt discovered, and as I've said from the beginning, Hazel Ginachere is the mastermind of all of this." Pointedly ignoring Ginachere, Sullivan's eyes bored into mine as she hissed, "You don't believe her, do you?" She scoffed. "No, with your naivety, you probably do."

I rolled my eyes. "Director Ginachere has been quite cooperative. And I've assembled a long list of links. Direct links, Madam Under Secretary. And the game is up."

Appleton placed her left elbow on the polished surface so that she could pivot her body to fully face Sullivan, and the SAC laid out the charges. "Genevieve Sullivan, you're under arrest as a co-conspirator in the murders of Heather Rourke and Abdul Hamid. You will be charged with the impersonation of a government official for your deception by posing as Hazel Ginachere to JJ Gansett. You will be charged for computer and wire espionage for your cooperation and abetment with Doctor David Curtis. You will also be charged with treason for fabricating an order of attack to the United States Navy against an innocent vessel named *Almaz*, and for the murder of all souls aboard that vessel. Due to that final charge, you will be considered an enemy combatant."

Sullivan didn't bat an eye, maintaining her demure composure. "That's all quite ridiculous," she sneered to Appleton. "Those charges are more appropriately leveled at the person sitting across from you. At Hazel Ginachere."

My phone chimed with a text notification. I scanned the brief message from Louis Lewis, and I holstered my Glock. "I've got everything I need to close this down," I said, scooching to the side and pushing up against Ginachere. She slid from the chair and stood, and Appleton and I followed suit.

"Under Secretary Sullivan, these misdeeds have been pinned on Director Ginachere from the very beginning," I said elaborately. "This has become quite tiresome. Let's go."

CHAPTER
78

I WAITED PATIENTLY, watching as the SAC took efficient control of the logistics to secure the scene on the slick tarmac. Appleton, declining handcuffs, detained Sullivan in a Bureau vehicle. Pointing at her Ford, Appleton gave an agent the Georgetown address and instructions to hand over the keys to Havens. Finally, she met my eye and caught my prompt.

I politely asked Ginachere, "How 'bout a ride back to Maryland? Appleton and I left a Suburban at your home, as you might remember."

"Of course," Ginachere replied pleasantly. "Looks like my schedule for the day is shot. What a way to begin a week," she cackled.

Ginachere took the front passenger seat. I sank into one of the familiar rear captain's chairs of Ginachere's Suburban and tapped out an update on my device to send to the Attorney General. After taking her time to secure the scene on the tarmac carefully and thoughtfully, Appleton eventually climbed aboard, and we set off.

Following the frenzy of the morning, it was pleasant to enjoy a quiet and civilized ride. From my perch in the passenger side rear seat, I soundlessly angled my phone to my left, toward Appleton. The SAC subtly peeked at my screen and read the various messages that I scrolled through.

The contemplative, peaceful, and serene mood that was set by the drive all changed when we arrived at Ginachere's home, where we found two local police cars, a second Bureau Suburban to go with Appleton's identical vehicle, and a black Lincoln sedan waiting in the driveway.

As we disembarked and stepped down to the gravel driveway, Ginachere protested, "What's the meaning of this?"

Appleton cleared her throat. "Ah, Porter, this is all yours."

With permission from the SAC granted, I stated, "I didn't think it appropriate to arrest the Director of the Central Intelligence Agency in a public setting such as Reagan National Airport. Shall we go inside?"

Ginachere's expression was dark; her eyes flared behind the lenses of the round, black glasses. "That is ridiculous," she snarled, all pretense of cooperation gone.

"Funny, that's the exact word Sullivan used. And to think we didn't even rehearse," I cackled, doing a pretty good imitation of the D/CIA. Wiping the smirk from my face, I added, "Doing this in public would irreparably damage the credibility of the United States and its intelligence services. Let's go inside. The Attorney General would like a word," I concluded, bobbing my head in the direction of Bart Williams as he exited the rear of the Lincoln sedan, accompanied by a woman with an Asian complexion whom I recognized from LinkedIn. It was Sara Lin. She opened an umbrella to shield herself and the AG from the rain.

"This is my home, and you're not going inside," bleated Ginachere.

"Suit yourself," I replied, spots of drizzle darkening the fabric on the shoulders of my borrowed Georgetown sweatshirt.

"This is preposterous. Sullivan ran from the State Department building, Porter. Explain to me why gunshots were fired inside a government building." Ginachere's confrontational words didn't match her body language, I observed, as she put her weight on her heels, sliding her right foot, unconsciously, perhaps, slightly backwards.

"I'd run, too, if armed FBI agents were busting doors open on the floor below. You don't think word got out within that wing in a matter of seconds that there was an intrusion? The fourth floor was being evacuated. And Sullivan's bodyguard—because the fourth-ranking person at State is considered valuable enough for personal protection—did his job. Simple as that."

"Really?" Ginachere halted her retreat and, emboldened, advanced slightly toward me. "That's it? That's all you've got?" She snorted. "I'm done here."

"Not so fast, Director," I replied pleasantly, enjoying the moment in the rain. "You see, you slipped up. On several occasions, in fact. Want the list?"

Ginachere crossed her arms defiantly. She was figuratively and literally digging her heels in as I began. "Let's start with Gansett in Salem. That was your first mistake. Initially, I thought that only two people knew that Gansett was the John Doe in the Salem Hospital and therefore could have sent Curtis to kill him. I told Sullivan it was Gansett. Later, Appleton and I disclosed the same to AG Williams."

The Attorney General confirmed my recollection with a curt nod before I continued, "The times didn't line up. The AG couldn't have gotten Curtis to Salem in time. Therefore, the AG is exonerated, leaving Sullivan as our suspect."

"Exactly!" exclaimed Ginachere. "It had to be Sullivan. Enough with this charade."

"Not so fast," I cautioned. "Sure, even then, I thought everything pointed to Sullivan. But a third person knew, and that was Chief Mary Miller. You said her name when we spoke here this morning. And that's when it hit me—you sent Curtis to Salem. You're the mastermind. Except . . ."

I let my voice trail off before I said firmly, "Except at that point, I knew I didn't have a case. I needed more evidence. Which, in fact, you provided."

Ginachere remained silent, her lips thin. Drops of rain clung to her eyeglass lenses.

I noticed that, at some point, Lin had handed off the shared umbrella to the AG. Lin was tapping notes on a tablet, and I confirmed, "You're recording this, too, right?" Lin nodded.

Satisfied that our record-keeping would be complete, I spoke again. "Your second error also relates to Gansett. As soon as you learned that we were in possession of Gansett's device, you freaked out. You knew you must have it in your possession because if we managed to crack it, surely we'd find it linking back to you. You should have let Lewis escort the phone to Langley, which would have preserved the integrity of the evidence. You purposely broke the chain of custody for Gansett's device. That alone was suspicious. But that worked out pretty well in the end."

"Oh," Ginachere jeered, "and why is that?"

"I'm getting there. But I do have one compliment for you. Honestly, it was a masterstroke on your part to accept the call from Curtis's device. I wanted him to show me how the comms worked in case I needed the device later. I didn't expect you to answer!"

I paused and exhaled. "Oh, wow. When you did that, I had second thoughts. I thought, maybe I'm wrong, because you played along so well, pretending to be Sullivan—even though you had to know it was me calling from the doctor's device. Even though you knew that the doctor was inside that house in Georgetown while you were sitting in your car outside. And—remaining in character when I was making shit up like putting Havens and me in the morgue at Reed? You were magnificent." I paused before suggesting earnestly, "You know, when you're in prison, maybe you should consider doing a little acting to keep your mind occupied. They do theater in prisons, right?"

Ginachere's expression remained stoic as I boasted, "Really, though, I thought I was pretty good, too."

"Uh, excuse me," Lin said, entering the discussion. "I don't understand why you kept talking on that call, if you knew Sullivan wasn't the target?"

I smiled at Lin. "Because you never know what comes out of an interview. In this instance, I was thinking that if I could keep Ginachere talking, when I caught up with Sullivan, it would be obvious that it wasn't Sullivan on the connection. Or maybe I could stall the auction. In the end, though, Sullivan bolted, and my intent for remaining on the call was foiled, but it turned out that didn't matter."

I faced Ginachere. "The call worked out to my advantage in a different way." Her eyes clouded as I rushed on, not wanting an interruption to throw off my cadence of allegations. "This brings me to your third mistake—when you mentioned my bullshit line about improving the range of the protocol. I suppose it's possible that you heard my end of the conversation on the headset from the speakerphone connection that Appleton carried, but you couldn't have understood the context without hearing the other side. That's when I knew for sure that it was you on the call, not Sullivan."

"You're an ass, Porter," Ginachere blustered, but I sensed it was only that. Bluster. Posturing for the sake of posturing. I knew I had her on the ropes. Time to deliver the knockout.

"In the event that you care, I'll admit I'm fallible, too. Want to know my error?" I checked to make sure Lin was keeping up and that the AG was paying attention. "I didn't anticipate you closing the auction early, and therefore at that time, I couldn't know if a bad actor had bought Curtis's protocol. I wanted to control that protocol. I suppose we could have been proactive in preventing its use, but it would be far better not to have it out there in the wild."

"Pardon me?" Williams interrupted. "This is very concerning. You're saying you don't know who won the auction?"

I admitted, "I took a calculated risk. You see, leaving Louis Lewis behind, like I said earlier, really worked out. I had instructions relayed to Lewis to win that auction no matter what the cost. When the auction was closed early, Ginachere was unsurprised, and she even said that she had it, quote, under control, unquote. I suspected Ginachere was bluffing. Then she doubled-down on her con when she said that a CIA-controlled account was the winning bidder."

I paused to make eye contact as best I could through Ginachere's foggy lenses. "When you told us that the winning bidder was from Syria, I was almost positive you were still lying, because I instructed Lewis to enter the auction by spoofing a Damascus IP address." I grinned at the sodden woman. "Oh, and speaking of faraway places, I knew about Sullivan's trip overseas a week ago, but you arrogantly assumed I was unaware of that. Nevertheless, we were forced to suffer through the chase to Reagan, to keep up the ruse in the event Lewis did not win the auction, which would have moved us into damage control mode, not yet ready to charge you."

I concluded, turning first to Williams, "We were on Sullivan's plane when Lewis texted me confirmation that he won the auction with FBI funds and with a bid of twenty-six million dollars. In return, Lewis received Curtis's protocol, so we possess that element of evidence, too."

Ginachere's shoulders slumped. The game was up.

Staring at Ginachere, I declared, "Therefore, the litany of accusations that Appleton laid out to Sullivan are all meant for you, Ginachere."

Appleton pulled a set of handcuffs from her jacket pocket and cuffed Ginachere. Under the oversight of the Attorney General, Appleton recited the charges.

As Appleton, Lin, and the AG escorted the disgraced woman to the waiting Bureau Suburban, I couldn't resist one more dig. "Hey, Hazel," I yelled, using her given name for the first time, as I trotted to catch up. "One more thing. I knew for certain that you were a liar when I asked about the picture of the puppy on your mouse pad in there." I pointed at her home. "Your pup didn't die. Page Six reported—*with the same picture*—that you lost custody of that dog two years ago in your divorce. The dog is living with your ex-husband and is very much alive."

I couldn't help myself. I added mockingly, "You know, you're a terrible spy."

I could see Appleton suppress a smile as she guided the wet, manacled, and defeated woman into the waiting car. But even though my sweatshirt hung damply, and I felt cold and exhausted, I wasn't finished. "I have one final question, though. What did you do to *Almaz*?"

The soon-to-be-former D/CIA bared her teeth and snarled, "I sank it. I sank it because you, Porter—you and your people—were getting too close to Curtis. I've been refining this protocol with Curtis since 2019. It was perfect, not only because Curtis thought I was Sullivan, but also because I had unfettered access to develop and hone a near-perfect assassination methodology. And you, Porter, don't understand the importance of that for national security because you are a nobody—a husky desk jockey who doesn't comprehend the complexity of the balance of power around the globe." She scoffed. "You're still in play not because you're smart or because you outwitted me. You survived Gansett at the beginning only because that redhead drove the car."

I goaded her, "Is that so?"

Ginachere clearly couldn't resist my baiting tone and continued menacingly, "You and your team—Quadrant," she spluttered, "have been an outlier to my intelligence operation—a pesky, impertinent thorn in my side. When I learned that Sullivan, that lightweight career bureaucrat, was flexing and deploying you, it was only a matter of time before I found the opportunity to sink that fucking boat. My only error was that you weren't on it, Porter."

"I've heard enough," Williams intoned.

So had I, and finally understanding—and substantiating at last—that Macallister, Volkov, Lockwood, the crew on *Almaz*, Hamid, and Rourke were all murdered by Hazel Ginachere in her callous, twisted power grab, I snarled, seething in anger and dismay, "Ginachere, you'll pay for those lives for the remainder of your life. Rot in hell."

EPILOGUE

IT WAS THE THIRTY-FIRST of March, sadly the day that I was to reunite with my team aboard *Almaz* in Port Said, Egypt, when the Department of Justice formally charged Hazel Ginachere for treason, murder, espionage, and dereliction of duty. The final allegation was added when the investigating teams discovered that the former D/CIA tasked her agents to steal a van owned by the Seabees and to target Leroy Havens and me. In doing so, Ginachere engaged CIA assets in an illegal operation on American soil.

Ginachere's house of cards collapsed in a matter of two days.

After I finally changed from a wet sweatshirt into clothing more appropriate for meetings at the Bureau's headquarters, Appleton, Havens, and I decamped from the Georgetown pied-a-terre to a conference room at the Hoover Building. There, with assistance from the Department of the Navy, we were granted access to the order, signed by Ginachere herself and then sealed "in the interests of national security." Expeditiously unsealed by the signature of the Attorney General, the order revealed the Ginachere targeted *Almaz* by tasking a US Navy Los Angeles class attack submarine, *Ezra Lee*. The ship's log reported:

```
Position: 40° 49.49' N, 025° 21.43' W
Time: 0132 ZULU.
Target was verified via visual identification
at periscope depth approximately 7 hours
ago, during the last hour of daylight,
and has been tracked continuously since.
Target was also confirmed via AIS and
cross-checked with the satellite images
provided with the orders received. The
validity of those orders was examined and
cleared as per the operations manuals and
security codes.
```

The audacity of Ginachere's treachery was exposed in the plain words that read as cold as the North Atlantic water. *Almaz* had been hunted, tracked surreptitiously for seven hours, and then, eight minutes after two torpedoes were fired from *Ezra Lee*, *Almaz* sank to the bottom of the ocean. The follow-up account by the sub's captain revealed that a watch was maintained for several hours, but no survivors were spotted.

By the thirty-first, Doctor David Curtis was stripped of his license to practice medicine. The so-called deal that I made with him was toothless. Upon review, the attorneys at Justice determined his confession to the murder of Senator Abiaria bore no relation to the case at hand and could be prosecuted separately. Furthermore, Curtis lied during his confession inside the pied-a-terre; it was Curtis who had trained Gansett on the methodology. The doctor finally admitted to the connection I made the very last time I spoke with the team aboard *Almaz*: Curtis, the top toxins specialist at Reed, was waiting to intercept Rourke's body when it arrived at his morgue. The only way he could have known to anticipate that was by possessing advance knowledge of Gansett's poisoning attempt.

Hindsight can be frustrating. Devastating. Especially when that red flag became visible early on, and yet we—I! —overlooked its significance.

One bright outcome, however, was my dinner last night, on the evening of the thirtieth, with an attorney from Justice, the captivating Sara Lin. On that topic, I could go on and on and on, but we're already in the Epilogue, and now's not the time for that. Anyway, Sara and I promised each other that we'd remain in touch.

On the other hand, I doubted that I'd receive a holiday card or another call from Genevieve Sullivan. Though she was indeed instrumental in initiating the operation to expose Ginachere, Sullivan's methods left much to be desired. She was neither transparent nor cooperative. Sullivan was motivated not by national security but rather by her aspirations and self-interest. That revelation came courtesy of Attorney General Williams at 8:00 A.M. this Wednesday morning, this last day of March, when he met with Appleton and me.

Williams reported in his booming voice, "Sullivan will be demoted significantly. In fact, I doubt she'll last long at State before being forced to resign. You see, as I've reviewed this case, Sullivan operated in bad faith all along. She knew about Ginachere's connection to Gansett, and she knew about the Saudi assassination plot. But instead of taking her allegations to the Director of the FBI through the proper channels, she attempted to manage the investigation herself, using her knowledge of the off-the-books Quadrant operation to do her bidding."

Appleton sighed. "In retrospect, had she not tried to benefit personally from Ginachere's ultimate downfall, we could have avoided this entire mess."

"And the Quadrant team would be alive," I observed sadly.

The AG concluded, "Unfortunately, none of us saw this evolving the way it did. Sullivan has unclean hands; she withheld crucial information in order to boost her own career."

"Talk about cold," I observed. "I now understand, first-hand, what British historian Lord Alton suggested when he wrote, 'Power tends to corrupt; absolute power corrupts absolutely.'"

Appleton's lip curled up slightly. "That's one of the access quotes to my bunker." The thin smile faded from the SAC's face as she added, "And here's another one. 'If you do not take an interest in the affairs of your government, then you are doomed to live under the rule of fools.' That one is a quite a bit older, circa 400 B.C., I think."

"Plato," the AG rumbled. "Indeed, good advice from a long time ago that remains relevant today. And, speaking of the present, SAC Appleton and Mister Porter, you're a formidable team. This discussion of your collaboration as I foresee it will continue, but I have other matters pressing today, and Mister Porter has a flight to catch."

The crowning blow to Ginachere's demise would be administered by her own accomplice, which is how I found myself on the commercial shuttle flight from D.C. to Boston that the AG arranged. I rented a car at Boston's Logan International Airport and drove to a small town on the southern coast of Cape Cod.

Arriving at my destination at 2:56 P.M., I leaned into a blustery southwest breeze, pulling my coat tightly across my chest with the air temperature barely reaching sixty degrees. Following instructions, I walked to the left side of the white, two-story, bluff-side home to its rear patio, where I found a man once known as the CIA's most deadly contract assassin.

"Mister Gansett," I called, not wanting to startle him.

"Ah, Mister Ben Porter himself," he replied with a lopsided grin as he stood up slowly from a white rocking chair, tugging a blanket around his frame. "If it wasn't so damn painful, I'd applaud your creativity with that nail gun." He dropped into the chair with a groan. "Have a seat and enjoy the view."

Selecting an identical rocker next to the assassin, I did just that, taking a moment to watch the regular pattern of the whitecaps marching toward the bluff from Nantucket Sound, building into steep waves in the shallow water of the beach at the base of the cliff, and crashing into the sand. "I'm not sure why you'd leave a spot like this to skulk around a hospital," I observed, without facing Gansett.

"I own a nice condo apartment in D.C., too," he said in a matter-of-fact tone. "Work is work. My profession requires a journey beyond the warmth and sanctuary of my homes."

"Why do you do it?"

Gansett remained silent for a beat, then two. "Initially, it filled a void. Hate and anger begets hate and anger. It's a vicious cycle, sadly. Ultimately, it consumed me and became my identity."

"You're having second thoughts." My tone made it evident that I proposed a statement, not a question.

"Yes," he confirmed, "which is one of the reasons I asked to speak with you. That, and of course, I can read the writing on the wall. My career is certainly over. My freedom, almost certainly so. I'm quite surprised the Bureau allowed me to be discharged from the hospital to recuperate here."

"You know there are a dozen agents here, don't you?"

"Nine, actually. They started with fourteen yesterday but became complacent. I imagine a few were reassigned to more pressing tasks than guarding an injured has-been who is currently having great difficulty walking and who has a lung punctured by a three-inch nail." He grunted as he squirmed in the rocker to a more comfortable position. "The pattern is so predictable. I could sit here for two more days, and there would be only four or five agents remaining. That's a manageable number to eliminate or evade, and then I'd disappear."

His resolve was evident in his voice, so I debated, "You make it sound straightforward, but all the same, you missed Appleton and me. You've lost your touch."

Gansett laughed cheerfully. "I don't think so. In fact, that's why you're here. You see, I began to question Ginachere's latest assignment. She claimed that she and a pathologist developed a foolproof assassination method. But before deploying it, they would test variables on a series of FBI agents who had gone rogue." He looked at me square in the eye. "The first target was you, except that Rourke drove the car that day. And, after the outcome, Ginachere wanted a different test. That exercise targeted Hamid."

I broke eye contact and looked out to the waves. "Exercise is an awfully clinical word to use to describe murder."

"Indeed," Gansett agreed. "But be that as it may, in my former line of work, that disassociation is required." After a reflective pause, he continued, "I've never regretted a mission. I began to feel second thoughts about Rourke and Hamid."

I wasn't going to give an inch, and in a venomous tone, I challenged him, "Small consolation, now, isn't it?"

Gansett seemed unaffected by my ire. As if I hadn't said a word, he resumed speaking evenly, "I've never worked on domestic soil. That alone should have dissuaded me from accepting the mission. Then the targets—FBI agents? I became increasingly uncomfortable." He leaned his head forward so he could catch my eye again. "Chivalry isn't dead, but it can be dangerous. At least, it was for Appleton. It was nice of you to hold the door for her, and it worked out quite well for me. That was not a kill shot, as you know by now." Rocking back in the chair, he muttered, "I don't miss."

"You missed twice. Once in the street, and the second time when you targeted Appleton in the hospital."

Gansett chuckled. "You don't get it yet, so add this to your evidence collection: I didn't use the Digoxin technique on Appleton, as you must know. You see, Curtis developed several routines to alter the output of the vitals monitoring systems. One technique was employed with Hamid; to spike a drink with Digoxin, and then to alter to vitals system output in a way to suggest a second, fatal dose of the same drug. However, the risk there is, of course, that the initial dose would be discovered. A second technique was to get the target into the hospital by any means, then to inject Digoxin in the patient's IV bag. The vitals system would be triggered to report the patient was in distress. Then, the attending doctor would dose Digoxin or a similar drug unnecessarily and in excess of the existing, hidden Digoxin in the bag. It would be a fatal overdose of toxicity. Quite clever, really. Undiscoverable, or if it was discovered, blamed on the doctors."

That piqued my interest, and in a less antagonizing tone, I asked, "What's the technique you used with Appleton?"

"It's less effective than the double-dose Digoxin sequence. The machines would falsely show cardiac arrest, and the patient would be dosed with epinephrine or shocked with a defibrillator. Appleton would have survived, I believe." He paused and grumbled, "I didn't miss."

"What about me? I'm still alive."

Gansett chuckled. "Yes, that's self-evident, isn't it?" He gazed out at the sea wistfully. "As an assassination technique, diethyl phosphonate has been tried before but failed. The target was an overseas arms dealer, as I recall. It's interesting, clinically, in that you suffered the same hallucinogenic episodes as the arms dealer reported. During one of those episodes, Curtis was curious what would happen, so he suppressed the signals from your vitals monitor back to the nurse's station as an experiment. Obviously, you survived without intervention, and after you made it through that episode, Ginachere decided to favor the Digoxin protocol."

I listened to the regular roar and hiss as the waves rolled onto the beach below, waiting for Gansett to continue. At length, he said, "Ginachere was misguided and egocentric, a terrible human. I'll concede that she helped me with my demons, at first, and I'll further admit that I was under her witch-like spell for far too long. This last assignment, however, opened my eyes."

Gansett scooched his chair closer to mine and, in a low but steady and clear voice, concluded, "I can give you everything. Not just names and dates. I'll expose the entire den of corruption that Ginachere built—and don't think for a second that someone won't rise to assume her place. You may have cut off the head of the snake, but another one will most certainly materialize from the den." He rocked backward and listed, "From bank accounts to bad agents, from plants and spies both domestically and abroad, and from operations that never should have existed—including, I might add, other events where Curtis's protocol was employed by Ginachere— I'll catalog it all. The Department of Justice will be able to disassemble her network of deception."

When the Attorney General asked me to conduct this interview, I knew something like this would be on tap, but Gansett's description was far livelier than the dry prep that was outlined by Bart Williams: "Gansett claims there's more to the Ginachere case."

"Okay," I offered, as a prelude to the question that the AG wanted answered, "but what do you want in return?"

Gansett stretched his right arm out and swung it broadly from right to left, his forefinger pointing at the horizon. "This. I want this."

He paused and dropped his hand into his lap. "I'll sell the place in D.C., and I'll stay here. You can put a GPS bracelet on my ankle. Hell, you can implant a tracker in my arm. I'll remain right here, the Attorney General sends his people to interview me, and I blow Ginachere's world to bits. After all, like I said, with her gone, someone else is bound to take it over. We don't want that to happen."

I nodded. "I'll take it back to Justice, but that sounds reasonable enough to me."

"Good. You're quite reasonable, too, Porter. And resourceful. I wish I had the chance to work alongside you. Perhaps that day might still come," Gansett said wistfully before he straightened in the rocking chair. "Hey, will you join me for a drink? I have some nice whiskey."

"Sure," I agreed. "Why not?"

Gansett disappeared haltingly into the house as I watched as two agents, weapons drawn, materialize from the perimeter. I ignored them and gazed at the horizon, idly watching the march of the whitecaps.

I felt a brush on my right arm and turned to see a rocks glass filled halfway with a brown liquid. "Jameson Eighteen. I believe you polished off a good portion of a bottle with SAC Appleton."

It was a statement, not a question. I snorted. "You're good, Gansett. I'll give you that. How in the world did you know that? You were in the hospital. Appleton was declared dead at the time."

Gansett scoffed and groused good-naturedly, "I've lost my touch, huh?" He chuckled. "Perhaps not."

The assassin and I conversed late into the night as the skies darkened. Together, we drained the whiskey bottle bit by bit, eventually sipping from our glasses hearthside at a roaring fire pit on the patio, the crackle of the flames interspersing with the relentless, repetitious crash of the waves below—much like the wave action 2,313 miles from the bluff, where a small, battered, and smoke-scarred yellow life raft scuffed a rock-strewn, narrow beach on the north shore of the island of Ponta Delgada. Under a gray sky in the local pre-dawn, early morning hours, a single hand brushed across charred rubber and stretched wearily from the raft, reaching for the solid mass of land.

THE END

THANK YOU

I am very grateful that you've spent your time reading my story. Please permit me to ask one other thing of you.

Like all authors, I rely on online reviews to encourage future readers. Your opinion is invaluable. Would you take a few moments now to share your assessment of my book on Amazon or any other book review website you prefer? Your opinion will help the book marketplace become more transparent and useful to us all.

If you are new to Ben Porter's world, please check out the prequels to this story, *False Assurances*, *Threat Bias*, and *Subversive Addiction*, available in print or e-book via Amazon, Apple Books, or Barnes and Noble, in print by order through your local bookstore (distributed by Ingram), or in audiobook format on Audible, Amazon, or Apple.

For insight into my world, please check out my website and social media presence. You may not know this, but I'm an independent author. I am not backed with the resources of a ginormous publishing house, nor am I insulated by layers of staff, agents, and hangers-on. It's just me—and you!

Thanks for reading! I hope to see you back for Book Five in Ben's series, and I trust you caught the hints of what's to come in the Epilogue!

www.RosowBooks.com
Instagram, Facebook, and Twitter: @RosowBooks

ACKNOWLEDGMENTS

THIS IS THE FOURTH Acknowledgments section that I've written, and I'm still not sure what the "rules" are. Do you express thanks in ascending or descending order? Build tension and suspense? Make a list? I have no clue, so I'm going to do it my way, and start with the most important thanks of all.

In prior Acknowledgments, I've closed with family; with this one, I start with them. Meghan (the love of my life!), Maggie, Keilan, and Connor have all contributed to not only this book but also to my journey. At one point in this story, Ben muses, "There's a fine line between perseverance and stubbornness," and that's really me saying that. My family has enabled me and encouraged me to persevere; they've shared in the ups and downs with unwavering support. Words cannot express my gratitude and love.

Likewise, my cheerleaders—Mom and Dad, a/k/a Jeanne and David—have stood with me all the way, offering advice, encouragement, critique, and compliments. Their support has been nothing short of exceptional.

And, speaking of consistent support, let's talk about James Patterson. I am proud to have his words on a fourth cover. I am deeply grateful for his encouragement—and for his ongoing advice. Jim read an early manuscript of this story, and his recommendations are woven within. I cannot thank him enough.

My editor, Ryan Steck, has also been someone to lean on often. His enthusiasm picks me up, and his insight makes me better. Ryan is a unicorn, I think, in the world of publishing and writing. He's created bridges between writers and readers that shouldn't exist in such a competitive landscape, and yet they somehow do, all because of the strength of his convictions. His first book, *Fields of Fire*, comes out in August 2022. You should consider reading it; I will (well, he better send me a signed copy . . . hint, hint, Ryan!).

One of our mutual friends is, of course, Ted Bell, who kindly graces me with a blurb for this book. Ted read the very first manuscript of *False Assurances*. It was pretty rough, I freely admit, and yet Ted saw its potential back then, as did, of course, Mister Patterson—I don't think any of us thought that there would be four Ben Porter stories, soon to be five, and yet here we are! How cool is that . . .

Another founding member of the Ben Porter fan club was the late Rush Limbaugh, who talked about the first books on air one day in May of 2020 and put Ben on the map. Rush endorsed not only Ben's everyman persona but also my self-publishing initiative; no surprise given Rush's passion for a "can-do" spirit. I dare say that sentiment surely supersedes any political affiliation. I was thrilled when Rush's brother, David, looked at the first pass of *Vital Deception* and embraced it.

Further from the spotlight, I rely on a team that has been crucial in the behind-the-scenes process of actually putting a book out. First, my beta readers and sounding boards, who both reached out to me after the first books were released and who I then reached out to for help: Patricia "Tink" Harwerth is an educator who has a keen eye for nuance like character descriptions and language (and who has a far broader vocabulary than I!), and John House, an Air Force veteran with electronics and computer science expertise, who corrected, among other things, my early passes at topics ranging from snakes to surveillance.

Next, Doug Metchick, who I rent my one-room office from, and who has lent his marketing flair to my endeavors, selflessly taking time away from running his skin care company (get out, stay out, and protect your skin with Dermatone – how's that for unashamed product placement?!). Doug also introduced me to Sarah Shropshire, who created this book's cover art. Allegedly, there's a collab coming up with this group that has to do with rum. Count me in; I'm always happy to take a break from writing for an afternoon rum tasting :)

Speaking of rum, I've raised many glasses with my dear friend Doctor Phillip Dickey, who was my medical advisor for this book. He read the very first draft and corrected many of my mistakes; as always, anything that's off base is my fault, not his. Phil has been in all four acknowledgments, and I'm looking forward to weaving something that only Phil can help with into book five. Set some time aside, Doc, for another manuscript, please. In the meantime, let's do some miles offshore aboard *Flying Lady*, the boat that got all this started.

Reflecting on this manuscript, two characters come to mind: David Curtis photographed me for a headshot in exchange for a character, and at first, I envisioned that character with a small but important role. "Doctor Curtis" became too much fun to write, so that role grew significantly, and because of that, I think Dave owes me another headshot. On the other hand, when I created "JJ Gansett," I knew upfront that he'd be a big personality with a lot to offer, much like his namesake, Jon Jodka. JJ will reappear in book five so, Jon, let's put back a couple of Narragansett beers together sometime and talk about JJ's future with Ben.

Last but not least, thank YOU. The reader. The Ben Porter fan. The person who dove into the book. You're the reason I do this.

Really, that's true. A lot of authors talk about the "lonely journey of writing" or something like that. I don't see it that way. The best part for me is hearing from readers. It's not lonely at all. It's exciting, it's gratifying, and most of all, it's fun to share a common experience through the written word. I am so very grateful that you've chosen to join me in this story.

— Christopher Rosow, March 30, 2022, Southport, Connecticut

ABOUT THE AUTHOR

Christopher Rosow is an independent author who has self-published four novels. After being rejected by the mainstream publishing houses, he decided to forge his own path. Turns out those publishers were wrong; Rosow's first release, *False Assurances*, became a best-seller. Three sequels have continued the story of Rosow's unique and compelling protagonist, Ben Porter.

When not writing, Rosow still works full-time in his "day job" in the design and construction space. And, when not working or writing, or enjoying time with his amazing family, he's probably found out on the water somewhere, sailing. He lives in Connecticut with his family, his dogs, and way too many boats.

www.RosowBooks.com

Facebook, Twitter, and Instagram: @RosowBooks

The Ben Porter Series by Christopher Rosow:
False Assurances — Book One (2020)
Threat Bias — Book Two (2020)
Subversive Addiction — Book Three (2021)
Vital Deception — Book Four (2022)

Made in the USA
Monee, IL
15 July 2022

99726455R00198